TO

DIE

IN

PROVENCE

TO
DIE
IN
PROVENCE

NORMAN BOGNER

A Tom Doherty Associates Book
New York

TO DIE IN PROVENCE

Copyright © 1998 by No Inc.

This book is printed on acid-free paper.

A Forge Book
Published by Tom Doherty Associates, Inc.
175 Fifth Avenue
New York, NY 10010

Forge® is a registered trademark of Tom Doherty Associates, Inc.

Design by Bonni Leon

Endpaper photograph of Sault Plateau, Lavender Fields, Provence, France. © Marche, Guy 1997.

Library of Congress Cataloging-in-Publication Data

Bogner, Norman.
    To die in Provence / Norman Bogner.—1st ed.
        p. cm.
    "A Tom Doherty Associates book."
    ISBN 0-312-86628-3 (alk. paper)
    I. Title.
    PS3552.045T6   1998
    813'.54—dc21   98-23592
                                                        CIP

First Edition: September 1998

Printed in the United States of America

0   9   8   7   6   5   4   3   2   1

To my darling Bettye,
with love

I floated on a wild river I could not master,

No longer guided by the pilot's compass.

1

MONT
SAINTE-
VICTOIRE

CHAPTER 1

The morning sun was cooking the town of Aix-en-Provence to a fine pink. It had been an odd unsettling year around the world. El Niño boiled up the seas, sun-flare convulsions and comet sightings had roused astronomers. Grand discussions of black holes encased in mysterious dark matter, dangling on invisible strings, served to further alarm the public and fetter anxiety, banishing prospects of immortality to those attuned to cosmic visions.

In Provence, eccentric blame was laid on obscure air flows which vented the powdery sirocco as it flailed off the Sahara and blustered up the North African coast during the spring and summer. While channeling over the Mediterranean it had gathered mists and seeds of cumulus, creating oppressive humidity. These sulky disturbances had, it was said, influenced the violent mistral. It almost seemed that little chuffs of air reflected and inspired unpredictable behavior and a soulless drift. In Aix everyone was irritable, rheumatic complaints were rife, and domestic squabbles needed divine intervention. Perhaps it was a case of pre-millennium jitters and dire prophecies.

Located on a square off the small Rue de la Masse, Chez Danton, the locals' favorite restaurant, was reluctantly coming to life. Despite the prevalence of evil and foreboding soothsayers, people were going to eat. Michel Danton tweaked the elderly handle of the forest green awning while his father stood at the delivery entrance with the butcher. They were having a glass of wine from the latest shipment of Chambertin and dawdling over wine talk. They had just restocked the *charcuterie* next to the restaurant. Fresh strings of Arles sausage and legs of jambon de Bayonne slyly waltzed on their hooks in the window.

Michel had come in at six and waited on the early trade and prepared several picnics. He saw the silhouette of a girl, in an apartment across the street, her fingers plucking the strings of a harp. The velvety purr of Debussy glided down to the street, breaking through the stillness of the summer morning. It was late July and the music festival had filled the city with tourists. The restaurant survived without them and took a certain snooty pride in refusing their reservations even after they had located the unlisted telephone number.

He went back inside, nipped at a glass of Armagnac and sipped his cold espresso. He made a dismal effort to clean up behind the bar, and scribbled on a chalkboard the names of diners who had called on the machine to book tables. This was normally his mother's job, but Nicole Danton, Aix-en-Provence's doyenne of cuisine, was still in the hospital, recuperating from gallbladder surgery. She had suffered from this condition for years and blamed it on the goose *confit* in his father's cassoulet, which merrily swam through gurgling deltas of fat. It was delicious and deadly like all the chef's classic concoctions.

Michel had been trying to make himself useful, but it was a futile exercise. His mental condition was one of buried ambivalence when his fiancée trooped into the restaurant. Yvette had gone missing. Now that she was back, he wondered why he had complained about her absence when he hoped he would never see her again.

"Make me an iced latte, please. It's so hot, you can't swallow. Tourists everywhere. Deux Garçons ran out of ice."

"Where the hell've you been?"

"Don't use that tone with me, Michel. I'm not a suspect in a murder case. I was in Paris and you know it."

"You were going to stay overnight—that was ten days ago."

"Something happened." She unwound the cable on her laptop and looped the wire over the bar. "My battery's low, I need a charge. Plug it in, will you?"

He scowled at her, dumped some espresso grounds into the metal cup and turned on the large Gaggia machine. He made a latte for himself while he was at it and joined her at the bar. An alley-cat staredown momentarily defused his anger. Yvette's icy gray eyes had the stark lambency of a fishmonger's red mullet or a corpse in the morgue amazed by death. Except for the buzz of the big fan, there wasn't a stroke of breeze. The slop-joined brick walls oozed in the heat.

Yvette hiked up her skirt and wheeled onto a barstool. "Can we have some air?"

He switched on the air conditioning. When his father heard the unit, he'd charge in like a maddened bull and start screaming about the fact that they were closed for another two hours and the bills that summer had been astronomical. The world was getting on Michel's nerves. At times like this, he would've liked to shoot anyone who spoke to him. He'd begin with Yvette. It would make a perfect head-line for the newspaper.

Le Clairon's Chief Crime Reporter Shot by Insane Commander of Special Circumstances Section

"It's over with us, Michel. I've moved out."

He had suspected something of the kind and decided to tough it out.

"Is there a sweet note on my pillow?"

"I was going to fax you."

"I've heard of cutting corners, but that makes even my blood run cold."

Yvette was having a problem breathing. When she shook her head, a drizzle of sweat hopped through the heavy air.

"It was the only way."

He took her measure for a moment. One hundred five pounds of steel. Modish, all angles, striking, with a short mannequin haircut and the pointed sideburns of a page at court. In profile, wearing a pants suit, she was often taken for a young man, a type never out of fashion.

What character flaw had brought Yvette Molyneux into his life? She had sprung from the new breed of pushy crime reporters. The publisher of the local scandal sheet had poached her from a paper in Lyon and serialized some of her tripe about sex cults. Nevertheless, it was not just an increase in salary and expenses which had lured Yvette to Aix, but a TV program arranged by the paper.

Exposure, she called it. For fifteen minutes a week, she did a round-up of slashings, grotesque farm murders, sensational accidents, the sexual practices of Basque sheepherders, topping it off with any bizarre rapes she was able to cull from the four corners of France. From these shaky palisades, she was launched. Her telegenic face and silver-tongued chatter were in marked contrast to the foul content of the program.

"What were you really doing in Paris?"

"Hemorrhaging."

"Not emotionally."

"No, from my lousy abortion."

Abortion, had he heard the word? No, the heat was affecting his hearing. They hadn't made love since Christmas.

"Slap me just once, Michel."

"It's not my style."

"I need to cry."

"If this is one of those immaculate conceptions, let's report it to the archbishop."

"The man I've been seeing didn't know I was pregnant."

"Oh, so it was a man and not some *in vitro* experiment."

"Do you want me to admit that I'm disgusted with myself?"

"I never found out what does disgust you . . . the truth would suit me. Who is he?"

"Don't ask."

"Where are you moving?" He'd ferret it out. "I may want to fax a reply."

"Stop . . . Denise Casson offered to let me move in with her until I go back to Paris in September."

"You can get your hair done free and keep track of her gigolos." Yvette refused to be baited. "Is this really a permanent career move to Paris?"

The mention of her profession brought a smile to her face and provided a moment of detachment, an escape from the poisoned hot-house air.

"Yes, I signed a contract with *France-Soir.*"

"You'll be writing editorials."

"Damn it, Michel, stop goading me. Crime stories with my own assistant and a photographer assigned to me."

"Can we backtrack for a moment, since I'm not officially taking notes? You mentioned an abortion. Have I met the grieving father in this heartbreaking soap opera?"

For once the slickness Yvette exhibited on TV deserted her and she was as fogbound as one of the bumbling crime victims she liked to grill for gruesome details.

"Don't force this."

"It's not an interrogation, simply a human issue."

"It won't make you feel better."

"You're not an authority on my feelings."

To keep busy, she began clumsily twisting the tangle of wires from her various communications gadgets. She couldn't connect anything. At his apartment, he would unravel her from the bondage of cables.

"I suppose I'm not." A dress rehearsal smile appeared on the ga-mine mouth. "What the hell was I supposed to do? You haven't come near me since New Year's."

"I thought it was Christmas Eve. I'll have to check my diary." He approached her without violence or murder in his heart. "I was actually convinced it was from the shooting trauma. Now I know why I couldn't go near you."

"Murder me. You're a great detective. If anyone can get away with it, you can."

"You wouldn't fit into my category. Ruthless people make dull victims."

To his surprise, humiliation set in. He repelled his feelings of remorse and sought a flimsy unity within his soul. The fact was he had considered giving Yvette her walking papers and instead was served with his. It was a stiff tariff and not in keeping with his sense of personal dignity or an honorable parting. She'd slipped in, grabbed her gear and whatever she considered community property, which meant just about everything he had owned before she moved in.

"Tell me who he is, please. For my own peace of mind."

"You won't confront him?"

"What's happening now, a hostage negotiation?"

"It's tricky."

"*Chérie,* I was the more deceived."

"Damn you, it's Paul . . . Paul Courbet."

She waited a moment for this bit of bad news to sink in, but Michel was glacial on the surface, shocked to his heels below.

"That idiot on the local vice squad. He's been screwing Louise's girls for years. He's worn out so many of them that Louise must be paying him cash to operate."

Yvette was startled and grimly swallowed the dregs of her latte. The beads of condensation from the glass dribbled on her chin and Michel wiped it with the bar rag. A napkin was too good for her.

"You didn't know? You seem a little worried, Yvette." Michel took her hand. "My darling, even Paul's wife and kids talk about it. How could my clever little fiancée not know that she was sleeping with the prince of whores? That's how they coined the word viceroy."

"Seriously?"

One day he expected this piece of disinformation to turn up in her column. "Look it up."

"Jesus, the surgeon who did my abortion tested me for HIV." She was down to a sad croak. "I was negative."

Michel now realized how frequently Yvette and Sergeant Courbet had been at pains to avoid each other in public. They kept him or some other beard as a barrier between them, like a dentist and patient at a cocktail party. Only the drill brought them together. It would be weeks before Yvette returned to Paris. It was clear that she was moving to Denise's for "stolen moments" with Courbet. Michel was prepared for Yvette to make her exit so that he could guide himself through the melancholy grammar of the cuckold. But he had waited too long. She grew expansive.

"One night when I was waiting for you, you called to say you wouldn't be back. I'd had too much to drink. Paul wouldn't let me drive home."

"It's a Truffaut film we saw when we were kids." The bleak logic of his sexual predicament suddenly became apparent. "I know what happened to me now. I had a sense about it. When you visited me in the hospital and I was in a coma, you leaned over to kiss me—"

"—I was there for you, Michel."

"Really? I tasted another man's sweat on your lips."

He remembered the pain of this undefined perception and had tried to hide her duplicity from himself. The repression had, over a period of time, gelded him. Now that he understood what had been going on, he was relieved, liberated.

"I'd betrayed you. I feel so horrible now."

"Confession does that."

Yvette was crying bitterly with what appeared a flow of genuine emotion and his suspicions were aroused.

"Why the hell did you bother to come and see me today?" he asked.

"When you walked into the apartment and realized I'd left, I was afraid for you."

No, that wouldn't do. "Tell the truth. It's so much easier."

"I am. My car broke down."

He was still unaccustomed to the magpie flights of her conversation.

"What's that got to do with anything? After you seduce your new editor in Paris, he'll probably buy you a Ferrari."

She assumed the character of the guileless provincial. "Well, I did think you'd want to know about what happened this morning."

"I'm waiting."

"There's been a double murder at the Bimont Dam."

"I'm on suspension, sick leave, whatever. Let the locals mop it up."

"Paul and Claude are the investigators," she said solemnly. "I was sure you'd want to have a look, suspension or not."

"And give you a ride, maybe?"

"I wouldn't object."

Chez Danton's air-conditioning unit seemed to have had a stroke. It whined and bleated its way into morose silence. In its place there was the familiar sound of the chef's stuck-pig howl. Michel's father stood before them outraged, his hand frozen on the switch. Philippe

Danton had Popeye biceps and when he carried twenty-four chickens on the giant steel skewer to the roti, he reminded Michel of Anthony Quinn in *La Strada*. When he was angry with his father, Michel called him Zampano and played Mahler full blast.

"What's the meaning of this?"

"Since when does my behavior have a meaning?" Michel asked.

"Good morning, Yvette."

"Philippe."

Michel waited for the worthy chef to pounce. "Will you kindly supervise the *charcuterie*, Michel?"

"No, I've been in there all morning. I don't know why the hell I agreed to help you out at all. Hire some more people and leave me alone."

"Michel, don't talk to your father that way."

"This tart's left me for Courbet. Can you believe that?" Michel searched vainly for a hint of understanding from his father, in this their thirty-seventh year of familial alliance.

"I don't blame her."

"Thanks for all your emotional support."

The absence of sympathy was not surprising or anything new and, to drive his hot-headed father further along the path to dementia, Michel recounted his morning assignments.

"I've completely screwed up the reservation list; the ice machine is shorting out; the Gaggia is leaking; and I left the liquor inventory for René. Oh, before I forget, I also broke the bulb in the freezer. I think you should call the plumber, electrician and anyone else you can think of."

"Get out! I never want to see you again," Philippe shouted.

Michel grabbed his jacket and ushered Yvette out. He paused in the doorway. Murder always gave him an appetite.

"Oh, by the way, what's the special this evening?"

CHAPTER 2

The previous year on a multiple murder case in Corsica, unconnected to the island's revolutionary bombings, Michel had been blasted four times by a sawed-off shotgun as he was about to make an arrest. He had killed the hitman who had been employed by the island's *condottiere*. That Michel was alive was something of a miracle. It had taken him six months to recover. He had returned to work, but an incident shortly afterwards had resulted in enforced sick leave. He was seeing a psychiatrist at the hospital three times a week. His seductive charms had thus far failed to persuade the doctor to have him reinstated.

Michel Danton was chief investigator, with the rank of commander, of the Special Circumstances Section of the Judicial Police and covered the five departments of Provence. His assignments were confined to the most difficult homicides. In the office, his group was known as the Sextius Legion. This touch came from the station commissioner in Marseille. The two native sons treasured the history of the region and in concert decided to honor the Roman consul who drove out the barbarians and set up an encampment at Aquae Sextiae, the thermal springs, which led to the founding of Aix.

Vice and the drug world had never held any interest for him. He preferred higher stakes and puzzles. As a boy, he had always loved mysteries, lurking in the woods, hunting, laying snares, trapping foxes at the family farm. He was regarded as an eccentric by his schoolmates. When he graduated from the Sorbonne with honors in art and philosophy, his parents were elated, expecting a glorious career for their prince.

However, Michel began to drift. He traveled to the United States for a month and stayed a year. He found a variety of jobs, made friends, lived in a crash pad in Chelsea with eight other students who were at NYU. That summer in New York he worked at Yankee Stadium selling hotdogs and developed a passion for baseball which never left him.

It was in late July that one of the girls in the group was murdered in the apartment. The New York police gave up on the case after several fruitless weeks. Michel became obsessed with the girl's death and one evening at a nearby bar, he heard an older man mention her name. Michel followed him home, not quite knowing what he ought to do.

When the man left his apartment at three in the morning, Michel tracked him to a brownstone in the East Village. The man picked a lock, broke in, and moments later a naked woman was at the window screaming. Michel had no time to call for help. He burst into the apartment and disarmed the man, who was eventually convicted of murdering his roommate.

On his return to Aix, Michel decided he wanted a career in the police. His choice of profession stunned the restaurant's family of patrons, not to mention the hive of relatives. His mother's cherished hopes were destroyed and she was inconsolable. She went so far as to cancel her cooking classes and took a leave of absence from her newspaper cuisine column. The boy she and Philippe had coddled and whose brilliance they had nurtured must be having a nervous breakdown. Not so. Michel was in love with murder. Oh, he'll get over it, they said.

But he thought of it differently. Murder was a fine symphony with themes, movements, and orchestral arrangements. Ultimately, it was the structure which intrigued and attracted him. The rhapsody of death, no matter how thoughtless or seemingly random, always had a form that possessed a composer's signature and the passion of narcissism. The process and the solution of the greatest crime bewitched him, creating a perverse triangle with the practitioner and victim.

Knee-high black metal posts corseted Aix's narrow pavements to ensure that pedestrians would not be splattered by maniacal drivers like Michel speeding along the single-file streets. He loved his Citroën Maserati. It was a 1974 model, painted a British racing green, with a V-6 engine which he kept tuned as if it were a Stradivarius.

With Yvette in the passenger seat, he turned down the regal Cours Mirabeau, crammed with tourists in berets and Pernod T-shirts, pretending to be French during the music festival. In another six weeks the residents would have the town back to themselves and this mob would be home watching their videotapes in suburbia and bitching about their Am Ex charges.

"You're being very understanding, Michel, and I appreciate it," Yvette said.

He laughed at her and himself. "It's a good thing we're not in California or the lawyers would be sharpening their knives."

"You never proposed, it couldn't be breach of promise."

"Lawyers always find something. Are you going to sell the wine Louise gave us?" His godmother, Louise Vercours, had presented them with a case of Pétrus for Christmas. "Shall we split it?"

"Actually . . . I sold all of it this morning. I needed a new wardrobe."

"I thought you'd put it in a vault to save for your brat's education when you decided to keep one."

"I can't have children after this and I'm not sad. They'd probably turn out as selfish as me."

For a fleeting moment, he liked her better than he ever had. Her honesty was as rare as a vacant hotel room during the season.

Mont Sainte-Victoire came into view when he swung onto the highway. A blur of woods, hillsides of bright yellow Spanish broom and small farms furled by, with fields of lavender, mauve globe thistles, stunted oaks—all of it driven like fuel in a mad bellows during the mistral. The land then gave way to *garrigues,* stretches of stone-filled moors, kneeling in the Arc Basin. Over the centuries at the water's edge, *calanques* had been slashed into the rock, impassable inlets below sheer drops of the limestone range. Cézanne had given it all an heroic geometric expression, but to the naked eye the landscape was without rhyme or reason. It was beautiful and there was no explanation.

Michel turned sharply into a spot, and flipped down the sun visor with its police card. Yvette already had the door open and was shouting to the TV crew, who had beaten her to the murder scene. They were shooting filler of the beefy gendarmes catching a little sun on their paws. She was out of the car with her recharged laptop before he had switched off the engine.

Michel's bones still ached when he moved suddenly. He was a large man with an olive hue to his skin, huge hands, a shock of black curly hair with an occasional gray outlaw. His dark blue eyes were suffused with a pensive weariness. But it was the Roman nose that gave his face a dignity and weight that was worthy of striking a coin. Local women considered him stately and, when given the opportunity, stroked the cleft in his massive chin. He was too big for soccer, too slow for tennis, but he could hit a golfball from his office roof in Marseille into the harbor. It would be some time before he could walk the course. Still his chipping and putting had improved. That's what he should have been doing instead of butting his nose into a case that still fell under local jurisdiction.

He didn't see anyone from his office on the scene. It had already been compromised by Claude and his crew. Cigarette butts and sandwich wrappers were scattered on the ground. Not a latex glove in sight. He took out a pair from the box he kept on the backseat and slipped them on. The uniformed men saluted him and he made his way under the taped knoll of grass.

The view above the Infernet River was dazzling and the water shimmered with fiery cobalt streaks. Below on a towline were divers. Boats were not allowed in the water, since this system of dams and canals fed the arid plains and provided Aix's water supply.

"I hope you didn't send your troops down there to poach trout, Claude."

"They're searching for a man's head."

"Really?"

Michel lifted the heavy black plastic body covers. A well-built young man had been decapitated and his hands tied with bootlaces. Maggots were already eating through the severed ribbons of pulpy flesh. Alongside this corpse was the niveous face of a red-haired girl. Her tongue protruded and her eyes stared vacantly at the bright expanse of Provence sky. She had a plastic bag over her head. A man's expensive alligator belt had been twisted around her windpipe and used as a garrote. He recognized the young woman.

"Claude, I didn't know that you were assigned to homicide cases," Michel said.

"With all these tourists in town, we're short-staffed."

Michel's relations with Claude Boisser, the superintendent of vice and public morals, were usually amicable, so long as they weren't working together. With his hooded brown eyes and liverish bags that puffed out like mildewed plastic shower curtains, Claude was a popular raconteur. From his vast nocturnal storehouse, he regaled the troops with obscure descriptions of frottage, transvestism and, of course, workaday diddling.

"What are you doing here, Michel? I thought you'd be hitting balls on the driving range."

"I gave Yvette a ride."

"Oh no, the scorpion's here already?"

"She's in makeup."

Closing in fast and glistening with sweat like a thoroughbred after winning at Longchamps was Claude's sergeant, Paul Courbet. Skin tanned to a fine mahogany, silk shirt opened to reveal the pelt of hair on his barrel chest, Courbet was Aix's Tarzan and boule champion. In his excitement to report, he didn't see Michel, who was still stooped over the bodies.

"The divers found something, Claude."

"Have them hoist it up," Michel said, from his kneeling position.

"You . . . ? Did the shrink run out of current for your shock treatments?"

"Yes, Sergeant Courbet. A power failure."

"What's the world coming to, Michel, when you can't have a bonk at a picnic?"

"Or in my apartment."

Michel rose from his crouch and tested his reflexes with a thunderous left hook to Courbet's solar plexus. Paul Courbet dropped in a *Swan Lake* swoon. He writhed on the ground, gasping for breath. His suntan now matched the limestone cliffs.

"I can't believe this, Michel. I'm going to have to arrest you," Claude said with embarrassment. "You'll have to help me with this. I've never arrested a superior officer."

"There's no protocol, so don't bother." Michel seized Courbet by the slippery ends of his pomaded hair and turned him belly up. He pressed his muddy Nike against Courbet's throat. "Yvette said use a condom next time. Everyone else does."

"Oh, *merde*, she told you!"

Claude pulled Michel away. Triangles were not his métier. "Please don't shoot him, and have your breakdown on your own time. We already have two bodies."

Michel spotted the olive brown shopping bag which was imprinted with CHEZ DANTON, *CHARCUTERIE*. Amid shoots of yellow jasmine and rosettes of dark purple anemones now blowing in the river breeze, the lovers had picked an isolated spot for their final embrace. And so had their killer.

"They're an American couple. I wrote up their picnic order this morning."

"Were they married?" Claude asked.

"I didn't see wedding rings. The woman had a Trusardi handbag and the man paid cash. She mentioned going to Picasso's grave. You could ask at the Château de Vauvenargues. Someone might have followed them. A walk and a little homage would do you good, Claude." The delicate nuances of violent crime had been squandered for Michel. He yanked the Gauloise out of Claude's hand, spattering the ash on his prodigious belly. "The couple ordered two beers, Stella Artois, and drank them on a terrace table. I didn't see either of them smoke. Have someone clean up the butts and find out which brands your men smoke."

"Yes, of course. Sorry, Michel. This was all so unexpected."

"Not for the killer." France was a wonderful place for a homicidal maniac. The provincial cops seldom caught anyone. "Look, even though I can't work on this case, you really should call my deputy in Marseille and bring in our team."

"That's up to our chief. He's afraid the publicity might scare the tourists away."

"It's a little late for that."

"Michel, I do what I'm told."

Courbet had gotten to his feet and was dusting his trousers and jacket. He listened for only a moment, then sheepishly tilted his head and produced a fatuous teenager's smile to demonstrate he was a good sport and wouldn't hold a grudge.

"Michel, I want to say—"

"One more word out of you, and they'll be fishing *your* head out of the dam."

On his way to his car, he passed Yvette, pancaked for the camera, rehearsing her copy. Over her shoulder he noticed her mud-encrusted Deux Chevaux on the muddy verge.

"How'd your car get here?"

There was the familiar glint of smirk. "It's a little awkward."

"What is?"

"When we left Chez Danton, I signaled the movers. They were in a van outside Chez Danton. I'm sure they'll be gone by the time you get back to the apartment."

"So dragging me here was a diversion."

"I suppose. Haven't you enjoyed yourself?"

Finding himself filled with admiration for the brazen bitch, he kissed her on both cheeks. By the year 2000, Yvette and her clones would rule the earth and there would be a certain justice in that. There had always been more of them and the majority ought to make the rules.

"I'll miss our games," he said.

"I'll have Paul to play with."

"With two bodies, and you to come to home to, he's over-matched."

Michel took her hand and looked at it. For her thirtieth birthday he had given Yvette a cameo ring.

"Are you going to return my grandmother's ring?"

"You'll have to cut it off my finger."

2

THE
THREE
SKULLS

CHAPTER 3

His name was Darrell Vernon Boynton, but everyone called him Boy. He hadn't intended to kill the couple up at the dam. It had simply been like the old wheel-of-fortune game at the carnival back home. Their number had come up.

He had spent the morning wandering through Aix-en-Provence's steamy maze of streets, unable to focus on anything. He flitted around, darting in and out of cafés and shops, clamped in a fugue state.

When he hopped on the bus, he recognized that he had no recourse but to go with the spell. The bus cranked up hills, taking on and disgorging passengers, but, as far as he was concerned, the world was made up of fragments, shimmering glimpses from the other side. He would find himself in two places: observing from beyond, and in the eye of the event. These magical passages halted time and he could lose himself.

He was down to fifty francs, about ten bucks. If he were in the States, he would have found a money trail by looking through the newspaper. It wouldn't matter where he was. He'd read the personals, the classifieds. Somewhere he'd unearth a stray, hunting for a date and a shag. Some gal with smoking pants sitting an open house and trolling. Maybe a housewife looking for a handyman and romance. Obituaries were taste treats he devoured. He'd roam through funeral homes among the mourners, dressed in his blue suit and rep fraternity tie, searching for a gal who needed his special down-home comfort. But he was trapped in France and he couldn't even ask where the Coke machine was located or find the damn toilet.

The bus driver bellowed, "Mont Sainte-Victoire . . ." and Boy lumbered through the aisle, shoved by sweaty locals who oozed garlic and sour wine breath.

In the dead stillness of late summer, the livid heat bit through the mountain wind, heaving up clouds of hissing limestone dust. The bright red clay on the country road reminded him of the small town in Oklahoma where he had grown up. But there were no mountains, only sulfur-baked rolling hills, nothing like this gently undulating white limestone range with its tiers of plateaus and deep gorges. He sniffed the air, suffused with wild herb bushes and lavender. He spotted some lizards darting from the coverlets of grass and, in the luminous chalky blue sky, a pair of eagles made for a mountain nest.

He didn't know how long he had been walking through the pinewoods when he heard voices carrying from below him.

Americans.

From a car radio, he recognized Barbra Streisand singing "The Music of the Night." He saw a vaulted river dam through the trees and a couple lounging on a blanket filled with food and cold drinks in an ice bucket. They were hugging and laughing.

The girl had long natural red hair and a lithe, kittenish figure, the man older, maybe thirty, stocky with curly black hair.

". . . Look, there are no kids to consider, so it can be a clean divorce."

"Nothing's ever clean with my husband." She had a wan expression now. "If he finds out it's you, he'll go crazy and drag it out forever."

"I think I can overcome his stubbornness. I'll give him a million dollars to take a walk. It should cure his heartbreak."

"You'd really do that?"

"I love you, don't you get it?"

A million dollars! The sum registered on Boy. He spied the man's Gucci attaché case and the girl's fancy handbag. They'd have a kickful of dough. Boy smiled to himself when she embraced the guy and ran her nails down his neck.

"I'm mad about you," she said. "The way it goes on . . . more every day."

They kissed hard. The man had his hand under the girl's yellow blouse and was unhooking her bra. She helped him place her white breasts in his hands. They gained momentum, going from trot to canter, and began to gorge on each other.

"Two little piggies feasting," Boy said to himself.

Boy watched the couple a bit longer, and shackled his own excitement. He was a qualified professional when it came to threesomes, the more the merrier in fact. Too bad Maddie was grinding away in French conversation class at the university. His little dragon would have loved this action.

Boy opened his backpack, jacked out his knife and hatchet. He slowly took off his clothes, then jammed his long hair into a swimmer's cap. Chords from the nightmare fugue raced through his brain. Brandishing the hatchet, he raised it like a baton. He had decided to join the party.

Boy was furious. The little redhead only had a purseful of coins she'd been saving for her kid sis's collection back in Aspen. Mr. High Roller, who had offered to buy her a divorce for a million dollars, gave up thirty bucks' worth of francs. The stories guys spun and the gals who swallowed that line didn't deserve to live. The big-shot had offered to write Boy a check back at their hotel. He was some kind of commodity trader. He advised Boy to buy pork belly futures and make his fortune.

"What I don' know about pork bellies ain't worth knowin'," Boy had said.

Boy had let the wimp watch an expert do his lady.

Nevertheless, this open-air excursion hadn't solved Boy's monumental problem. He'd counted on Maddie Gold, his great score. Maddie had lured him from Los Angeles with promises of an all-expenses-paid European vacation. She'd be taking French courses at the university her parents had booked. He could not get back to the States until September because the airline refused to change his ticket. He was broke and trapped in this miserable French market town with rich Maddie. Her allowance had been gutted by her parents to twenty-five dollars a day and no plastic or traveler's checks to her name.

Maddie had learned of the arrangement after they were both on the plane to Marseille from L.A. The princess was in first class and he was squashed next to a load in the deadbeat section by the toilets in the rear.

After the plane took off, Jennifer, the tutor Maddie's folks had hired, had handed Maddie a letter from them.

Boy heard Maddie's screams from first class but was powerless to do anything, since the purpose of the trip was to keep Maddie clear of him.

Maddie was running down the aisle of the plane like a feral cat.

"If they were here, I'd open the door and throw them out!" she screamed, alarming the befuddled passengers. Jennifer and the flight attendants calmed her down with a pair of Xanaxes.

This jaunt with Boy had taken months of planning. Whenever Maddie was home from college, she had rifled through the Golds' caches, beaten the maids for supermarket change, even squirreled away her allowance to be able to spring for a coach ticket for him. Now her funds were in the clutches of her tutor.

Nothing had worked out for Boy.

Maddie had even turned tricks at Madame Louise's fashionable brothel one afternoon to get him some money. She came back crying the blues, claiming the two customers she'd serviced raved to Madame about the new American girl. But Maddie had not been paid by the guys and the madam had stiffed her.

Boy continued his vigil from a café table across the street from Louise's house. He was steaming and couldn't wait to fix this madam's ass. The trip had turned into a nightmare. He was living in the back room of a house owned by a middle-aged hairdresser and working in her salon as a gopher. He'd let her pick him up outside the town spa and take him home. She gave him a job sweeping hair, nails, shit like that, sometimes shampooing or running to the post office to collect cartons of samples.

"Get me some milk, cold milk," Boy barked, waving the little metal pitcher at the waiter. He'd been drinking abominably strong coffee. *"Leche fría."* The waiter finally got it. "Prison Spanish is what you understand here, huh?"

Boy sipped the coffee. It tasted even worse with the scummy milk he added. He got up as though to stretch, but he couldn't beat the check. The waiter was watching him. Boy was ready to gag. It was his last fifty-franc note, and he hated to part with it. Like a monte shark, the waiter scooped up the change before Boy could move on it.

"Cooks at Soledad could teach you mothers a lesson. Like how to make chili. But you'd probably mess that up too."

Boy roved down to the cathedral and stared at the figures of well-dressed men, faces bloated with satisfaction, escorted in and out of Louise's house by the madam herself. Leaning against the gritty old cathedral wall, he listened to them arrogantly sniggering. The sound pierced him like the bullwhip that had once been laid on his flesh. Their laughter would soon end.

CHAPTER 4

In frustration Michel listlessly roved through the market stalls. He was intoxicated by the smells of his native land, with its bouquets of thyme, rosemary, fennel, basil, lovingly packed in print sachets, the braids of rosy garlic; the sacks of almonds; the fresh catch from Marseille of mussels, shrimp, red mullet, langoustine and loup made him long for his mother's bouillabaisse. When it was available at the restaurant, she sometimes added cuttlefish, piercing its black inky sacs which spread a fragrant brininess through it. He visualized the dish and mentally added a thick creamy *rouille* slathered on *mar-ette,* the crusty toasted bread, softened by the broth until it became spongy and he could scoop it into his mouth like a sea gull.

He had to make a convincing case to his psychiatrist so that he could be allowed to go back to work. He would admit to being unstable; that was common knowledge. But how could his personality have been different? If a man spent his life investigating murders, he was entitled to kick up his heels and have a soprano's temper. The double homicide would never be solved by Claude and his pathetic bunch. If anything demanded his Special Circumstances Section, it was this case.

Much as Michel preferred to ignore it, underneath the lush sunshine, corruption flourished in his town. It was, however, like examining a friend too closely and he chose to ignore it.

He bought some tangy black Nyons olives, a slab of creamy fresh Banon Chèvre, a few slices of Dijon ham, speckled with parsley, and a baguette for lunch. He ate it while selecting a bouquet of sunflowers for his mother, then strolled over to the hospital.

The nurses had changed Nicole's dressing and she was sitting up in a chair by the window wearing a sunflower peignoir. Michel leaned down to kiss her. She had beautiful, velvety skin, a fine aquiline nose and sensuous lips. She was fifty-seven, twenty years older than he, but at night when she dressed in her Chanel or LaCroix at the restaurant, she might have passed for forty.

She noticed his air of preoccupation and that he was wearing his pager.

"Something going on?"

"Two young Americans were murdered near the dam. Brutal. And the local branch is wrecking the investigation."

"Have they asked you to take over?"

"If Dr. Stein clears me."

He filled a vase with cold water and arranged the sunflowers.

"Darling, thank you for the flowers."

"You match."

He wasn't quite sure how to broach the subject of Yvette. Nicole had never interfered in his private life and he admired her clandestine talent for evasion.

"Your father called and broke the news."

"Are you upset?"

"Me? I liked Yvette in spite of her shallowness. I thought she'd outgrow it when she felt more secure about her career."

"She was having an affair—probably still is—with that imbecile Paul Courbet."

"I know."

"The detective finds out last. Yvette said goodbye to me by taking most of my furniture. I have half a sectional now."

"I hope she took your bed. You could use a new one."

"That's what they all say. Maybe it's true."

He felt a curious sense of despondency overwhelm him. This was usually a precursor to a panic attack, but he managed to remain calm. The public knowledge was mortifying. He had the local gossip to look forward to.

"When did you hear about Yvette and Courbet?"

"Louise told me before Yvette left for Paris. I didn't think it was worth worrying you about."

"Were you waiting for me to read it in the papers?"

"No, of course not, Michel. But there are things a man has to find out for himself. I don't like informers or blackmailers."

"Blackmailers? What's that supposed to mean?"

"Louise wants to see you. In fact you just missed her. She's in a difficult situation."

"What would you like me to do?"

"Help her."

"How?"

"I'm not the policeman."

He was for once guarded with his mother. Nicole Danton was not in the habit of soliciting favors from anyone.

"I don't think I can interfere if there's some kind of investigation going on."

"There's a threat of one. She's terribly anxious and not herself."

"I'll see. . . ."

The nurse came in carrying a metal tray on which a syringe lay like a sleeping snake.

"What's that for?" he asked.

"My antibiotic. Gallbladder's miserable surgery. I'm still draining."

"Well, your kitchen partner should assume some responsibility."

"How's he doing?"

"Wrestling with Louise's last shipment of steaks."

"Was there a marbling problem with her new Charolais?"

"No, there was enough fat to bard the roasts."

He thought his mother was ready to spring onto the wheelchair and fire her range.

"Did the *saucisson* arrive from the farm?"

"Yes, it's wonderful. I did a tasting before hanging them in the *charcuterie*."

"Are you quarreling with your father?"

"I thought he'd go for the cleaver when I quit. But there was a witness."

Nicole laughed and held her side. "He's impossible to work with."

"I never understood why you married him in the first place?"

"It was a sexual attraction and you were basting," Nicole replied with a cynical smile. "I'm sorry. But the attraction is still there."

"At least I know why you never divorced him."

"Michel, be kind to him. Poor thing, he feels helpless without me. He couldn't really cook at all when we met. He was only a grill man in the navy for admirals."

"Congratulations, you saved them from scuttling the fleet again."

CHAPTER 5

With murder in mind, Boy waited for Maddie across the street from Louise's house. The five-foot-four miniature Samson stood staring at himself in a boutique window, striking weightlifter's poses, the cherub as discus thrower. He had streaked, shoulder-length blond hair, a button nose, and a playful smile that brought out an androgynous mystery in his personality. When they'd met last Christmas, Maddie had told him he was a ringer for Brad Pitt. Boy had heard it all before.

As usual Maddie was late leaving class and arrived on the run, breathless, sweat running down her neck. But he liked the hunting smell of her.

"The professor went on for another hour."

"Why didn't you cut out?"

"It's my favorite course. I'm doing a paper on the symbolist poets. Actually, it's you. You're my Rimbaud."

He'd heard the name before and didn't like the sound of it.

"Oh, yeah, right."

"Françoise grabbed me on the Cours Mirabeau. She's hysterical." There was a flinty coldness in Maddie which he had cultivated. "Louise fired her and shipped her out."

Françoise was one of the madam's regular sirens for sale. She and her Arab boyfriend had befriended them when they'd first hit town. Françoise had introduced Maddie to Louise's brothel.

"Jennifer filed a complaint with the police about me working there."

"What? How'd Jennifer find out?" Maddie lost it and crumpled in his arms. "You told her!"

"I'd had so much hash to smoke. My eyes were rolling behind my brain. And I was upset. I hate to see you doing these dirty jobs for a hairdresser. You're so down."

"That's a certified fact." His anger would not abate. The wide smile he hid behind blistered into rage. "Your freakin' tutor Jennifer has ruined our summer."

"I made a joke out of it. I never thought she'd take me seriously. It was just some girl pillow talk, that's all."

"Pillow talk. Did Jennifer get excited or anything?"

"No."

"Did you try to lean your head on her thigh?"

"She pulled away when I tried it on."

"You've got to jump-start Jennifer. She's got a cold battery is all. But she's curious about what it would be like."

"Not from me," Maddie replied, forlorn.

An early plan of Boy's which involved Jennifer's seduction by Maddie had come to nothing. If Maddie got her in the sack, that would have given her some leverage and access to her funds. Boy was ready to explode, then held back and appraised Maddie.

With her cyanic blue eyes, Maddie's looks still fascinated him. In her Pembrooke College T-shirt and cut-offs, she was a gorgeous, fresh, virginal, sinuous waif with tawny hair. At the cafés and wine bars, the men couldn't keep their eyes off her. Boy saw them lick their lips and sniff. They strained to walk beside her four abreast on the main drag. She was the finest piece of tail in the city and she couldn't work.

"My fault. I should have done something about Jennifer in California."

"My folks wouldn't have let me come without her," Maddie protested. "They trust her."

He could see the kid squirming, wondering how she could continue to protect her teacher.

"Please, Boy, don't start again. You promised you wouldn't hurt Jennifer."

"I don't know why I give in to you."

A dazzling tableau flashed through Boy's mind. He'd have another picnic on the grass. This time with Jennifer.

"Maddie, you head over to Louise's house and plead with her. Speak softly. You're hurt, the injured party. You did these guys as a demo. You were promised a job by Françoise—her main lady. And Louise broke her word to Françoise. You have to do a number on Louise. You turned your tricks."

"I practically OD'd from the garlic those guys had for lunch."

"Exactly my point. Turn on the waterworks. If Louise is any kind of human bein', she'll lay some money on you." Boy had thought this out. "See where she goes for it. There has to be a safe. Find the location. I saw her on her roof garden. Diamonds and emeralds flashing. She's got more rings than I've had hot dinners."

He spotted Louise driving off in a Rolls-Royce and shoved Maddie away.

"Let's get goin'. Never mind. We missed the boat."

Maddie banged her head against the cobblestoned cathedral wall and cried, "It doesn't matter, Boy. I went to see her yesterday and she threw me out on the street like a dog. If you want me to try again, I will."

"Believe me, sugar, she's going to have to explain her behavior to me." He peered at the Rolls, throttled in traffic. "Hey, she's stuck in this parking lot. We can follow her on foot."

As Michel was leaving the hospital, a silver gray Rolls-Royce pulled up at the curb and the driver blew the horn at him. He'd had many rides in Louise's car and owed a great deal to her. It never failed to puzzle Michel how his bourgeois mother and Louise came together when they were students at the Cordon Bleu. Nicole's family owned a herb farm along with almond orchards and olive groves outside of St-Rémy-de-Provence. From childhood Nicole had a flair for taking anything that grew on the farm and combining flavors into some daring and unusual dish.

Louise, on the other hand, decided that handling dough massacred her nails and formed disagreeable lumps on her silk dresses. In fact, learning to cook was superfluous training for a woman attracted to emeralds and large yachts sailed by wizened businessmen. Along with marrying well, to be wealthy, beautiful and permanently young were her lofty ambitions. Still, the handmaiden of Escoffier and the courtesan remained the dearest friends.

Louise Vercours was a majestic woman in her midfifties with a svelte figure, her long blond hair twisted in a braided knot. She was now thought to be the richest woman in Provence, with estates that dazzled the eye, shimmering like cities of gold through the luxurious lavender horizon; vineyards in Burgundy; herds of prime Charolais gamboling along the Loire which Chez Danton bought at cost and served to eager patrons.

She was said to run an abortion mill on one of her distant estates. It was rumored that this was the original source of her wealth: bovine field girls to whom she promised husbands. It was rumored that Louise replied furiously to the accusation: "Novices have to begin somewhere and they've already been branded."

Thus, the feudal passage resumed, from apprenticeship to journey-dame. Then to craft and ultimately a room in Louise's guildhall in Aix. Afterwards, who knew . . . an apartment for those with strong backs and courage? Her complexity divided the locals into rival camps. To those who were envious, she seemed to be a queen whose domain was merely an arid plain of materialism. But to Michel and her friends, she was a benefactor. To put it kindly, the Dantons were loose change in her pocket.

It was impossible for Michel to be rancorous about her. When he got into the passenger seat, he leaned over and kissed her with the unsullied affection of a child greeting his rich aunt. Louise had been mistress to many but mastered by none. Her face delighted Michel, its luminous façade concealing many secrets. She put down the cellular phone that seemed nowadays, like her emeralds, to accompany her everywhere.

"Thank God for air conditioning," he said, mopping the sweat off his brow. "I was on my way to see you."

She always smelled so delicious and tantalizingly seductive. She had godmothered his first amorous experience with one of her new ripe, country plums brought in from the Midi.

"Michel, I'm so relieved I caught you."

"What's happened?"

"An American woman by the name of Jennifer Bowen registered a complaint about me with Paul Courbet. This lunatic accused me of procuring her student." Louise reached for her notepad. "This Bowen woman is some kind of professor and tutors a girl called Maddie Gold. It's a canard. I've never heard of either of them. I asked my manager—you know Gerard—?"

"Oh, him. He owns a porn store in Aubagne—with an Algerian thug."

"Yes. But Gerard's very efficient. He questioned all the girls and he thinks one of them made up this story, or possibly brought in a friend. But that's unlikely. I mean to say, it's all slander. These damn girls prattle and lie about everything."

Michel waited for Louise to continue her performance as the coy innocent.

"An *American* working for *me?* Have you ever heard anything so crazy? With all the unemployed French girls, it would be unpatriotic to engage foreigners. That's the counsel I offer Gerard. He does the hiring and he suspects one of the girls has a grudge against him and is using me to start trouble."

Prostitution had been wrapped in the banner of chauvinism and economic necessity. Michel detected no irony in Louise's tone or expression. The country was in a dizzy economic crisis. Buy French, simple as that. One would have thought she'd been elected to the Chamber of Deputies. And that was the way she distanced herself from the trade, through rationalizations and intermediaries. She never gave orders, merely whispered requests. If there was a chain leading to her, a link would be missing. Louise ran a men's club, and the members were some of the most important landowners and politicians in Provence.

"Did you ever meet Maddie Gold?"

"No, of course not," she said peevishly.

There was no reason not to believe Louise.

"Now Courbet is demanding a hundred thousand francs—or he'll take it to the examining magistrate and have me charged."

"Are you serious?"

"I could go to prison."

"Does Claude know about it?"

"I think he's a silent partner. He keeps a dog but does his own barking."

"How do I get in touch with this Jennifer?"

"I'll drive you there."

Michel did not like this situation. Since a murder wasn't involved, he might have talked to the officer who took the report. A friendly backscratch.

"I don't have much influence with Courbet. You already know Yvette's had an abortion."

"I sent her to my man in Paris. I didn't want you to be upset, so I did it quietly."

"Yvette didn't mention that." He didn't know whether to slap Louise silly or to tell her he appreciated the gesture. "Everyone's so concerned about my feelings."

"You have sensibilities, Michel, they're deeper than feelings."

"Maybe that explains my killer reviews in bed."

"I can do something about that if you like."

Michel glanced into the rearview mirror and saw a couple of young people chasing the Rolls. Maybe they thought film stars were in town. Louise also spotted them; she turned the car sharply, freeing herself from the traffic, and left them in the summer dust.

"Thanks for the offer. But there're some things I have to do for myself."

Troops of indefatigable tourists were lined up outside Cézanne's studio, shoveling croissants into their mouths and smearing their faces with sunblock. Come September, they'd be gone. Louise turned off on the Boulevard du René Roi and pulled up at the porte-cochère of a resplendent old Rococo mansion near the university. Like many of Aix's historic buildings, it had been sliced up into expensive flats. The friezes and pediments had been cleaned and the wrought iron balconies painted a dark green. Some of them had been turned into small gardens and were laced with trellises of bougainvillea. A number of locals evacuated in the summer and rented their apartments to students and pilgrims. He was surprised that a teacher could afford such a luxurious accommodation.

Louise stared at him for a moment, touched his hand, petting him, more like it, he thought.

"I'll wait for you?"

"No, I'll walk to the psychiatric hospital afterwards. It's one of my high maintenance days."

"I'll be seeing you for dinner at Chez Danton. With Denise as usual."

"If you need a reservation, don't use my name."

CHAPTER 6

Michel had expected Jennifer Bowen to resemble one of those shriveled sacks of dried figs entwined on a wooden stem and wrapped in dusty cellophane that morose people with bowel trouble buy in health food stores. Instead he found himself confronted by a ravishing thirty-year-old sensuous blonde. Her hourglass figure would please Renoir. She looked anything but prudish.

"I was expecting Sergeant Courbet."

"He has a full plate. I do the tourist run for him."

"Oh, you're sort of a PR who speaks English." Michel presented her with his identity card. "My God, you're from the Police Judiciare."

"We do our best to impress visiting scholars."

"Jesus, this is something. I'm astounded."

"Isn't this a life-threatening situation?" Michel said, boiling over. He was humiliated, wasting his time on this fool's errand instead of investigating the murders.

Jennifer Bowen backed off. "Not exactly. But you know in California you could lie in the street with a bullet through your brain and the police would drive around you."

"Well, your TV reporters give first aid, don't they? They always beat the cops to the scene."

"Unfortunately, you're right."

She was striking, with a pleasing density, lime-colored eyes, and succulent coppery skin. She led him upstairs to a dark, bleak attic above the main apartment. Of course, she had the maid's quarters. An au pair exchange of sorts.

"How'd you learn to speak such excellent English?" she asked, a bit superciliously, he thought.

"It may come as a shock to you, but we have schools in France that teach foreign languages. Like English. Some of us have even been to the United States."

"*Bien dit* . . . I guess I deserved that."

She gabbled away nervously. Her French had a haughty Parisian roundness, nagged by its very faultlessness. She had spent a year at the Sorbonne in her junior year on an exchange program they had with Stanford. She went off on what seemed to be a tangent that witnesses develop when facing authority. Poor Cézanne had been the grand old saw of her Ph.D. dissertation. Her suntan bore witness to picnic excursions along the path of Mont Ste-Victoire. She had probably counted the rocks; they made a living publishing that sort of rubbish in American universities.

Didn't this woman understand that he didn't give a damn about her complaint? But he had nothing better to do. He could kill a few hours playing lightning chess at one of the cafés around the university. Drive into Marseille and drink at the golf club until his appointment with Dr. Stein. He'd better not come in staggering like the last time.

At last she turned to the subject at hand.

"Maddie Gold is one of my students at Pembrooke College. And I'm supervising her during a summer course here at the University of Aix."

"How lovely for you both."

Jennifer's duties, apart from coaching Maddie in French art history and poetry, included the maidenly but martinet duties of housemistress. And not to put too fine a point on Jennifer's skills as a chaperone, she was worried. The girl might conceivably have picked up something, heaven forbid, HIV. Jennifer would have a problem explaining that away to Maddie's parents.

"Maddie Gold is upsetting the natives. Frankly, I don't give a damn if she wants to work as a prostitute. I'll arrest her if you like. But don't go running to the vice squad with lies about her working in a brothel for a distinguished citizen. There are no brothels in Aix!"

"There aren't?"

"No, Miss Bowen, they're against the law. You must be watching old movies."

"I do watch old movies! Is that okay with you? Look, I'm having a helluva time handling Maddie. I wanted to come back to France. Thanks to her father, I got this trip to Aix—all expenses paid. I never would have been able to afford it. Her father is Adam Gold, the American TV producer." Jennifer removed several typewritten sheets of paper from a bureau drawer and thrust them at Michel. "Please, please, would you read this? It explains what Maddie's parents had to say about the situation she got herself into a home. They gave it to me at LAX as we were leaving."

Michel scowled at her. He didn't want to get further enmeshed in this ludicrous affair. He gave the letter a perfunctory glance.

From the Desk of Adam Gold

Dear Jennifer:

My lovely daughter hates her mother and me. She is our only child and we have spoiled her rotten. But Maddie's smile can bring a tear to my eye. I will do anything to prevent her from ruining herself and the fortune that she'll inherit.

I'm supposed to be a tasteless TV hack writer who got lucky. Well, I have eight Emmys for my lack of taste. Yes, I got in on the ground floor, but does that make me a villain? No, I'm not Norman Lear or Aaron Spelling, but I certainly pitch in their league. I am not the carnival buffoon my daughter makes me out to be.

Short of sending Maddie to France with an escort of security people, I let her go with you. I don't want to make my daughter a prisoner. The point is, we have been through hell with her. Drug rehab, an abortion, psychiatrists, counseling. My wife and I did not mention these problems to you before you undertook the trip with Maddie. Frankly, we were afraid you'd run for cover if we told you this up front.

Maddie's involved with a young man who worries us. Since she was so secretive about him—and he spooked me— I hired a private detective to follow him on a date up at Ojai. It turned out to be an expensive and dangerous assignment.

On the mountain road above the lake—when you turn off the 101 to Pembrooke—Maddie had stopped her Porsche. According to the detective, Maddie and this character got out and went down the side of the hill.

The detective parked and tried to track them. He was worried about Maddie. He couldn't find either of them. Then out of the blue, his car was pushed off the side of the road into the ravine and exploded. We both found this behavior hard to believe. It was no accident!

In any case, my attorneys ran a check on you, and you are a fine scholar and an outstanding person who I know has suffered a personal tragedy. If only you could exert a positive influence on our daughter.

P.S. This is from me, Karen!!! Maddie is irresponsible with money. But let her have a little extra if she needs cosmetics, hairdresser or wants to buy some clothes.

Have Fun,
Adam and Karen Gold

Michel handed the letter back to Jennifer. His head was splitting. Cluster headaches had succeeded panic attacks in the pantheon of his mental health. He was, however, relieved that Maddie herself was not there for him to question, since then he would have learned the truth. That might have led to more complications. Now he'd move his knight and trap the queen.

"Does Maddie ever lie?"

"Sometimes."

"You're absolutely certain she was telling the truth this time?"

"No, I'm not."

"By the way, how old is Maddie?"

"Nineteen."

"Good, she's not a minor." Michel was beginning to enjoy himself. He'd rescue Louise and give this self-righteous, repressed, soap-opera fan something to write home about. "Okay, here's what we're going to do. I'll have two of my men pick Maddie up at the university. You'll both come into Marseille with me—"

"Hang on, Commander." Panic overcame Jennifer.

"Wait till I'm through. I have the power of subpoena and I'm going to bring you before an examining magistrate so he can prepare a case. You'll need a bilingual attorney. Let's see, someone from the American embassy in Paris will have to fly in. Since Mr. Gold is so important, the ambassador himself will probably have to appear. Do you want to call Mr. Gold now? Better still, his public relations people. They'll want time to prepare a press statement? Oh, damn, I'll also have to contact our Foreign Ministry."

Jennifer fell back as though she'd been poleaxed. "Oh, Christ, am I in trouble?"

He let her squirm. "What do you think? This is an international incident."

"I don't know what to do."

"Nor do I. You and Maddie want to press charges against an imaginary madam in an imaginary brothel?" Jennifer was hyperventilating.

"You made this story up and reported it Sergeant Courbet to protect yourself, didn't you? Why, because Maddie was fooling around with some guy?"

"It's called watching your ass at home."

"Professor Bowen, you can't come to a foreign country and make wild charges against respectable citizens. There's hell to pay. This is France, not New Jersey. Our society is built on law. You've set off machinery . . . when it begins to grind, it makes a terrible racket."

"You're so angry." His belligerence unnerved her. "I had to get on record."

"You succeeded and launched an investigation!"

She was so intimidated that she trembled and fell on his mercy.

"It was almost impossible in this job market to get a job after I got my Ph.D. from Stanford. I had to teach crammer French. I finally wound up at a two-year no-name institution called Pembrooke College. When a girl's grades and SAT scores aren't good enough, they come to us. This job gives me time for research. And it pays the bills." She winced and her body bunched up into a ball. "I can't tell you what it was like to scrounge for a year."

Jennifer Bowen gave off an aura of what he could only think of as fertile, a roundness of shape and innocent generosity that had about it something medieval. She would have been at home as a figure in a tapestry. Whereas he carried within him the comfortable and resilient country thickness of someone whose ancestors had tilled the soil and turned the olive presses for a thousand years. In spite of his irritation, his sympathies were engaged, but he forced the issue. He had to get Louise off this dangling hook.

"Does Maddie want to make a statement?"

"I . . . I don't think so."

"Good. Call Sergeant Courbet and tell him you'll drop this charade. Apologize and say it was a practical joke. You're an American. You think it's funny when someone slips on a banana peel or gets whacked with a pie in the face."

"You're confusing us with the Germans. And I don't like your anti-Americanism."

"The fact is, I love America."

"You could've fooled me."

She was building a head of steam and he realized he should have quit earlier. "The French have made a god out of Jerry Lewis," she said.

"You don't think he's funny?"

"Try Sid Caesar's old *Show of Shows.*"

"Who . . . ? Professor Bowen, you've got such a fantastic imagination. Call Courbet . . . A brilliant woman like you will think of something."

She became wary. Maybe he'd overplayed his hand.

"Really? If we're down to bartering, you can take me to dinner."

He glanced around Jennifer's attic room. It held a travel clothes line with her insinuating lingerie drying. He watched her self-consciously folding her underclothes.

"Dinner? Is this your usual method for dating? Some kind of New Age California technique you're introducing me to?"

"I'm lonely. And good French husbands always wear wedding rings."

"Maybe I have a girlfriend—or a boyfriend."

"I don't think so." She had caught him staring too long at her lacy black bras. "Maybe you can tell your Jeanne d'Arc you have a murder suspect and you're busy with an interrogation?"

Something personal and unexpected was trapped within Michel. He felt a resurgence of desire. Jennifer Bowen had aroused him. The pure pleasure of an erection couldn't be presumptuously dismissed. Jennifer put her undies away in a drawer. She seemed at home in these surroundings. But behind her bravado was a gloomy quality that touched him. She had a beguiling face, with a broad forehead, full lips and an upturned freckled nose. He wondered why the scent of an unloved woman clung to her. What had Maddie's father meant by her personal tragedy? Jennifer Bowen did not look as though she was dying.

"Hello there . . . Do I get an answer? I'm going to hang up my jeans. You probably want to follow me into the wardrobe and do a strip search."

Michel couldn't believe her gall and wondered how to react. He looked at what Jennifer's dinner would be. It was an old spinster mélange: On a wobbly table, resting on a curiously folded moth-eaten cloth, a mummy-wrapped tallowed wedge of Port-l'Éveque cheese, yesterday's grim baguette, a compote dish with peaches and apples organized on a chipped plate. The requisite bottle of wine stood sentry.

"I was trying to create a still life that Cézanne might have painted."

"*Alors* . . . we're on for dinner on one condition. Pour out that old Nouveau Beaujolais."

She was again unhinged. "What's wrong with it? Is this part of some sadistic ritual for you to make me totally crazy?"

"Exactly. If you're going to drink *that*, it has to be in early November in the year of its birth. Your bottle is four years old."

"Don't give me any heat. I buy what I can afford."

Their eyes locked in a war of wills which he regarded as clumsily adolescent. Who would give in? Jennifer grimaced, finally drizzling the wine down the sink as though it was Christ's blood.

"Michel, Commander, whatever . . . I think you're definitely the person I can trust to complete my education."

He took out a crumpled card, the back of which contained the address and map to Chez Danton.

"I'll see you there about seven-thirty."

She smiled in triumph. "I'll be on time. Oh, is it dressy?"

"Yes, and very plush."

"Any Michelin stars?"

"No, they keep a low profile. It's the aristocrats' favorite spot. Get yourself tarted up."

"Sounds like Donna Karan time."

"And don't bring any more criminal complaints."

"We'll see about that."

Michel observed her swaggering and found his senses reawakening. He fought against it, but dammit, she made him smile. Like chess, he knew that it was fatal to give ground at the opening. Yielding to her could lead only to another debacle. He realized the seduction had begun: an itinerant academic counting dimes and a detective whose house specialty was murder. His dinner dates had seldom been made from such capricious preludes.

CHAPTER 7

Boy pondered his next move. Earlier he had forced a protesting Maddie into Denise's salon to get her hair dyed, then he hitched a ride out to Aubagne from a driver shuttling an empty produce truck back to the farm.

"You're going brunette," Boy had ordered Maddie after they had fruitlessly chased Louise and the burly passenger in her Rolls halfway across town. They finally sat down under a cool plane tree at the Fountain of Nine Cannons on the Cours Mirabeau. They were surrounded by crowds of students planning their evening entertainment. Boy had sloshed water down Maddie's neck and bought her an ice from a crippled peddler. He guided the truant back to Denise's shop.

"Why should I change my color?"

"I don't want anyone to recognize you."

"Why?"

Boy dug his thumbs into her elbow until the pressure was unbearable.

"You're hurting me."

"What about me? I had a life and it's five thousand miles away. I'm sleepin' on a metal cot in a box room and sweepin' hair in a shit town because of you. Do you have any common sense? I mean, what a place this is. They can't even grill a hamburger. When I'm nuts enough to order one, it comes out raw and costs me twelve bucks!"

Maddie fell back wounded, tears exploding down her cheeks. "I love you so much, it's killing me."

Boy gave her his magnetic field con. He slipped his tongue into her ear, sucked on it and made the hissing sound she loved. "You know, Maddie, when you're our age, sex is everything. We can't get enough. You'll look gorgeous with dark hair. And my lady, I will waste you."

"Oh please, yes." She broke the spell and looked at her watch. "I've got a class. Then Jennifer for two hours of conversation. If I'm late again, she'll be waving the flag from the terrace."

"I don't care."

"Aw, Boy, give me a break. Brunette?"

They were at the entrance to Denise's salon entrance.

"Hey, relax, we're going to collect the money that bitch Louise owes us."

"Oh, stop dreaming."

He pecked her on the cheek and she clung to him. "I stopped dreaming a long time ago! Now once you're in the salon, don't say a word to me. We're strangers, got it?"

Shop girls were coming in for a quick wash. Maddie noticed a few of them smiling and giving Boy long looks. Denise was hustling them over to assistants.

"Are you seeing someone else?"

"No way. I've told you, never be jealous. Everything I do is for us. Us! When you did those johns at Louise's, it was business, Maddie. I wasn't jealous. Now listen, I want you to meet me outside Chez Danton, soon as you shake Jennifer."

"Why?"

"I heard Denise speak to Louise. She made a date to eat there with her."

"I'll try."

He gave her a cold stare. "Suit yourself."

"Oh, Boy, stop this. I can't bear it when you're angry with me."

He considered her state of mind. One more push and she'd be over the edge.

"Maddie, I want tonight to be special. Remember me telling you about valiant deeds. Experiences that shape you—if you've got the grit and spirit. Your problem is you've never stood up to your parents. Or even Jennifer. You have to take command, Maddie."

"You know I want to." She was aroused by the thrill of breaking down the barrier of rules which had always imprisoned her. His eyes flashed and she sensed the danger. "I'd kill for you."

"I'll give you a chance to prove it."

"You know you can count on me. Where're you going now?"

"Out to see Karim."

"What for?"

"My business."

There was another aspect to Boy's plan. Women were unpredictable, even the best of them, and implicating Maddie in murder would bind her to him permanently. Once they were finished with Louise, she would be the first woman he could entirely trust.

* * *

Shortly after arriving in Aix, when he'd run low on cash, Boy had met Karim Hassad and his girlfriend Françoise Artois. Boy had horned into a new model apartment on Pont de l'Arc. He had flimflammed a real estate agent, persuading the man he was the wealthy scion of an Oklahoma oil millionaire and the family might buy a bunch of apartments. After several days there, he had persuaded Maddie to try to turn some tricks. At first she balked. But when he let loose a tirade, threatening never again to see her, she turned to butter.

It would be the old badger move. Maddie would lure in a guy and get him to strip. Boy would take his money, then tear his eyes out.

He had given Maddie a pregame pep talk.

"Now strut that tail, wild thing, and give 'em that L.A. sunshine smile."

"I'll deliver, you better believe it."

It had worked. Maddie was seeing the reflection of herself in his eyes; her self-respect was his to generate or to extinguish. She would be one of the countless millions who could never understand "clarity of intent."

The idea of turning Maddie out was a real clunker, especially in a strange territory and with an inexperienced rich girl as bait. A total washout. Maddie didn't have a clue. She hit on an Arab in his twenties as her first mark. Really! The girl didn't know a slave trader from a Persian carpet. In two minutes Karim had been joined by a leggy, dirty-blond degenerate in leather shorts so tight that her thighs bulged out of them like jelly doughnuts.

The three of them went into Boy's model apartment. The two hustlers had excellent fleecer's English. When Boy bolted out of the closet with a tire iron, the four of them fell down laughing. Brilliancy prize for Maddie. Boy sends her out for a john, she comes back with a pimp and a hooker. But that was how Maddie got to Louise's.

At Deux Garçons, Karim had sprung for sandwiches and beer, and Françoise had made a proposition to Maddie.

"I'm a working girl and the madam always likes fresh faces. After I pay the house, I sometimes bring home as much as four hundred dollars in a day."

"Don't even think of such a thing, Françoise!" Karim snarled. "Louise would never take in an American girl."

Karim had pitted prune skin, wore baggy designer suits, a silk shirt and some kind of curried cologne. His ebony eyes were at once mysterious and tormented. Boy thought he must use sardine oil on his hair.

"Four hundred, cool," Boy said. "My little Maddie will pounce on a stick for that."

"It's not what you think," Karim said sharply. "Françoise does this work because she's supporting a great revolutionary cause . . ." Karim turned political and the rebel flounced into being. Maddie leaned forward earnestly. "The Algerians—and I am proud to be one of them— deserve equal rights in France. Instead we're thrown into hovels, abused by the police . . ." Maddie was lapping up this bleeding-heart bilge. "Now there's a horrible civil war going on between the fundamentalists and the military in Algeria."

And on and on Karim the Arab went: coups, bomb plots, noble sentiments. Boy switched off. Nothing but trash talk. He wanted to ask the patriot just one question: "Is your girlfriend Françoise selling her ass for the great cause, or to keep you in threads?" He kept quiet though. Karim was paying. The customer is always right.

En route to Aubagne, Boy sat on bunch of old burlap sacks and nibbled something he thought to be celery. It looked like celery, had a bulb with stalks, but turned out to have a horrible licorice flavor. The French couldn't even grow celery. They reeked of garlic, ordered chartreuse-colored piss drinks in cafés, pigged out with anchovies on oily bread. And their women! Lots of them didn't shave their legs or under their arms. They'd have to go to a Mexican jail to get laid. Everything sucked and was a rip-off. Bars wanted a sawbuck for a shot of Jack Daniel's.

The scenery, however, enchanted him. Fields of lavender and wild herbs, sunflowers, all billowed in the gusty wind. He had to admit Provence had it over the States when it came to landscapes and postcards.

He thought wistfully of Mystery Man and their good times together and how much his redeemer would have enjoyed the vista. He had rescued Boy from a childhood filled with unspeakable torture. If he were with Boy, he would have relished working on Louise with him. Boy had a sudden longing for the old team that had coupled when he'd been growing up in Oklahoma: the narrow escapes, the tense sense of danger they felt on their forays in search of valiant deeds.

"Snakes and burns / Make you do crazy turns," he droned in a singsong voice to himself.

*   *   *

The major's real name was Eldon Royce Calhoun, but to this day, Boy thought of him as Mystery Man. He'd be rocking toward sixty by now, but his back would be ramrod straight and his posture that of an officer on parade, taking salutes. He had been Boy's mentor. Under his tutelage, Boy had discovered the possibilities of what the major referred to as *fate control*. There had been the diligent lessons in snake handling: when to trust a diamondback and when to span his neck with the forked stick. Boy fed them and played with them fearlessly. When he and the major were going out on a mission, Boy would boil up the mushrooms and peyote they got from the Indians and add it to the snakes' drinking water. It fired them up. The major brought in kraits and mambas from Africa which he ordered like catalogue seed and they'd collect them from seamen on freighters in Galveston.

Major Calhoun would say: "Snakes, why they are the easiest, tamest pets in the world. Only treat them right. Bunny rabbit for Easter and a nice meaty hen for Christmas. Why your household kitty'd be more likely to claw you or Rover to nip you than a snake shooting venom at you. World-class sleepers, made for survival. You must make a friend of the leader of the pack because they have a leader like every living thing. Then none of the others'll go for you."

He had given Boy his first real home in his ranch house. And privacy! No one pounded on the bathroom door when he was inside. The Mexican maid cleaned up after him, did his laundry, and cooked up storms of enchiladas and carnitas. Hand-made her own tortillas on a little griddle in the kitchen. The thought of them made Boy hungry.

The major had a pork-packing operation. He supplied the bughouses, Indian reservations, here and there an army base. Boy started out in the gut shanty working offal, pig's hearts and livers, cleaning the intestines for sausage casing. The trotters were pickled and sold in large jars to bars. What cattle they had were "downers," the sick oldsters that dropped to the ground of fever or disease. After slaughter, they were sold to markets in the barrio.

The newspapers labeled Mystery Man as part of the Dixie Mafia. They dared not use his name, but referred to him as a distinguished former army officer. Nobody could prove a damn thing. Where was the evidence of hijacked cigarettes from North Carolina which New Jersey ginzos bought; or the charges of bootlegging and manufacture of thunderclap? The major never went near a still, he just collected protection from the moonshiners and would put in a word with the sheriff or some good old boys at the state AFT branch. Yes, he sold some of the Indians' loco weed, and gave them their fair share. When the bikers got out of line running crank through their whores, it wasn't no damn sheriff who read them the riot act. The bleating lawmen would haul ass over to Major Calhoun's front porch, and he'd have a quiet word with the bikers and they'd tone down the volume.

He had been a Green Beret, captured by the Vietcong, eventually escaping with the help of some French legionnaires left over from Dien Bien Phu. When he returned home, Major Eldon Royce Calhoun was a world authority on torture. But he never spoke or complained of his experiences.

On Saturday nights the major ran a hi-low game at Shorty's market and on Sunday the big fiesta took place in his barn. The cockfights were exciting devilish bouts with hundreds of men betting and rooting for their *hombre* to carve up the opponent. Boy sharpened the swords and attached them to the cocks' legs and let the best man win.

Promotion and adulation followed Boy like a lucky star. He was the major's sunshine and at fifteen was appointed chief collector of the sums the major generously loaned out to the gamblers and workers.

"Now, Boy, you let a man, or a woman for that matter, welsh on a debt and your honor's besmirched. He starts in talking to his *amigos* and sooner than later they'll all be spittin' on your boots."

Boy traveled alone in the major's Caddy convertible, parked it right in the center of the barrio. He'd get out his satchel and snake basket and walk right into the Refresca Cantina or track down a delinquent to a mudhut. He always came back with something: the money or somebody's hand.

If someone turned Boy down flat and he knew it to be a righteous debt, he'd calmly offer him up some of his special thunder tequila. He'd already hit it with a dash of battery acid and peyote and the man would be seeing Tiger Woods's first thousand-yard drive.

"No hard feelings, *amigo*. Have a drink."

The man would drop to the ground and Boy would hook up a hair curling iron to his car battery and listen to the mooch squeal. Then he'd take out one of the slaughterhouse knives from his satchel, which were honed to cut paper, and he'd read that person the lesson of life. If you owed, you paid. Madame Louise was going to hear that message loud and clear.

*　　*　　*

Boy had been to La Sex Boutique once before. It was the size of small supermarket. It had a garish pink neon sign of a naked girl, viewing booths strewn with gummy Kleenexes and rows of videotapes and skin glossies. With the infernal sun flaming, a brisk lunch trade took wing inside.

Karim was bagging some porn tapes for a courtly gentleman. Boy did a casual browse; all of it, of course, made him yawn. In prison he had once read an article in *People* about actors' residuals. And how they paid off. With all the films and photos taken of him, by his reckoning, Boy should have been a millionaire and had an HMO. Instead he was still scabbing for bucks in a hardcore stall. He hung in one of the aisles, trying not to be noticed. Just check the lay of the land.

Behind the till was the owner, filling his pockets with franc notes.

". . . But Gerard, I unpacked the new merchandise and didn't have time to dress the window," Karim whined.

"Do what I tell you or clear out."

Gerard was a round-shouldered, bearlike man in his late thirties, with a ratty ponytail and expensive, unstructured suits that flapped like sails on his stocky frame. He had a soft, oily voice, a twiglike wheedle. He worked at Louise's as master of the foxhounds. Karim's ole lady, Françoise, claimed Gerard treated them like he was a concentration camp commandant.

Boy didn't understand the language, but picked up on their beef.

A pair of droning, parboiled Englishmen brought some gadgets to the register. Gerard smiled at the customers and let the argument with Karim simmer. He and Karim spoke English to them. Gerard asked about their holiday while Karim assembled their vibrators and loaded the batteries for their adventures in marital orgasms. Gerard rang up their purchases and Karim bagged them in an oversize sack. Soon as the johns were gone, the argument resumed.

". . . First you send Françoise away to Cannes and I'm only one person in the shop."

"Cannes! Is Cannes torture?" Gerard bellowed. "Françoise brought in an American girl and now there's hell to pay with the police. Louise is hysterical."

"Françoise didn't bring in any American girl! She knows better than that."

Boy listened intently. Françoise had been shipped out. Karim, Mr. Revolutionary, was getting his ass kicked and Gerard was the storm king. Tail between his legs, Karim lugged some cartons to the front, took his shoes off, and climbed into the window. A rabid, sweating pack of Foreign legionnaires bustled through, demanding change for the video booths from Gerard. The Legion had a barracks in Aubagne. Boy used them as cover to slip outside.

Last time they had drinks, Boy had spotted an automatic peeping out of Karim's jacket pocket. He lived behind the porn shop in a decaying cottage that reeked of horrid spices, teas, and old lard caked like dam walls in the fry pans. While there, Boy had scouted the place for weapons or anything that might have value.

Karim had laid some hash laced with opium on him a few days ago. Doing his good deed, Boy had brought it back to get loaded with Maddie. Maddie had gone back to the apartment Adam Gold had rented for her and Jennifer. She'd been so stoned she had blabbed to Jennifer about her session at Louise's.

The moment Karim started to dress a mannequin in the window, Boy whipped out of the shop. He wove through the parking lot and slipped into the alleyway to the back. There was a broken window on the side of Karim's shack, filled with a lumpy piece of Styrofoam. Boy removed it and climbed inside.

Boy went through the obvious places: under the bed, the dresser drawers, suit jackets. He didn't see any of Françoise clothes, but he found a box of surgical gloves and an eternity's supply of douche rinses.

He'd been searching for close to three minutes. Mystery Man had schooled him well. Four minutes is danger, five and get ready to shoot your way out. He hit paydirt at the top of the closet. A wooden box had been jammed into a breeze-block crack. Boy yanked it out. It was a beautiful piece. A loaded S&W .45 and a box of ammo.

He was thinking quickly and decided to make a switch. He opened his backpack and removed the clawed, bloody, camping hatchet he had used on the commodity trader and the redhead. It was clean of prints and, if he needed it again, he knew where to find it. He'd used a condom with the girl. No way physical evidence could link him to the murders. Not even a strand of hair, if these yokels collected evidence like that.

He replaced the Styrofoam and slunk around the block to check the shop. Karim was still in the window, draping chains and handcuffs over a female mannequin wearing a leather mask. Gerard was outside, directing this fashion show in perversion.

Boy stuck his thumb out to the dusty road and happily sat with a bunch of yammering kids in the back of another farm pickup that was lugging lemons to the market in Aix. He revised his opinion of the French. They were champs to hitchhikers.

The gun was essential and felt comforting when Boy snuggled against it in his backpack. When he had gotten into real trouble, he could trace his problems to ignoring the wisdom of Mystery Man.

"You might kick a dog, or take a forked stick to a rattler, but if you want to get the attention of a human being, don't be flickin' some Jazz-bo knife at them. Boy, you jam a loaded gun between their eyes and cooperation follows. . . ."

CHAPTER 8

Still fuming, Michel left the police station. The bodies of the two young Americans had been sent to Marseille for autopsy. He didn't know if they had been identified. As far as he was concerned, it was a total blackout. He had tried to see Aix's chief but had been turned away. He was in a meeting with the mayor and city council about the crowd control problem at the music festival. According to his secretary, a delegation of merchants was ahead of him, whining about the tourists' double-parking, which held up deliveries to the shops. The traffic officers had run short of tickets and half the tow trucks were being repaired in the municipal garage.

"Does anyone here give a damn about murder?" he had shouted to the duty officer on his way out.

"Michel, why don't you go to the spa for a massage or switch on *Baywatch?*"

"France is going to hell because of people like you! By the year 2000, we'll be buying our computers from the Congo."

Michel hurried down the Avenue de l'Europe to the psychiatric hospital, dreading his time with Dr. Stein. What a miserable summer this had turned out to be. In the musty entry, the usual group of schizophrenics were lined up, waiting for their drugs. Nowadays, everyone was an outpatient because the government was broke.

"Ah, Michel, you're early and I'm running late," Dr. Stein said. "How are you?"

"I've been having wet dreams about bouillabaisse."

"Doesn't everyone? At least you're sober today."

He put an arm around Michel and led him into his office. Their bonhomie was genuine, antedating the patient-doctor relationship. Leon Stein was on his fourth wife and had a gaggle of children. Invariably broke, he foraged for alimony change, working as a forensic consultant with the Special Circumstances Section in Marseille when they had a nut to crack. He loved the cops-and-robbers adventures. How else did a pudgy man somewhere around sixty get to race through lights, flash a windshield card advertising police business, and double-park when he was at dinner with some patient he was trying to seduce?

"I'll slip Jung in today and see if we can find a few fertility symbols in a bouillabaisse."

"Frankly, Leon, I haven't got time. There's been a double murder. I can't work on it until you reinstate me."

"Anyone we know?"

"No, two young Americans. Ordinarily, I'd head the investigation. But the chief in Aix hasn't called our office yet. And I'm persona non grata with him."

"Go on." Stein flicked the switch on his sputtering air conditioner. His desk was piled high with professional journals, which he tossed on the floor along with his cigar ash.

"Yvette's been shacking up with Paul Courbet under my nose. Another thing. After she told me, I was mousetrapped into a date with an American teacher I'd never met before."

"Congratulations. At least you don't have an eating disorder."

"I don't think that's funny."

"I can see that." He paused and regarded Michel with sympathy. "Actually, I thought Yvette would leave you at Christmas during the kitchen wars between your parents. Frankly, I think all the Dantons are crazy. It runs in families."

"Oh, stop it." Michel pulled him up short. "Did you know about Yvette?"

"Sure. You did, too, but you didn't want to see it."

The insight calmed him. "Leon, I've got a suggestion. You're in a financial bind. If you slip me back on duty, I'll see that you're put on the payroll to work with me on the case."

"That's a very attractive offer. I've got some free time. But as your doctor, I'm not certain you can handle the pressure."

"Sitting on the sidelines for six months has been torture."

"There were no options. Michel, don't you realize that you've been unbalanced? You almost murdered an innocent man."

"I had a flashback of the scene in Corsica. The man I went after could have been the twin brother of the killer who shot me."

"But rationally, you knew you'd shot the assassin and he was dead."

"Not at the time. Look, Leon, I promise it won't happen again."

Michel stood at the window looking out beyond the gray fortress to the blistering sun-drenched streets.

Stein pulled a chart from the dusty sill. "Your lab work is back."

"Yes?"

"All normal. Except your testosterone level. It's in the high to normal range. Any more anxiety episodes or panic attacks?"

"I thought I was having one earlier."

"What were the circumstances?"

"When I made this date. I was as nervous as schoolboy."

"Take her to a film, that's the place for a grope."

"She's . . . I felt sorry for her."

"Weren't you attracted?"

"She excited me."

"That should make you feel better. How long has it been since you were intimate with Yvette?"

Michel blanched and retreated. He mumbled, "Six months . . . or more."

"Much too long for someone your age. You're a very desirable man, Michel, with needs."

"They didn't coincide with Yvette's. I had . . . trouble—" He broke off, mortified.

"Michel, I always believed that there was a neurotic component to your sexual relationship with Yvette. After being shot, you came back to life, so to speak. At that time the neurotic attachment to Yvette dissipated. She recognized it but you didn't."

"I wanted a passionately romantic relationship."

"You thought you did. But it was doomed from the outset. Yvette's a crime reporter, you're a homicide detective. It was never possible. She used you and you let her. Now if you want my advice, go to the music festival with this American girl. Take her out to your farm. Don't get emotionally involved, and give her a good screw."

"I need something more than that. I have to be tested again. Sharpened like a good knife."

He could see that behind Stein's easygoing smile the psychiatrist was unhappy with the simile. It was an uncomfortable moment for them both.

"I'll declare you fit for duty only if you continue to see me."

"My word. Fax Marseille . . . tell them I'm all right."

Stein lit a Havana, scrupulously allowing the flame to winnow the end into a perfect glow.

"My theory is that the only way to succeed with women—and killers for that matter—is to let them coax you into them catching you."

"I'll try that tonight on Jennifer."

"Bring her to the Provence Club after dinner."

"Are you thinking of giving her a Rorschach test?"

"I just want to make sure you're in good hands."

CHAPTER 9

Maddie stared vacuously into the hairdresser's mirror, not recognizing herself. This was a far cry from Beverly Hills where Michael Rosati took hours snipping and coloring her locks. A runty hairdresser, chewing gum, was combing her out in Denise's salon. Maddie's natural soft auburn hair was now a mousy brown. Boy had been in the back cleaning the sinks. Now he was pushing a broom under the chairs and scooping up the hair in a dustpan. He nodded with approval when he passed Maddie. She was enthralled by him and knew she'd do anything to please him. He was bringing her to new levels of consciousness and daring.

At the reception desk register, having a laugh on the phone, Denise Casson stood beneath a large framed photograph of herself and the illustrious Vidal Sassoon at a competition. Since then Denise's figure had waxed into a sun-dried medley of indeterminate lines with a sagging cleavage, goosed up by a Wonder bra so that her breasts resembled yesterday's doughy brioches sold by bakeries at a discount.

"Un moment, mademoiselle," she said as Maddie waited for her bill. "Well, I'm glad you've got good news, Louise. You can buy the champagne. *À bientot, chérie."*

Denise was enchained in a swag of bangles, and Boy had slipped in beside her to dust the costume jewelry in the glass showcase. Denise gave him a friendly rub with her hip and Boy smirked as though to say to his patroness, Not here . . . later. Maddie was about to explode with anger as she watched Boy operate. He took a shiny curling iron in his hand and was whipping it through the air and tickling Denise. They were both giddy with the childish game. When he put down the iron, Denise wove her fingers, not quite professionally, through his long thick textured hair.

She turned to Maddie. "Ah, sorry to keep you. We're so frivolous here. But it creates a good atmosphere, doesn't it?" she asked.

"I wouldn't know."

Denise took Maddie's money and rang it up, but she couldn't take her eyes off Boy and he continued his flirtation. The conqueror of lonely old hearts had her juices going.

"You want a good . . . umm, steak, I think," Denise said to Boy. "Tonight I'm having dinner with a friend. You can join us at Chez Danton."

Boy played her while Maddie fretted and looked through the selection of hair mousse.

"Chez Danton's a real popular place," he said.

"The town's favorite restaurant." Denise was ready to wrap him up as an early Christmas gift to herself. "They try to keep the tourists out. But they'll make an exception for you."

"You sure are spoilin' me, Denise." Boy peered at Maddie. "The Lancôme's real popular with all you ladies at the university," he said to Maddie.

"I'll have it," she said, gritting her teeth.

"André, I'll have to start paying you commissions." Denise refused to call him Boy and used the French code name Maddie had given him to outfox Jennifer.

Maddie again waited for change, which Denise took from a red pouch under the desk.

"I don't think I can make it. I've got a lot of reading to do. French poetry."

"Poetry, eh?" Maddie couldn't believe the way he was sucking up to Denise and caught her breath. "You could stop by for a drink afterwards."

There was another call and Denise flicked open the appointment book. Maddie stormed out and Boy trailed her, pushing his broom on the sidewalk through the rush of pedestrians.

"Hey, sugar. Your hair's fabulous. Boyfriend's going to love it."

She was having no more of his smooth talk. "Oh, really, will he? Why are you screwing around on me, Boy?"

"I'm a door away from homeless. Denise took me in off the streets. You think I enjoy strokin' her?" His voice was calm and she saw the child in him trying to please. "I guess I can't expect you to understand me. I've been let down before."

Her heart went out to him. "I'm so mad about you and I dragged you here."

"My lady, you can kiss me goodbye right now if you're not outside Chez Danton by eight. Oh, why am I botherin'? This is all about *your* honor and you don't get it."

* * *

Michel had to be careful of the inflection of mood swings, particularly the elation that accompanied him to Chez Danton. His apartment had looked like Hitler's bunker after the Russians arrived, but it didn't matter. He was dressed in a pale blue Cardin suit that he thought had been lost. Actually, it was the only complete suit he could locate. Yvette's idea of domesticity—which she had volunteered for when she moved in—had taken a perverse form. She would take a suit jacket *or* the trousers to the cleaners, but never in tandem. Thus, his wardrobe consisted of some jackets, some trousers, and he had taken to hiding his clothes even from himself.

He came in through the back of Chez Danton, and removed the wooden plaque over the boule court wall which hung in tribute to the annual champion. Last year after three consecutive victories it had been renamed PLACE DE PAUL COURBET. Michel disdainfully flung it into the trash and replaced it with the weary old Pernod sign. From the kitchen screen door, his father had been surveying these proceedings—one eye on the steaks grilling, the other suspiciously on his erratic son. Michel joined Philippe at the range. The chef had on his summer lightweight toque, and his grand barrel chest bulged through a starched jacket on which the blue-stitched MAÎTRE said it all. At times, Michel forgot their own animosity because of his father's devotion to Nicole.

He glared at Michel. "What the hell's going on outside?"

"I don't need any reminders of that bastard Courbet. By the way, I owe you an apology."

"You're thirty-seven years late."

"You want me to say I'm sorry for being born?"

"It won't help," said Delantier, the tottering headwaiter who was employed for catering parties when butler tinsel was called for. "Louise and Denise want the double Chateaubriand with *béarnaise*, Philippe." Delantier was in full regalia, with hair resembling oilcloth, parted in the middle, and his sommelier medallion swinging from his neck like a noose when he bowed. Philippe pulled a horn of ruby beef off the tray and set it on the back of the grill's flaming branches of olive wood.

"Save the alcove booth for me, Delantier."

The old waiter flapped a menu as if it was a distress flag and his Bay Rum aftershave made Michel gasp. "Impossible. It's reserved for the mayor tonight." Delantier had been a navy buddy of Philippe's, mess chief or something equally useless. "While we're at it, Michel, I did the books in your mother's absence. Your account is ten thousand francs in arrears." Philippe shied away from this delicate, dirty family business and began filling orders.

"I haven't got that much cash on me. Will a check do?"

"The last one you gave us was returned by the bank."

"I've got a solution. There's been a large seizure of cocaine in Marseille. I can get some for you. And you can double your money."

Delantier scowled, then straightened up with effort and Michel heard the creak in his bones as they struggled on calcified hinges. He departed on feet so outwardly splayed that he could traverse the entire stone floor without touching a join.

Philippe had been listening. "Are you going back to work, then?"

"Tomorrow."

"The murders of the Americans?"

"To start with."

"That means we won't be seeing you very often."

"Correct."

"In that case. Take the booth. Delantier will be waiting on you."

Michel was outraged. "Look, I've invited a lovely woman for dinner. And that's really a dirty trick, even for you. Delantier has two methods of service: everything in fifteen minutes or three hours and no in-between."

"That gives you a choice. *Bon appétit,*" his father said with a mocking grin.

Jennifer was dripping wet from the shower when the doorbell rang. She wrapped a large towel around her. "Oh no, what have you done now?"

"Like it?" Maddie asked. "I needed a change."

If ever there were a subject which could drive Jennifer stark raving mad, it would be another conversation about Maddie's hair. In the year and a half they had known each other, Maddie's coiffure had gone through a variety of colors and styles: kelly green spikes; a fuchsia chop with a touch of purple; some shade of shoe-polish black smarmed back like patent leather.

"Look, I'm really sore, Maddie. I've been waiting all afternoon for you. I was going to take you to Avignon with the girls down the hall."

"It was either getting my hair done or a nose pierce."

"Don't tell me . . ."

"Nah, you'd squeal."

No matter how Maddie cajoled her parents, they drew the line at a nose pierce. Pembrooke College expelled its nymphs for piercings. *Das Boot* and that was it. The Golds would of course go ballistic.

Maddie had, however, secretly beat the system. For a bon voyage treat when Boy got his passport, he had taken her to the Venice boardwalk. An old Okie friend of his operated a leather and spike emporium. Garrett Lee Brant was a piercing wizard, tattooist, makeup artist and tormented painter. In these circles gender was a matter of perception, and Boy had told her that at home Garrett was called IT. It and Boy had concocted a salve with fragrant oils and flake cocaine. Boy rubbed it on Maddie's clitoris and the specialist fit in a ring.

"At long last, your hair's normal, Maddie. If your father saw you, he'd have a heart attack."

Jennifer returned to the apartment's one large bathroom and Maddie followed her inside while Jennifer dried herself.

"Wouldn't that be nice. Between me and those greasy deli sandwiches dripping with fat he chomps, one of us ought to be able to take him out." She giggled. "And we'll FedEx him up to the drama twilight zone where he can shoot the shit with his hero Rod Serling. My father's punishment should be watching his own programs for eternity. Did I tell you that he made a video of his will? He wants a TV antenna and the *TV Guide,* the one with his picture on the cover, brassed on his mausoleum."

Jennifer snickered in spite of herself. "You're a hoot."

They were both dressing: Jennifer for her first date in two years, and Maddie for her regular dinner with "Andre." He was purported to be a young French rock musician she had fallen in love with after three torrid weeks. Jennifer still had not met him and she had stopped pressing for an introduction.

Jennifer had dutifully written to the Golds that Maddie was behaving herself. She came in late every night, but what the hell, the girl was nineteen and this wasn't a prisoner-and-escort brig deal she had signed on for. Let her breathe, Jennifer thought.

At the mirror, Maddie was flicking her hair back with her fingertips into different looks.

"Jen, I'm so glad you're finally going to have some fun. We cannot live by reading Colette alone. Believe me, she would be having a ball down here." She opened her eyes wide, ragging Jennifer. "Who's the lucky man?"

"Someone I met."

"Ooooooh, tell, Maddie." Maddie took a dry towel and wiped the back of Jennifer's neck and surveyed her figure. The two could not have been more differently shaped. Jennifer was all fluid curves, and Maddie had the waifish, hard flatness of a gym nut, though she never worked out.

Jennifer felt a hand on her breast. She pulled away, jumpy and exasperated.

"Come on, don't do that."

"You're so voluptuous and firm. No floppy belly or stretch marks. Wait till he gets his hands on those double-D's."

"You're not funny, so cut it out."

"Oh Jen, can't you take a joke? Stop being so self-righteous. Sugar, you got to give it up. Honestly, you really need to get off once in a while. You act like you're always on the rag."

"Don't talk to me that way."

Jennifer slipped on her robe, incensed. They seldom shared the bathroom, except at makeup time, but this afternoon the traffic pattern had changed when Maddie returned late.

"You're only what—eleven years older than me—and you behave like you're fifty. Let it go, the ship's going to sail out to mysterious ports and leave you on shore waving your fist. So don't be saving up your good times."

"You're a full-time responsibility."

"You booked passage on this cruise, lady," Maddie said sharply. "I didn't think you'd turn out to be my nanny."

"Me neither."

Maddie's sarcasm continued. "At long last, the new DKNY is out of its garment bag."

Maddie picked it up by the hanger neck and gyrated like a swishing stripper. On a layaway plan at a local Ojai shop, Jennifer had squirreled away her salary for months in order to buy this pale yellow dress with its slit skirt. It would be just the thing for a summer evening out. She rescued the outfit before it was gassed to death by Maddie's Giorgio perfume.

"Maddie, everything comes a little too easy for you and you don't appreciate it."

"Oh, here we go. Gratitude 101, the final."

"Let's get serious for a minute. I want to ask you one last time, was there any truth to you going into that brothel and working there? There've already been problems."

Maddie made her madwoman's face, spittle dripping on her lips, twisting her features into a parody of an old crone's. When Jennifer did not respond, she edged out of the bathroom.

"Can we pleeeze stop talking about this! I lied to you. André and I had a few beers and we passed the place. And I said I was curious about what it must be like to work in a place like that. The truth is, I was never in any whorehouse. I was putting you on." She winked. "Although I'm still curious, aren't you?"

"No, I'm not."

"Awww, listen, Jen, I was with André all that night and I knew you'd be pissed at me for coming in so late."

"I guess André's an improvement over that character you were seeing in L.A."

"That goof, yech."

What could she do with this impossible girl and her wacky buoyancy? "You spent the night with André? And that's it?"

Now Maddie smirked lasciviously. "Well, the box score reads something like this: double-digit orgasms. You see, André's got this amazing staying power and he's huge."

"Oh, we're back to your favorite game: 'Let's bait Jennifer.' I'm fed up with it!"

"Get your head out of the sand, lady." She danced around Jennifer. "Sex is natural, relaxing, intoxicating. André is fantastic in the sack. I've never seen anything like his monster."

Jennifer hated this smutty description, but she tried to swallow her disapproval like foul-tasting medicine. It was useless to reason with Maddie or rebuke her again. Most of the girls in the dorms at Pembrooke talked the same way. Jennifer slipped on her dress.

"I'll zip you."

She didn't want Maddie to touch her but could not avoid it. "Maddie, I wish one day you could think of love in connection with all this."

Maddie bellied up against her forcefully.

"But I am. That's the point. I love André to death. Isn't this something the poets *maudits* used to write about?" She was determined to nail Jennifer to the cross of scholarship. *J'accuse . . . !*" Maddie stabbed her finger at Jennifer. "Weren't you the one to introduce me to Rimbaud and Verlaine? And didn't Rimbaud talk about art as the disorder of the senses? 'I have seen the sunset, stained with mystic horrors.' "

Jennifer yielded. *"Touché, ma petite."*

Maddie stretched out her palms. "Sister, can you spare a dime?"

"I gave you a thousand francs yesterday."

"It went on my hair. Please, I'm broke."

Jennifer hated the accounting but made a notation in the book she kept for Adam Gold. She handed Maddie two hundred francs.

"Doesn't André ever pony up?"

"No, that's bullshit. I'm a liberated woman. I pay for him."

"Where do you think you're going at night with your backpack?"

"To a picnic under the stars with my poet."

CHAPTER 10

"Thanks for destroying the ice machine," René the barman said, by way of greeting Michel.

"René, I'd like to take you home and put your head on my dartboard."

"Along with the rest of the staff, eh? I suppose you want a pastis."

"No pastis! The Krug Special Cuvée eighty-two," came Louise's imperious voice as she approached.

The rake-thin barman's cough spattered the ash of his Gauloise onto his broad mustache. He was about to hack up a lung. "Madame Louise, that's running two thousand francs a bottle. We only have four left."

"Chill three. Nothing's too good for my Michel."

The prodigal gesture was part of Louise's diva style, like her cool celadon Armani suit, which blended with her emeralds. She had spoiled him all of his life and Michel loved her. She took a seat beside him and kissed him. Her generosity had an uncontrived elegance. Louise Vercours had paid for his trip to New York; she had first outfitted him at Charvet's; on his return to Aix she had bought him a Citroën Maserati for his birthday.

"Thank you, Louise."

"I want you and your new lady to really enjoy this evening. By the way, do I know her?"

"Not yet."

"Is she local?"

"Professor Jennifer Bowen."

Shock firmed the rorquals on Louise's throat. "Is this a joke?"

"The price of freedom. I talked her out of dropping the complaint she made to Courbet. We bartered, I lost. The tariff was dinner with me."

"That's a stiff one. I adore you, Michel." Louise was still puzzled. "What exactly was this all about?"

"The girl Jennifer is tutoring happens to be a pathological liar, with an enormously wealthy father who pulls the strings. Since she can't punish him, she's selected Jennifer." Michel looked over the crowd and saw Denise chatting from table to table. "I spent most of the afternoon thinking about how I could get back at Paul Courbet . . . for both of us. Normally, I'd file a report. Have a team come down from Paris and investigate him for extortion. But I can't, Louise. You do run a business and you wouldn't pass the test as a witness."

"Do I pay Courbet?"

"Leave him to me. He won't bother you again."

She was alarmed. "You're not going to—?"

Michel raised his glass and Louise tapped his. *"Cincin."* The champagne had a silky flavor and the body of a goddess. "In our professions, answering questions isn't an option."

Delantier shuffled over and bowed to the queen. Louise tipped him lavishly and he behaved himself when he was around her. "I'm sorry to interrupt your tête-à-tête. There's a foreign lady out front. I don't know whether to allow her to come in or not. She's either lost or with Michel."

"Bring her in, and keep your hands off her."

Delantier slugged down a scotch neat. He kept a bottle hidden near the bar hatch. "No one can keep up with Michel's taste in women—from Modigliani to Rubens overnight."

Jennifer peered in. She hadn't waited for the pompous major-domo and was already nervously searching the room for Michel. He left the bar.

"Glad you could make it."

"Hi, am I okay?" she asked.

"Perfect."

"I love the lighting. Look at the wood moldings."

"They're mid-nineteenth century from Napoleon the Third's coachhouse."

"My God, I'd eat a salami sandwich here."

"You may have to," he said, taking her arm.

"Do we have a table or a wait at the bar?"

"The bar. I owe you a drink after the Beaujolais incident."

"You don't owe me anything. And we're going Dutch."

"We'll see."

Amid the honeyed timbers and the dim lamps of Chez Danton, Michel watched Jennifer innocently looking around at the courtly landowners. It had become a mark of coming of age for these feudal lords, some of them with archaic titles, to introduce their sons to Louise's delights at the appropriate age. Somewhere around sixteen, usually. Everyone scrutinized this newcomer when Michel brought her before the queen.

"Do you have any hobbies or special interests?" Jennifer asked.

"Murder, ballroom dancing."

"What a selection. Is that it?"

"Since we met, you've renewed my interest in romance."

Jennifer's body shook with laughter. He enjoyed watching the parts jiggle as she stared down the help.

"You're kidding. Do I get fed or are we getting drunk?"

"Both."

"Lead the way."

"Madame Louise Vercours, Professor Jennifer Bowen."

Jennifer's luminous light hazel eyes popped in disbelief. Louise was silent, like an alchemist weighing gold or expelling dross. Jennifer was about to retreat when Louise graciously said, "We'll need another glass, René."

"Louise, you two ladies have started out on the wrong foot. I've retained Jennifer as my Cézanne expert."

"I didn't know you needed one."

"You can't live in Aix without having a specialist on your doorstep."

"I should know. I have three of his paintings."

Jennifer was flabbergasted. Her contrition dissolved into awed veneration.

"Three Cézannes?"

"At home."

"I hope you'll forgive me for the trouble I caused you, Madame Vercours."

"Michel said it was this student of yours."

"Yes. She drives me crazy. I never know what to believe."

"When you sign on as a hand on a tramp steamer, dump the cargo the moment you begin to list," Louise advised her.

"I gave her father my word I'd stick it out."

Louise offered her hand. "Don't let this girl trap you again."

"I'll try not to." She sipped the champagne. "This is wonderful."

"It's Louise's way of bribing you."

"She's succeeded." Jennifer raised her glass to Louise. "Madame, I'd be very grateful if you'd let me see your pictures one day."

"If you make Michel happy, you can ask him. He has the keys to my house."

Denise came to the bar giggling and whisked Louise away. Her voice carried from the entry. Jennifer stared at her champagne, then looked up at Michel.

"It was idiotic of me to accuse her of anything."

He had no choice but to continue lying on Louise's behalf. "True. Listen, she has a major collection of paintings and is as you've seen a very grand lady. She's my mother's closest friend. But you're forgiven."

His eyes dove into Jennifer's ravishing, plunging neckline. As he touched her hand, Delantier shoved the large show menu between them.

"Your table is ready, Monsieur Michel."

"Thank you. Will you put on the heavy-duty Piaf tape?"

"Could we have some Aznavour as well?" Jennifer asked.

"I'd planned to play Bach. Isn't he suitable?"

"Not tonight," Michel said. "And I want you to take my order before the kitchen closes."

The cathedral clock of St-Sauveur tolled nine o'clock when Boy nudged Maddie out of a pharmacy doorway across the street from Chez Danton. The evening balminess with its concentration of flowers and summer herbs gave way to a spur of wind which carried the effluvium of rotting fruit. The clangor of garbage lids by *clochards* and cats foraging for food intruded on the stillness.

Soaked with wine and laughter, Louise and Denise were walking arm in arm. Denise's voice boomed through the quiet old quarter.

"And what do fantastic soufflés and great blow jobs have in common?"

"Knock-knock," Louise said.

"Two things you can't get at home."

"That's what keeps me in business," Louise replied with a throaty chuckle.

Boy and Maddie kept close to the building and followed the two women.

"Sure you want to go through with this, Maddie?"

Without hesitation, she responded, "Anything you say."

As they strolled shoulder to shoulder, weaving through the sparse crowd of tourists and students, they stood apart in a union unknown to the entire world. The intensity and rage of Boy's old humiliations were encapsulated in the moment of reckoning that awaited them.

"We won't get caught?" Maddie asked, suddenly chilled by Boy.

"I haven't so far." Boy took her hand. "It's your first time. Virgins get all the breaks. I envy you the experience."

"You'll tell me how it all began for you . . . all the things about how you got to be you? Your secrets?"

"Every one of them." Boy felt the excitement of the chase.

"I'm ready to serve you," she said, hypnotized by his voice.

"Valiant deeds and clarity of intent will bring you to new heights. You will walk with the gods. After this, nobody can ride you. You'll be in charge."

When the women paused on a corner, they slunk into the entry of a pâtisserie and huddled together, whispering.

"Can you understand what they're saying?" Boy asked.

"Something about a cruise with a woman called Nicole. I didn't catch it all."

Maddie was beginning to feel shaky, her voice sounded shrill, all the sounds of night in the deserted back streets of the quarter were amplified. The women stopped outside of Denise's dimly lighted townhouse, embraced and kissed. *"Bonne nuits"* carried like thin flutes. Louise, a bit tipsy, crossed the street and walked slowly, looking up at the night sky.

"Let's beat her to the house," Boy said.

He and Maddie walked very quickly. But they were alert to faces and witnesses. Boy scouted the windows above him for nosy insomniacs. The Café Printemps opposite Louise's house was shuttered. Her private entrance was around the corner. They stopped alongside the wall abutting Louise's mansion.

"Put these on, Maddie." Boy handed her a pair of latex surgical gloves.

"Why?"

"You want fingerprints left for the cops?"

"You've thought of everything."

At the other side of Louise's house merry sounds were coming from the Hôtel Estaque, which housed the brothel. In a moment, they heard the clatter of heels; then they stopped.

"C'est vous, madame?"

"Night watchman," Boy whispered.

"Oui, Benedict. Dorms bien, mon vieux."

When Louise resumed walking, Boy huddled with Maddie against the wall and kissed her. As Boy had planned, Louise saw them immediately. Her heart was light with the young lovers' ardor. The girl was half hidden in the shadows of the wall. Boy, holding Maddie's hand, moved closer and smiled cordially.

"Do you speak English?" he asked.

"Perfectly. Ah, *mes enfants*, are you lost?" she asked, opening her arms to embrace them.

"No, you are, my lady."

Boy rammed the automatic between Louise's eyes. The barrel jarred her back.

"This is a mistake," Louise said in a quavering voice.

"You made it, darlin'."

"How?" She beseeched him. "We've never met."

"No, this is our first date."

"Open the gate," Maddie said when Louise began to stall. "Or he'll shoot you right here."

Louise had her key out, nodded and docilely walked ahead.

"Turn left to the elevator," Boy said.

"How do you know about the elevator?"

"I do my homework. Do you have an alarm code to punch in?"

"No, I never needed one—until now."

He had clearly studied the layout of her house. Louise was quiet with dread, becoming more frightened by the terrible purpose she sensed. The elevator door opened. It could hold four people and was ornately decorated with old brass rails, painted mural screens and an inlaid gate.

"Any cameras or recording devices?" he asked.

"No."

In the light, Louise observed surgical gloves on the two children. She sagged forward, trying to keep her composure and not cry.

"Let's go upstairs and visit, Madame Louise."

CHAPTER 11

In the plush booth the rosy velvet cushions made a stunning Renoir contrast with Jennifer's outfit and skin hue. The dress she wore was a stretch fabric which wrapped around her curvaceous figure. The soft opalescent yellow shimmered like an exotic seashell on the beach. There was a stormy grandeur about Jennifer.

"You look positively gorgeous," Michel said.

Her breasts came alive, vibrantly. Compliments clearly were not tossed freely at her. She was a woman ruled by penalties. Underneath her reserve, something was simmering. It was not obvious, but he liked those generous earthenware pots slow to boil.

"Three bottles of champagne. Isn't that a lot to drink? Jennifer asked.

With a look at the lurking Delantier, Michel said, "You'll drink yourself sober by the time dessert arrives."

"You won't hear me argue. This is the best champagne I've ever tasted."

"You deserve it for being so understanding."

"Weren't you going to arrest me for making false charges?"

"I could have. That's serious stuff here in France."

"You spooked me when you came in to question me. Not many people have that effect on me. I can get very tough when anyone tries it on." She pressed on to convince him. "I had to learn how to defend myself. I've had two years of karate."

"Thanks for the warning. I'll be very careful. Did you find out why Maddie lied?"

"You're a terrific teacher. I sweated it out of her. She never went near a brothel. She was putting me on."

"What a strange girl she must be."

"She is. I thought with a new French boyfriend she'd calm down. He's a musician called André."

"I'm speaking on behalf of all of Aix when I say we hope Maddie returns to Los Angeles correctly conjugating her irregular verbs and not carrying anything alarming out front."

"That's her parents' problem. I had a call from them. They're thinking about coming to the Riviera for a week."

"You'll be relieved of your bodyguard duties?"

"I hope so."

Jennifer was all smiles, peering around at the *soignés* locals nodding and waving to Michel.

"The way they bow and scrape for you."

"There may be an ulterior motive."

"You're so suspicious of everyone."

"I'm in the crime business."

Delantier again presented menus and more champagne.

"Michel, this is my first date in several years," she said with a candor that surprised him and made him like her even more.

"Something wrong with American men or do you have different preferences?"

"Nothing like that. Oh, never mind."

Michel quickly totted up the score. First date in years, personal tragedy, added up to loss. Her nose crinkled when a platter of gurgling escargots passed by.

"They have a few nongarlic dishes, but you'll have to bring a note from the doctor to prove you've got allergies."

He made her laugh and considered this a good sign. She trusted him. He'd been ready for a change and hadn't realized it. Jennifer had quickly banished Yvette's ghost.

"I love garlic."

"Good, we'll be swimming in it tonight."

Should he mention that this was the family establishment? He decided to continue in the role of local celebrity. She scanned the menu, searching for something.

"I don't see it . . . Oh, well . . ."

"Can't you find anything to tempt you?"

"Everything sounds marvelous. It's the wrong season, I know. But I've vowed not to leave France without eating a good cassoulet. I lived on it when I was a student in Paris. I've never made it very well at home."

Michel almost choked on the mere sound of the word. "It's been discontinued here. If Shakespeare were to return and write another tragedy, it might make a fitting subject."

"That's an obscure explanation. Tell me."

"The owners quarrel about cooking. The chef's a beef man, his wife's an artist in the kitchen. Last Christmas they came to blows about which cassoulet to serve. His or hers. All the town's dignitaries were here. I almost had to make an arrest. She's in the hospital now and the rumor is that his cassoulet was found in her gallbladder."

With an unsteady hand, his breath inflamed by scotch, Delantier took their order.

"You decide," Jennifer said.

"Gigot Nicole," Michel said. "It's baby lamb encrusted with sesame seeds and infused with herbs, garlic and mustard. One of the wonders of the kitchen."

"As Monsieur well knows, it requires a day's notice," Delantier said.

"Tell the chef we're in no hurry. Make up a plate of a few starters. Tapénade-stuffed eggs. Cold mussels, a *pissaladière*." He turned to Jennifer. "That's a flan made with anchovies, onions and olives."

"I'm spellbound."

Michel was as well. He moved closer to her. No panic attacks brewing this time, but rather a rich, erotic affinity with her. While Delantier scribbled furiously, Michel laid his hand across Jennifer's tanned arm and she leaned down hugging it like a cat. Nothing suited the possibility of a new romance more than the death of an old one. Yvette and Courbet might spend their time eating sandwiches between dirty sheets at Denise's house. He was drinking champagne with an American beauty.

With the Matisse *Odalisque* hanging over the platformed bed which she stepped up to as though to a throne, the suffusion of bright needlepoint pillows, the black satin coverlet, the intimacy of her boudoir seemed the wrong place to Louise to be attacked by these young people. She watched the girl's Nikes sink several inches into the shallows of her Aubusson carpet as she left the room and climbed the spiral staircase to the roof. Louise thought about rushing out and screaming, but the young man blocked her way. She loved music and hated the traffic noise. Damn, she had soundproofed her apartment. Privacy was everything to her. She trembled and prayed that her panic was not obvious. She was desperately playing the gracious hostess, in the hope of calming down these maniacs.

"Can I offer you some wine?" She flourished a bottle to Boy. "I bought a few cases of Pétrus in Bordeaux last month. It's so dense and rich, you can sense the tobacco and ripeness of the herbs and berries in it. Exquisite, like velvet." She was becoming frantic. "Please, let's all have a glass."

In his turbulent eyes, she saw something deeply troubling and aberrant. He knocked the bottle out of her hand and glass splat against the wall, showering fragments over the bed. He craned his head out to the partially opened French window. "Maddie, what's on the roof?"

"A pool and a greenhouse," came Maddie's muffled voice as she tiptoed down. "No one can see us."

"May I stretch my legs?" Louise asked. "Maybe you'd like a swim."

"Just be quiet," Boy said with a smile more menacing to Louise than his surly manner.

Maddie climbed down. "There's a walkway to the hotel. I saw guys sitting in a large room with liveried waiters serving drinks."

"It's a men's club."

Boy peered out. "What are those girls doin', then?"

"Gentlemen make arrangements and pair off."

"And you grab all the money."

"No, I only get a hotel fee. I don't take anything from the girls."

"She's a liar, Boy. Is there any way to shut her up?" Maddie asked.

"Gabbin'. It's nerves, they all do it."

Boy pressed Louise to the carpet, dug his knee in her back and slapped her. He yanked her by the hair, shoving her through to the balcony and up the short flight of stairs to her roof garden and pool. The shrill rasping of cicadas unnerved her. An environment of plants and creeping roses offered Louise no reprieve. She thought frantically. The poolman had been there and had left two canisters of chlorine which he had forgotten to put in the shed. The previous day, Michel had come for a swim and carried them inside. She was losing her train of thought. Michel, if only he were here.

Boy pulled her to the edge of the railing. "Scream, and I'll heave you off the roof. You'll hear the sound of your head splatterin' on the cobblestones."

Looking down at the street gave her vertigo. "There's Beluga caviar in the fridge. Let me get it for you. We'll have a pool party. A barbecue if you like."

"She's just like your folks, Maddie, trying to control us."

Maddie slapped Louise with the back of her hand and sent her reeling back against a chaise longue. Louise's hand went to her bleeding split lip.

"There's money in the safe downstairs." Louise pointed. "Behind the Matisse painting over my bed. The combination is six to the left, thirty-one right, and fourteen left. I have chips from the casino in

Monte Carlo I didn't cash. About ten thousand dollars. Untraceable. Take it, take everything."

Boy knew from past experience that Mystery Man would not have bought into this trap, and he was not about to be conned by this old smoothie. Louise's superior attitude sent a vent of steam through him.

". . . My jewelry's worth a fortune."

Boy peered through a beautiful old brass telescope Louise had on the roof.

"Some men's club," he said contemptuously. "There's a bunch of naked gals goin' round the room, havin' an orgy."

"It might be a bachelor party. You have them in America. Good fun."

Boy knocked over the telescope in a fury. "What do you take me for? Some halfwit? My ole lady made a contract with you. You think you can have two guys fuck her simple and not pay?"

"This little girl told you that?"

"It's true, Boy, I swear."

"I know, sugar."

Maddie stood back in awe. Boy's temper was terrifying.

"Then you have the gall not to pay her. And you tell her to take a hike. Is that the way you do things in Provence? A woman like you who makes your money from sex?"

Louise heard herself pleading. "This is a terrible misunderstanding."

"I've heard that one before," Maddie said quickly.

"My manager—"

Boy dragged her down the steps back to her bedroom. Maddie trailed, looking around cautiously.

"That cheeseball pimp who works in the porn store with Karim?"

Spitting blood, Louise tried to forget the pain. "All right, have it your way. My pimp, Gerard, mentioned that Françoise could have brought in a new girl. Maybe I wasn't paying attention."

"I came back and begged you for some money and you had them toss me out like I was a piece of garbage!" Louise was shocked by the mad accusation. What was this little girl talking about? "I had to go back to my lover and tell him how I'd been humiliated. We didn't have ten bucks between us. And I performed. I worked my ass off for the money with those two dirty bastards from Paris."

Boy was proud of Maddie and egged her on. "Feel it, the current buildin', don't you, darlin'?"

"It's a rush."

Maddie closed in on Louise, who retreated and fell back against the mirrored wardrobe. She cringed and was gasping with terror. Maybe there was a way out?

"I can get you girls, boys, fantasies—anything you want! They'll be here for you in a minute. I'll pay everything you think I should. Please, be reasonable."

Silence enveloped Louise. She gaped at the young man untangling an extension cord; then he plugged in a curling iron which he had taken from his dirty backpack.

"What's that for?" Louise cried. "Forgive me, I beg you. I don't know what I did wrong. But it can be fixed. I can call Marseille if you want drugs. I'll give you anything in the world. . . ."

Boy swung around and turned Louise so that she faced the mirror.

"No one but Maddie gave me a break. The others shoved a fist into me. Take that pretty suit off. Let's see how you're put together." Maddie clung to Boy's neck, overpowered by the sexual excitement she sensed. "I have been laid, relayed and parleyed by rich scum like you who did anything they wanted to me. Like I was freak. With no feelin's . . . I know what it's like to put my ass on the line and be stiffed!"

He was raving and Maddie shrank back for a moment, unsure of what he meant. Boy lashed out wildly, gnashing his teeth.

"You like sex, Louise, it's your business. Tonight, you're going to have more than you ever dreamed of, dear." He said, stormily waving the hot curling iron in her face.

"What's that curling iron for?" she repeated as he moved closer.

"I do some hairdressin'. Denise showed me how."

The final movement of Mozart's *Jupiter*, which was being played in the Archbishop's Palace, spilled into the air. Louise had given her tickets to some of the girls.

"Let's get those pretty panties off, Madame Louise."

"You want *me*?" she asked in disbelief.

"You're a fabulous-lookin' woman."

Maddie drew closer to Louise, mesmerized by Boy's powers. Louise dropped her jacket, unzipped her skirt, then carefully undid the buttons of her blouse.

Boy ran his fingers down Louise neck. "Bet you're a specialist, like me."

"I'm flattered," Louise said, trying to make a joke of it.

Louise felt hope ebbing. She was an alien swimming to the promised land from exile but the shore constantly receded. Naked and bleeding, she moved between the two of them. Boy placed her hand between Maddie's thighs.

"What a body's she got," Maddie cooed, bending over Louise's breasts.

"She swims all the time on the roof. With that big guy she picked up in her car."

Boy stuck his hand under Maddie's pants. He liked the damp feel of her. Maddie crooned when he started to play with her. He placed his fingers behind Louise's neck and she was trapped in a vise. But she responded to the signal. She dropped to her knees and placed her mouth between Maddie's thighs.

"Let's get her in the sack, sugar."

Louise looked up with a smile, trying to gratify them.

"Yes, it'll be more comfortable for you."

She lay on her majestic bed, and Boy danced around her, flashing the curling iron in her eyes. He observed the familiar sea change of disbelief in her dark eyes. All of his victims had reacted that way. This could not be happening to them. Then the realization was driven home and their minds retreated, drifting into oblivion.

Louise wiped her bloody lips and nostrils with the white sheet.

"I'll please you, if you let me."

"Let her do you, Maddie. I want to watch her workin'."

Boy removed a huge knife from his backpack and brandished it between Louise's thighs. She rolled over, face down, and knew she was lost.

CHAPTER 12

Michel was saturated with Krug champagne and his hand drifted on Jennifer's knee. He had already brushed a kiss on her ear and not been repulsed. Neither of them was in the mood for coyness. Jennifer's clean perfume cut through the herbal garlic filets the patrons were devouring.

"I'm so pleasantly surprised. You're such a honey, Michel."

This was the last word he would have thought to describe himself these last few months with Yvette. She'd boxed his ears off and try as he might, he was still smarting from the crude way she had discarded him.

"You bring out the courtly Provence tradition in me. You're in the land of troubadours."

"So I am. There's so much I want to find out about you. Forgive for me for asking, but why did someone with your intelligence and education become a cop?"

"That's still under investigation." He didn't want to scare her off with tales of murder. "Tonight, forget about what I do. I'm your friendly suitor. A tourist attraction if you like."

For his peace of mind, he needed clarification. He was not about to bull his way into a situation in which he'd become the obtuse angle of a triangle. He had been jarred by his ignorance of Yvette's affair and some emotional circumspection was in order. Michel drifted for a moment into the wasteland of the past. Here he was two and half years later at the same table where he had drunk Christmas Taittinger rosé champagne with Yvette.

"Is something wrong?" Jennifer asked.

"Not really. Just the morbid pursuit of a trivial memory."

"It's not easy to let go, is it?"

"My turn, if you don't mind," he said somewhat defensively, since she was so quickly attuned to him. "I can't believe you don't have some terrific man in your life. Or that you're not seeing someone. I'm not asking for a confession," he said to relieve her vigilance. "We can always talk about food."

The gaiety illuminating Jennifer's pleasing, round face was abruptly snuffed out. Ruled by modesty, she was quick to erect barriers. He could see her wavering through the conflict, the indecision of making him a confidant.

"Actually it started with food. I was engaged to be married. Three years ago this November thirteenth. We'd set the date because it was Harry's birthday. It also fell before Thanksgiving and Christmas so our families and friends wouldn't have to change their holiday plans."

She polished off her champagne and he poured her another glass. His intent look seemed to alarm her and she fell back on a girlish reticence which he found beguiling. She was not a modern woman with that caustic, competitive manner he was encountering everywhere.

"The engagement was broken off because of food? Come on, trading secrets with strangers can be healthy."

She nodded, stirring at last.

"Harry and I were graduate students together at Stanford. He was two years ahead of me and we became friends. He had a fellowship in creative writing and I was in art history. We didn't even have enough money to rent an apartment together. I was in student housing and he bached it with three other graduate students. Intimacy became a big deal because it was infrequent. When we could get together, it was something of an event.

"Then we got a wonderful break. Harry was offered an assistant professorship in English at Stanford! I can't begin to tell you how remarkable that was."

"Like being taken on at the Sorbonne."

"Exactly. It meant he wouldn't have to go trooping through Modern Language conventions sucking up for a job at some academic backwater dump and have me thousands of miles away in California.

"We were going to celebrate. We were maxed out on our credit cards and I did some creative accounting. Harry booked us a room at the Stanford Court in San Francisco. Oh, I'm talking about places you've never heard of."

"No you aren't. I spent three months in Los Angeles on a course with their Special Investigation Section and another month in San Francisco with the FBI. I've had dinner at Fournier's Ovens in the Stanford Court. I know the geography. Go on, Jennifer . . . if you can," he added kindly.

She leaned over, clutching his hand.

"We decided to go to Chinatown for dinner. Not anywhere fancy. I love the atmosphere. Wonderful Peking ducks swaying in the windows. Everyone scurrying around from one dumpling house and shop to another. I used to roam through the herbal pharmacies on my eternal quest for a miracle pill to keep my weight down. We always had such a good time on these expeditions.

"Harry and I drove in from Palo Alto for our big night on the town. When we came around the Peninsula Road, we remembered that none of the places we liked to eat in took credit cards. We had about nine dollars in cash. So Harry parked and I waited. He went around the corner to a bank to use the ATM. I was sitting in the car for five minutes and I thought, Hell, the computer's down or he can't remember his PIN or whatever. Then it became ten minutes. Finally, I took out his car keys, locked the Bug and went to look for him.

"He was lying in a pool of blood. Dead! He'd been shot while trying to take out fifty dollars to pay for goddamn Chinese food!"

The memory stirred her to tears. Michel gently wiped them off with his handkerchief.

"I'm so sorry. I feel like I've sprung a bear trap."

"No, no, it's okay. You're really a very generous man."

"Did they catch the killer?"

"The following day. He was some middle-aged, deadbeat career criminal out on parole." She shook her head. "The bank's surveillance camera immortalized the horror. In court, I watched Harry being murdered on videotape."

Michel filled her glass again and she needed it. Jennifer mused over the champagne and became ferociously angry.

"The court's sentence was astounding—second-degree murder. The killer claimed he hadn't meant to kill Harry. There was a struggle for the gun and it went off. Bottom line, this murderer will be out in another four years. And I, as one of the taxpayers, paid for his defense counsel, prison and rehab."

Michel wanted to hold Jennifer but knew consolation was impossible. Harry's presence—the good young man who had hoped to marry her—lurked in the mists of her thoughts.

"Did the chef forget about us?" she asked.

"He's probably having a nervous breakdown."

At that moment, brusquely shoving between them, with a rattling trolley, was Delantier, sweating profusely and definitely drunk.

"The waiter from hell," she whispered.

"That's considered praise for him."

"Gigot Nicole, Monsieur Michel." Delantier flicked the carving knife in the air as though practicing a tennis serve and Jennifer ducked. "Shall I carve?"

"No. Chez Danton isn't insured for self-inflicted wounds."

At Les Deux Garçons, Boy was doing two doubles of Jack Daniel's and Maddie a champagne split. Boy had run over to the *tabac* for a carton of Marlboros. Until their visit to Louise's, they would have had to share a beer and bum a cigarette. A few of the college guys started hitting on Maddie. Finally, she turned on a persistent clown, "When my ole man comes around, you'll wish your ass was a million miles away."

She had been on crank, grass, coke, and had free-based before meeting Boy; and there was a big difference in the highs. She loved Boy's implacable resolve. Lots of men pretended they were tough, sitting in front of the TV enjoying and condemning the daily spectacle of violence dished up by the news. They'd say, "If one of those gangbangers tried to grab my car, I'd move so fast with my tai chi, he'd be out like a light before he hit the ground."

The real difference was that Boy had been there. Nobody messed with him, and if he were the one demanding the car, he'd blow your brains out in an instant if you got cute. When Boy spoke, you listened. Best for a man not to make eye contact with him and *never* smart-ass him.

When Boy was behind the wheel of her Porsche and some dude tried to hassle him—his size, color or gang didn't matter—Boy would not back down. Once he asked the question "You got a problem, man?" the person at the other end had one.

Her father had hired some dumb detective who tried to play tagalong with them at Pembrooke when Boy was visiting. Boy had pulled off the road above the lake and they had scrambled down the side of the hill. Boy knew the detective would follow them and he and Maddie doubled back and rolled his car over the embankment, then sped away in the Porsche.

Maddie giggled at the memory. Imagine the detective trying to explain that one to his insurance company! What was beautiful about the move was that Adam Gold could not mention the incident to her.

Boy said to her afterwards, "My lady, first time I landed in the big dark place with those old cons, one of them thought he could scare me. Throw a saddle over me, *me!*"

"You were helpless, what could you do?"

"Helpless, me? My lady, I carved my initials on that Big Bad Boy's nose. The point of that little exercise back there, was that nobody makes a puss out of me and lives to brag about it."

When Boy arrived at the table, the asshole pestering Maddie was dangling his legs on Boy's chair and keeping up a nonstop pickup line.

"Think you better find another seat, cowboy." The student ignored Boy for a few seconds. Boy waited for a response, then calmly pressed his thumb into the kid's eye. With a howl, he jolted to his feet and ran.

"Not a dude in town can stay away from my Keeper of the Flame."

"I do feel different now."

"You're giving off the scent of power, sugar." Boy raised his glass and sniffed the Jack Daniel's. "Jesus, finally a decent drink I can pay for—and a Marlboro," he said, puffing away.

"In a few weeks, we'll be home."

"And, Maddie, we'll make some different housekeeping arrangements."

"Believe me."

"How's it feel to be God Almighty?"

"Greatest rush ever." Maddie sighed pleasurably. "She was awesome, Boy."

He nodded. "She was supposed to be."

"A sex machine."

"Yeah, like a world-class athlete who devoted her life to a sport." Boy added some soda to the highball. "Let's be real careful about money. Don't start buying clothes or being flash. I don't want Jennifer to start with her questions and snoopin' again."

"I'll watch myself."

Maddie had been initiated and brought to the magical frontier of the secret knowledge of life and death, and there was a chilly tranquility in her confident demeanor.

"I'd like to be with you all night," she said.

"Stick to the game plan. Nothin' impulsive. Head back to your place and crash."

"I'm too excited to sleep."

"It'll take a while, but sleep and the dreams will come."

She was enthralled by the radiant dynamism her hero projected. "Will you tell me everything . . . about how all this started and you got to be you?"

"My lady, when I was a kid, I was blessed to have found my savior. His name was Mystery Man. Now I have you."

"Will I ever meet him?"

"He'll give you away at our weddin'."

"Mystery Man," she said with fascination.

CHAPTER 13

Michel had taken Jennifer to the Provence, a private club, where tangos were not unheard of and rap was banned. Neither of them could walk a straight line or sit without slumping over and dropping to their knees. There was only one answer. Like a pair of wounded elephants, they thumped out to the dance floor and clung to each other. Despite Chez Danton's infusions of food and the sorcery of Louise's champagne, Jennifer's perfume still carried a tantalizing hint of vanilla or was it almonds, he wondered. Her flesh did something intoxicating with it, liberating the admixture into something as ripe and lush as the tropical savannah.

He felt at home with himself and an unfathomable surge of hope. His desire for Jennifer became almost unbearable as he held her tightly in a tangle-footed tango. The emotionally insolvent inner man had opened a new account in an offshore bank.

"You're a sensational listener, Michel. You know everything about me, and you haven't told me a word about yourself. Now where's your lady?"

"Since we're being open . . . she moved out. Fled in broad daylight with her Romeo and my furniture. Not to mention my grandmother's ring."

"You're serious?"

"Yes. I was very confused about this woman, Yvette. We spent more than two years playing out what my shrink calls an approach-avoidance scenario. Whining, friction, squabbles. No fires, lots of thunderstorms. The last six months were a period of glacial indifference. I could probably dig for fossils or those nuggets of insight that tell me nothing. I was lazy, she wasn't. She found she could be a freebooter while I gave her shelter. That's more or less how the last dance of my love life ended. Ashes in the wind. I'm not carrying a wound like yours."

His lips rested on Jennifer's warm ear and she pressed against him.

"Do men like women . . . bountiful?" she asked out of the blue, not prying him loose from his undignified thoughts.

"I don't know about bountiful. But if you mean your breasts, they're not for the timid. I don't find them offensive at all," he said with amusement. "You're the kind of woman men have to pay attention to. Ready for more compliments?"

"Mm-hm."

"I'm captivated by you. I feel like a spectator of my past. I'm back to being a schoolboy again who's caught sight of the new Venus."

"Did you fall in love with Venus?"

"No, I was too young and I let her go. I saved up my hopes for tonight."

"That's lovely."

Jennifer moved closer to him, belly to belly. Her skin tingled from the flush of his appeal, which she knew was quite distinct from her own yearning to be held, adored, and ravished. As Michel warmed to his task, ready to go on with more drunken tributes, he was tapped on the shoulder.

Dr. Leon Stein had a smoldering redhead on his arm. Probably some schizophrenic he was giving new hope to. He handed Michel a rumpled piece of paper, slippery as eelskin.

"Sorry I missed you at dinner, Michel. Here's a copy of the fax I sent to Marseille."

"Thanks for my ticket."

"Don't let me down. We'll continue once a week."

"Whatever you say, Leon. By the way, Dr. Bowen, this is Dr. Stein, our local witch doctor." Michel smiled at the redhead. "Leon casts spells with the best of them."

"Nothing's sacred. Your crew obviously read my fax, Michel. And let's not forget our arrangement. I'm available for consultations. You and Dr. Bowen will join us, I hope," Stein said. "It's Michel's coming-out party."

The girl with Dr. Stein suddenly kissed the psychiatrist, and he wrapped her in his arms and they began to tango away. Michel and Jennifer were enveloped by clamorous laughter. A large party of the Marseille gang had blown in and waiters were annexing tables with furious speed. Michel looked at Jennifer grimly.

"It's *The Wild Bunch* . . . incoherent detectives and dancing coroners. They're going to be rude and psychotic. We won't stay long."

Merrily loaded, Jennifer danced with the skillful Charles Laurent, the chief medical examiner. He told her how he had cradled hundreds

of dead bodies and weighed tons of vital organs and how light she
was on her feet. He was supporting her back and dragging her hair
along the floor in a ferocious dip. She had no idea what to say to the
keeper of the dead. Emerging from the smoky blue Gauloise haloes
above the table of drunken French policemen, Michel reappeared,
staggering over to retrieve her.

"Definitely not prom night. I really should get back," she said.

"Bed check for Maddie?"

"No, I don't want to pass out in public in front of your friends."

Noisy wet kisses bid them farewell. Michel lifted a bottle of Armagnac off their table. When they were outside, he couldn't remember
where he had parked his car and they hailed a taxi. The driver negotiated the narrow streets in a fury, hurling them together. She kissed
Michel impulsively.

"I liked that," he said.

"Me too."

"Please don't stop. I need a woman who takes the initiative."

"Later . . . I'm curious about something. What was in that fax Dr.
Laurent passed to you?"

"Duty roster."

"Come on, tell me."

"There's been a double murder."

"Will you be working on it?"

"I'll be running the investigation. It's total chaos." Michel leaned
forward and tapped the taxi driver. "Jean, pull up for a minute."

"In front of Louise's *maison*?" came a shocked thick voice. "Are
you sure?"

"Yes."

They got out of the old Mercedes and Michel brought Jennifer into
the lighted courtyard. She was awed by the scandalous frieze of maid-
ens copulating with demons, an addition, Michel explained, made by
Louise, but aged to look old by artisans and lashed into the *ancien
régime* style by the mistral. Jennifer peered over the railings next door.
A man wearing a white liveried outfit with leather cuffs walked a
poodle.

"The dog looks like he's in drag. What is that place, Michel?"

"A private club."

"Maddie must've thought it was a brothel when she was out with
André." She was on the scent. "I've been to all the famous old mansions. The Forbin is my favorite. I'm a sucker for wrought iron balconies. I wonder why this one isn't in guide books."

"It's not the real thing. Just a restoration," he said to divert her.

A scent of a spicy lemon trees snuffling in the wind crossed Pont de l'Arc and crept over them, permeating their skin.

"Another thing, I've never seen Louise's Cézannes listed in John Rewald's catalogue, or any other reference book for that matter."

"Louise doesn't like publicity. Not many people know she owns them. She prefers to remain anonymous."

Jennifer pressed her lips against his again. "You know everything, don't you? I can see it in your face. I'm taking you home with me."

Above Mont Sainte-Victoire, curling ribbons of lightning and distant rumbles of thunder brought a welcome hint of a summer storm to the heavy night air. Michel paced nervously outside Jennifer's apartment, clasping the bottle of Armagnac and waiting for her. The issue had nothing to do with keeping Jennifer chaste or his code of honor. The fact was that serious adults did not frequent parks, pastures or check into shady hotels in the middle of the night.

Jennifer crept out of the doorway. "Maddie's sound asleep. But the floorboards in my attic squeak. She'll wake and come upstairs."

"What happened to her night under the stars with her poet?"

"I don't know."

"My place . . . ?"

"Yes, all right."

"No, we can't go there. It was totally trashed by the enemy. It's not even worth a visit for flea market scavengers." As St-Sauveur tolled three, a great thought arrived. "We have a farm in St-Rémy."

"How do we get there?"

She had rattled him. Emotions storming. Some detective, he couldn't find a bed on his own turf.

"I remember where my car is. It's behind Chez Danton."

"You can't drive. How about going back to Louise's place? We could sneak in and look at her pictures while we're at it?"

"When we're sober."

"Oh, the hell with Maddie! You have to come up with me. I don't want this evening to end." He was on pins and needles, his flesh on fire. "Wait, wait," Jennifer said. "I've got the keys to the apartment next door. The two girls renting it went to Avignon overnight. They won't be back till tomorrow afternoon."

Upstairs, the obstacle course began when a large, crippled wardrobe almost fell on them as they hunted for the light switch in an alien bedroom.

"Any mines or old torpedoes to watch for?" he asked.

"I hope not."

Jennifer extended her arms, groping for the location of the bed, which once established, enabled her to switch on a lamp. It made everything glow in what remained of the stars. Raindrops pinged off the high old windows. Michel took Jennifer in his arms and they rolled in a large pile in the middle of a four-poster which had a downed wing on the left side and threatened to capsize.

"I don't have AIDS or any protection," he whispered.

"Nor do I. Now you're at my mercy." He peeled off her dress while she was snapping the buttons off his shirt. "You'll just have to come visit your baby in Ojai next year." Jennifer felt something that frightened her. "What's that?"

"My job accessory, a Glock twenty-one."

"Jesus, I still can't believe how you can be in this business. Oh, Michel, I'm falling for you. Even if it's only a summer romance. Or a night, it'll be worth it."

"Yes, I feel the same way."

She gave herself to him with a frenzied abandon which, much as she hated the thought, was fueled by Maddie's erotic chatter. Like some mad conductor entering a secret place, filled with her heat and fragrance, Michel was driven by the need to prove himself and the sensation of belonging to Jennifer and only her. They flawlessly hit the high notes of love and found themselves engaged in perfect harmony.

Muffled voices from next door intruded on Maddie's nightmare, which was haunted by demonic visions of Louise crawling on the floor shrieking. Night sweats had soaked the bedding. Maddie lifted her sweaty head. She was disoriented, squinting at the strange surroundings before she realized she was *not* in Louise's bedroom.

The head board from the room next door was banging against the thin wall. As Maddie drifted back into a dream, she imagined she saw the specter of Louise and heard her voice.

"Ah, *mes enfants*, are you lost?"

CHAPTER 14

A smiling, freshly perfumed Denise welcomed Boy with open arms. She was relieved to be rid of her other houseguest. Yvette had not stopped wailing since Denise had come home from her dinner with Louise. Denise had impulsively invited Yvette to stay with her after the breakup with Michel. But she had not been prepared for the emotional fireworks. Yvette finally had cried herself into a temporary stupor.

"Where have you been, André?"

"Just boppin' around the clubs with some students."

"It was a girl." She stroked his chin. "The pretty one who came into the shop for the coloring. Ah, reckless love. Aix is the place for it. As long as you don't forget about me."

Denise cupped her hand over Boy's ear and in a wet whisper explained that the woman groaning in the salon had broken up with her fiancé.

"Well, I better get out of the line of fire. I didn't mean to intrude."

"I'll join you shortly. I missed you at dinner. I had a dear friend who wanted to meet you. She's a fantastic lady and very sexy. We ate royally, but I kept thinking of you."

Snuffling, Yvette came in, wearing a shabby robe and embracing Denise's old tabby.

Boy extended his hand. "Hi there."

"Hello," Yvette said gruffly. She had, of course, known that Denise entertained young men at all hours, but having a visitor tonight of all times seemed to her grossly insensitive and made her even more surly.

"Try to get some rest, Yvette."

She watched Denise clasp the young man's arm and pilot him through the rabbit warren of rooms in the rear of the house. At least this one was clean and smelled of soap. His hair was still wet; he must have just jumped out of a shower to pick up a few hundred francs. Trusting, dumb, innocent little gigolo.

Damn, damn Michel! Staying with Denise had been an act of desperation but a way to have a handy rendezvous with Courbet when Denise was at her shop. But Paul Courbet had become skittish and fended her off with excuses.

Rising from the back of the house, Yvette heard "Te Dire Adieu," a weepy old Aznavour song she had danced to with Michel. A rollicking volley of laughter followed. Someone was being tickled.

Yvette sobbed. "Slaves to our appetites."

Tell Maddie how he became him? Boy reflected in Denise's bedroom. He stood by the mirror slowly removing his clothes until he was naked. Denise hid in the closet, enjoying the voyeuristic game.

"You're a little shy tonight, André."

"Really?"

"Shall I give you a massage and get you in the mood?"

"Whatever . . ."

He had been a beautiful child with golden hair, luminous emerald eyes, and an endearing docility. But this natural softness did not prevent his mother from giving him up for adoption. Through a bureaucratic error after being jettisoned, Boy had been cast in a cell of the most incorrigible and violent children in the Albermarle Children's Home. Providing combustion in this charnelhouse were rabid biters, an epileptic, a mad girl who pulled her hair out and never stopped shrieking, and the mutant who stuck pins into itself and anyone approaching it. This entity was so fearfully different, that it defied classification in the mind of a five year old.

Before he was six, Boy was again taken out of the Albermarle Children's Home and dished up to his third family. He wound up living with Cissie and Lyle Boynton, middle-aged white trash, who rented a clapped-out shell of a house in an unincorporated, red-dirt inferno beyond West Guthrie, outside of Oklahoma City.

Cissie had a booming voice with a phony laugh hitched to it that could cut diamonds. She worked as a bingo caller outside the Indian city in Anadarko. She and Lyle fed him, filched his clothes from the Salvation Army, and collected a monthly allowance for his maintenance from the state, which Lyle, a horse degenerate, blew at the racetrack. Sometimes Lyle worked the fairs, guessing people's weight, or with a traveling rodeo, time-keeping for the bull rides. He was also said to be a member of a select gang and fingered the high rollers for a murderous biker crew.

Mostly, Boy was left on his own, doing errands for the Boyntons' close friends Herm and Velma Gortz, who owned a small trailer park down the road. He'd run to the market and buy them beer or whiz through the five and dime shoplifting a yo-yo for himself and picking up jars of hair-setting gel for Velma.

Boy found himself especially busy on Wednesdays, the day of the swap meet the Gortzes held. They'd give him a handful of pennies, which he'd jingle in his pocket while he watched Velma wrenching her curling iron in a vain effort to put a wave into her hair. In the oppressive heat, it hung down like the bodiless canned spaghetti he used to wolf down cold.

"Ain't you through doin' you'self up?" Herm would bark as Velma fussed with the pudding rolls of fat on her face, gluing on the butterfly lashes and ladling pancake on her cheeks like breakfast syrup. While Boy zipped her and helped her primp, the scent of hair burning from the curling iron still lingered.

Lyle always roared in for the occasion on his big Harley and came stocked with bags of loco weed which he peddled. He had the gait of a gorilla, a bushy red beard that seemed to sprout from his chest to his chin. He wore black bike goggles even indoors. When he was around, fear enveloped the community.

Sometimes Cissie would take the day off from the bingo game. How Boy looked forward to seeing her. She would bring him jelly beans and Almond Joys. Shower him with boxes of Good n' Plenty. She had a washed-out complexion, brawny, with full, sagging breasts and thighs like a state trooper. Her glasses drooped over a button nose, but her sly inviting smile struck a chord in Boy's soul. She'd once been a Bible teacher and was always teaching him right from wrong. He trusted the warmth and cuddles she so freely gave. She had thought of adopting a girl, but gave up on that notion when Boy arrived.

"Can't help it, I just love this kid to death. Couldn't think of having anybody but him around."

They had dropped his real name, Darrell, and called him Boy. He didn't mind, just aimed to please his new folks. The horror of being returned to the orphanage again was still fresh in his mind.

The secret swap meet was a cash cow for the Gortzes. As many as fifty people would turn up.

$5 PER HEAD, SINGLE WOMEN $2.50.

That bought a ham dinner and a naked swim in a prefab pool Herm and the Indians had built for the event. Most of the folks brought the supper dishes they got free for going to the show Monday night at the Criterion in Oklahoma City. They could also bring their own booze, usually white lightning, and tag it with their names, or pay a buck a beer from Herm.

And, of course, a man could swap his wife or girlfriend at the meet.

Velma rented blankets for fifty cents; a cot in one of the trailers went for a deuce; and anyone could screw anyone who said "yes" till dawn.

"Now you haul ass out of there, Boy, and stop helpin' Velma preen," Herm bellowed from his post outside at the cash table where he was counting out the float, the air choking with his Old Spice.

The fan snorted in the dusty heat while Velma smirked at her image in the cracked mirror. She'd give Boy a friendly little grope and whisper things he didn't understand.

"I want first crack at them oysters when they're fired up."

A final glance at her ensemble, broad-brimmed "Casablanca" hat tilted at the right angle, just over her eyes, she surveyed the yards of aqua muslin encasing her stout body. She would peep out and put a dainty rhinestone boot down on the first step of the trailer and croon, "How do I look, Herm?"

Herm would wipe the sweat gully under his nose with the back of his wrist and yowl a hog call in his county fair falsetto. "Why, Mama, you is a sight. We gonna party till the snakes take cover."

The first time *IT* happened was at the Labor Day Swap, the frenzied finale of the summer meets. In the middle of the night, Boy had wakened from a nightmare, crying, frightened. Hearing the wild grunting in the darkened bedroom he had crawled into bed with Cissie who was being hammered at both ends by Lyle and Herm. For a time, they did not know he was there. The heat of their flesh was comforting. Then without anyone realizing which end was which, Boy found himself locked in the middle of the naked traffic jam.

Now that he was in the line of fire, there was no escaping. They got him to touch them. When the pleasure of his company became fully appreciated, the men dared one another.

"You first."

"No, you."

"Lyle's kin. He gets the honors," Cissie said.

The men took turns.

The violence of it, the violence still haunted him.

He knew he was powerless. The God-fearing state of Oklahoma sent the monthly allowance so long as nobody opened their mouths, which Boy was hardly able to do. Lyle and Cissie, like mechanics in some hi-low game, happily split the pot.

After Thanksgiving dinner, Velma Gortz came up with the idea that transformed Boy's life.

"We're always answerin' them cheesy ads in the swingers' papers," she said. "And all we get for our money are burned-out stag films or deadbeats lookin' for action." She held up a tattered copy of *Southwest Adult Activities*. "Now there's a market for films. But it's got to be stuff that's unusual."

Boy's eyes retracted when she fondled him on her lap.

"Too dangerous," Herm said. "What adults do at the trailers is their business and our people keep mum about it."

Cissie looked at some ads. "They use code words for that sort of thing and have a P.O. Box. Here's one talkin' about 'Cubs and Wrens.' Another says 'Baby Talk.' How 'bout 'Toilet Training and *Discipline*'!"

Lyle lifted Boy off Velma's lap. His thick-veined tattooed arms enclosed Boy like a bear trap. "He sure as hell is a beauty."

Boy did not understand the discussion, but the following weekend when the group reassembled, he knew something terrible was brewing. Lyle and Herm were in the garage pounding nails and sawing. Cissie and Velma were at the sewing machine, clothes patterns strewn on the carpet.

Boy sat frozen, hiding in a cubbyhole beside the bookcase. He shivered when the men came for him. He was brought into the garage where a makeshift platform had been built. There were bright floodlights, and a camera stood on a tripod pointed at the rickety stage.

Some time during Christmas, with the roving carolers outside, one of the bikers riding the dope trail with Lyle worked out some kind of arrangement with Cissie, who had become Boy's keeper and trainer. The man agreed to develop and distribute the films they had made of Boy.

Boy was well treated by his handlers, given prime rare steaks and fresh vegetables, bought cowboy outfits and high-heeled boots. Before long, under their schooling, Boy became a luminary on the kiddie porn circuit all through the South.

When video cameras arrived, the filmmaking techniques became less complicated, and Boy starred in his first let's-pretend snuff movie. They'd make him up, put wigs on him, dress him up as a girl. One of the shows Boy especially enjoyed was a switch on this theme. The child victim was given a make-believe knife and "murdered" the couple who had violated him.

By the time he was twelve, Boy was robust, too big for the baby stuff, and Cissie decided to whisk him off on the party route. She'd made a number of contacts through the adult ads. These adventurers loved his perfectly formed body, the wide cat-green eyes, spacy and innocent. Private Lear jets glided in from Dallas and Tulsa for the Sooner Saturday games carrying special clients willing to fork over five hundred dollars for an evening of hijinks and handcuffs with Boy.

The performance artist, with his King Arthur haircut, was in great demand for these Big Daddy and Bad Mama fiestas which were filled with rapacious adults who couldn't wait to get their hands on him. These events ultimately became the reality of his childhood.

Boy was a shy young man, always polite and with a broad, lively smile. He struck everyone as very bright, normal but distant. He couldn't make friends or get close to kids his own age and he was saddened by this failing. On the other hand, his radiant friendliness made him a favorite with teachers. He had good grades and was not a problem.

He had been groomed by Cissie never to open his mouth about his career. Lyle plugged in the chain saw in the garage and warned him they would chop him into pieces if he ever said a word. In the neighborhood, everyone praised Cissie for the job she had done raising him.

"I just teach him fundamental values is all," Cissie said matter-of-factly.

In the dark vault that was his mind, Boy waited for the chance to escape.

One night in January with the wind screeching and the sand devils tearing through the scrub oak and blackjack trees, blowing off the scraggly antennas, Lyle and Cissie became testy. They couldn't even raise snow on the TV and joined the Gortzes in their trailer for a drink. Boy was sent down the road to the bootlegger for a few bottles.

There was a long line at Shorty's market and filling station, which served gas along with booze. Everybody griping about the TV. They'd all be missing *Jeopardy*. When Boy was finally served, he took two bottles and was glad to get them because of the run that night. It would have been hell if he came back empty-handed, moods his keepers were in.

When he came out, he looked to thumb a ride. Out of the funky, swamp shadows, a man with a slouch hat covering his eyes took his arm. He stood beside a dusty Caddy convertible.

"You load up my car, I'll drop you back."

"Yes, sir."

Boy had never seen the face before, but something about its very unfamiliarity in this locals' territory told him the person was important. This was confirmed when several of the wise-asses passed by and tipped their baseball caps. Indians turned away and the Mexican women shivered. Boy knew he'd finally laid eyes on Mystery Man.

Bouncy with the thrill of being in the company of the celebrated outlaw, he shunted two cases into the backseat of the Caddy. Mystery Man handed him a twenty-dollar bill. He was short with a powerful torso, sandpaper skin and demonic ice-blue eyes. His stare made Boy turn away.

He took Boy by the hand, opened the door for him, and graciously eased him into the front seat. Boy nervously juggled his bottles of white lightning as the big engine zoomed out of Shorty's down the dark dirt road.

"I'm goin' up to the Gortz trailer park, sir."

"I know all about you, Master Boynton," he said, adding another dimension to the mythic powers attributed to him. "I been waitin' on you."

"Well, it sure is a pleasure, meetin' you."

"We'll see."

The man lit a cigarette with his Zippo lighter and the car clouded with a blue haze. Boy was getting antsy, not knowing what to expect. Despite the cold night, sweat trickled down his back. They cruised down land reputedly owned by Mystery Man. Fields with workers' dormitories; machines churning in his pig slaughterhouse; a guard tower with searchlights which illuminated two men with rifles patrolling on a catwalk. The entire area was enclosed by barbed wire.

"He who will not deliver *himself* shall always live in fear," he whispered obscurely. "Are you game?"

"For what, sir?" Boy asked, frightened of the eyes.

"The deed. Now is the time."

Boy was uncertain of the meaning of these words, but he was in thrall, mesmerized by the intensity of Mystery Man and the power he emanated.

"Do you know who I am?"

All Boy could think of were the unspeakable acts attributed to Mystery Man. His mouth went dry with alarm.

"I believe I do, sir."

He gave Boy a narrow, menacing smile.

"Would you like to learn? Study life by my side?"

"Yes. Yes, I would."

"That's real good, sugar. Now follow what I say closely. The valiant deed is born in hell and brought forth by *clarity of intent.*" Mystery Man's voice was rasping but pleasing. "Now tell me this: what are people afraid of?"

"I don't know. Pain, maybe?"

"It's not pain. That is a reality they can endure. It's the anticipation of it. The unknown space that hollows out the soul."

"I believe that."

"Tonight will be your trial."

"Seems to me, my whole life's been nothin' else."

Mystery Man did a sudden U-turn and slued the car back toward the Gortz compound. As they approached, he placed Boy on his lap and let him steer. Then, passing one nondescript trailer after another, he gradually slowed down and asked Boy to point out where the party that night was to take place. Boy indicated the Gortzes' wood-shingled leviathan. He backed up the Caddy to the campfire grounds at the edge of the woods behind the trailer and cut the engine.

"Are you ready?"

"Yes, sir."

Mystery Man squinted in the gloom and reached into the backseat and brought out an old oil can with a metal nozzle. He took Boy's liquor from him, spilled out some and adjusted a funnel to the mouth of one bottle, then the other. Boy watched him carefully pouring a few drops from the oil can into each one. When he was finished, he handed them back to Boy.

They sat quietly for a few moments and Boy joined him in a smoke.

"You feeling primed for the great occasion that awaits you?" Mystery Man asked.

"I feel, I don't know"—he groped for a word—"I feel haunted, sir."

"I'll accept that." The man screwed up his eyes, like he was guessing weight at the fair. "Boy, I will use you. But you're going to learn the supreme lesson of life from me."

"Be my guide."

"You can never turn back after the valiant deed."

"I don't want to."

"Soon as you get in, turn the radio on. After they've had a drink, let me in."

Silently, they left the car, and Mystery Man did not have to tell Boy any more. At the entrance to the Gortz trailer, Mystery Man gave him a long smile of approval, then kissed him on the lips.

"I've watched you from afar for a long time, Boy. And fell in love with you at first sight. You've bewitched me. Know that I love you."

"Love me?"

"Yes. This bunch have done ungodly things to you."

"I know that."

"We must alter the course of destiny. It's called *fate control*. After this, you will walk with the gods."

Boy caught some heat for being so long. But all he could think of was that someone loved him. He placed the liquor bottles on the cocktail bar and took four Mason jars off the shelf.

"Lots of folks were down at Shorty's, carrying on," he nervously explained. "TV's are out everywhere. We're missin' all the great programs." He looked at his watch and fretted. "*Jeopardy*'s startin'."

Lyle barely glanced up from the bong he was loading, Cissie's eyes were glazed, and the Gortzes were stripping down for action. Velma lustfully smirked at him while working the curling iron through her pompadour.

"Anyone mind some music?" Boy asked.

"Suit yourself," Lyle said, drawing on the bong. His bearded cheeks were puffed up like a trumpet player's.

Boy fiddled with the dial, caught some static, until he found the country-music station which came in loud and clear.

Herm was eagerly sizing him up. "Come on, Boy, let's git it on."

"Well, just for once, I'd like to watch you all get worked up. You drink up and get *me* in the mood." He heard his voice crack, but forced himself to continue. "I'm ready for some real heavy action tonight."

Four sets of small red pig eyes hungrily roved over him. On the blue French buffet table, Velma's equipment was laid out for the feast.

"I want to do that number on Boy Cissie tol' me about." Boy's eyes glazed. "The one you performed for that oil man," Velma said breathlessly. "I read in *Adult World* them porn stars is doing that at the O'Farrell sex shows in San Francisco."

"What's that all about?" Herm asked.

"You'll see," Lyle said.

Boy popped open a can of Coke for himself and, like a fawning waiter, passed drinks around on a tray. He had been tutored in obedience.

"Now you sent me out on a night like this, you all drink hearty."

He could hardly catch his breath, but this stunt would be worth a whipping with the strap with copper nailheads. Give them all green-apple bellyaches. He watched them clink glasses and drink.

In about two minutes, their faces started to lose color. Boy found himself churning with elation as the convulsions and choking began. Tongues protruded, shrieks were drowned out by Elvis crooning "Love Me Tender" on the radio.

When they were squirming on the floor, Boy rushed to the door. Mystery Man bolted in. Now seen in good light, he was dancing on bandy legs with a large wicker basket as his partner. Boy couldn't make out what he was saying. He was babbling in tongues. Finally, Boy stopped him.

"What was in the can?"

"Venom and battery acid, a little toddy for the sinners. You'll see."

"Are they dying?" Boy asked with mounting excitement.

"Not yet. They be waitin' on you." As the four people writhed and gagged in agony, Mystery Man handed the basket to Boy. "Now here's sundown for these folks."

With curiosity and just a bit of fear, Boy removed the lid. Six rattlers, furiously hissing, uncoiled. Boy stood back in awe as they slithered on the trailer floor toward the groaning foursome, locked in a final daisy chain.

"What's burning?" Mystery Man, still dancing, asked.

"Velma's damn curling iron."

Boy stomped on a smoking pillow and was about to unplug the iron.

"Don't do that."

Mystery Man picked up the burning iron and smiled at Boy.

"Snakes and fire/Will halt desire," he chanted in a mystical voice like a prophet. "You shall give them all that lesson."

"Ohh, this feels so good," Boy shouted.

"Remember what I told you, Boy. Clarity of intent. Now take your time."

And he did. . . .

Boy brushed back the pageboy bangs which were obscuring his vision. He picked up the curling iron, hissing with burnt pillow feathers and hair. He waved it like the fiery, noble sword of a conqueror. Slowly, he brought it first to Cissie, then to Herm and Lyle, anointing them. Searing their flesh. Lastly, he stood over Velma's purple face, circling her while the rattlers closed in.

"Them oysters just exploded, Velma darlin'," Boy raved in an ecstasy of triumph.

When the deeds were completed, Boy felt a profound sense of liberation and exhilaration. Yet he was troubled by the intrusion of reality. He could not gain the attention of Mystery Man. With a forked stick, his guide rounded up the snakes. Boy was astonished at how calmly they returned to their basket.

"What do we do about the bodies?"

"They will be purified."

In the howling, ghosting wind, Mystery Man laid a trail of white lightning to the trailer's gas tank and handed Boy his Zippo lighter.

"Darkness falls more swiftly than light shall arrive."

From Mystery Man's car, Boy surveyed with reverence the painting he had created. He lovingly embraced the images. Through all the savage turns of his short life, it was the beauty of the fire, the creeping fronds of flame slowly planting their images in the sky, that thrilled him.

As Mystery Man drove away from the inferno, Boy turned to look back at the roar of the explosion. The belly of the trailer ruptured into a fireball that brought him to satisfaction and the knowledge of manhood.

"I came! I came! For the first time," Boy hollered proudly.

He leaned over the wheel of the speeding car and passionately kissed Mystery Man on the lips, entwining his tongue with the whisky breath of his savior.

"Valiant deeds are rewarded," they sang like reverent choirboys.

None of the officials from the Albermarle Children's Home gave Boy a hard time. Mystery Man had spoken to them, and Boy learned that he was a patron of their charity. He signed some documents and Boy was able to move in with his benefactor.

Some of the regular dwellers at the trailer park might have suspected something funny, but now with Mystery Man as Boy's protector, they kept quiet at the memorial service. Maybe a dozen of Lyle's biker buddies rode over to the field behind Shorty's for the event. They were solemn and one of them played taps on a bugle.

They looked Boy over with curiosity. He was wearing Mystery Man's green beret and a silver star on each shoulder of his denim shirt.

One of Lyle's buddies got pissed off and was about to rake Boy over the coals, then stopped in his tracks. Boy had a .45 on his hip and a commando knife in a sheath. Boy eyeballed him, ran his knife down the man's ponytail and slashed his black leather jacket. Mystery Man leaned his head out of the Caddy to watch his protégé. Boy sashayed out into the middle of the assembly of wild-eyed, furious bikers and started to dance to music only he heard.

"Anybody got a problem they want fixed?" Boy asked. "They can dance with me till dawn."

*　　*　　*

"André, André! It's very late, *mon petit chéri.*"

Boy stared at himself in the mirror. Over his shoulder he saw Denise. "What? André? Who's he?"

"You, *mon ange.* Your pet name. We'll see each other in the morning. You need your rest."

CHAPTER 15

There might have been a knock on the bedroom door, but Michel couldn't be sure. His eyes were closed, hands clasped around Jennifer's bare arm in the shelter she had located last night. He stirred when a hyenalike laugh detonated through the open doorway. The sound rudely pulled Michel and Jennifer out of wonderland. Neither of them knew where they were. It was a case of amnesia that gave way to bewilderment. The tilted vessel of the night was clearly not seaworthy. It had nearly capsized and listed on its side.

"Lazy otters sunning on a rock," Maddie said perkily. "Good girl, Jen, you took my advice! No guts, no glory."

Michel's eyes fluttered open and took in the small, dainty urchin before him. Jennifer still drifted in and out of a fog. Michel turned to Jennifer with an arid twisted tongue. "Who is this?"

Raising the raunchy old blankets to chest level, Jennifer said, "Madeleine Gold, this is . . . Michel—"

"Love it. Not even his last name. Jen, you've got to read the Pembrooke AIDS brochure. And by the way, for purposes of identification, this gentleman is Commander Michel Danton of the Police Judiciaire. Now I expect a complete report."

"Michel Danton, of course," Jennifer said. "I'm so glad I have you to look after me, Maddie."

Maddie winked at Michel and handed him his beeper. "You dropped it in the hallway with your credit cards." Maddie's voice reached a crescendo. "You sure made a racket. I thought you were going to knock down the walls."

"You have fine French construction to thank for your safety. Built to mistral code." He smiled at her. "So you're Maddie. Any new adventures in white slavery to report?"

"Ah, I make up stuff that Jen swallows."

Through neuron clouds Michel recognized the smell of coffee and identified a tray with croissants coming toward him along with strawberry preserves. He was not in the mood to bitch at Maddie for invading the sanctuary. She placed the breakfast tray on his lap. He was grateful and offered up some fingers.

"*Alors, mes enfants.* Eat up, as my dad would say. We'll be seeing him and my mom. I also got a fax, Jen. I can't wait for their invasion of the Riviera. I'll speak perfect French to them and maybe they'll buy me emeralds."

Jennifer's eyes were a mass of ruby capillaries. "Thanks for the breakfast, now please clear out."

"See you after class, Jen."

Staring into the sunlight creeping through the dusty shutters, Michel and Jennifer drank the coffee.

"Maddie's not what I expected. She's amusing and wholesome."

"Underneath it all, a savage."

His beeper sounded. "I have to check in with my office."

His haste disappointed her. "I thought you might stay a bit longer. Can't you?"

"We'll have lunch. And if I get off early, I'll take you over to Louise's. We can have a swim. She has a pool on her roof garden." He hardly recognized his suit amid the mound of clothes serpentined on the floor.

"Did I disappoint you?" she asked.

"No. You're a wonderful lover. I adore you."

"Do you?"

"Yes. Damn it, we're both so insecure."

She held on to him. The night with Michel had transformed her sense of herself.

"I feel beautiful."

"Jennifer, you are."

"Maybe now. Silly of me. You meant everything you said last night?"

"Do you need confirmation?"

"Lots of it."

"I was an unhappy, miserable man until yesterday." He rescued a trouser leg. "I can't go out looking like this. I'll need an iron."

"I'll press for you in Ojai."

"We'll find a French laundry."

Wrapped in gummy sheets and clenching their bundles of clothes, they made their way through the corridor and into Maddie's apartment.

"You shower first," Jennifer said.

"Not together?"

"You're the one in a hurry."

"What's the razor situation?"

"New Bic, on the top shelf of the medicine cabinet."

He looked at his watch. It had stopped. Seiko, they were all crap.

"It's seven-thirty," she said. "I'll be upstairs in my room."

Twenty minutes later and with only a few nicks, he was bundled in a pink terrycloth robe and padding up the spiral staircase. Jennifer had her hair pinned up and was at the ironing board, a flower of domesticity. He looked around: suit pressed, shirt with missing buttons and yesterday's sweat. Shorts soaking in soapy water in the sink. She handed him one of her blue denim shirts and, although snug, it had buttons, unfortunately on the left side. She touched the scar routes on his back and chest, nasty stippled troughs of bulbous tissue. The striations formed a crazy quilt design on his chest and shoulder.

"Can I ask you something?" He nodded, knowing where this was leading. "What are these?"

"I was shot four times in Corsica last year. The guilty parties were dealt with. I was out on sick leave until last night. They said I had a nervous breakdown along the way, although I didn't agree. Thus, Dr. Leon Stein three times a week delving into my childhood. Completely untraumatic."

Her mouth gaped open with bewildered concern. His beeper went off again and he was spared.

"Why didn't you mention it?"

"After you told me about your fiancé, I didn't want to spoil the one perfect evening of my adult life."

"Oh, Michel. I can't let go of you." Eyes somber, growing misty she kissed him. "Please be careful."

"I always am. Discussion of war wounds to be tabled until I can spring free of whatever it is they want me for."

"Is it serious?"

"It's this murder investigation. The American kids."

"Christ, I washed your briefs." She rushed to her unstable dresser and the drawer almost dropped on her foot. She pulled out a variety of panties. He selected the least offensive white ones, high-cut with frilly borders.

"I've always wondered what it would be like to wear a woman's undergarments. I'll have to ask the vice squad about that. Well, I'm off, transvestite on the premises. Now I have a secret life that only you know about."

"Lunch? Where?"

He wrote down his numbers in Marseille and his emergency beeper code. "Better still, I'll call you."

"I'll murder you if you don't."

"You're a magnificent woman. Last night—"

"Was a toe-curler."

"I don't think there's a French translation for that one."

He gave her a loud kiss with easy familiarity. He was mad about her. Damn, he wanted her again and was huffing like a teenager.

"Thanks for the use of the clothes. We'll save for the baby's college tuition shopping at Unisex."

3

THE

BATHERS

CHAPTER 16

Michel hit the klaxon of the Citroën Maserati, scattering the people on the street. He was intoxicated by his vitality and heading back to the whirlwind of his career. There was something miraculous about finding a good woman, no question. Jennifer had cleared his vision in a hurry and done wonders for his confidence.

The call had informed him that he was to go to Louise Vercours's establishment. Had one of the girls committed suicide? No, he wouldn't have been notified. More than likely some ancient cretin had been suffocated with a plastic bag over his head striving to achieve his annual orgasm at the hotel she owned next door to her house. This was a new form of recreation made popular by British cabinet ministers after threading coke up their noses. Louise really ought to get out of the business. Take millions from the Corsican syndicates in Marseille and call it a night.

The troops were out in force: ambulances, Laurent's coroner's wagon; parking meter Gestapo busily adding to their bonuses, writing tickets.

A gendarme directed him. "It's upstairs, you'll have to walk up. The elevator's been sealed off."

"To Louise's house?"

A nod. Michel clambered up the S-curved staircase to her roof garden. He was momentarily baffled by the chaos. The forensic technicians welcomed him back. Dr. Charles Laurent emerged, looking outlandish in plastic surgical boots.

"You're finally here. Welcome back."

"Who's dead?"

"Louise."

"What! That can't be."

He handed Michel gloves and boots. "Follow me."

Shock waves resonated within Michel. He'd been with Louise last night, kissed her. He realized he had a grotesque hangover and he was not alone. The Marseille team were already there and their chalky faces revealed they too were in rotten shape. So much for partying.

"The ferocity of the murder is as gruesome as anything I've ever seen, Michel. Put on the boots and we'll go in. Claude and Courbet are already muddling things."

Louise's living quarters had been flooded and reeked of chlorine. Summer sniffles going around—allergies, or was it the chlorine? Only a few days ago, he had put the canisters away for her. The techs were shooting videotape and the still photographer was lighting the room from a power pack.

"Electricity's off, Michel."

"How are you, Patrick?"

"About to dish up my eggs. And you missed this work?"

There was no way for Michel to adjust to the scent of this murder scene. The invasive climate of sexuality, its fluids, the hidden memories now obscured, clothes, curtains, inanimata, the silence of Louise's great art, the essence of obscure secrets buried for now, but likely to disclose their hidden power. What always struck Michel about murder was the debasement which filled the canvas, obliterating the subject. Death fused with life. Which of them was real and which the impostor, he thought for the thousandth time.

Trudging through more than a foot of bloody, putrid water, Michel entered Louise's bedroom. No defense wounds; her hands were bound tightly behind her with a thick red patent leather belt. Her fingernails were black as though dyed. A bloody towel had been jammed in her mouth. He stooped down to get a closer look at her. She lay on the floor, naked and bloated. She had been gutted.

Burn marks had seared her thighs and ravaged what had formerly been her female organ. Almost as though from a branding iron. Her intestines were coiled out in front of her like groggy snakes. A bottle of Pétrus wine had been smashed against her head. Shards of broken glass floated on the dead sea.

Michel looked away, stupefied by the horror. This was different from the anonymous population of corpses he had seen through the years. The defiled body was one of his. Memories of Louise's generosity and love flooded back and he felt his flesh severed by the same wounds. Something within him had died with her.

Claude was peering into the open wall safe with a flashlight.

"Claude, let me tell you right now: If you touch evidence or steal anything, I'll throw you off the fucking roof and then arrest you for compromising the case."

Threats were good for Claude's posture and he snapped out of his habitual slouch.

"Damn, Michel, I'm sure there was a robbery. Her safe's been cleaned out. And don't treat me like a suspect."

"Maybe Paul Courbet is."

"Now this has to stop. Because he's with Yvette and you're not, you're acting in a very unprofessional way for someone who's now in charge of three murder investigations."

"He tried to extort money from Louise about some American girl sleeping with her clients."

"Prove it," rang Courbet's cutting voice. He was crouched behind Michel, ready to spring. "I took the complaint and asked Louise if she'd be willing to pay off this idiot teacher and get rid of her."

"We'll leave it for the moment. Now get out."

Michel was convinced that Claude had been looking for a diary or an account book which listed payoffs Louise had made to the vice squad. He was so deficient in common sense that Michel felt a tinge of sympathy for the bungler. If Louise had such a document, it would be in the possession of her lawyer. Let Claude find out for himself.

"Has Denise Casson been notified?" Michel asked.

"Not that I know of," Claude said.

"Or my mother?"

"No one yet," someone shouted.

"Who called this in, Claude?"

"Old Benedict, the concierge, told the maid that there was a flood coming from Louise's roof. He thought her pool had overflowed or that the sprinkler system had broken."

"It was Celeste who discovered the body."

"Wonderful, Celeste is dotty and Benedict's got cataracts." Michel needed some privacy to regroup from the shock. "Claude. Please wait outside. I need a few moments alone."

Louise's eyes protruded and the graven agony on her face was not softened by death. Michel closed her lids and kissed her forehead. He puddled over to the wall safe which had been concealed by Matisse's *Odalisque*. It too had been hosed down, but fortunately the glass had saved the painting. Blood spatter distributions on the once ocher walls were imprecise and would not assist the investigation.

He headed for the kitchen, all new. A rank odor permeated it. He looked at the sleek black Amana oven and had a man check it for prints. Clean as he had anticipated. Still he used a pencil to lift the handle. Inside the grill cavity was a bloody glutinous gel that reeked of burnt rubber.

He told the ambulance attendants to bag the body and walked through the cordon of police chattering on the roof.

They quieted down when the station chief of the Marseille office strode in. Richard Caron was an aloof man, imperious, admired, never adored. He had something of the de Gaulle autocratic style. Many years ago he had been a member of the general's corps of personal bodyguards, and the praetorian manner was evident in his gaunt face and hawk eyes. Now sloping toward retirement, he had been Michel's sponsor throughout his career and had anointed him his heir. That was a dim possibility, for Michel lacked anything resembling political skills.

"Send someone down to the Café Printemps for a pot of coffee and aspirin," Michel roared.

"Lovely girl you were with last night. Pity you left so quickly. I wanted to dance with her too."

"Laurent wore her out with his tangos."

"And you afterwards?"

"Something like that."

"Is Yvette in mourning?"

"No, she's been doing Courbet on the side."

"That halfwit grafter?"

"I can't account for her taste—or mine. Why are you here, Richard?"

"I wanted to see you. Are you up to this, Michel, or do you need more time off?" Caron asked with paternal concern.

"Up to this! I never should have been farmed out. I knew Louise all my life and loved her." Michel leaned shakily on the wall. "No one knew her better than me. Dammit, the local cops shouldn't be here in the first place. They've already pulped the homicide scene with the American couple."

"It was out of my control. The prefect finally called me in Marseille and asked for you. But be reasonable. Claude is the Municipal Police's homicide representative. You know their local politics. Don't humiliate Claude. You'll be in charge."

"Okay, let's look this all over."

Murder had nuances and an ambiance which Michel regarded as the most essential aspect of the early investigation. He had to re-create the *mise-en-scène* before he could proceed. With a seemingly dreamy look on his face, he wandered around familiar territory: the greenhouse; the coiled hoses; the sprinkler timers; the empty canisters of chlorine. He stood at the edge of the pool staring at his reflection. He was handed a large cup of steaming café au lait and aspirins.

"Suspects, thousands," Claude said. Michel wanted to clamp his mouth shut, but he continued musing. "Anyone who worked for Louise or was a client over the years."

"Claude, I do this for a living. Now get yourself some coffee."

Claude threw up his hands in exasperation and waited in vain for Richard Caron to reprimand Michel. "It's futile, trying to work with you." He ambled off to the table where someone had put a jumble of sausage and cheese, fetched from the market below.

"Who do you want to work with on this, Michel?"

"I'll need two women. Say Annie and Corinne if she's back from holiday."

"Last week. Annie would be good choice. Corinne is in her first trimester but hasn't put in for leave."

"Couldn't be better. I'd like a sympathetic pregnant woman on this. She'll have hundreds of Louise's girls to talk to. The golden-age retired and the new flock."

Caron shuffled into a more tranquil spot with Michel behind him. He paused at the bougainvillea trellis and looked down at the street. Canal Plus TV cameramen were doing color with market people and snatching samples off the fruit stalls.

"Any ideas, Michel?"

He tried to sort out his thoughts. "I stopped off here with Jennifer on the way to her place. I wanted to show her how an old classic *hôtel* had been restored. It was three A.M. No noise, nothing usual. Benedict took Louise's poodle for a trot after closing. There was nothing to make me suspicious. She was probably dead by then."

Michel looked away. Images formed and he felt the rush to put them in some kind of order. He signaled a tech. "Oh, Albert, I'll want a check on her telephone calls. *Toute de suite, mon ami.* And bring Louise's answering machine. It's a Panasonic by her bedside."

Michel turned back to Richard Caron. "Sorry. Well, a great impresario has been at work. He's not a virgin composer of this sort of music. It's too depraved and it's tainted with revenge. Yes, lots of experience, talent, and the ability to improvise. The physical evidence has been contaminated. Our man put his surgical gloves in the microwave to melt. Everything was hosed down and chlorine added. Someone came to kill Louise, slowly, then turned it into a sex party."

"More than one?" Caron asked.

"I doubt it. A male for sure."

"Could Louise have known him?"

"I don't have any answer for that. Odd, the way madams keep their sex lives quiet. No one knows a damn thing about Louise's lovers. I certainly don't. I never met a man with her."

"Do you think she picked up someone?"

"It's possible. She left the restaurant about nine with Denise Casson."

"Would she do something impulsive?"

"No, that's Denise's style."

Laurent was beside him. He had picked up a puffy roll filled with sausage. He always snacked at murder scenes.

"I'm going to take her back to Marseille for the PM, Michel."

The air-conditioning units at the cafés were already dripping and the porters were mopping puddles under the awnings.

"Keep her cold. And no stories about running out of freon."

"Michel, you've hardly been back and you're still an utter pain in the ass."

"Laurent, on this case, you'll please spare me your exotic South American poison theories. Another thing, I don't want you spending a month doing a spleen analysis and air-mailing organs to the FBI."

"Thanks for the tip."

"Can you tell us anything now?"

"My guess is the cause of death was a right-handed severance with a very long-bladed single-edge knife. Sliced into the right carotid artery. Then it was sawed very deeply into the jugular. It's practically a trench."

"What about the American couple, have you done the autopsies?"

"The woman was strangled. A hatchet was used on the man for the decapitation."

Michel shivered in the steamy heat. "Would Louise still have been alive when he disemboweled her?"

"Possibly an antemortem wound. I'll know better after the autopsy. The stab wounds below the left breast measure roughly one hundred-fifty millimeters in diameter. And there was foreplay—perhaps an electric waffle machine. Or an iron."

"It's the wrong configuration for a waffle or an iron. The striations of burns have no indentations."

Richard Caron smiled. "Quite right, Michel."

It was horrible to contemplate. "We'll see if there's a fire poker missing in the inventory."

Michel's mind drifted. What a day this would have been for a picnic with Jennifer at the family farm, walking through the countryside, a dip in the deep lake that meandered through the property and then love in the lavender pasture. He'd wrap her in boughs of herbs. Rapture gave way to reality.

Michel took out a five-hundred-franc note and handed it to Laurent.

"Do me a favor when you get downstairs, Laurent. Stop at Sylvie's stall. She once worked for Louise. Buy some flowers and put them beside the body."

Claude, chomping a roll, wheeled around the periphery, not wanting to miss a word. Crumbs hung off his lip. He had his cellular phone peeking out of his jacket pocket and was hovering.

Michel whispered to Richard. "I'm going to give him a false lead. Or if he has a wild theory, please encourage him. He'll believe you."

Michel spiked his hand on the bougainvillea winding over the greenhouse door.

"Claude, you've given me an idea. Louise was always using a cellular phone. I don't know who would handle the billing," Caron said in a friendly tone.

Claude pondered. "A hacker could be involved."

"That's an interesting possibility."

"Tapped into her line, got personal information . . . We've had a ring of Russian thugs playing with car phones."

"Excellent, could you look into that for Michel?"

Claude's hooded eyes came to life and he smiled at the praise.

"Might be a Russian." Claude became pensive, dancing with this notion. "The town's full of those cheap bastards. I'll have my people work on that."

"The Russian idea is a penetrating insight." Richard clapped his shoulder. "I'm happy to have you looking after Michel."

"See, Michel, you're not the only detective in Provence."

When Claude had joined Courbet at the freeloader's table, Richard guided Michel to the back of the greenhouse.

"We found the passports of the two Americans who were murdered at the dam. Do you think there might be a connection with Louise?"

"I'm not sure at this stage. I think the couple ran into bad luck on a picnic. That was an opportunist's murder. Louise's is different. He came looking for her."

Michel turned away tearfully, devastated.

CHAPTER 17

With Claude dispatched on a frivolous pursuit, Michel continued to rove around the interior. He and Richard peered through the French doors at the pandemonium in the street. Bedecked with flowers and followed by tearful stallkeepers with hats off, the meat wagon began its tortuous journey through the old quarter. Louise had been generous to everyone and a friend in need.

"I want to go back through this scene a lot more carefully, Richard."

"Want company?"

"Yours especially."

"I missed you, Michel. There was nothing I could do to get you back sooner."

"I know."

With the techs and the other local detectives gone, Michel had the opportunity to regain his focus.

"We have a man capable of brilliant improvisation. He sees a hose, he uses it. Then rewinds it the way a gardener would.

"He takes a swim in the pool afterwards, to clean up. And I'll bet he wasn't on drugs. No, far too methodical. Drugs mess you up. And he has to concentrate, stay cool. He certainly planned to burglarize Louise. She would have let him take anything. There wouldn't have been a battle over her emeralds or the combination to the safe. She has more millions than she could've ever spent. So, knowing Louise, she'd cooperate with him. But for some reason the man loathed her."

"He must have, or he simply hates older women. She might have reminded him of someone," Richard Caron said.

"Since we're speculating . . . He may have believed she'd injured him—his girlfriend or mother who had worked for Louise."

"Assume he has a gun?"

Michel was silent. Did Louise know the killer? Was she accosted in the street? Did he break in, or was he already inside, waiting for her?

"A gun sounds right. But this doesn't have the feel of one of those robberies when someone panics. He came to kill her. He has a gun, in theory, but decides against using it."

"The noise, of course."

"Yes. But there's something more to it. It's a vulture's feast."

Richard Caron was attentive. "He knows police methods. Military background possibly?"

"That's reasonable. Let me go on, please. It's a program killing: a distorted tone poem.

"First movement: taking her hostage downstairs.

"Second: *allegro non troppo.* Humiliation, verbal abuse, then sexual games, building to torture.

"Final movement: cymbals and drum rolls and the *coup de grâce.*

"Coda: destroying evidence. It's not a showcase murder, but rather another bravura performance. There's a sense of orchestration in which the killer uses all of his craft and his entire repertoire. It's a concert for tough critics. In other words, us.

"This man doesn't lose his head. He looks around and finishes with a little flourish. Nothing ostentatious, mind you. He sees chlorine and he methodically swamps the place. Anything to create confusion and destroy the evidence." Michel was dazzled by the virtuoso. "Beautiful technique. The point being, he wants to go back on stage to conduct again . . . when it suits his purpose."

Richard Caron was pleased by the hypothesis. "What about a time schedule? He's operating in, say, the two-hour range?"

"Or longer, if he's been watching Louise. She has very regular habits."

"Could Denise have known the man?"

"I'll find out."

He and Caron were back in the swamp of Louise's bedroom. The Aubusson carpet was ruined. Broken glass everywhere, crunched underfoot. There was a terrible ineluctable logic about the killer's methods. Michel opened Louise's closet. Dresses, shoes, suits scattered on the floor, some cut up. The caustic smell of urine was overpowering.

"This is helpful," Michel said.

"What, that he was a savage?"

"That's really the point. He doesn't care about great art, designer clothes. Fine wine means nothing. Richard, in your wildest dreams, can you imagine a Frenchman slashing a Chanel suit, turning a hose on a Matisse? A man who wouldn't bother to drink a bottle of Pétrus?"

Michel sensed that in this case he might track this monster by his relationship to the food chain. They trolled back and forth through a variety of theories and tried to pinpoint national types. Caron was superb when it came to volleying ideas. He was flexible, no ego problem, with a fine imagination.

"We have a man who knows everything about murder and is ignorant of the good things in life," Michel continued. "He doesn't understand what is quality and what's trash. So to begin with, I'd suggest he had limited schooling and certainly no college degree."

"From one of the former communist states? An English or German skinhead?" Caron reflected.

"It's unlikely that he was a European. A Russian would have grabbed some of the paintings. Her art is worth millions. He would have taken Louise's clothes and flogged them at a flea market. Or given them to his girl. There was a grudge here, and a seasoned killer didn't want anything cumbersome to unload. He took cash and jewelry."

Michel was never wedded to a theory, but trusted his instincts and powers of observation.

"Richard, we're looking for a man without our civilized traditions. On the other hand, the man might have his own beliefs. A religious fanatic." He checked up. "No, I'm unhappy with the idea of an Islamic fundamentalist being involved. Louise wasn't political. This man had a grievance of a different kind that has to do with his character and something that happened in his own life rather than a cause."

Richard Caron was delighted to have Michel working. There was nothing better on a murder case than a detective who was well educated, poised, and ingenious.

"I'll have Claude send the uniforms out to check the hotels and pensions. In the meantime, apart from Annie and Corinne who else do you want from the Legion?"

Michel scanned the faces of the two detectives who had arrived from Marseille. The ferrety Pierre Graslin, a law school dud, was nevertheless a fastidious interrogator. Émile Briand, ten years older than Michel, but his subordinate, had a kindly avuncular manner. He'd be effective with the locals.

"The ladies. Pierre and Émile. Oh, *merde.* I almost forgot. I promised Leon Stein I'd use him as a consultant when I had a case. Psychiatrists always need money."

CHAPTER 18

By eleven, Denise had finally left the house to open her salon and Boy was able to do a thorough inventory of Louise's jewelry. The sour, whining bitch who had stayed in another room down the hall from him had rushed out very early after a phone call. Later Boy had seen her on TV doing the news outside Louise's house. He had stashed everything in the garden shed he had commandeered to do household jobs. It was filled with rusted tools which he had found useful. With a rusty flashlight, he examined Louise's emeralds, diamonds, rings, and stones he could not identify. He had no idea of their value and he wasn't about to begin getting appraisals while he was in France.

Mystery Man would unload the spoils through his people at home. Boy would not get a beat count from his protector. Should he Fed Ex the jewelry to him? No, that might cause a problem with customs snoops. Where was his head? Of course, Maddie would carry the goods home. If there was a hassle, she'd do the explaining and he'd walk.

Boy cleaned up, then scouted around the hotels and pensions. The cops were everywhere. Gendarmes cruised the reception desks, flicking through registration cards. He decided to stay put. The students were at classes and Boy had a table to himself at Deux Garçons where he studied *USA Today*'s foreign currency exchange. He did his long division slowly and methodically. He had sixty thousand francs plus thirty-five thousand more in chips from the casino in Monte Carlo. That converted to about eighteen thousand dollars. It was the most kickable cash he'd ever had in his life! The thrill of having a stake made him giddy. He could be independent. Maybe buy some land on the Gulf. He'd always found Galveston accommodating. He and Mystery Man had traveled there on several hunting expeditions and to collect snakes.

But then he reconsidered his circumstances. This was really chump change compared to the kind of money Maddie had. To top it off, he was in love with her.

The gift of Mystery Man's wisdom came back to him.

"Women, you keep 'em befuddled, then web 'em."

Maddie merrily swanned down the Cours Mirabeau. The colossal plane trees, believed to be the oldest in France, provided a curtain of shade from the dazzling light. She was still high from her night with Louise. Boy was right. Once she entered his kingdom, she became omnipotent. She stopped at the Fontaine Chaude whose thermal spring water was thought to benefit people with rheumatism or gout. Believers were dipping in their hands and some were filling up their jars from the chiseled rosette spouts. She turned her face up to the sun. She and Boy could use some beach time, a holiday. Now that she had committed the primal act, she felt in control of the cosmic powers of the universe.

When she saw his legs arched over a chair at the café, she said, "Oh, to be nineteen and madly, wildly in love."

"Yes, my lady." Boy stood up, bowed gallantly, and pushed a cane-backed chair in for her. He grabbed a waiter's arm. "Get us a couple of light coffees. Not that black silt."

"*Deux cafés au lait. Un verre du lait froid aussi, s'il vous plaît.*"

"*Oui, mademoiselle.*"

"Such a smart-ass."

"Nobody's smarter than you, Boy. We'll get you everything. French lessons, you name it. The world is ours." She clutched him under the table. "When *they're* gone, we'll have everything."

Boy played dumb and let her think the remark whipped over his head.

"Cops are out sailin' and scratchin' their chigger bites."

The coffee was delivered. Boy had a yen for a big New York onion bagel with cream cheese piled two inches high. He got a flaky croissant instead and sulked.

"Two men in my life—you and my father—always griping about food."

"We have much in common."

"Not for long," Maddie said, stroking him under the table.

"Don't do that. The dragon gets very angry and spits fire."

"Oh, really." His relationship with Denise nagged at her. "Did you save some for me?"

Boy knew she was sex crazy as usual and jealous. He had yet to find a way to extinguish the fire of possession. Maybe he'd been wrong to turn her on to threesomes. They all had to start somewhere before he could get them to calm down.

Maddie was still petulant. "What goes on with you and Denise?"

"Elle est charmante," Boy replied with a decent accent.

"If that bitch's touched you, I'll chop her up and I'm not kidding."

It always happened with amateurs. One kill and they ruled the world. Let her be queen for a day. Boy kissed her fingertips. The courting students at the university did that with their ole ladies. Always put stars in their eyes.

"Denise likes lookin' at me naked. I stand by the window. For the Peeping Tom society in this freaky town, so they'll know she has a young guy. It's her ego." Maddie was still extremely agitated. Boy laid it right in the trough. The truth for once. "Ole Denise, she's afraid of AIDS. She works the giant Toshiba on herself. Makes more goddamn noise than the exhaust on a Greyhound bus. Wake the dead. I'd hate to be on the receivin' end of her electric bills."

Maddie bought it. No options.

"It's eternity for us, you know that."

"Hoped and prayed you'd ask me for more'n a Saturday night mountin'," he said lightly. "What's that word you JAP ladies call it?"

"A *shtup*. Yeah, you got that right, Darrell Vernon Boynton."

"I serve only you." He touched the top of her head. "You had your coronation, my queen."

"That's how I feel . . . Now I have breaking news that'll freak you out."

"I saw the TV coverage. I understood most of that pig Latin, too."

"No, not that. Listen to me. I have a plan. Guess who's coming to dinner?"

Boy cupped her face in his powerful hands, smiled and bided his time.

CHAPTER 19

Sitting across from his parents in the hospital room, Michel was deeply affected by their palpable shock and the tears that accompanied his disclosure. His mother's soft, caring face seemed to lose its structure.

"When can I see Louise?"

"Not for some time. She's been taken to Marseille by the medical examiner for an autopsy."

"What about funeral arrangements?" Philippe asked with a degree of forlornness Michel had seldom observed in his father. "She had no blood relatives, Michel. The three of us are her family."

"I know," Michel said, sharing their anguish. "We'll do it in style. Now don't be alarmed, but one of my investigators will be here shortly to take your official statement. It's Pierre. He's been to Chez Danton with me. Go back in time and see if you can remember anything about Louise's past that may help. Was there an old lover? Did she have an enemy she might have mentioned? Maybe there was a silent partner in her *maison* who had a grudge? Anything . . ."

They nodded meekly, rattled by Michel's ominous tone and saw a different side of their son. They were overwhelmed by the power and authority he exuded.

"You'll catch this beast?"

"I'll do my best, Papa. Oh, before I forget, let me have the chit for Louise's dinner order."

Philippe had brought yesterday's checks and the books for Nicole to do because it was Delantier's day off. He located her order on the spindle. Receipts would be reinvented, for Chez Danton had successfully resisted credit cards and a computer. His parents were afraid the tax people would swoop in and catch them fiddling. Everyone paid cash, like the old days.

Philippe handed him Delantier's drunken scrawl. "By the way, Louise not only paid for your champagne, she settled your account with

Delantier." Louise's munificence never failed to astound him and he was speechless. "Otherwise, you and that American woman would have been given scraps from the kitchen."

His mother's inconsolable keening rang in his ears and her voice broke.

"She loved you more than anyone, Michel."

Maddie returned to the café with a map she had bought at the bookstore on the corner. Boy was plowing through a cheese omelet.

"You know these idiots have never heard of a bagel. And French's mustard in France, forget it."

"Tough it out for a few more weeks, Boy. I'll be feeding you with a silver spoon."

"Sorry, this bullshit food is just a killer on my stomach." Maddie's face had an intriguing guile which tantalized him. "What's up?"

"Jennifer's walking on cotton candy," Maddie said. "She got her rocks off big time last night. I was dreaming and thought it was a seven-pointer and the building was going to collapse."

Boy was delighted. "Maybe now she'll stop leaning on you."

"I'd say."

"Is this your big news?"

"No, be patient. I'm giving you a dose of your own medicine."

Maddie took out a Michelin map and spread it on the table. She had too much jittery energy. She was jumping from one subject to another. Getting flaky. He'd have to be sure that she didn't smoke hash or drop acid. She'd go off on a riff and they'd be locked up in ten minutes.

"I said before, 'Guess who's coming to dinner?' but you weren't paying attention." Boy had caught her drift but chose to wait her out. "Mr. and Mrs. Adam Gold." Maddie pulled out a sheet of paper. "I've got faxes coming out of my ears. I picked this one up at the university after French Civilization. Here's their itinerary. Three days in Cannes at the Montcalm; two days at the Hôtel du Cap in Antibes; three days at the Hôtel de Paris in Monte Carlo."

"So, you'll cut school for a few days and have some fun."

"We will, Boy. The beach, some sun on our bodies. I will drench you in Bain de Soleil. My father will be going to meetings with foreign distributors. My mother"—Maddie shook her head with scorn—"will be wearing her 'Give Me Shopping or Give Me Death' T-shirt. Wouldn't it be nice to grant her wish?"

Boy laid a misdirection move on her. "You know, I'd really like to head back to L.A."

"You can't! Don't you realize what a chance this is?"

"To do what? Follow you around and hide out in some greasy pension? I'm stayin' put until Air France puts me in my seat."

"We can have it all."

He let her lead the horse to water. "Tell me another one. What's your father worth?"

"According to the *Wall Street Journal* at least six hundred million dollars."

The number meant nothing to Boy. Five or ten million made sense, had reality. Not this astronomy. "Cut the crap." He gazed around suspiciously. She was getting on his nerves. "And lower your voice."

"Okay." She dropped down an octave. "Now listen. I am the sole heir to the estate. Last year a cable company offered him six hundred mil—and you heard right—for A. G. Productions. It was an unsolicited offer. My father's business manager and his lawyer did an analysis of the offer and they concluded it was a too low. It doesn't matter, my father won't sell."

"How'd he get so rich?"

"We're living through an electronic revolution and my father is a supplier of programming content, if you can call the garbage he churns out content. He claims it's the tip of the iceberg. He can make video games out of his shows, put them on line for computers and now they're digitizing everything. There are also hundreds of satellite channels that need programming. Mr. Adam Gold and producers like him are in the catbird seat."

Maddie continued to explain the financial implications to Boy. Since 1968, Adam Gold had created seventeen one-hour episodic television series which had run for years. After two network showings he retained ownership and sold them to local stations in the syndication market. There were hundreds and hundreds of episodes that ran and reran. Seventy countries paid royalties for these rights; they in turn churned them to death. An entire floor of employees in the Adam Gold Building on Cañon Drive in Beverly Hills did nothing else but sell, track, and collect fees on these rights.

"You know an awful lot," Boy said, surprised by her commercial sophistication. "How'd you get so sharp about all this TV rap?"

"Thing is, Boy, all during my childhood, I heard nothing but how they sell TV series. My father used to drag me along to his network pitch meetings, his office, everywhere. I grew up in this business." She kissed his nose, then his mouth. "You have been sleeping with the golden goose, my love."

Boy had been waiting for this, holding two pair close to the vest. She had just dealt him the full house, aces up.

"Maddie, I fell for you before I knew you had two cents to your name." He wiggled the line and she took the bait. "I thought you were a brain-dead goofball from all the dope you'd done. The Porsche you had the first night could have been some guy's, or hot." He drew her in deeper, watching her moisten her tongue. "I didn't know or care. I fell in love with you, darlin'."

He had her hyperventilating. "Me too. When you took down that gangbanger and walked over him, I knew I'd found my man. Even if his name was Boy."

He glanced down at the map on the table and got her back on track.

"Cannz?"

"Cannes. The *s* is silent."

"*Can* like in a can of chili beans."

"Exactly the way it's pronounced."

Running his finger along the coastline from Marseille, he said, "And there're beaches there?"

"Gorgeous ones. Water's warm. Beachboys will wait on us hand and foot. I'm going to give you the treat of your life."

He leaned over and kissed her. "You already have, sugar. When do Mom and Dad come for their summer vacation?"

"Two days. And I'm going to cut their throats."

"No, you're not. You're going to listen to me, my lady."

"Oh God, when you call me 'my lady,' like on our first night, I get so excited."

"I'll give you all you can handle later."

"Nice and slow, drop by drop. I'm so hot, Boy. Listening to Jennifer getting off made me wild."

Boy assessed the possibilities critically and came to the conclusion that Maddie would have to be gentle and compliant with her parents.

"Maddie, here's what we do. Go back to your natural hair color. I don't want Mommy and Daddy bent out of shape. Miss Goody Two Shoes is going to charm them. You have got to be snowy clean with a perfect alibi. You know doin' the folks in France gives us an edge over the States. The cops here are lazy and dumb. They never stop eatin' and boozin'. Leave it to me."

"Yes, yes."

"The other thing is, if by some chance you were spotted as a brunette last night, they'll never recognize you when you're back as a redhead. Change the color before you arrive in Cannes. Not here, though. I don't want you runnin' back to Denise's."

She nodded submissively. Then her eyes wandered. Her mouth twisted into a vicious snarl. "There's that animal Karim. Boy, kick his ass."

"No. I'm going to buy him a beer."

"Françoise, I could cut her eyes out for bringing me to Louise's."

"I'll fix their wagons when the time comes." He ran his fingers up her damp thigh and she shuddered. "Françoise went to Cannes."

"How do you know?"

"Never ask me questions. I want to find out where Françoise is stayin'. It's important." He squeezed her arm until it hurt. "Drag your ass up and charm Karim. It's hugs and kisses time."

"Yuck, his aftershave makes me want to barf."

"Maddie, this is business, behave yourself now."

"*Alors, mon vieux, ça va, Karim?*" She opened her arms wide and kissed the gritty, unshaved cheeks of the young Algerian.

"We've missed you, pal. Have a drink on me."

CHAPTER 20

The manicurist was giving Denise a fill when Michel arrived at the salon. Her face was barely visible under the hair dryer. Denise smiled at him and held up one finger. With a pen, she was underlining a cabin price for a cruise. Michel gestured apologetically and switched off the dryer.

"Oh, damn it, couldn't you wait?"

"Can we talk privately?"

Denise motioned to the manicurist, who rolled her table away. Both women were miffed by the inconvenience. Clearly, Denise had not heard about the murder.

"I'm sorry about what I'm about to tell you . . ."

He observed Denise's reaction. She might have been hit by a shotgun blast—he knew firsthand how that felt. Her recoil was instantaneous; shock waves registered; her hands jerked spasmodically. Her head rocked back and forth and she leaned on his shoulder.

Over coffee in her office, she emerged from this state and into the irrational vengeance phase.

"When you catch him, let me give him a manicure!"

"I'll do better."

Michel did not need to jog Denise's memory.

"Louise and I were going to try to book a world cruise together during the mistral season. She was going to bring your mother along as a surprise. That's what we were discussing when you and your new friend said good night."

"Was anyone privy to your plans?"

"The travel agent."

The direction was becoming a bit clearer to him. "You and Louise frequently cruised together, didn't you?"

Denise looked away. "Yes, on and off."

"The two cruisers."

"Well, yes, we were dear friends, you know that."

"Did you share a cabin and split costs?"

She hesitated, another bad sign. "Sometimes."

"You both like your privacy?"

Denise's face instantly flushed. Her hands played with a pen and she scribbled nervously on the margin of the brochure. His question remained unanswered.

"You and Louise are extremely attractive women, very much in your prime. Assured, intelligent with designer clothes. Not short of money."

Her throat pulse vibrated. "I'm a bit lost, Michel."

"So am I. I was thinking of dancing. Two years ago when Yvette threw a little New Year's soirée, you dropped by and we danced together."

She laughed. "Till three. I hope you've refined your technique."

"I'm still a Seville bull." He smiled. "You're a wonderful dancer. I'd imagine on cruises you were a champagne-hour champion."

"Louise was better than me. One of us usually won a trophy."

A bewitching childhood memory of Louise unexpectedly trespassed, stinging Michel. He was wearing baby pajamas that came with little padded feet. Louise was holding him in her arms at a birthday party and dancing with him. How many candles had he blown out? Three, four?

"You and Louise didn't dance together on cruises?"

"Of course not."

"You found partners?"

"Naturally."

Private cabins, gigolos, or whatever they called these night crawlers who freebooted cruises and were expected to administer a slap and tickle to the lush ladies. Denise and Louise were traveling accomplices above and below decks. They foraged for men in ports of call. Both of them were too prudent to waste their time shopping. Tip the concierge at a deluxe hotel and wait for the bundle he sent up.

"Did Louise ever meet someone on your travels that she liked? Someone who admired her more than she was prepared to be admired?"

Denise shook her head sadly. "What are you intimating?"

It was time to take the belt off as a threat to an uncooperative child.

"Denise. I don't have the time for tender feelings and frankly I don't give a damn about your indiscretions. But if you'd been the victim, and Louise was the last person seen with you in public, I'd be asking her the same questions."

Denise rolled around her middle-aged secrets like poker dice. Frowning when they hit the bar counter and she lost.

"How dirty would you like it, Michel?"

"I'm not here to pry. I'm investigating her murder. Don't take me around the world with duty-free shopping trips. Louise was murdered between nine-thirty last night and seven this morning when the maid found her."

Denise still resisted. What was so terrible to mention? He had one more blank to fire before he loaded with bullets. The appeal to honor, rather than squealing.

"Do this: Imagine you're Madame Curie attempting to cure a disease and there are thousands of slides to stain and place under the microscope. But your intuition tells you which one takes precedence. Now use your knowledge."

A box of open-face sandwiches was delivered from the café. Denise got first dibs before distribution to the ravenous clients in for a quick wash and set. She pecked at the Bayonne ham, he the Scotch salmon. The cold glass of Meursault was better than coffee, she thought. Just like the cruise deck with a gallant steward leaning over and having just a hint of zipper undone below his starched white jacket.

"Do you think there might be a possibility that the killer was looking for you? And he found Louise instead?"

The ham dropped on her lap and she started to screech.

"Stop it!"

"I can't help it, Michel. When Louise soundproofed her apartment, she said it was partly for me. When I have a climax, I shriek. Or when someone upsets me as much as you have."

It was an unearthly sound. Two more minutes of denial followed before the Travelers' Tale was unraveled: Rabelais and Chaucer might have collaborated on the sizzling book of this sexual sing-along. The geography of the ladies' encounters was as he had surmised. Above and below decks: on shore with shop clerks, bellmen, bartenders, and here and there a naked room-service waiter tossing their salads. Previously, it had all been done at sea, then the landlubbers came to a decision. Why wait for Greenland when Eden was around the corner and soundproofed? Whoever found the stag telephoned the other. They were secretive, discreet. Denise claimed they had only one such assignation since the gentleladies' agreement.

"We met someone almost a year ago."

"Nationality?"

"A mutt."

"Did you see him again?"

"No, he got back on his ship and we never heard a word."

"Where did this all take place?"

"We were gambling in Monte Carlo."

"Did you give him your address or a check?"

"No, phony names and cash and carry. We decided to arrange these events together as a form of self-protection. If it got out of hand, there'd be two of us."

"Buddy up."

"Don't put it that way. It was a precaution."

"Are you sure Louise didn't have a different *plat du jour* without you knowing?"

"Don't be disgusting. There was nothing emotional about our arrangement. You have an appetite, you feed it, then get on with your life. I can't spend eternity at the table or in bed, can you? In any case, the program was discontinued for the summer."

"Who usually made the selection?"

"Louise, naturally. She could tell in a minute who was worthwhile and what was trash." She paused, wretched about having committed herself, but under his scrutiny continued. "It would be like asking your father to grade a side of beef."

"Of the two of you, who was the more . . . enlightened?"

"Louise was a queen. No one could touch her art."

"Art?"

"Yes, art. It didn't matter which cruise, which man. Once Louise had knighted him, he wouldn't wander. I'd be thrown in as an afterthought. There are women who think they know something about making love, but Louise was incomparable. After a man had slept with Louise, he wouldn't come looking for me. He might find a younger girl at the university for a night. More beautiful. A black, Oriental, it wouldn't matter. In the end, he'd sprint back to Louise. We once had a gigolo who gave her back the money in return for another night. She trained the girls at the Hôtel Estaque."

Michel tried to imagine the soft, alluring Louise conducting sex classes and lost his trend of thought. When he was recovering from his wounds in the hospital, he'd waited for her visits. Louise would arrive bearing fruit, chocolates, sit by his bed for hours, reading him the newspaper when the tubes were in his chest and he couldn't move. In spite of the angelic care he was given, she tipped the nurses munificently, stuffed thousands of francs in the hands of nuns to light candles. No, Louise was not a saint, except to the Danton family.

"How's your new houseguest working out?"

"I hope you're not annoyed that I let Yvette stay with me."

"Not at all. Is she making her bed finally and scraping the plates?"

The glimmer of a smile peeped through Denise's distress.

When they left the salon, the locals were outside their shops discussing the murder. On the terraces of the small cafés, cliques were bragging about how much they knew about Louise Vercours. Everyone had the special edition of *Le Clairon* with large photos of Michel and Louise on the front page.

"It's a good picture of you. Before they shot you up," Denise said.

"You're turning my head." She kissed him. He always disarmed his witnesses, but now he had another surprise for Denise. "Denise, this won't get in your way. But one of my detectives is going to spend some time in the salon."

"Are you trying to ruin my business?"

Striding toward them, carrying a briefcase, was the plump-faced Corinne Toulaine. She was thirty-two, pert, dark-haired, amiable and unthreatening, with the manner of a school guidance counselor.

Michel kissed her affectionately. "Congratulations. Richard told me you were pregnant."

"One of those happy accidents."

"Are you all right with this?"

"Sure. I'm so happy to be back working for you. You look well, Michel."

"The golf course and going crazy agree with me, Corinne." As the social director of the mixer, he forced the match. "This is Detective Inspector Toulaine, Denise. She'll sweep hair clippings and listen in for a few days. They still gossip at the hairdresser, don't they?"

Jennifer was at the bar of Les Frères Lani reading the newspaper. She looked at Michel speechlessly, daunted by Yvette's headline article.

"My God, Louise was murdered. That's why you were called."

"Yes. It's a ghastly situation. My parents, me, we're all broken up by this. I knew Louise all my life. She was like a sister to my mother."

"I'm sorry. I believe I know how you feel."

"Probably better than anyone."

He leaned over and kissed her. She was in shorts, sandals and a Stanford sweatshirt, hair pulled back in a ponytail with a barrette, She reminded him of the unattainable coeds he had seen at college football games in America.

"Let's have a drink and talk about our future." Michel signaled the barman. "Two Manzanillas. We'll pick at some of the cold hors d'oeuvres, if you don't mind. I'm on the fly without my Superman uniform, unfortunately. Just Clark Kent."

He took her hand and felt it tremble in his grasp.

"It's a miracle you're still alive."

"God saved me for you."

"Michel, please, please, don't make a joke out of this."

She was about to cry and he comforted her. "Don't . . . you've had enough tears and you're out of mourning."

"When I read this story, I was terrified. I don't want to lose you."

"You won't."

"I was granted a pardon. Maddie's going to visit her parents. I'll have time off."

"I liked Maddie. Spunky. She's not the dragon-child I imagined."

"She's a con woman." Jennifer flourished the newspaper. "Will you tell me what you were doing in Corsica when they shot you?"

"Read on. Yvette always lards her pieces with prehistory."

" 'After a long recovery from near fatal wounds, received during an arrest in Corsica, Commander Michel Danton of the Special Circumstances Section will lead the investigation into the three murders.' What does this mean?"

"I do murder, only murder."

Jennifer blanched at the word and he regretted his frivolity. "When are we going to be able to see each other?"

"Cops have to go to bed and eat. The first free moment I have, I'll take you out to our farm in St-Rémy and ravish you *en plein air*." The chilled dry sherry was lively and made his lips pucker. "We'll have a naked picnic on the grass, à la Manet. We'll talk about Cézanne's brooding geometric rocks. Did you know that D. H. Lawrence said that Cézanne's apples were more valuable to society than all of Plato's silly ideas?"

"Stop it, now, Michel! Are you in danger?"

"You're not listening, Jennifer. I have an army of cops protecting me. I'm the lead investigator. What happened in Corsica was an error in judgment on my part. I never thought there was a risk."

She turned the newspaper page. "A man with a sawed-off shotgun fired at you in a crowded café—"

"I've changed cafés."

She sulked over tiny plates of sardine *paupiettes* and barely touched her marinated fennel.

He looked at his watch. "I have to dash to Marseille to visit your tango partner from last night."

"The coroner?" He nodded. She was shaking and he took hold of her. "You're going to an autopsy."

"No, I've got files to go through. Charts and trivia. Relax, will you? You can come and take a walk around the port. The Roman docks are being rebuilt. And there's an old maritime museum near my office. You'll enjoy yourself."

They stopped by her apartment so that she could throw some clothes in her carry-all and leave a note for Maddie.

"I'm in a hurry. No trying on dresses. Grab your makeup if you like. I don't turn back for lipstick or bras."

Jennifer burst out of his car and returned while he was still searching through old eight-track tapes.

"Good, five minutes. You can anchor the relay team."

Along the N8, she leaned her head on his shoulder. He put on a Charles Trenet tape of "La Mer" to soothe her.

"I'm a rational woman, but I'm thinking in a completely illogical way. Michel, I feel something very special and deep for you."

He was moved by her honesty, mad about her, but terrified of exposing his vulnerability.

"Your glands are talking."

"No, they're roaring. But it's more complicated. It's something profound—almost mystical. I'm falling in love with you."

"You've saved yourself from the Roman dungeons." She placed her hand on his thigh. "That feels good, Jennifer."

"Do we have time?"

"Can you keep it friendly and snug for me?" he asked

She gave him a heedless smile. "No, I want you to slip your hand between my legs and put this car into cruise control."

"Cruise control in a Citroën Maserati? Please!"

"Is murder really more important than us?"

CHAPTER 21

Nothing in this ungodly universe, not the stench in the major's gut shanty of hog spleen, chitlins stew, or menudo, smelled worse than the Algerian restaurant Karim had selected for lunch. Karim's dark eyes nervously darted around as he wolfed down some horrible pilaf concoction. Curled onions looked like barbecued bugs. Boy and Maddie had offered to spring for a meal and were ready to weep. He and Maddie pushed away their untouched kebabs. The wine tasted of turpentine.

"Boy, let me ask you something."

"Shoot."

"Did you come out to my place?"

"Nope."

"La Sex Boutique in Aubagne?"

"He said no!" Maddie screeched. "He doesn't need porn tapes, he has me."

"True. It's just that if you had visited, I wonder, did you see someone going into my house?" Boy stared blankly at him. "Someone broke in and took some very valuable possessions of mine."

He and Maddie laughed. What could this pauper have that was valuable?

"You get beat for your hash?" Boy asked.

"No."

Boy threw him a curve. "The Islamic Front might be after you. Ask Gerard if someone's been snooping."

Karim shook his head. "No, it's not them. And Gerard and I are finished. I quit. I'm going to Cannes to meet Françoise. I can peddle tapes on the Croisette."

Boy gave him a broad smile. "Well, Karim, isn't this a sunny day. Maddie's going to be in Cannes for a few days visitin' her parents. And I'll be her tag-along."

Karim perked up. "How are you going to travel?"

"They're sending a limo for me," Maddie said, to the manner born.

"And where will you stay?"

"My parents have a suite at the Montcalm."

Karim's dirty fingernails strummed his T-shirt. He gave Boy a knowing look. "Ooh-la-la, very expensive."

"Hell, I can't afford it either. And I'm not going to mooch off her folks. I'll be looking for a place. Got any ideas?"

"I know a wonderful pension in the old port. We can share expenses."

"That'd be great," Boy said, "you're a *bon ami*."

They listened to Karim theorize about Louise's murder. He had heard a news flash over the radio. He hoped that there was bad blood between Gerard and the madam. He also revealed that Louise had undoubtedly made a number of enemies over the years.

"You can't be dealin' girls and have them all happy campers, now can you?" Boy asked.

"Who cares? Boy and I can't wait to hit the beach." Maddie caught the "be nice" signal from him. "We really ought to have ourselves a great dinner, then go dancing with you and Françoise in Cannes. It'll be on my father. Champagne, the works."

"You are a very gracious lady, Maddie."

"We'll hit the clubs, Karim!" Boy said. "Even revolutionaries like to dance once in a while."

"Françoise and I would love to be with you both."

Karim wrote down the pension address on a corner of the paper tablecloth and tore it off. He looked longingly at their untouched kebabs. "You're not hungry?"

"No, we ate somethin' last night that upset our stomachs," Boy said.

"In that case, may I take them?"

Boy paid the check and the three of them strolled out. They stopped at a stand where Karim bought the newspaper. He anxiously read the front-page story as they continued down the Cours Mirabeau. When he looked up from the article, he was still agitated.

"Allah be praised. They didn't mention Françoise."

"Why would they?" Maddie asked.

"She and Louise had a terrible argument. Françoise was thrown out by Gerard. I don't understand why. And Françoise said she didn't either." Boy read the situation instantly. Karim was stewing about the implications. "Please don't mention this to anyone."

"Come on, cheer up, Karim. Your belly's full of all those Algerian goodies. This can't be anything serious. Say, when are you leaving for Cannes?"

"Some time tomorrow."

"Are you keeping your place?" Boy inquired.

"Yes, the rent's paid for the month. I'll be staying with Françoise. If you want to use it, I'll be happy to let you."

"No thanks. See you in Cannes." He grasped the fleeing Karim. "Could've been Gerard who tossed your place."

"I wondered about that myself."

"Well, don't take any crap and lay it on him."

"I'm afraid. He has dangerous friends."

"See you in Cannes. Give Françoise a big kiss for us," Maddie said.

They watched Karim scurry down the street, glancing furtively behind him.

"Scared shitless and he sure acts guilty," Boy observed.

Maddie began to giggle hysterically and flashed the newspaper photo of Michel at Boy.

"Hey, Mama, I've seen this dude coming out of Louise's. I thought he was a client." Maddie started to skip crazily and Boy lost his patience. "What's shakin'?

"This is a hoot. Commander Michel Danton, chief homicide investigator of the Special Circumstances Section. I brought him coffee in bed this morning. He's the one who fixed Jennifer's plumbing."

"Oh, I love it. The detective with a dick."

"He's our alibi, Boy. Jen came in while I was sleeping to see if she could sneak him upstairs to her room. They used the apartment next door."

"My lady, I'm going to do something devilish to you."

Boy kissed her passionately in the heart of Aix, amid thousands of onlookers. They were young, in love, and getting away with murder.

CHAPTER 22

The Special Circumstances Section was housed in Marseille's Vieux Port in a late nineteenth-century warehouse on the Quai des Belges. Each morning, Michel could hear the fishermen hawking their catch. The building retained its shabbiness of the past on the exterior, but inside, it was as stylish as Pompidou Center. All the modern technology equipment known to man was available. Even the FBI criminalists who visited from Washington paid compliments. The French loved their crime and were diligent in apprehending their killers. They didn't tolerate the American claptrap of extradition from Michigan to Wisconsin. It was a functioning federal system run by the Judicial Police, but the local cops still resented the intrusion of experts like Michel.

When the wind cannoned in from the east, Michel thought he could smell the Ethiopian galley slaves and hear the lash of the whip as the Roman consul chanted the beat. Marseille's poet laureate had been Marcel Pagnol. Michel loved the sentimental novelist and the delightful *grande dame* of French cities he had immortalized. Still, Marseille was inhospitable to foreign tourists, unless they wanted to eat bouillabaisse; those who came to explore for heroin soon found themselves in the odious prison.

Dr. Charles Laurent was running late as usual and Michel was exasperated when he settled in his office. He removed Yvette's photo from his oversize antique desk and tossed it, frame and all, into the trash. He dusted his bookshelves with his jacket sleeve. Most of the office staff were delighted to have him back, a few not so sure he wasn't still loco. He booted up his computer, and the screen filled with outdated memos, which he promptly deleted. He looked out the window at the stream of ferries and fishing boats that painted the harbor.

Somewhere down there, Jennifer would be wandering, thinking of him as he was of her. She was a breathtaking woman, but in her cardinal-red Stanford sweatshirt definitely still a college girl. The agony columnists were right: keep plodding along; get out of sour relationships and sooner or later one's luck was bound to change. If there was hope for him, there was hope for the world. He'd rebuild his life. But how? Jennifer would be back in California in four or five weeks. His life's savings would go on keeping Air France aloft.

Laurent tapped on the door. He looked very official in his long white lab coat. A clean one for a change.

"It's three-thirty in the afternoon," Michel said. "You got back here at least five hours ago. Did you have time for a siesta?"

"Michel, let's go to the lab. Forensics is running some tests you must see."

Under a massive domed skylight, running thousands of square feet, were the fruits of French criminal technology. From forensic anthropologists who could reconstruct a body from a shinbone to the most sophisticated DNA analysts, scientists worked around the clock on murder cases. Patrick and his assistants had developed the still pictures and had them displayed on a large-screen wall monitor. The images struck Michel as some wrathful art installation and revived the gruesome horror of Louise's murder. Richard Caron came through with some politicians from Paris and introduced Michel to them. They were all in a furor about budget cuts. France was tightening her belt. In a moment, they were ushered out by one of his assistants.

Andrea, the lab's Eurasian siren, and its hair and fiber specialist, moved out from her electronic microscope and received Michel back into the fold with a kiss. She lined up a slide for his inspection.

"What am I looking at, Andrea?"

"Hair comparisons."

Michel could clearly see two different kinds and colors. He stepped back and Laurent gave him a churlish smile. "I extracted a number of these hairs lodged in Louise's right canine tooth and her back molars."

"Michel," she said, "it's female public hair and not the victim's. The pigmentation indicates the woman is Caucasian."

"Another woman?" His shock gave way to grisly anguish. "You're sure this isn't Louise Vercours's hair?"

"Yes."

"From the uprooting of the hair, could you judge where Louise's head would have been during this . . . ?"

"I think the other woman . . . had mounted Louise."

"Louise was beneath her?"

"That's my guess."

"This is impossible for me to believe."

Andrea said, "If you go back to the microscope, you'll see that this one has a waxy finish."

Richard Caron was less mystified. "So we have a young woman who wears bikinis, loves her beach tan, and doesn't want loose ends to show."

"Does she have a boyfriend, Andrea?" Michel asked.

"I can't confirm that yet."

"No male hair?"

"Not yet."

"Did you finish the tests on the American man who was decapitated at the dam?"

"The results are with your secretary."

"Did you find any male's hair that wasn't the victim's?"

"No, only the victim's. And traces of rust from the hatchet. It was very old."

"What about semen?"

Laurent interjected, "In neither case did we detect any male secretions."

"No semen or another male's hair?" he asked. "Isn't that odd?"

"Claude and Courbet were collecting the samples, so anything's possible," Andrea said with disgust. "The prefect in Aix let them botch the evidence."

The very absence of semen in all three murders revealed more than Michel had anticipated. Frenchmen hated condoms and the government's AIDS campaign was stillborn, compared to other European countries.

Andrea put another slide in. "Women in their summer bikinis," she said wistfully.

"What's this, now?"

"More female hair—this came from the head of Louise's partner. And it was dyed, with good strong follicles. The roots are intact. I've got enough exemplars to have Timone do DNA tests on it."

"Any idea of how old this woman be?"

"Come on, Michel. My eyes are popping out."

"Give me an estimate."

"Twenty to forty range."

"Very good, Andrea," Caron said.

At another bench, Timone, the lab intellectual, a molecular biologist by trade, observed the proceedings with an amused sneer. Even in clothes he looked like a skeleton. He was heating beakers with his Bunsen burner.

"What are you cooking, Timone? Coke to free-base?"

"We did that yesterday, Michel. I'm surprised they released you."

"The insane asylum did me a lot of good. I dressed in leather and read *Madness and Civilization* again."

"And what was your conclusion?"

"It's all a ship of fools. With nuts like us running things."

"That's the truth. Welcome back," Timone said, clapping his shoulder. "Louise had vaginal fluid in her saliva and on her gums. And it wasn't hers."

"Are there live cells?"

"Yes, hundreds of them."

"Can you run a DNA test?"

"It'll take about ten days to do the polymerase chain reaction test on the hair and the fluids. We can use degraded cells if necessary. The odds then become one in a million that the female you find will be the one who was with Louise."

"I assume I've got to collect all the Pap smears between Aix and Marseille this evening. And when I'm not doing that, I'm sneaking around beaches filching pubic hairs in the bathhouse."

"It's in character, Michel," Timone said and brought a laugh from the trenches. "The DNA tests will turn out to be a treat when you've got a suspect."

Devoire, the serology specialist, approached. He had a clubfoot. The country surgeon forty years ago did a shoddy job on him. Devoire claimed he had run into Charles Bovary's reincarnation.

"There's an office pool on how long you'll last this time," Devoire said. "My ticket says a week."

"Maybe I'll retire at full pay and fly jumbo jets for Air France."

The women in the room tittered and one said, "I'd fly with you."

"Careful, Sophie, I've got elevated testosterone levels." He turned back to Devoire. "What have you got?"

"Louise is type O-positive. So far, there's no other blood group, but we've sent people back to the scene to start collecting more samples. And we'll do the luminol tests tonight."

Michel continued down the line of technicians. He stopped at Faure's bench. "Thank you for the anniversary gift. Pity you couldn't make the party."

"The invitation called for black tie and I was in a straitjacket at the time."

He held on to Michel for a moment. They attended chamber music concerts often and played lightning chess afterwards. "You seem just fine."

"I am. What about the glob that was cooked in the microwave?"

"Latex. You were right about the surgical gloves. But I think the murderer had on a rubber swimming cap also." He held up a small piece of stippled rubber. "Only about ten million of them sold every year."

Michel pondered over these disparate grains of information. The man probably used a condom, shaved his public hair and wore a swimming cap. The woman hadn't been as careful. Why? She had no police record, and the man did.

Michel addressed the room of technicians. "Does anyone have any idea about the type of instrument that was used to cause the burn marks on Louise?" He was enveloped in cheerless silence. "I'm sure someone will figure it out. I'm really happy to be back working with all of you. I missed you." Michel paused at the laboratory door and smiled at his family of associates. "Oh, while you're doing your exotic tests, find out what Louise had on her fingernails. It smelled like iodine to me."

Nana, the lab's specialist in physical chemistry was a hulking, middle-aged woman with tiny feet. She daintily tiptoed over and presented a small bottle to him.

"This was recovered from the scene. It *is* iodine. Your killer certainly knows about halogens. He, or she, applied it to Louise's nails and swamped her in chlorine afterwards. Most of our physical evidence is worthless. Michel, with this one, I'd start saying my Hail Marys."

In the elevator back up to his office on the third floor, Michel found himself perplexed by this chain of events. He tried to reconcile the slender threads of evidence with a female killer. She had to possess the strength of an Amazon. She'd be depraved and powerful enough to capture the young couple, overwhelm them in a life and death struggle. What kind of a frenzy could make a woman torture them and chop off the man's head with a hatchet?

He was looking for a congruence in three murders and he was on the wrong track. The couple had been murdered by a man; Louise by a woman. He wondered if the killers could have known each other.

CHAPTER 23

It was agreed that Richard Caron would handle press relations and, more important, the legal matters with the *juge d'instruction.* Michel had problems with them. They were worse than their American brothers, the slick-talking DAs who filed their information and got indictments or slammed a suspect with a grand jury subpoena. In France, the legalities were still adornments of the Code Napoléon. Incontrovertible evidence was required before a suspect was brought to court.

He and Laurent adjourned to Michel's office.

Laurent was smug. "No, Michel, I had no siesta today."

"Didn't I apologize? It's my first case on my first day back."

"You're still rude. You ought to be on Xanax or some kind of tranquilizer."

"Leon Stein stopped them last month."

"What about Prozac?"

"It had the reverse effect on me. Gave me insomnia and suicidal thoughts. Let's get going, Laurent."

Louise had been pregnant many years ago and had undergone a hysterectomy, according to Laurent. She'd had liposuction on her stomach but some stretch remarks still remained on her hips. Based on the undigested contents of her stomach, he estimated the time of death between midnight and one A.M. Michel took out the Chez Danton dinner slip and handed it to Laurent.

"She had beef of some kind."

"Chateaubriand rare. Sauce *béarnaise,*" Michel noted.

"The entrance wounds confirm that the killer was right-handed and very strong."

"Are there any differences in the wounds that would suggest two different people stabbing here?

"No, but there are a series of slash marks under her breasts that might have been foreplay. "At the moment, it looks as though your killer is a powerful woman who lifts weights and must work out all the time."

Michel spread out the photos of Louise on his desk. He had been blindsided. Could Louise have been a lesbian? Was Denise covering up for her to protect herself? He felt compromised by his mother as well. She and Denise would have known about Louise's predilection. Still, he wasn't convinced. He'd have to hear it directly from them.

"I know at this stage there's nothing to support a male perpetrator except my own suspicions . . . but look at these here, Laurent." He pointed to a pre-autopsy blowup of the evisceration. "This longitudinal cut really bothers me."

"Why?"

"When I was a boy, I used to help out in the restaurant. As you did, in your father's surgery."

"I sterilized his instruments and dusted his medicine cabinet."

"That's exactly what I mean. Now part of running a restaurant like ours is to make certain you get the best-quality meats. Visits to the abattoir aren't especially pleasant, unless you're in the trade." Laurent leaned over and studied the photo. "You visited operating theaters with your father, I've seen pigs slaughtered. This is the type of cut only a pig butcher would make."

"A pig butcher?"

"Yes," Michel said decisively. "I don't care whether it's Denmark, England, or Germany. They all cut a pig in precisely this way after they've stuck it. It's a universal technique. There's no other way to get the intestines out for sausage casing without damaging them. And then you section the pig and trim it: loin, trotters, spareribs, leg, butt and so forth. In all these years, I have yet to see a woman on the line in a slaughterhouse gutting and disemboweling a pig."

"All the evidence points to a woman. Maybe two women were involved."

"That doesn't fit these murders. The murders at the dam involved a *ménage à trois* with two men. The American girl didn't have any trace of being with another woman. He did the killing. We could argue that either Louise was willing or resisted. I'd like to think she was forced into it."

After considering Michel's theories, Laurent nodded. "You have a brilliant killer on your hands."

"I know I do." Michel stared out of his window down at the old port below shimmering in the sun. It buzzed with trawlers and people scooping food from vendors at the stalls on the quay.

"I have a personal favor to ask. How soon can we have Louise's body back? My father's going to contact Louise's attorney regarding her will and funeral arrangements."

"I'll need it for at least a week."

"Laurent, please. We're her closest friends. My mother's bereft."

His secretary, Robert, peeped in. The resident opera lover's freckled face had an expression of perverse amusement.

"There've been several messages from a lady. She's in reception and asked if she could change her clothes. Do I arrest her or what?"

"Robert, bring her in, dammit. And don't forget to give me the file on the American couple."

"I can't keep up with you. Did you find this one at a therapy session?"

Michel hurriedly scooped up the set of autopsy photos and the videotape, shoved them in an envelope and buried Louise Vercours in his dusty attaché case.

"Please show Professor Bowen in."

"I guess she's the first volunteer for the public hair samples we're advertising for," Laurent said to Robert, sniggering.

"Michel always comes up with new investigation techniques." said his secretary.

"Both of you, get the hell out!"

Jennifer crept in, curious, but tentative. Her hair was windblown and her skin a blaze of copper.

"You remember our local Valentino, Jennifer?"

"Dr. Laurent. He's impossible to forget. Are you behaving today?"

Laurent gave Jennifer a raunchy look. "Just leaving, Professor Bowen. I didn't mean to tie up your changing room."

"Think about the burn marks, Laurent."

The moment he was outside, Michel kicked the door closed, swept Jennifer in his arms and kissed her.

"What was that all about?" he asked.

"Oh, he gave me an old-fashioned grope when we were dancing last night."

"Good thing you didn't dance with my psychiatrist."

She clung to him. "I took the ferry tour to the Château d'If and didn't hear a word the guide said. I can't think straight. My mind kept racing. All I wanted to see was you. I missed you."

He lifted her in his arms and carried her to the window. "You have a choice: the sofa or my desk?"

Jennifer gave him a wanton smile. "I'm the tourist. The view, please."

"That's easy." He sat her on his desk. "And I dusted."

CHAPTER 24

The only building in Aix that attracted Boy was the Natural History Museum where, on his nomadic wanderings, he had discovered an exhibit of large dinosaur eggs encased behind glass. He understood nothing of the fluvial basin or the science of paleontology, nor did he care. He was an expert, having seen *Jurassic Park* six times. He tried to imagine these giant creatures emerging from their shells and ruling the earth. The size and power of monsters held him spellbound. He was convinced that he possessed their strength and dominance. His was the thorned fist of Goliath. The contemplation of murder amid these prehistoric beasts set him aglow.

"Boy, can we go now?" Maddie pleaded.

"All this stuff turns me on."

She was edgy and horny. He had not kept his promise, but frittered away their afternoon in the museum. Occasionally he asked odd questions about her parents and their habits.

He finally made a move to the exit, still enthralled. In the street, he got back on track.

"The Hôtel du Cap won't work. Gettin' in and out of long driveways is a problem. You don't know who you're goin' to run into. And the hotel in Monte Carlo sounds like there's a lot of security."

Maddie caught his drift. "The Montcalm is more casual. People go in and out all the time. Once you walk out the door, you're in a large terraced bar in the heart of town. It's always packed for cocktails and has a street entrance."

"How do you know so much about Cannes?"

A pretty shop girl gave Boy the eye, and Maddie caught him winking at her. She had to rein him in, but didn't know where to begin.

"My father used to take me to the Cannes Film Festival."

"The what?"

"It's a market for film buyers. They go there and shop for movies to distribute."

"What a weird business."

"Let's concentrate."

"I'm scopin'. Okay, doesn't matter which country, which town, the cops look first to the family. *You,* Maddie, you're going to be the suspect. So you have your dinner with Mom and Dad, then cut short your visit and head back to Aix. Tell them you've got to study for an exam.

"And don't upset them. 'Yes' them to death. Be affectionate in public. The cops will ask if they were havin' a beef with you."

She was growing anxious. She would be alone. Her role was becoming too complicated.

"The hotel—what's it called again?"

"The Montcalm. It's a big white battleship on the Croisette."

"The maid or security will eventually call the police after they find your folks. The cops will be a pack of local cowboys. They love those big, rich places. They can steal a little and mooch dinners."

"And then what?"

"They'll look for suspects and find them."

"Not us?" she cried with alarm.

"No, Maddie, not us. Never us."

They strolled back to her apartment. He waited downstairs. After several minutes, Maddie signaled from the terrace. Boy tiptoed through the entry. The old concierge was watching TV and chuckling at a Murphy Brown tirade. He crept up the stairs stealthily. Maddie waited in the hallway.

"Where's Jen?"

"In Marseille with Michel. She left a note. She'll be late."

"I can't wait till it's her turn. If you think what I did to Louise was excitin', wait till I fix Jennifer for us."

Boy had been in Aix for a month and this was his first house call. He peered around the large living room and ran a finger on a beautifully carved pine country table. The old grace of Provence was still preserved in this lovely, grand apartment. The buildup of repressed animosity transformed him. It was a caste system and he was always the outsider. He was not good enough for Adam Gold's daughter, that's what it boiled down to.

"You're so far away, Boy."

"Just thinkin', darlin'. And gettin' pissed off. We could've had a ball here instead of me scroungin' at Denise's," he said with the somberness of a man doomed to life in the underclass.

"That letter my parents wrote to Jennifer did us in."

"They sure had a hard-on for me. Well, give them lots of hugs and kisses when you say goodbye."

"You do it for me."

Jennifer had changed into a low-cut Provençal print blouse and a short skirt before they returned to Chez Danton for dinner. Michel had a perfect view of her magnificent legs. He attempted to be discreet, but her enticing hourglass figure continued to arouse him. He looked at the clock over the bar.

"My troops will be strolling in shortly. And they won't be singing Frédéric Mistral's *chansons* like troubadours. Don't be upset if I have to leave you for a while and talk business."

She picked up one of his giant hands and kissed it. "As long as you come back."

Jennifer's turned-up Irish nose sniffed the air, redolent with a simmering garlicky thyme-scented stew served with large beef marrow bones and crusty toast.

He was curious about her background. He learned that when she was twenty, she had been accepted by the Barnes Foundation to study the Impressionist collection annexed by the redoubtable Dr. Barnes. The admissions committee approved of her background. Her mother was a widowed high school French teacher and the Bowen family had originated in Montreal; Jennifer's mother was now teaching in Sausalito. However, after three months, Jennifer was dismissed by the foundation. She was found to be insubordinate and subversive. Michel was not surprised. He fished for more information. Intimate, this time.

"Harry was your first lover?"

"And only. You're the second man in my life."

"Is that true?"

"All through school, the girls did a number on me. I was considered a chronic, outdated virgin. My parents had a loving marriage and were strict. But in a good sense. They taught me not to waste my time or waive my rights. There's only so much of a person to squander."

"Unless it was worth your while," he said smugly.

Her animated eyes darted over him. "Everything's perfect now—oh, except maybe my weight."

"Diet talk is forbidden in Provence. And I like a growing girl."

Nicole had demanded a release from the hospital. Head to toe in black, his mother was hovering, out of sorts and sullen. His father wore a black beret and armband and looked like a leftover from the

Resistance. Michel was also in a black suit with an armband, incongruously turned out on a sultry night in Aix. The Dantons had decided it would be impossible to close the restaurant. Too many people were traveling in for dinner who hadn't left phone numbers with Delantier.

Philippe was nettled when Michel set up a large trestle table and benches for his men on the boule court. He had fed the Legion galley-rowers before, and this was how Michel had run up his enormous bill.

"Your mother tried to smile at me. She looked like she'd just had root canal."

"Gallbladder. She should be in bed." Michel struggled to keep everything in his head. A courtship and three murder investigations made for an impossible equation to balance. "She's in mourning and very angry with me. My mother's in charge of Louise's funeral arrangements. And I can't release the body for a week."

He was on his fourth Johnnie Walker Black Label and Jennifer was still sipping her first glass of a Côtes de Provence rosé from the celebrated Domaine Ott, which his father had recommended to the mayor.

"Jennifer, I have an awful job ahead of me. It's very awkward for a man. And frankly, I don't know how to broach the subject. I've never encountered a situation like this one."

"What is it, Michel?"

"It's about lesbianism."

Jennifer's mouth froze. "What brought that on?"

"I need some insight. I have to be very delicate when I bring it up with my mother."

He was making a hash of it. Jennifer was uncomfortable but determined to help. "You can trust me."

"I do. You see no one knows that years ago, my mother, Nicole Sourire—that was her maiden name—and Louise Vercours lived together in Paris while they were at the Cordon Bleu school."

"Oh, no . . ." He saw the conflict in Jennifer's eyes. "Delicate is an understatement. You're going to ask your mother if they were lovers? Jesus . . ."

"I have to. Tell me the way it works, if you know."

Jennifer related accounts of many such couplings during her school years. Once the young ladies were away at college, free of parental control, some of them fell naturally into a relationship. The women were considerably more sensitive and less promiscuous, in her view, than the gay men.

"It was always the guys in the closet who seemed tormented. For some reason, men believe there's more at stake with their sexuality than women do. Maybe in the States we're still demanding and expecting young men to be like their fathers.''

"Isn't that always the case?"

"Possibly. As a student and later as a teacher, I've always found that mothers were more understanding about being gay. The fathers are the ones who're tough to handle.''

"Is my mother going to be understanding about me interrogating her?''

"I don't know your mother. And from her attitude, I probably never will. But if some man told me my roommate was a lesbian, I'd be upset by the implications.''

How could he skirt around this? He could be aggressive with Denise. But he had to find out the truth from his mother.

As they were about to go outside, he saw a lone figure standing on the court nervously holding a boule in one hand and the smaller target ball, the *cochonnet*, in the other.

"Jennifer would you ask Delantier to keep separate bar accounts for my men? I'll settle up afterwards. And please bring out a bottle of Black Label.''

This would take time, for full bottles required inventory notations, and Delantier was busy. Michel strode outside toward the man who, seeing him, retreated. With the PLACE DE PAUL COURBET sign down, the local boule champion was disoriented.

"Practicing your stroke, Paul?"

"Have I been exiled?" Paul Courbet asked, flinching under Michel's cold eyes. "The sign's down.''

"Since you've been screwing Yvette, I didn't see any reason to be reminded of your skill with other people's balls.''

Courbet flicked the sweat off his lip. "Michel, I wanted to tell you a dozen times. Yvette always stopped me. After you came out of the clinic, she said it would break you. I didn't have the heart to do it. Was I wrong?''

"There's always a case to be made for deception.''

"Yvette made the first overture.''

"She raped you?''

"All right, it wasn't very gallant on my part.''

"Since when was gallantry your strong suit?''

"I fell into the trap of the married man. I found an attractive woman who led me to believe she was available.''

Michel moved closer and Paul Courbet backed away. "Where are you running? I won't take another poke at you?''

"What, then?''

"Did you try to extort a hundred thousand francs from Louise?"

"No, I told you before, she misunderstood. I thought this Jennifer Bowen could be bought off. Honestly, Michel, when I took her report, she was hysterical. She was afraid her student had picked up the clap or something worse."

"Where were you last night between nine-thirty and three A.M?"

"With my wife. But don't tell Yvette. I said I was working on the homicides."

"But you're no longer on the case."

"She didn't know."

Michel slapped him on the ass. "Okay. Go have your dinner." Yvette slid in like an eel, still parking in the staff spots behind the restaurant. "Is this a family reunion, Yvette? Or a night on the town for the new couple to go public?" Michel asked.

"I hear you found a pair of floppy American tits to hide behind."

"Floppy, they're not. See for yourself. She's inside."

Two other local cops whirled in, accompanied by Claude, who as usual was retailing some lewd gossip.

". . . This man who shall be nameless was about to make love to his wife and she asked, 'Why are you using a condom after all these years?' And he replied, 'My girlfriend made that a condition. If I get you pregnant one more time, she'll dump me!' " Bawdy laughter resounded. Still guffawing, he spotted Michel. "Just the man I want to see."

"How are you doing with the Russians? Anybody ordering hot borscht and blinis in the cafés?" Michel asked. "Just the thing in a heat wave."

"You'll see. Some Russian Mafia thugs are at the university pretending to take courses. They want to take over Louise's business. Believe me, Courbet and I will find the killer."

Michel waited until Yvette and Courbet snuck away toward the kitchen door.

"Based on forensic evidence, we're definitely now looking for a woman, twenty to forty. She'll be involved with a man."

"A woman with Louise?" Claude was intrigued by this tidbit. "The uniforms have been looking at the dump and out in the country ponds for the bloody clothes of a man."

"Call them off."

"Why?"

"I believe the killers were naked when they murdered Louise and left their clothes outside."

Jennifer carefully carried a large tray with the scotch, glasses and ice. She placed it on the trestle table.

"Jennifer, may I present Aix-en-Provence's crack law enforcement team and our prize-winning crime journalist watching you from the kitchen door."

Jennifer sized up the previous mistress. "Yvette, of course."

"Yes. You'll find that Michel's a great favorite with the summer student trade at the university. He's a mine of local information."

"He hasn't gotten to that part yet. I thought he just enjoyed dancing and wild sex."

Yvette vainly attempted to contain her hostility but descended into brittle sarcasm. "That's national news. I'll have to run that as an exclusive story."

Michel was elated. He was amazed by the fact that it had taken Jennifer only seconds to obliterate his humiliation.

CHAPTER 25

To discourage Michel and his party from lingering over dinner, Chez Danton's cross-eyed dishwasher had been assigned to serve them. People scattered when he slammed down the plates. Still nobody complained about service over the massive platters of Camargue Cowboy veal stew and the Côtes de Provence wine. At first, the group of cops had been somewhat timorous and reserved with Jennifer in attendance, but no one quibbled with Michel's judgment. Michel had asked Jennifer to remain inside while he discussed the case with his team.

Émile Briand, the graying, professorial detective Michel had assigned to the case, sopped up the last puddle of gravy with the heel of bread he had been saving. Émile had the soft, cajoling voice of a friendly doctor. He was someone people trusted. He had been out to La Sex Boutique in Aubagne where he had interviewed a wary and frightened Gerard David.

"Gerard's a schemer, but I don't think he'd have the guts or stomach for murder. He did mention there was a problem with a girl by the name of Françoise Artois," Émile informed him. "If that's her real name. Louise told Gerard to get rid of her."

"The girls change names regularly. Especially if they've been booted out of one of the Corsican brothels in Marseille," Corinne said. Michel smiled at her across the table. He was glad to have selected her for the case. A pregnant detective would be less threatening. "I interviewed some of Louise's regular girls today, Michel. They get their hair done at Denise's salon. They all say the same thing. Louise was loved. She was generous with money and advice. If a girl needed an advance, she gave it to them. They bypassed Gerard whenever they could. He was very hard on them.

"When the girls had their monthlies, the practice of bringing in a substitute wasn't tolerated by Louise," Corinne continued. "Each month a fund was set up. And based on the time the girls worked, they shared in the pool. Françoise was caught sneaking in an understudy a couple of times. She has a greedy Algerian boyfriend whose name is Karim Hassad."

"He worked for Gerard at the porn shop and they had an argument," Émile added. "Gerard fired him."

Michel was beginning to see the symmetry he had imagined. He had a man and woman with a motive and on bad terms with Louise. "Where is the lovely couple?" he asked.

"Françoise went to Cannes. Gerard assumes Karim is on his way there."

"Good, I'll call Richard and drive down tomorrow. Let's keep the Nice office informed but I don't want them involved. They've got enough to do on the Riviera."

"Those *cons* are out buying sunblock," Pierre Graslin said, arriving late. Everyone laughed and welcomed him. He was a balding, reedy man with coarse features and cheeks filled with ruptured winy capillaries. "Where's my dinner?" he growled.

"The *plat du jour* is history," Michel advised his seedy lieutenant. "Order the filet with the garlic *confit*."

Annie Vallon, the team's other female detective, bolted in.

"I just came from a gay ladies mixer. I was the star of the show." Annie said, sliding next to Michel on the bench. "I'm supposed to have discovered my true nature. There wasn't a whisper about Louise being a lesbian, Michel," Annie said, dipping bread in a bowl of tapénade.

She was in her forties, a tall, angular woman and the bohemian of Michel's group. She was a nudist and vacationed in Sylt with the rich Hamburg gentry. They loved the Fassbinder types, neurotic and funny. What delighted Michel about Annie was that she fit in wherever she happened to be assigned. Her multiple personality went a long way in Legion investigations.

"One of our puzzles is a possible link between the murders of the American couple and Louise." Michel opened the file. "The man's name is James Walker. He owned a commodity firm in Aspen, Colorado. The young woman, Carolyn Davis, was a researcher in his firm. She was married to an attorney in Aspen.

"The day before they were murdered, the couple checked into the Mas d'Entremont. They'd flown from Paris where they'd stayed at the Ritz."

In a single voice, the team shouted, "The husband!"

"The American Embassy checked with the Aspen police. He was at home. He had no idea that his wife was having an affair with her boss.

"Now tomorrow, Annie meet me at the dam in the morning. I want to see if I can find anything Claude missed. Corinne, you stay with Denise at the shop. Pierre can start going through Louise's list of girls; and Émile, you rework Louise's house with Forensics."

The dishwasher thumped down a cheese tray that looked as though it had been scooped from other customers' plates.

"Two filets—" Michel began. "Never mind, I'll get them. Cook them if I have to."

Michel, the perennial bad boy, whom only Louise had tolerated, always saved the worst job for last. Ordering steaks on his account would again cause a row with his father. He passed the bar where Jennifer sat talking to some functionary from the mayor's office about Provence's politics. He squeezed her hand and she looked up at him.

"Have you put the bodies to bed? I'm sleepy."

"Me too."

"So Louise *was* a madam."

"Just a rumor."

"Truth in advertising has a new definition in Aix."

"Don't be tough on me."

He burst into the kitchen. Nicole was on the phone, weeping; his father, closing down the grill and listening in. He learned that Denise was complaining to his mother about his rudeness.

"Say goodbye, Mother. The worst is yet to come."

The last embers fluttered on the grill before being suffocated by the porter who was waiting to scrape and scrub it. The filets had been put to bed. A T-bone, meant for a giant, caught Michel's eye. He snatched it and quickly brushed it with olive oil and tossed it on. He'd cooked thousands of them when the Dantons thought he might be kitchen material.

"I'll do it," Philippe said, somber but in command. "Michel, why do you ask ladies such disgusting questions?"

"I haven't begun."

The firestorm took about a minute to develop. Nicole Danton grabbed Michel's wrist as she had when he'd been a naughty child, crawling under the card table and examining the ankles and darkened interiors of the ladies playing bridge.

"Didn't Denise give you a favorable astrology reading?" he asked.

"Don't be flippant with me."

"You really shouldn't be on your feet."

Nicole pulled him into her office, a sunny room with a vaulted skylight and languid ferns that overlooked the boule court behind which was an ivy-covered cottage that was their town home. The fragrance of gardenias and lavender pervaded the room.

"Why are you going around asking middle-aged women about their sex lives?"

"Louise was murdered. Her habits, intimate and public, are relevant to the investigation."

His mother winced. She was very proper and hated smut. "This is very offensive."

He sprawled on a wicker chair. "We agree."

"Michel, are these investigations always so grisly?"

"Invariably worse. It's just that we're emotionally involved. And that makes it even more unpleasant."

Nicole Danton accepted the explanation. She was, after all, a dignified person, illuminated by reason and sensibility. He had a towering respect for his mother's accomplishments. She'd been left twenty-five ragged hectares in St-Rémy which she had transformed into a working farm and sausage factory for the *charcuterie.*

From his vantage point by the door, he observed Jennifer. She had been intrepid enough to come into the kitchen and was chatting to Philippe at the range. Yvette abhorred kitchens. She would sit regally at her table, commanding the staff.

"Mother, I'd like to remind you about how honest you are and how much I respect you as a person. When I was a teenager on the prowl, you had Papa mention it to Louise and I was rewarded with an afternoon that boys never forget. Over a period of time, you told me about your Cordon Bleu year with Louise. And you were candid. Two gorgeous charmers from Aix kicking up their heels and staying up all night in Left Bank cafés."

She nodded. "What do you want to know?"

"Was Louise ever involved with other women? Love affairs?"

"No! No! How could you think such a thing?"

Nicole suddenly raised her hand and flailed at Michel, trying to slap his face. He ducked away, but his cheek had been grazed by her nails. Nicole stormed after him. At that moment, Jennifer barged in. She seized Nicole's wrist and pushed her against the wall.

"Don't hurt him, Madame Danton," Jennifer shouted.

"Jennifer, it's all right. She's upset."

Jennifer's fury overwhelmed them all. She released her grip on Nicole. The melée spilled into the kitchen. The staff froze, and waiters ignored their orders.

Nicole shouted at Jennifer. "Get out!"

"Jennifer. This is difficult for her."

"Sorry." Jennifer was trembling. "I blew it for us."

"No, you haven't."

No question of the Irish in Jennifer's temperament or her reflexes in hand-to-hand combat. Michel put an arm around both women, desperate to defuse the situation.

"Mother, I think it's time I introduced you two. Nicole Danton meet Jennifer Bowen, fighting out of Ojai, California, in the red corner."

"That's not funny," Jennifer said, glaring at Nicole.

Philippe was surrounded by a covey of prying waiters. "Out, out, out! No interruption of service will be tolerated."

When his order had not been obeyed, he flashed his hot tongs like a pair of banderillas. Michel disarmed the chef, took Jennifer by the arm, and returned to the grill in time to flip the steak. These American women had pluck, there was that to be said for them, Michel thought. The Dantons stood by, infuriated. Finally, Nicole pulled herself together and approached Jennifer.

"I'm worried about my son. Do you understand that? Michel's been very ill. He's a sick man, but you wouldn't know that or recognize the symptoms. He needs to go back to the hospital. I'm calling Dr. Stein. The last time, they took him away in a straitjacket. He asked me if I was a lesbian! Or having an affair with my dearest friend. That is sick."

"He also asked me about lesbians. It's a hideous murder. The woman was *your* friend. Michel has to ask these questions."

"Mademoiselle Bowen, please wait at the bar," Philippe said.

Delantier toddled by the range. "The mayor is still waiting for his T-bone, Philippe."

Michel was too quick for his adversary. He snared the steak from the grill and set it on a large platter. He whipped through the kitchen piling potatoes and asparagus on the border.

"With Michel around, sell the place before he puts you out of business," Delantier said by way of commiseration. "Now please, Philippe, cook another steak."

Michel headed outside with Jennifer to the table. His detectives had ordered champagne in his absence. He sliced the steak for Pierre and Annie and served them. He took Jennifer aside.

"We're both exhausted and need a night's sleep," he said.

"Does your mother always slap you around?"

"Only on special occasions."

"I guess you hit the bull's-eye when you asked about her and Louise."

"Louise was a man's woman, as I thought." He held Jennifer against him and she nestled her head in the hollow of his shoulder. "I want to be alone with you. Maddie can look after herself."

"I don't know about us, Michel."

"Why?"

"I got so angry when I saw your mother strike you. I feel lost. I could have killed her. I had this flash of my fiancé. If I'd been with him, maybe I could've saved him."

"Let's spend the night out at our farm." He tried to read her but he could not penetrate the emotional barrier that had sprung up. "Please, Jennifer."

"Is this your idea of a courtship?"

"You can wear my underwear this time."

CHAPTER 26

Maddie was brooding, verging on panic. She wouldn't be seeing Boy for two days. They had made love for hours and she hoped she was pregnant. If she had his baby, so much the better. Boy came out of the telephone booth at the bus station, Yankee baseball cap jauntily to the side, eyes alight with deviltry. He picked up his backpack and adjusted the straps over his broad shoulders, another floater traveling Provence's byways. Maddie knew enough not to ask whom he had called. It would put him in a rotten mood.

"I've been going over it, again and again. Boy, you're brilliant."

"Makes three of us who agree. It's all simple and clean."

"I hate the thought of you on a bus half the night," she said.

"Life's always getting on a bus and catchin' the rainbow at the end."

"I love you so much. You're my Apollo." Maddie ran her hand through Boy's beautiful shoulder-length hair. "Are you going to be all right?"

The ultimate survivor gave a mellow laugh, music to her. "Don't worry, my lady, I have a map, my Berlitz and there'll be sunshine for us when I'm through. Now you know what to do."

"Oh, I meant to tell you. I found the letter my father gave Jennifer—the one that mentioned you. She hid it."

"We read it ages ago."

"I know. But afterwards, when the police begin to investigate, Jennifer might turn it over to them. She had it filed. I destroyed it."

"You're a real quick study."

"I'm hitting my marks."

She was afraid to admit that she was terrified. Louise's murder had excited and empowered her. But now if something went wrong, Boy would be alone. Having set him in motion, there was no way to stop him or extricate herself. At the last moment, she had pleaded with him to call it off.

"You drew from the deck, so don't start tweakin' your cards." He studied her, gauging her mood. "The pot's on the table and we're both all in, Maddie." Her eyes plugged with tears and he frowned. "You're not afraid, are you?"

"A little." Her voice was small with the solemnity of the undertaking. "For you."

"Valiant deeds and clarity of intent are sobering to the soul."

"I'm yours for life, Boy."

"Don't forget to dye your hair back to its natural color before you see your folks. I don't want them sassin' you about anything."

Her brow furrowed when he waved out of the grimy bus window. With a belching backfire, the bus moved out of the station and into an uncharted realm of space for Maddie. She knew now only too well that this was territory previously explored and conquered by Darrell Vernon Boynton.

Boy had telephoned Mystery Man from the station. They spoke in their personal code. His gravelly voice was filled with encouragement. The fire was still there. He had returned from Africa where he had collected a new brood of snakes. He had advised Boy to stay put when he returned from Cannes. He did not know the terrain and had no allies outside of Aix. He could not let the police search for him.

"It's a face-off from the get-go," his mentor had said. "A question of wills. Yours and the Frenchman's. He's not in your league, Boy. Nobody is."

"Makes me feel better comin' from you. I'll be countin' on you, Major, to be best man at the weddin'."

"I will be there in dress uniform."

"You'll also be my first houseguest."

"Never mind that. You bring Mrs. Boynton down to visit us country folk. Once she's got you in her will, we'll give her a tour she will remember in eternity."

"Yessiree. Love you, Major."

"Mutual, my darlin' Boy."

His guide in these matters had endorsed the agenda. Boy thought back to the thrill of the first expedition after Cissie, Lyle and the Gortzes had eaten fire.

Shortly after Boy's sixteenth birthday, on a sweltering, sunbaked June morning out at the major's ranch, chiggers couldn't sleep, breeze a theory, Mystery Man was in the mood, had a yen, which Boy picked up on real quick.

Major Eldon Royce Calhoun didn't have to say a word. He got that faraway look in his deepset rock-blue eyes. His mind enveloped Boy's, which was part of the mystery. Telepathy or something. They'd pack up the van with their equipment and tell everyone they was goin' fishing. Leave very early and get to their destination no later than three, when school was out. The major's strategy was ingenious and Boy paid attention. Like the army, this was a period of orientation and indoctrination.

They dropped down to El Dorado in Arkansas.

". . . Got to be a population over ten thousand, twenty's better. No small towns, everyone notices everything. They got nothin' better to do than to sit in their cars and count off the number of people checkin' into the motel. Spend their lives waitin' on the postman.

"Over fifty thousand, there's a police force to speak of and a hangout with state troopers droppin' by. Good communications wired up to the state capital and the FBI. I'm talkin' national now, Boy. They're all the same, doesn't matter which state. So population is very important. And you got to know where you're going before you act. How to get in and out."

Major has his ordinance maps. It is though he is setting out on maneuvers, checking topography and what have you. They cruise gently down a road, looking for someone out strollin'. Slow down at the bus stop on a peaceful country lane. There are two girls, hot and bothered, waiting for the bus to get them home from school.

"Roll down that window and give them little ladies your best smile."

Boy obeys. He is the bait.

"Howdy, girls, hotter'n than my gran's biscuit oven," Boy says. He has an almanac of easy weather lines. "Me and my daddy give you folks a ride?"

The first time, it was a pair of sophs from the high school, smirking and giggling over the beer Boy took from the ice chest in back of the van and handed them.

"We got to cool down, Boy."

"That's for sure, Daddy."

The girls thought that was a good idea, especially when Boy produced towels and ladies' swimsuits in all sizes. When they asked how he had such a large selection, he explained.

"It's our business. Daddy and me. We drive through all the towns with the new-fashion swimsuit styles and sell 'em to the general store. These are samples and you charmin' gals can have 'em free."

The major checks his dashboard compass and map. After a drive and more beers, spiked with some peyote juice for the guests, radio tuned to a stomping country station, they'd be at some river the major had scoped out.

The major, always courtly, likes to reassure youthful company. "We got our suits under our jeans. You little ladies can change in the back in privacy."

It was fishing in the parlor aquarium. In about two minutes, when they know the girls are in that awkward stage of yanking off their panties and shoes and with the peyote rumbling through their brains, Boy springs the back door open and gets inside. Major slides a bolt in the door from the outside. He scoots into the driver's seat. All with military precision.

Major watches Boy in action, shouting encouragement as he goes to work on the girls, in one, then the other, sometimes with one of them screaming, sometimes enjoying him. When he is finished, he and the major gag them. Boy studies the dread in their gaping eyes.

They drive down to the riverbank and stop under a spinney of trees. The underbrush is thick as a jungle's. The girls are shivering. They are struggling but it's all wasted effort.

Before the Major and Boy leave the van, the master opens the snake basket and locks the girls in. The big snakes are steaming, sweating musk, and crazed. They've been licking peyote juice, too. The snakes go for the girls' heads, digging their fangs into their eyes.

The exercise takes about five minutes for the toxic shock to kick in. On this, his first mission, after Cissie and company, Boy wants to celebrate his initiation.

"I don't see why I can't carve my initials on them," Boy says.

Instead of blowing a fuse, the major speaks serenely in measured tones and not in the spirit of an officer chewing out a raw recruit.

"No fancy Dannin', this isn't some oak tree where you tell everybody 'John loves Mary,' and leave a return address. You save your prancin' and dancin' for me in the bedroom.

"See, Boy, problem is you're tryin' to be clever and think you can leave a signature and the dummy lawmen will never figure it out. But they could."

Boy listens attentively to his elder. All eventualities are considered. Nothing is left to chance.

"Remember the odds against gettin' away with this are always a

million to one. Plan. Plan. Plan." The major checks his chronograph.
"There's also something we in the military call a timetable. Be sure
you got a partner who'll swear you were with them. Feedin' your face
or someone sittin' on it."

They wrap the bodies in a canvas tarp and carry them no more than
fifteen feet. They toss them into the river where the current is strong.
They lay out the girls' clothing and personal articles and books on the
bank.

"When they find these gals, they'll have looked like they got careless
when they went for a swim. They got snakebite. That's why I brought
water moccasins along."

Boy opens the basket and drops the snakes into the river and
watches them wiggle in the cold water as they sober up. The team
makes sure there are no footprints. Before leaving, Boy uses the shovel
to chop up the van's tire tracks. Soon as they get back to the ranch,
the tires will come off and get a hosing.

"Water and fire do not reveal their secrets easily."

Boy was filled with admiration. "You think of everything."

"I hope so. Remember my words, for I am your redeemer. The act
of murder is its own statement."

They arrive back at the major's ranch by seven for supper. Boy has
never eaten with such a good appetite. Many such events were to
follow, but none as exciting as those designed for pure pleasure to
educate the young scholar of death.

The bus deposited Boy in Cannes at 3:30 A.M. He had no problem
following the map from the station. People were still up and around.
He was on a broad boulevard called the Croisette—whatever that
meant. There were lights atop the Hôtel Montcalm in the casino and
a few stragglers at tables on the terrace bar. Only a few feet away, the
hooker patrol, like a pack of hyenas, was still grinding for tricks. He
scanned the faces, searching for Françoise, but she was not among
them.

Boy chuckled to himself. Not a one had given him a tumble. The
joke was that he had five thousand dollars worth of francs stowed in
his kick. He wove through the streets, scrutinizing everything, and
eventually found his way to the Pension Martell. Karim would be
meeting Françoise there. It was across from the old harbor, pocketed
between fish restaurants. He'd have to be a damn fool to try checking
in anywhere, especially this dump. There'd be a registration card to

fill out and he'd have to hand over his passport. The night clerk would remember him.

There were large pleasure boats moored, with midgetlike Arabs partying with big blondes. As he walked out to the point, he carefully surveyed which boats weren't in use. He looked over the dusty tarps of a forty-foot Chris Craft. He undid some snaps and crawled underneath. If the harbor people rousted him, he could buy his way out. No, this wouldn't be vagrancy. There was always his deckhand number.

"Skipper told me to sleep over. I'm going to be interviewin' for a crew job." He'd hand over a few hundred francs and he'd be on his way.

Nodding off to sleep to the gentle rock of the moored boat, Boy ran his hand through his lush golden curls. Tomorrow they would be gone.

CHAPTER 27

A cawing sound echoed through Jennifer's dreamscape. With an involuntary lurch, she slipped deeper under the covers. Human flesh, a hand, caressed her bare breast and she shifted her weight toward the comforting sensation. Her eyes peeped open.

"Wake-up call for me," Michel whispered.

For Michel, it had been a night of prodigal lovemaking which was even better and more satisfying for them both than their first night together. It had been a feast, talking late into the night and listening to the mellifluous and seductive quartets of Ravel and Debussy. Afterwards, he guided Jennifer through the prickly-leaved juniper trees and the clumps of stinging nettles that bounded the lake. They plunged into the cold lake water beside the olive orchard, dried each other off and made love on the grass. With a murder to start the morning, this combination would ordinarily have been a perfect mood elevator for him. But this time the victim was someone he had cared about and he was unsettled.

"What's that noise?"

"Stendhal, our cock."

Jennifer spread out her arms and luxuriated in the space. Sleeping with Michel was heaven after the narrow cot with its marshmallow mattress in the cramped attic above Maddie's apartment. Michel's farmhouse bedroom was palatial and painted a luminous chrome yellow. The furniture was oversized, pale honey, real country pine French. The shutters were a soft lime green and the straw chair reminded her that van Gogh had painted a masterpiece using such humble objects. But it was the light and landscape of Provence which inspired great painters. She gazed at her surroundings and realized she had never been in a room that was so tasteful and serene. There was a pair of eighteenth-century commodes with hand-carved serpentine fronts and gently curving sides; the armoire was decorated with nests of turtledoves, enjoined hearts and other symbols of marital bliss. The classic *panetière*, a see-through wooden cage which hung on the wall, originally intended to keep the bread dry, had been modified and a small CD player had been installed.

"No, don't leave. I want more of you."

"Go back to sleep."

As her lids closed, he kissed them.

Michel strolled over a meandering hillside of lime and olive trees. He was surrounded by his mother's herb gardens, fields of lavender, groves of plane trees and greenhouses. The mix of early morning fragrances intoxicated him. Michel regarded the stone farmhouse covered with fragrant, pink, climbing roses. As a boy, he'd helped clear the land and planted herbs with his father and uncles. When the new wing was built, they had all traveled up to the Alpilles Mountains to gather stones for it.

At the bottom of the hill was the sausage factory, Nicole's Saucisson. It was a longish rectangular stone building, which had originally been a crumbling barn. When Michel clattered in, the staff were drowsily stirring, dipping claws of fresh baguette into their bowls of café au lait.

"Oh, duck everyone, Nicole has sent the big boss to investigate the missing Arles sausage," said Amélie, the surly plum who managed the enterprise. "What brings you down here without Yvette?" the busybody inquired.

"I've changed dance partners."

He heard applause from the workers on the line. Wiping her mouth with a corner of her spotless apron, Amélie brought him over to the long marble counter where an assortment of dry sausage lay, destined for testing. He was tempted to start sampling tidbits, but decided that garlic breath before breakfast would be a barbaric prelude to kissing.

"What can I do for you?" Amélie asked.

"I came to visit."

Amélie was distrustful. "When we saw you arrive last night, we thought Yvette had sent you to examine the headcheese. No farm laborers have been incorporated in these, Michel. Although I must admit they give it a kick and preserve well."

"I'm only foraging, Amélie."

He took the ruddy empress aside and spent ten minutes discussing pig butchering.

"It's a man's work. I once tried to do it, but I don't like it."

"Why?"

She thought for a moment. "It's like cutting up a woman. And with the sucklings, it's even worse. You feel like you're killing a child."

"Thank you, Amélie. I don't remember us ever slaughtering here?"

"Rarely. Then one of the men attends to it."

The machinery was switched on along with music tapes to keep the employees happy. No talk shows or TV. At the beginning of this enterprise, a finger or two had been lost over political arguments.

"What about the intestines?"

"The *abatteur* delivers the casing clean. Your mother is an artist and we always run our own saline solution through it. He sends the spleen and the rest of the muck to Lyon. They talk about their cuisine, but your mother and I agree. In Lyon and in Caen, they'll eat shit and call it a regional delicacy."

"I wouldn't argue with you two."

He selected a new entry for breakfast: a long sausage stuffed with pork, herbs and spicy olive bread that his mother had created.

"Please send this up to the house with some eggs, figs and baby melons. And have your husband fix breakfast, then drive Jennifer back to Aix."

Amélie ground her tobacco-stained crooked teeth. "All this for an American, Michel! What's wrong with you?"

"I don't know. I think I'll try being happy for a change."

Before leaving, he peeped in on Jennifer and slipped a note on his side of the bed. Her long blond hair was splayed across the pillow and he shivered with emotion.

I've found the love of my life, he thought later as he drove out through the wooden farm gates.

He arrived at the Bimont Dam murder scene before Annie Vallon. She'd still be on the traffic-choked road from Marseille. He had read and reread the file on Carolyn Davis and James Walker. They had been happy and in love when they had ordered their last meal on earth at the *charcuterie*. As an afterthought, Walker had asked for a large tub of crème fraîche to go with the wild strawberries he had bought at the greengrocer while waiting for his order. He had taken two bottles of Cristal champagne from the cooler while getting the cream. He paid with a platinum American Express card. Michel envisioned the couple kissing before they drove away in a Mercedes convertible with the top down, smiling at the sky.

Laurent's autopsy had revealed that they had eaten most of the lunch, but there had been no evidence of strawberries or seeds. The empty pannier of strawberries had been listed in the inventory. The killer had eaten the strawberries and cream and drunk champagne.

Michel tried to reconstruct the scene. He roved through Cézanne's trees and studied the clearing from various angles. He took out his Zeiss binoculars, slowly scanning the landscape. Annie pulled up in her new Renault. How could she afford it on her salary? Some German she'd met sunbathing nude must've bought it.

"Annie, I'm here," he called out.

"Good morning. I brought coffee and brioches."

"Wonderful. I'm roaming around. Sit on the blanket I put in the glade."

"Facing you or what?"

"No, lie down."

"Pierre and Émile are going to be late. You in the mood for something quick?"

"No, dammit, keep your clothes on." He took off his shoes and socks and padded barefoot on the cool grass. "Point a finger in the air if you can hear me moving."

Annie lay on the blanket, resting on her elbow. Michel moved closer until he had reached the best angle to observe the setting without being seen. With a stick, he batted at the trees.

She pointed. "I hear something now."

"Okay."

Michel found a broad branch which was strong enough for him to sit on. "Any sounds?"

"No. The brioches are getting cold."

He quickly shimmied down the tree, rushed to his car and called the police garage in Marseille where the car had been towed and was still impounded.

"Georges, it's me. You're working on the Hertz Mercedes rental car. Yes, that's the one. Now switch on the radio and tell me if it's tuned to Radio Luxembourg."

Annie handed him a plastic cup and poured her thermos of coffee.

"My God, it's Hawaiian kona."

"Freshly ground for you from Colbert's."

Sweat drizzled down his cheeks as he waited.

"Pink Floyd is on Radio Luxembourg," the head mechanic answered.

He hung up, sipped the coffee first, then tore off a piece of brioche and dipped it in the fragrant coffee.

"Annie, call Radio Luxembourg and find out what their music program was for Thursday afternoon. I think James and Carolyn never heard the killer; they were making love, and the music was playing from the car radio when our man crept up on them."

Annie puckered her lips as though from a sour taste and the sun creases shone like white filaments under her eyes.

"Michel, I don't understand. Everything in these murders points to a woman."

He put his arm around her fondly. "She'd have to be smarter than you."

CHAPTER 28

Boy had stashed his gear at a crew locker down the street on the Quai St-Pierre in Cannes. He had a scruffy two-day beard and his hair was still shoulder length. He found the public baths and cleaned up. He located a small, empty barber shop and had the man give him a crewcut. Hanks of his beautiful cherished locks flew through the air with the abandon of a cheap carpet installation in a squalid motel. It was chopped like underfelt. He left the barber feeling mean.

Earlier, he had done a reconnaissance at the Montcalm. The staff entrance was on Rue d'Antibes. He had helped a trucker unload some crates of fresh seafood and ran the dolly merrily into the kitchen. The waiters and bellhops had a dressing area and lockers. All the uniforms had *Montcalm* in green flowing script underneath the left pocket. When they cleared out, he grabbed himself a pair of clean starched overalls from a bin.

At a bar, across the street from Françoise's pension, he drank a couple of Cokes and ate a thickly buttered hard roll. Twelve bucks. The prices in Cannes insulted human intelligence. At ten, he called the number Karim had given him. He heard people yammering in different languages before Françoise picked up the phone.

"I'll be down in a minute," she said. "I have to talk to you."

Outside a café, he watched Françoise glancing around. She had on espadrilles and a flimsy see-through beach shawl which window-dressed a high-cut neon pink bikini. Wraparound sunglasses, drooping under a wide-brimmed Panama, completed the outfit. Her straggly blond hair was pinned up. On a striped beach bag, FRANÇOISE was printed large enough to read back in Oklahoma. Still, with those long sapling legs, she had the tantalizing, trashy veneer that might excite old guys.

Boy stroked her. "Hi, gorgeous, what a sight you are."

She gave him a perfumed kiss on the cheek. Good thing his asthma was in check.

"You cut your gorgeous hair."

"It's my summer Scout camp look."

"Come on, let's have a bite at the Carlton beach."

"Is it near the Montcalm?"

"Next door."

"Might be crowded."

"It always is. But they know me."

The sun was at twelve o'clock high with only a hint of breeze. They wove through tanned bodies slick with oil and glued to straw mats. The speedboats were doing figure eights; on the hotel docks, water skiers were lined up. Most of the hotels had a restaurant directly on the beach. Monster yachts, the size of cruise ships, were anchored all around him. Arabs with binoculars were leaning over the guard rails scouting for blondes. The town growled with money.

The headwaiter at the Carlton gave Françoise a big phony hello and led them to a table under a parasol. Françoise was astonished when Boy slipped her fifty francs to tip him.

"You've got money?"

"I'll tell you about it later."

After their order was taken, she leaned close to him. She emitted a sweaty muskiness which overpowered her perfume. It was the familiar scent of fear.

"You've heard about the murder of Louise Vercours?" she asked.

"Huh? Who's she?"

"The madam I worked for in Aix."

"Maybe there was something in the paper. Karim was kind of worried. What's it got to do with you? And by the way, where the hell's Karim? He promised to meet me. We were supposed to hang out."

"His car broke down in St-Raphaël."

"I wanted to discuss some business with him."

She blinked, puzzled by the remark. "What kind of business?"

"Oh, it's a surprise. I'm going to help him out. This guy Gerard really treated him like dirt." Boy unfolded his map and located St-Raphaël on the coast. The bus had driven through it. "What time'll Karim get here?"

"The garage is replacing a hose. He should be at the pension by three or four this afternoon."

Some decent sunnyside eggs and ham arrived. Françoise ordered a Bloody Mary. She couldn't touch her food and continued to look around for cops. A few of the bronzed men glanced up from the pool lounges. One of them, with no wife in sight, held up four fingers for an appointment. His missus would probably be getting slapped around by a masseur, enough of them hanging around the cabañas. Françoise nodded and wrote down the date time on a bar napkin. Trade first. The drill was second nature to Boy.

"Did you know about my problem when I brought Maddie to Louise's to work that afternoon?"

"Weren't you trying to get money from Louise for Maddie's session?"

"No, I couldn't. I never mentioned it to Louise or Gerard."

The pronouncement shocked him, but he buried it under the wide smile of a simpleton.

"Really? Then they couldn't have met Maddie and argued about paying her."

Françoise felt compelled to be honest with him. This American kid was so open and naive that she took pity on him.

"Darrell, I couldn't work. I had my period."

"Maddie never mentioned that."

"Women don't like to talk about it. You see, this was *my* idea. Louise would never allow a replacement. I thought if Maddie attended to my clients, you and she would have some money. And nobody would know."

"Let me get this straight: Were *you* paid?"

Françoise nodded ruefully. "Yes, but much less than the usual price. These two men were strangers I picked up near the baths. I thought there might be enough to share with Maddie. But they chopped me down to a streetwalker's rate."

"Maddie did the dates, you collected the money, and the guys beat you down?"

"Yes."

"Did Maddie know you got paid?"

"No, I gave her a story about Louise and Gerard." A sheepish grin appeared. "I needed the money for Karim. His mother is widowed. Karim's father opposed the fundamentalists in Algeria and he was assassinated. That's why Karim became a freedom fighter." She sipped her Bloody Mary. "I knew Maddie came from a wealthy family and that her parents would send her money if she really needed it."

Boy was stunned but concealed it. "You're dead certain Maddie didn't go to Louise and ask for money?"

"No, I begged her not to. I would have been fired."

Boy's tone was even and unthreatening. "So you had to lie to Maddie and she had to lie to me. Is that what happened?"

"Not exactly. Maddie didn't want to upset you. I told her to tell you that Louise turned her down. Forgive me, if I've created a misunderstanding. There was no way to collect more money."

Whores hadn't changed their style for two thousand years, he reflected. He waited for Françoise to elaborate and then coaxed her.

"Why weren't you up front with Louise? You could've told her Maddie was going to work your johns."

"Come on, Darrell. If I was an employee in a shop, say, I couldn't bring in a friend without telling the manager that she'd be replacing me. And on top of that, the boss had to pay my salary to this friend."

"I guess you're right."

"Somehow Gerard found out that something was funny. I don't know how that happened."

"I do. Maddie got loaded on the hash Karim gave us and blabbed to her teacher about screwin' two guys. She's not a pro and couldn't handle it. She had to blow off some steam and that was her way."

"Ah, so that's what happened. It was her tutor, this Jennifer, who informed the vice squad."

Jennifer! Boy knew he had to trust his instincts. He should have killed her the moment they arrived. But Maddie kept pleading for her. The craft of murder had its own script and when it was violated, disaster followed.

"Françoise, did you tell Karim that Maddie filled in for you?"

"No, he would've gone mad."

"So the only people who know what actually happened are you, Maddie and me?"

Françoise was guarded. "Yes. And we have to keep quiet about it, especially since Louise was murdered."

"Count on me. . . . Now tell me about the guys?"

"They were from Paris and cruising. I took them in the back way of the Hôtel Estaque with Maddie. No one saw us." She shuddered. "I'm frightened that the police are going to arrest me. They'll think I might be involved. . . ."

"Come on now, sugar, don't you worry. You did your best."

"Oh Darrell, you're so lovable and innocent. I was certain there'd be enough money for everyone."

Boy was now focused perfectly on the operation and detected no flaws.

"Why'd you come to Cannes?"

"I was forced to go." She shivered in the heat. "Gerard has a police officer on the vice squad who works for him. His name is Paul Courbet. When there's something unpleasant, Courbet does it. If a girl's boyfriend or her family starts trouble, Courbet goes to see them. He told me if I didn't leave for Cannes, he'd slash my face with a razor."

"Sounds just like home," Boy said with a biting laugh.

"It's been very hard on me here. I'm not connected to a man or a house. The street girls hound me. Security agents chase me out of the casino. If I pick up a client, I never know if he'll pay or beat me. It's terrible in this business not to have a protector. . . ."

A demonic sexual tableau from Boy's past was projected on the screen of his mind like a videotape. He soothed Françoise and felt a deep connection with her plight. He, too, had been a captive until Mystery Man had rescued him.

"I'm here for you. I know what it's like, darlin'. Nobody's going to touch you." Boy shuddered involuntarily. "When you do this kind of work and you're not paid afterwards, you want to kill the person, don't you?"

"*Oui, oui.* I'm sorry I didn't tell Maddie the truth. I can see it complicated things."

Boy took her hand and massaged her long bony fingers. He wanted to chop them off.

"No harm done."

He paid the check and gave Françoise a glint of his roll. Then he intentionally dropped a Monte Carlo rectangle casino chip on the wooden slats covering the sand. It was a shill ruse. He waited for her to move on it and she did. Would she steal it or tell him?

"Darrell, do you know what this is?"

"You take it."

"But this is a five-thousand-franc plaque from the casino in Monte Carlo!"

"I won me a few skins there."

They walked toward the exquisite Montcalm beach with its immaculate green and white parasols and lounges. Beach boys were hopping around the hot sand, catering to every whim of the guests. A surly young uniformed guard stood behind a wooden gate checking to see that outsiders did not dare to use the hotel's pool. Boy stopped and pressed a five-thousand-franc bill into Françoise's hand.

"I understand your business. Save this for the rainy day."

She was flabbergasted. "Thank you so much. May I call you Boy? Maddie always does."

"Sure."

"I would have left Karim for you anytime you wanted me. But I would have hurt Maddie." Françoise removed her glasses. Her eyes were blotted with tears. "She's so good-hearted and tortured. She loves you madly."

"Cash in the chip whenever you like. But promise me that you'll do what I ask."

"Anything."

"You've had a rough time and I want you to really treat yourself." He lifted up Françoise's hat. "You really should have your hair done. You'd look great as a brunette."

"That would be a good change. But the prices are very high here in season."

"I got a check from home. Didn't Maddie tell you my family owns Calhoun Oil and Gas in Guthrie, Oklahoma?"

"No, not a word. She's so secretive about you."

"I like it that way." He touched her limp blond hair. "You need a nice soft classy color to go with those brown eyes. Get a manicure and a massage. Let me spoil you." He thought for a moment, allowing her to get sucked into the riptide. "Top it off with a gorgeous new dress. What a treat you'll be, all dolled up. Fact is, I'm goin' to have you and Karim meet Maddie and her parents for dinner tonight."

Maddie had told him the name of the restaurant where she'd be dining with her parents.

"Le Moulin de Mougins. Did I pronounce it right?"

"Oh, yes. But the Moulin costs a fortune."

"Her parents are loaded and so am I." Boy baited his hook again. "You know what, we might all travel with the Golds for a week or so. How's the Hôtel du Cap and Monte Carlo sound?"

"You Americans are so generous."

"We get a bad rap, but we try to be the good guys," Boy said affably, then spiked the champagne fantasy. "Adam Gold's a very important producer and he's one great guy." Boy looked her over professionally. "You never know what could happen. Beverly Hills . . . Hollywood. He likes a good time."

He could see that he'd buttoned her. Françoise was breathless with the mirages that whores like Boy himself had also been led to believe. The fables of strangers with treasure. During his childhood, he, too, had thought, Let me be lucky this once. I'll give 'em my best.

"Boy, I don't think I can be back in time to meet Karim."

"I'll wait for him. We'll dress him up, too. Bet he'd look great in a white dinner coat, patent leather boots. Man, he'll knock your eyes out."

They climbed up the steps back to the Croisette. He had dazzled

Françoise. She was exuberant, bursting with optimism. "You're *fantasque.*"

"Listen, Maddie wants pictures of us dressed up in our best. She's got a photographer coming to meet us at the church in the old town."

"That's Nôtre-Dame-d'Espérance."

"Our Lady of Hope." He put his arm around her waist and knew his smile was irresistible. "Look, why not cancel the date you made with that guy on the beach? We don't want his pacemaker skippin' a beat."

She laughed gaily, *"Avec plaisir."*

"I'll bring Karim along and we'll meet up at the church. I'll get us some champagne . . . it'll be unforgettable. Six o'clock sharp."

"I won't be late."

CHAPTER 29

Denise's salon was packed with the local housewives. *Le week-end* always began with sets, rinses, pluckings, pedicures and the ghastly odor of henna, which invariably made Michel sick to his stomach. The mistress was at the costume jewelry counter trying to flog a necklace to a woman with three chins.

"You again," Denise snapped.

"I'm in a hurry. I need to talk to you right now."

"I'll throw out my clients and close down the salon."

"I may do that for you and take you into Marseille for a long interrogation."

"Michel, you infuriate me." She signaled the receptionist and told her to take over. "And don't keep the mayor's wife waiting when she comes in. She has a reception at noon."

They walked outside so that Denise could keep an eye on the shop and greet anyone coming in. "That woman Corinne had been hovering and talking to the customers. Now what do you want? More sex talk?"

"Yes, you get me very excited."

It was going to be another roaster for the tourists in their baseball caps rushing to their buses. In the sharp, brilliant sunlight, he stood squinting at Denise under a café awning. Her mood had become conciliatory when he brought up the taboo subject.

"Louise a lesbian? Not with me. If that was her dark secret, she gave a performance that would've won the Palme d'Or at the Cannes Film Festival. Michel, you really don't know much about women."

"That's part of my charm."

"We all thought Yvette would complete your education." She fanned herself with a *Paris-Match*. "But you turned out to be a pig trotting in the sun. Didn't you ever take any psychology courses at the Sorbonne?"

He strategically retreated. "Complete my education."

"Damn, Michel, if the timing is right, anyone can be ripe for a different kind of sex. But during our high seas adventures, Louise and I weren't kissing each other good night."

As she recounted their torrid encounters, it became evident that she and Louise were the pirates collecting booty inland and by sea. No gullible natives in this party.

"Your problem is that you've been treating Louise as a saint. Not as a woman who ran a brothel. She's not *your* mother.

"Look, Louise was brilliant. But she had as much interest in the sex business as Mother Teresa did. She cultivated her clients. This one tells her something about a farm going into bankruptcy; a financier who wants to get into her good graces drops a hint about a company on the bourse. Maybe they intend to announce a new product that will corner the market or take over another company. Some lecher is choking on estate duties or a divorce settlement and has a pair of Matisses. He doesn't want to pay a dealer commission. Or sell at auction. He'll take cash. Louise has it. It's a silent transaction."

Michel carefully considered how much to reveal to Denise.

"I don't believe a client or one of her girls murdered her. For just the reasons you've given me. Louise would have found some way negotiate her way out of trouble."

"Of course she would have."

She peered through the window. "I must go. Someone has turned Madame Sardou's hair into Chinese red." Denise stared at him for a moment, then shook her head with resignation. "I hope for your sake, your new girlfriend straightens you out. But if a French woman couldn't educate you, I don't have much faith in an American."

Yvette's Deux Chevaux grumbled to a stop on the pavement. She grabbed her briefcase and laptop.

"I'm early, Denise."

"We can wash you in . . . about fifteen minutes. Michel's wrecked my schedule."

Yvette looked wearily at him, for once with uncertainty. That lasted a few seconds. Michel turned away and gazed in the salon window, his eye skipping over the maddening jumble of ingredients and armaments women bought in order to prepare for an evening in a dark cinema. Perfumes gave way to a display of a huge jar of Alpha Hydroxy and this in turn stood guardian over hair dryers and hot curlers for the traveling beauty.

"I suppose I can use the time to interview Commander Danton."

Denise marched back into her salon, waving her arms furiously at an assistant. He watched her put on a pair of rubber gloves before plunging into Madame Sardou's dyed hair.

"Enjoying your new digs?"

"Since Denise's temp left town, it's been quiet."

"Couldn't he handle you both?"

"I'll never live this down, will I?"

"It would have been simple to dispose of me. All you had to do was to have paid a courtesy call before you left for Paris. I worry about people I care about."

"You're right, I behaved like a pig." She shook her head and her self-reproach was unfeigned. "How are these cases going?"

"We have no leads."

"That's hard to believe with the forensic setup you have in Marseille."

"No fingerprints, or physical evidence to speak of."

She licked her lips as though savoring caviar. "You've got a real clever one, then."

"Honors in murder."

"You think he's done this before?"

"No question."

"Will he continue?"

Michel was distracted and continued to gaze into the salon window.

"I have no way of knowing. I think he had a reason, deranged as it may be."

Her eyes had a wicked ambivalence that he remembered from their foreplay. Little puddles of sweat ran down from her hairline and he wiped it with his handkerchief.

"Michel, I have some information. Want to trade?"

"You first."

"Vincent Sardou is Louise's lawyer."

"Tell me something I don't know."

"When I asked him about Louise, he froze. He told me to mind my own business. Odd, don't you think? This is the biggest story of the summer and as the publisher of *Le Clairon*, he acts like he wants to cane his favorite journalist."

"He's acting properly."

"He knows something, Michel."

Across the street, Michel watched the forensic staff working on Louise's roof, meticulously itemizing her treasures.

"I don't want this in print yet, Yvette."

"All right."

"I'm looking for a young couple."

Seldom taken off guard, this time she was jarred. "A woman was involved?"

"My guess is that they're between twenty and forty. The man could be older than the girl. But I think they're peers, lovers for sure. If you print this, it will ruin the investigation."

"A woman . . . a woman," she repeated, shaking her head with incredulity.

"They've been known to commit murder."

"This isn't a payback? Disinformation? I don't want to look like a fool."

"You're talking to the fool."

"No, I was, Michel. Anything else?" Yvette's face flooded with orgasmic pleasure. "Is there a link between the murders of the American couple and Louise?"

"Not yet."

"But you think there might be?" Yvette spun around. "What are you staring at?"

"Was I?"

"You keep looking over my shoulder."

In an instant, Michel sprinted across the street. He dashed up the steps to Louise's roof and burst into the group of technicians.

"Anyone found a curling iron?"

"No, Michel. There was blood in the pool," Émile said. "Louise's."

"I'd bet the killers went for a swim afterwards, Émile. Drain the pool and start scraping it. Bring back samples and any residues you find."

"Where are you going, Michel?"

Michel bolted downstairs and burst past Yvette into the salon. He reached into the window, capsizing everything. Bottles of cosmetics exploded on the floor, startling the women in the shop. He yanked out a curling iron.

"I'll pay for this later," he shouted.

Denise tried to calm down the ruffled patrons. "He's totally mad."

"That's why I left him," Yvette said with a rueful smile.

Michel stabbed in the lab number on his cellular phone and waited impatiently until someone tracked down Charles Laurent.

"I want you to examine the burn marks on Louise's body again."

"Aren't you glad I didn't release it?"

"Yes, you're wonderful. See if they match a metal curling iron made by Profile."

CHAPTER 30

After Louise had arranged his introduction to manhood at fifteen, erotica hadn't interested Michel very much. When he had to look at it professionally, he became as bored as the actors in the videos. The current rage was S and M, piercings and tattoos, but he still resisted the potential for excitement that lured aficionados to places like Gerard's sex boutique. Several men were browsing through the schoolboy magazine section. Gerard was at the counter, busily unpacking videos with the ardor of someone counting cans of sardines.

"Oh, Michel, welcome to the neighborhood." He bagged a skin magazine of pierced, tattooed women for a young legionnaire.

"I thought you might enjoy a visit from me."

His thick lips pursed with indignation. "I've already wasted hours with your detective. I can't close my shop."

"Don't you have any employees?"

"I'm trying to hire some. You looking for a job?"

"Are you expanding?"

"I may be."

"I want to hear about this quarrel with Karim Hassad."

"It's not police business." Michel angrily swept the counter of the porn tapes. "That's vandalism," the alarmed Gerard whined.

"Would you like me personally to burn down the shop and make it look like you committed arson?"

Gerard rounded up the customers and told them he would be closing for lunch. There was a squalid neighborhood bistro with a few *routiers* outside, drinking beer and letting their trucks cool down.

"Let's have a drink, Michel?"

"I'll pay. Government courtesy."

A barkeep with a black eye pulled two bottles of Stella Artois off the ice and they declined glasses. They sat outside at a table where old rice pellets had hardened, giving the lino top a stippled relief. Like drug pilots, flies landed warily on this airstrip.

Michel was searching for a motive for Louise's brutal slaughter. There had been a robbery, but the valuable stuff had been left behind. These killers hadn't known what Louise's paintings were worth. They weren't stupid, but unschooled in fine art. Impressionism of all subjects. Even French farm brats knew something about Renoir and Cézanne.

"You don't like me, Michel. You never have."

"Forget my social preferences, will you?"

Rather surprisingly, Gerard became emotional and was close to tears.

"I loved Louise. She was my savior. If not for her, I would have gone to prison. I had nothing to do with her murder."

At one time Gerard had been a notary, but some fraudulent property transactions had caused him to leave the legal profession. Floundering, he had been scooped up in Louise's net. She had a place for a man like Gerard David.

"No one's accusing you of anything. I need information."

It was invariably difficult to compel innocent people to focus. With a guilty suspect, there was no such problem. They selectively told you what they wanted you to know. Gerard drifted morosely back to his fall from grace. As one of several notaries employed by Vincent Sardou in his law practice, large sums of clients' money were frequently entrusted to him. It might be the down payment on a property or a large commercial transaction. Gerard had not quite stolen money, he had borrowed without the lender's knowledge. Always repaying and balancing the books. This high wire act eventually came to Sardou's attention and for some reason Louise interceded on Gerard's behalf, sparing him prison.

"Why'd she hire you?"

"I'm a damn good businessman. And Louise knew that at this stage of my life, I could be trusted. I never cheated her."

"Did you keep client books?"

"No, Louise did it all in her head."

Gerard managed and hired the girls at the Hôtel Estaque and ensured that the so-called social club connected to it ran smoothly. He ordered food and wine, saw that the staff maintained the premises and functioned as a general manager.

"Sometimes I suggested investments when I heard something from one of the club members. She took my advice or ignored it. No question that she was smarter than me."

"Do you have a girlfriend by the name of Françoise Artois?"

A bleating laugh escaped from Gerard. "No, no. Louise knew I was gay."

"Do you have a special friend, then?"

"Several. But they have nothing to do with Louise. I pick them up in the shop."

"Was Karim one of them?"

"No, he's straight. He and Françoise want to get married."

"Why did you get rid of her?"

"There was this nonsense—a rumor I assure you, nothing more—about Françoise bringing in some American student. It was groundless."

Maddie Gold had turned up again. Michel was puzzled. "Did Françoise know this girl Maddie?"

"I have no idea."

Françoise had been banished to Cannes for the rest of the summer as a result of the gossip. Karim had caused a furor, and he and Gerard had argued about it.

"Karim's gone to Cannes to bring Françoise back. And we've settled our differences. We're on the best of terms."

He continued to sound out Gerard about the young Algerian. Not surprisingly, he was a political activist, a peacock strutter, decidedly argumentative, but Gerard had never known him to be violent. And Françoise was a sharp-witted hustler outside the brothel, selling American jeans and T-shirts at flea markets.

"Karim's going to be my full partner in the shop."

"Why this change of heart?"

"I can't be in two places at once, Michel."

"What other place?"

"I'm taking over Louise's business. From different premises, of course. And I'll put Françoise in charge of the girls. Youth at the helm," he added, as though explaining a corporate recruitment program in order to launch a campaign to sell a product to a new market.

Someone dies, someone advances, Michel thought bitterly. A group of new people would profit from Louise's death.

"The chain of succession, you make it sound almost constitutional."

"In a sense that's true. They need me in the city. Someone has to provide entertainment to stop the men from beating their wives and see that they get home for dinner."

Jennifer handed Maddie a makeup case as she was about to get into the Rolls-Royce limousine. In her white linen Armani suit and high heels, Maddie had a carefree, unstudied elegance. Jennifer was pleased with her reckless protégée. After four weeks, Maddie was on her way to becoming civilized. Her grades were excellent and the wildness had given way to a new maturity.

"I wish you'd change your mind and come to Cannes with me, Jen. My folks are going to be disappointed as hell."

"You need some time alone with them."

"Come on, this is Maddie. I know why you don't want to go. Michel's more delectable than dinner at Moulin de Mougins."

What was it about Maddie that invariably offended Jennifer? Or was Jennifer too quick, mistaking her frankness for a streak of vulgarity? Whatever it was, it unfailingly had an unwholesome element. No matter what effort Jennifer made, she could not really get close to Maddie.

"I guess you're right."

Maddie went into one of her riffs. "It happens so fast when it happens. I know the feeling when you get hooked on someone. Beats drugs. Nothing in the world like it. You think to yourself, How did I live without him? When André left for his music tour, I was blown out."

Jennifer smiled at her. "Take a few days off and travel with your parents. The Hôtel du Cap, Monte Carlo. It'll be fabulous."

Maddie shook her head. "I have to be back for the lecture on Rimbaud."

"I'll take notes for you."

Like an unexpected summer squall, Maddie's mood changed. She fell into Jennifer's arms, crying. "I love you to death and I don't want anything to happen to you."

"What is it, Maddie? I don't understand. Michel's not going to hurt me."

"Life can."

Jennifer was bewildered. They seemed to be speaking different languages. She watched the limo turning the narrow street corner and wondered about Maddie's future. Her hopefulness gave way to an inscrutable sensation of apprehension.

Michel pulled up beside her and opened the door. "Give you a lift?"

"Why not? I missed you at breakfast."

Jennifer got into the car and lifted the newspaper off the seat. She read the headline:

Killer Visits Aix for Music Festival

CHAPTER 31

"I want to stop when we get to Fréjus," Maddie instructed the chauffeur.

"Oui, mademoiselle."

Maddie sank into the soft leather folds of the Rolls-Royce's backseat and pressed a button that raised the window partition. Closing her eyes, she went over every detail of Boy's demanding plan. There was no margin for error. To succeed, she had to control her nerves. She had hated her parents since she could remember. . . .

During the Christmas break from Pembrooke, Maddie had escaped from her parents for a night. They had been watching her like hawks for any sign of drugs. She'd been so paranoid, she thought they were going to ask for urine samples. One of the dorm wantons at college had given her the address of a warehouse in Venice that held raves and played grunge. Maddie drove her Porsche Carrera out of the Bellagio gates like it was sundown at the OK Corral.

The place was crowded, noisy, smoky, with music so loud that the tin roof vibrated. Maddie paid her door charge and went exploring. Boy was working there and she glommed him like a Godiva truffle. "These old speakers should be in Arizona with their asthma," Boy was telling the rave's organizer during an equipment check.

"Well, what are we going to do?"

Boy fiddled around with them for twenty minutes and rewired the tweeters.

"What'd you do?" the man asked. He'd made the speakers snap like Dobermans.

"Put in new lungs. Would you like me to install a pair for you?"

Later, Boy admitted that he had kept tabs on her that night.

He finally made eye contact with her. He'd spotted the slinky, slim girl with the dope rings under her deep blue eyes and the sleek auburn hair. He watched her wave a hundred-dollar bill and score some ecstasy. She had a clever, luminous face and small, fine features; everything about her was delicate but he detected a coldly mutinous quality. She was swinging her hips and waiting on the nitrous oxide line with her balloon. Ten bucks filled it, and got the fans gassed enough to giggle for an hour. When the keeper of the nozzle asked if she had anything smaller, she fished out another hundred and waited for her change.

She was slam-dancing with anyone who came along, looking for the right one to fill her. At about three-thirty, the crowd thinned and she was sliding toward the door. He couldn't let go of the vision of that stack of hundreds. He had a sixth sense about girls who came from money. Like a Geiger counter that would start popping when it got near radioactivity.

Carrying his tool chest, Boy packed it in for the night and followed her out to the parking lot. He spied a huge black guy hitting on her. Maddie wanted no part of him. But the dude wasn't hearing and made a move that scared her. Boy snuck behind her nifty red Porsche and pulverized the guy's skull with a wrench.

Her gratitude was compromised by the shock of it. "My God, do you think he's dead?"

Boy took the keys from her shaking hand. "Does it matter . . . ? Are you in health care?"

"No. He said he was a gangbanger! I saw his tattoo."

"Well, I guess you'll have to hide me out."

Maddie surveyed the dazzling young man in the light. Long blond hair to his shoulders, tight jeans, lithe, strong build, with bulging muscles. He was about her height. The controlled fury of his face relaxed in an angelic smile.

"Can it be forever?"

"Come on, I'll drive you home, wild thing."

It was cold but he had the sunroof down and charged the Porsche down the Pacific Coast Highway. Maddie let go of her stifled feelings and floated up into the spark of the moment. A prince guiding her chariot through the celestial unknown.

She had a lulled, defiant lack of affect, a hard vacant place, his to occupy. He had picked up the shrink jargon from his many interviews and could gas about a diagnosis with the best the state had to offer.

She waited for him to move on her, but he had more information to collect. She had a shag blanket in the backseat and wanted fury on the beach. He'd had enough of women who never asked his name. This one would be sent home quivering and ungratified.

"Aren't you going to park at the beach?"

"Can't let the princess roll in at dawn with purple eyes. Mom and Dad'll start your day with a grounding threat that'll ring in your ears."

"My God! How'd you know that?"

"I channeled into your soul."

"That's outrageous. What's your name?"

"Darrell Vernon Boynton . . . the First."

"I'm Maddie, Maddie Gold."

"Pleased to meet you, ma'am," he drawled. "My friends call me Boy and that's not some nigra insult that makes me slap leather."

"Boy! Boy . . . Boy." She rolled the name on her tongue like sunshine. "I love it."

"Well, here's what I suggest, Miss Maddie. After what happened on the parkin' lot, I don't want you throttlin' around by yourself, these dirty, low hours. We'll drop me near your house. I'll catch me a bus."

Boy stopped abruptly. "Oh, wait, you got a car phone. Better still, we'll get you back to the ranch and call a cab from there."

Maddie looked at her watch—four-thirty. Boy did too, spotting a Rolex.

She thought quickly. Her parents would be going down to Palm Springs in a few hours. Some charitable organization in the desert was giving Adam Gold their Man of the Year award. He had lobbied for it for a decade. Another honorarium to go on the wall with the rows of plaques he collected. All of them informed the world that Adam Gold was a humanitarian and had reached the pinnacle in TV.

There wasn't enough time to do what she wanted to with Boy. She did not give up easily and decided to give Boy an off-speed pitch. She'd have the house to herself for three days. She'd put a stroke on those golden curls. She realized he didn't know what was happening, possessing only the courage of the innocent.

He winked shyly at her. Maddie was about to launch him into the adult world.

"You're right, Boy. I should get home."

"Thank you, my lady."

He drove carefully through the Bellagio gates and into Bel Air where the greenskeepers at the country club were shaving the emerald fairways with soft humming mowers.

"It's got the perfume of the fields from home." Actually the chemical field poisons had a slightly different aroma in Oklahoma. He used to cough his way through entire counties. As the fresh grassy air recirculated the last of the nitrous oxide, Maddie was so knocked out with him that she started quoting Shakespeare.

" 'It is the bright day that brings forth the adder; And that craves wary walking.' "

Boy slowed up, studying the dappled awakening of Bel Air. He stopped the car in front of a colossal white Colonial manor home, the size of Tara. Boy spewed out the words Mystery Man had given him.

"Snakes and fire / will halt desire."

"Wonderful, you're also a poet," Maddie exclaimed, beside herself with happiness.

"I write songs . . . that don't sell."

Her plan was for Boy to hide in the guesthouse until the Golds had taken off for Palm Springs. But Boy gave her a little shucking and jiving. No, that wouldn't be proper. He had a code of chivalry. She'd call him a cab and he would return at a proper hour.

"Bring enough clothes for three days. I'm not letting you out of my sight."

"Well, I got to pick up my bike at the shop and I'm being hassled by the mechanic. It's under house arrest. Have to see some people and round up some bread to spring my baby."

"What do you drive?"

"Harley."

"How much do you need?"

"Six hundred would do it."

Maddie snapped open her handbag and stuffed a pack of bills on him.

"Truly, you're wonderful," he said, sniffing at real bucks. "Now I'll pay you back. Count on that."

"See if you can score some blow."

"Will do, ma'am."

"Oh, and what do you like to eat?"

"A porterhouse would suit me."

She forced a kiss on him and was breathless with expectation. But he didn't encourage her.

"Barbecue at the pool, sir."

"I'll play a little country music for you."

When he arrived in the afternoon, he gawked at the Gold mansion, which was the size of some entire towns in Oklahoma. Thirty-five thousand square feet of marble and carpets and gilt furniture. Everywhere Boy looked, he was assaulted by statuary and paintings.

"It's called 'Belles' after my dad's first hit TV series."

"Oh, that was the one with the three gals who wore body huggers and were bustin' out of their bras."

"It was memorable for the fact that a lingerie designer won for best costumes."

A dick whacker for the prisoners, he recalled. "Guys in my school loved it."

He'd been out of Atascadero for seven months and was freelancing as a sound-system man at underground discos and raves. One job led to another. He had learned how to put sound systems together during a stint at McAlester Prison.

They were out at the Olympic-size pool. Boy had cooked a three-pound steak and was expertly slicing it. He'd been dying for good beef after months of Domino's and Big Macs.

"You are an extremely thoughtful and generous young lady, Miss Maddie Gold."

"You'll have an opportunity to reciprocate after we've dined."

And that's when the delicate moment arose. Boy floated up a knuckleball. He spoke to Maddie of a relationship, friendship, the danger of AIDS, although he himself was circumspect and could not remember the last time he had been intimate. His line was not working. She was dipping into the coke and scrunching her tongue at him.

"Hey, it's only our first date."

She was having none of it. "I beg you."

"I don't just drop my pants for anyone."

Women, he knew, simply couldn't believe it when he turned them down. Her hand crept up his thigh, then along the fly and her eyes bulged as though a hangman had put a noose around her neck and she was doing her first swing on the gallows.

No way out. It was tee time. "Got a room?"

"Thirty something."

The expert checked her out. He was all business and Maddie was driven and haunted by her own tumultuous desire for him. He gave her an hour in different positions. By the time he was through with her, slavery would follow, but it would be called liberation.

"Boy, it's so huge."

"Yeah, and its been abused by mercenaries," he said with uncharacteristic candor.

"I'll be kind to it."

"There is no kindness in sex, it's all about power." He had her squat over him. "Now hike up, Maddie, and come down hard on me."

Blinded by sweat and intoxicated by a multitude of orgasms, she became his vassal.

After New Year's, he visited her every weekend at Pembrooke and put her through sexual graduate school. He brought her dope and good cheer. She was running short of the hundreds. Living on a budget didn't suit Boy, especially when she started squealing about a shave in her allowance and telling him that Adam's business manager was threatening to chop her plastic. She was madly in love with Boy and he decided to find out if she was up for the test. He loved the breaking-in period with a new woman. When they ran out of money or he got bored, usually a daily double with him, he found another young thing.

He knew he had to take a woman's pride if he wanted submission. Showing them kindness, offering financial support—worse still, responding to emotional needs—brought out the poisons in women. The wrong form of dependency. Boy wanted them as allies to work with him and for him. To reach that point, they had to be lashed or else they'd crush him under the weight of their demands. He left the advanced training for the beginning of March, when he brought up a large chocolate Easter bunny.

Drinking Cuervo Gold shooters in the deserted cocktail lounge of the Ojai Pines Motel, he was playing some easy jazz on the piano to kill time. He wasn't bad, but not band quality. Listenable, he called it. He hated waiting until Maddie got out of class or finished her homework or went for counseling. It was her fault that he was bored silly. He'd been passively courting the statuesque barmaid who made it very clear that she had left her inhibitions in Dallas. She had an apartment out back; good-humored sort; liked to smoke grass and drink. She drooped over the piano, with a sappy smile on her face.

"Got to make a call, Dawn," he told her. Not true. He strutted into the restroom to primp and squirt Binaca on his breath. When he came out, Dawn was lurking in the corridor and working over her makeup in the cigarette machine mirror.

"You think you got stood up?" she asked.

"Anything's possible with you temperamental ladies." Dawn gave him a hug and he lightly kissed her mouth. "When do you get off?"

"Now's the hour."

"My little gal's goin' to freak out if I'm not here." Boy cupped his hand on her ass. "I'd sure like to get to know you better."

"Same here, cowboy."

"I don't think the girl's goin' to be any trouble. How do you feel about somethin' like that?"

"You got the lasso." She ran her fingers through Boy's hair. "Ask *her*, I'm game."

Maddie strolled in. When she made out the figures in the corridor, she just about had a seizure.

"Now calm down, Maddie."

"You bastard!"

"I have spent days coolin' my heels until you're through with your French class, or your therapy, or your other bullshit. Sittin' in the dark with just a local paper for company and an occasional warm, friendly face like Dawn's here."

"It's all been innocent, pet, so don't start accusing him or me," Dawn said.

Boy watched Maddie slowly retreat, eyes darting from his face to Dawn's.

"Dawn's invited us back to her place for cocktails."

"And we'll see what we can cook up," the busty barmaid said with a leer.

In Dawn's tidy little apartment, they relaxed over two joints, some blow, and a fifth of tequila. Wearing a red satin robe, the hostess came out of the shower, pink and smelling of a flowery talc. She sat between the two of them while Boy fixed another rolling thunder joint. He gave it to Dawn and lighted it. She passed it to Maddie who went piggy with it before laying it back on Boy. Dawn gave them both a steamy, inviting smile and put on smooth Joe Sample jazz. She wiggled her little finger at Boy. He got to his feet and they started to dance. He could see Maddie's resistance breaking down. She'd been challenged and he tapped into the hollowness he had detected in her character.

"Come on, little lady, dance with us," Dawn said.

Boy had his arms around both of them, then his hand glided down the slit of Dawn's robe.

"Ohhh, feel this, Maddie . . . it's so hot and luscious."

Maddie's big red eyes opened wide. She shook her head, reluctant to join in, until Boy let her feel him growing hard. They started dancing closer to Dawn's bedroom.

"I can't—I mean . . ." Maddie protested.

"You've got to experience everything with me, darlin'." He kissed Maddie's neck passionately and wheeled her over the threshold. "Dawn's got one, you got one. You have to learn to respect and comfort each other if all this feminist babble really means anything. Come on, Maddie, you know I got enough to fill two tanks."

Dawn didn't need encouraging. She went right to work on Maddie while Boy stripped off her bra. Maddie was aroused to fever pitch. And then she got the message and went after Dawn, who was splayed on the bed, legs wide open to take her offering. Boy mounted Maddie from behind and she started pulsating with excitement.

"You're like me, Maddie, born to it. Deeper . . . deeper, honey. . . ."

"Oh, yeah, look how hard I'm making her nipples."

He methodically dismantled every inhibition that had been foisted on Maddie.

Later, when they walked back to Maddie's dorm, he clasped her in his powerful arms, "Flyin' colors, my lady."

"I never thought I could do anything like that."

"It's just a rehearsal." He peppered her face with kisses. "Fess up. You loved it, didn't you? Strikin' when you wanted. Gettin' us both off together. In control."

"You and Dawn really knew what you were doing. It was fantastic."

"Sure it was. That's my idea of Sisterhood Unity. Now you never have to think about it and wonder. You've experienced a threesome."

"You gave me the guts, Boy."

"Had to get you out of your rompers and into the Ph.D. program." He remembered his own initiation at the Gortzes' swap meet and the final outcome when Mystery Man had showed him how to take charge. "One day, you'll be the lawgiver in one of these deals. You'll be able to decide someone's fate. Life or death."

"Will I? It's awesome, being with you."

Outside the dorm, he held her close, pressing her head into his barrel chest. He kissed her voraciously and the dorm snoops were impressed with the young lovers having a farewell kiss. Boy waved his hand in a grandiloquent gesture.

"There's only me. No family, no friends. I have chosen you to walk by my side and to explore the subterranean passages of mortality."

Maddie looked at him with reverence. "You are my light, my God, Boy."

"Keeper of the flame with me. . . ."

Maddie reached over to the ice bucket in the back of the Rolls-Royce. She opened a split of champagne and drank it from the bottle. She had truly become keeper of the flame with Louise. Now the fate of Adam and Karen Gold was finally in her hands.

4
CHÂTEAU
NOIR

CHAPTER 32

While waiting for Michel, Jennifer went into Deux Garçons. The interior of the café was divided into two gracious rooms whose glories inspired a clubby friendliness among waiters and the clientele. This genial ambiance prevailed despite the crowds and noise. University professors reading newspapers intermingled with grubby tourists barking for beer and sandwiches. Jennifer found a small marble table in the mirrored room overlooking the Cours Mirabeau. She sat opposite the expansive zinc bar and imagined Cézanne drinking coffee there, solitary and preoccupied. An ancient waiter appeared and smiled at her. He probably thought she was different from the run-of-the-mill tripper and now that she had Michel, she did feel different, almost French.

After an hour and three espressos, she idled her way down the Cours Mirabeau. The pure playful, insinuating melodic inflections of the fountains were an invitation to pleasure. For her, the street was a path to heaven, which, over the centuries, had been devised by mortals in their search for paradise. Embowered by double rows of immense plane trees, shrouding the sun's rays, the splays of flickering light through the mass of green leaves were magical. They mysteriously altered the features of people walking or sitting at café tables and invariably caught some aspect of character which might not otherwise be discernible. At sunset the last fingerprints of light reminded her of guttering candles on a birthday cake.

She roamed down the winding back streets of the university to get her mind off Maddie. In the eighteen months that she had known Maddie, she had not been able to get a fix on her. The girl was always in trouble, moody and preoccupied with sex. This trip to Aix had been a disaster for Jennifer, until she met Michel.

She stopped at a bookstore. Thumbing through dusty old shelves, her mind drifted back to America. Her small apartment in the college dorm was no place for a man like Michel. College rules prohibited men from staying the night. Where would they go? The five thousand dollars she was earning as salary from Adam Gold was now invested in a mutual fund. She had saved and scrimped but without this largess, she would have been broke.

Michel was obsessed with three homicide investigations and was stretched thin. She tried to be understanding and knew that she had become a prisoner of events. She wanted his time, needed it. This pull of circumstances—being acted upon instead of acting—created a degree of frustration she could not come to terms with.

After her fiancé's murder, she had learned that there was no such thing as saving up good times and spending them at leisure. She skimmed through a book by Gimpel, the art dealer. Unable to concentrate, she put it down. What made matters intolerable was the realization that these investigations were not isolated cases. Michel was consumed by his work. They lived in different countries, and their worlds were fundamentally incompatible. The predictable life of teaching, which kept her balanced and productive, was in conflict with his profession. She did not believe she could cope with a man whose steady diet was murder. She ached when she tried to conceive of a future for the two of them.

He had left her to interview Louise's attorney. It was all so disturbing, for Michel had reawakened emotions that she had buried and she was damned if she knew what to do.

Vincent Sardou was a collector of large legal fees and the fine furniture of Provence. His office was next door to the stately seventeenth-century Hôtel de Forbin. It shared the wrought iron balcony where the dukes of Berry and Burgundy, grandsons of the Sun King, had on cloudless days waved their perfumed lace handkerchiefs to acknowledge the monstrous taxes levied on the populace.

Michel passed a group of hand-wringing clients waiting for Sardou to discuss their divorces, or to learn how to steal inheritances, and stay out of prison. Fax machines and computers anachronistically hummed amid soft Baroque music.

Sitting behind a small table shaped like a scallop shell, Sardou switched off his automatic line of telephones and rose to greet Michel. He was an elfin figure in his midsixties, with a startling cockscomb pompadour and a beard shaped for a Van Dyck portrait sitting. Tailored by Gieves of Savile Row and with a paisley bow tie by Turnbull and Asser, he presented a figure at once florid and pompous. But behind the façade was a lucid intelligence admired by the late President Mitterrand for whom he had once served as an adviser. In his court robes, Maître Vincent Sardou's stature increased. He had a classically modulated voice, wit, and knew more law than most of the judges. News in Provence was controlled by his newspaper and TV satellite connection.

"Where are we, Michel, in this gruesome event?"

"I'm collecting information."

"Do you have a suspect yet?"

"No. Just ideas floating around."

"Is Louise's murder complicated?"

"Yes, very. I'm searching for a form. The killer was very experienced. And destroyed most of the physical evidence."

Sardou pondered this remark for a moment. "Could it be the work of the Union Corse? Someone from *le milieu*?"

"There's an entirely different modality to this crime. Would you expect a French criminal to smash bottles of Pétrus Eighty-nine? Lafite Sixty-one? Leave Matisses and Bonnards undisturbed? Ignore Cézanne?"

"No, no, I wouldn't."

"Nor would I."

"So your man doesn't drink wine or like art?"

"They don't understand them."

Sardou was confounded. *"They?"*

"A man and a woman."

Sardou was stunned. "Exactly how did Louise die? You haven't released any details. I've been hounding Yvette about it."

"I want the killers to stay relaxed and complacent. I took a chance with Yvette this time. I told her what we have, in case she gets a tip on a young woman."

"You can trust me as well. I'm an officer of the court. I wouldn't publish anything that would damage the investigation."

"Louise was tortured . . . with among other things a red hot curling iron. And then she was sliced open like a pig."

Vincent Sardou recoiled in horror. Michel rose to assist him but was waved away. Sardou reached for a small brown bottle and slipped a nitro tablet under his tongue.

"Are you all right, Vincent?"

"Angina. I tried the patch but it didn't work. The pills do the job faster for me." He slumped into an armchair and Michel sat opposite him. "Pour me a glass of Armagnac and please join me."

"Are you sure you want to mix the two?"

He nodded. Michel went to a gleaming marble-topped buffet table and filled two glasses from a thick crystal decanter. Sardou raised his glass to Michel's.

"To Louise Vercours. May her great good deeds be counted by the Lord." And then he returned to the business at hand. "Who's handling the local investigation with you?"

"I have my team from Marseille. Claude and Courbet are acting for the Municipals."

"They couldn't find a corpse in a morgue."

"Local pomp and pride. Richard Caron spoke to the prefect of police and he's got them on a short lead."

"Is there anything I can do? I can call the Minister of the Interior and get you more help."

"I don't need it."

Sardou was not placated. "This case is different for you, Michel. You and your parents are emotionally involved."

"True."

"Lawyers sometimes make mistakes when they have strong personal feelings about clients."

"I appreciate your advice."

"Are you sure you're well enough to handle this investigation?"

"I wouldn't have undertaken this—or any other case—if I weren't completely convinced I could do the job. The last thing I want is a bungled investigation. Vincent, tell me something about Louise that I could never find out."

Sardou's face took on an uncharacteristic vacant expression as he straddled the dilemma: to assist in a murder inquiry or retain his discretion. It was a moral question which dealt with the wishes of the dead. So long as the living were not compromised, did the dead have any rights? Michel thought he had found a chink in the barrister's armor.

"Why do you ask?"

"There was a grudge in her murder. There might be something from her past that led to it."

Slowly it unfolded. Louise had come back from Toulon to settle permanently in Aix in 1961. Vincent Sardou had been recently admitted to the bar after a long clerkship. He had also fallen in love with Louise.

"I thought she stayed in Paris." Odd that his parents hadn't mentioned it.

"No, she'd been in Toulon for some time after Paris. She fell in love with an American pilot. He was testing experimental new fighter planes for NATO. He was married and had two children. He and

Louise had a passionate affair. It ended tragically. He was killed on a flight in a Mirage jet. Louise was shattered, suicidal. Your parents pulled her out of it."

"What was the pilot's name?"

"I never asked. I doubt if she would have told me. The only person I can implicate is myself. I was married and had two teenage sons and a young daughter. Louise wouldn't break up a home. When she pulled herself together, all she was concerned about was making money."

Sardou had helped her find a location and raised the financing for the derelict buildings which she turned into a private men's club. Dues and club dinners, catered by the Dantons, were hardly profitable and so she added other amenities to the guttered old guesthouse known as the Estaque. It had been a seedy inn for commercial travelers but retained a license to operate as a hotel and sell liquor. This made it a valuable asset.

"It started as a men's club," Sardou continued. "I was like a busker. I brought everyone in. Willing clients, unwilling businessmen, senators, deputies. The prefect of police. Then reality and Louise's business shrewdness took over. All of these wealthy men wanted a pretty girl while they were in town. They weren't about to leave their wives or break up their homes.

"Louise hired exceptionally pretty young waitresses and barmaids. In a few months, she had a stable of them, willing to pick up extra money for favors. Her *maison* was the natural offspring. In a sense I paved the way for her to become a madam."

"And what did you get out of it?"

Sardou removed his tortoiseshell spectacles and wiped a tear from his eye.

"Once a month we met in Marseille: had dinner; took a walk along the Canebière; went to the cinema. Sometimes she wanted to go dancing. I would have given up my practice to marry her. God, I loved her."

"Thank you for being so honest with me."

The elderly barrister still appeared lost in the thicket of his youth and what might have been, if Louise Vercours had agreed to marry him.

"I'll want to talk to you to privately another time. It has nothing to do with Louise's murder," Sardou said obscurely.

Michel was puzzled by the remark and the dead ends that wove through the inquiry. They continued to entrap him. He knew more about Louise Vercours than he ever had. But amid the gossip and scandal, he had been unable to uncover a specific clue or a motive that would enable him to solve the mystery of her murder. More and more he found himself drifting away from the core of the search. But he remained convinced that the killers had not known Louise well.

He was searching for a rhythm, a melody line, but the case resisted any crystallized structure or form. Yet he recognized that the killers had their own convoluted theory of the aesthetics of death, a flight into magical darkness. They had to make a mistake.

In a daze, he walked toward Jennifer, who was at a bookstall. He idly watched her thumbing through some old magazines. For a moment she ignored him and he wondered if he were back in the approach-avoidance process Yvette had brought to a fine art. Had he also misread Jennifer?

"You're screwing up my first free time," she said finally. "For God's sake, we're in Aix-en-Provence. The weather's gorgeous. I assume we're crazy about each other. Do you have to spend all your time on murder?"

He put his arms around her and smiled. "No, of course not. I'm going to see my psychiatrist. I'd like company."

"Do you mean that?"

"We won't be long and maybe you can help."

"Is this your idea of quality time?"

"Don't you want to get to know who I really am?"

CHAPTER 33

The Hôtel Montcalm's army of concierges and bellmen leapt from their posts to greet Adam and Karen Gold, veterans of a score of film festivals. They trooped through the busy lobby bowing to Adam, who was barefoot and carrying crocodile loafers under his arm. He waved his hellos with a stack of hundred-dollar bills. A number of guests watched, fascinated by the raw display of power.

Boy had on a wide-brimmed sun hat and a pair of black Ray•Bans. He peeped up from behind a copy of *Sports Illustrated* to watch the Golds' ceremonious arrival. Bursting out of his safari jacket, Adam Gold was a short lard barrel, balding, with five o'clock shadow. According to Maddie, he could eat his own weight in pastrami. Karen's staccato voice pierced the lobby. She'd been a TV bit part player. Her sallow skin had a plastic surgery sheen, but she still moved with lithe grace and wiggled her ass. Maddie called her Plastic Polly and told Boy that her mother had always played a dead body. She didn't flinch or move a muscle when the camera was revealing her death wounds. Boy had laughed when Maddie related how Karen Gold's career had ended. A reviewer in *Variety* had noticed Karen's performance in one too many shows and commented on her many lives. "Like Esther Williams—'Wet, she was a star'—dead Karen Gold should get an Emmy."

Boy wore a pair of decent white shorts, new Reeboks and a green Lacoste shirt, which he'd bought earlier on Rue d'Antibes while getting the lay of the land. It was now two o'clock. They were on schedule. It was ninety-three miles from Aix to Cannes. Maddie was due at five. She'd stop along the way to get her hair colored. Dinner would be at nine at the Moulin de Mougins.

The Golds were walking to the elevator. Adam wanted to know about the TV reception and was assured it was perfect. Four Sonys had been installed for their visit. Boy observed the dial of the elevator. It went directly to the eighth floor.

He left the hotel and walked quickly down the Croisette to the Quai St-Pierre. Leaning against the boat where he'd spent the night, he phoned Françoise at the pension. They put someone on who spoke a jumbled English. But he was able to understand. Françoise was out. Then he asked for Monsieur Karim. No, he hadn't checked in yet, but was expected.

Boy looked up when he heard a clapped-out engine sputtering to a halt across the street. Karim got out of a tinny old crate and Boy dashed across the street.

"How's my main man?"

"Ah, Darrell, I'm glad to be here finally. It turned out to be a terrible trip."

"Got to get you some new wheels, Karim. Come on, let's grab a drink and some food."

Boy picked the crowded fish joint next to the Pension Martell. Nobody would remember them. Karim was in an ecstatic mood. He was going to be made a partner in the porn shop. Françoise was to get the plum assignment of recruiter for Gerard.

"See, I'm lucky for you."

"I believe you are." Boy had to avert his eyes. Karim was gorging on snails and mopping up green butter with hunks of bread. "It's a pity that all this is because of Louise's death. Until they quarreled, Louise was very good to Françoise."

"A real saint, huh. I'm sure everyone misses a madam."

Boy enthusiastically outlined their social agenda. He took out some cash and slipped it into Karim's greasy hand.

"What's this?"

"A gift from me and Maddie."

"Five thousand francs!"

Boy had him hallucinating, as he sucked him in with more goodies: Dinner at the Moulin at nine-thirty; Karim was to rent or buy a white dinner jacket and bring flowers.

"I'm so happy. I can't wait to see Françoise. Do you know where she is?"

"We had brunch at the Carlton. She said she's gone shopping for a party dress and she has a six o'clock date—"

Karim developed a sudden case of scruples. "It will be her last one!"

"Hey, a man has to live. It doesn't matter to Françoise. She loves you. You're a champion of political dreams. Arabia is bein' torn apart."

"Algeria," said the patriot. "Every penny Françoise earned tortured me."

Karim was wringing his hands, a little late as far as Boy was concerned. "Next case, Karim. We're on champagne time now. Maddie's parents are real eager to meet her friends. They want to take us for a vacation to Monte Carlo."

"Monte Carlo! It's hard to believe, Darrell, how fortunes change in an instant."

"You were stand-up for us from the get-go. We don't forget our friends. It's easy street for you and Françoise now."

Boy outlined his plans to an elated Karim.

"Ask for the Gold party at the restaurant. And do something dramatic. You know, like a romantic Frenchman. When you get to the table, pick Maddie up in your arms and kiss her. Her folks love all that movie stuff. It'll be a gas. I'll see you there at nine-thirty. And dress yourself up like the king you are."

"This is like a dream from the *Koran*, Darrell."

Boy sang a line from an old Karen Carpenter song:

" 'We've only just begun . . .' "

Maddie wrapped a scarf over her hair when she left the tacky hair salon in Fréjus. The color was excellent. The young hairdresser had worked quickly and had not been one of those noisy personalities who bent her ear. She knew it was a one-timer.

The chauffeur was sitting at a café table on the Rue Jaures where she'd left him. He was drinking a Coke and reading a real estate brochure. He rose without commenting about the delay. She had told him that she wanted to walk around for a few hours.

"How long will it take to get to Cannes?"

"It depends on the traffic. By five, I believe, mademoiselle."

She dreaded this final encounter with her parents, but she would play her role to the hilt. She would never let Boy down.

CHAPTER 34

Unlike Louise's lusty Chambertin, which achieved its maximum density after eight years, Michel knew that murders did not improve with age. The nose went first, followed by the clarity; ultimately all that was left would be a mucky sediment at the bottom.

Jennifer sat in a corner of Dr. Leon Stein's office batting the psychiatrist's cigar smoke out of her eyes. He was not pleased to have her present, but relented when Michel informed him he was back on retainer for the Special Circumstances Section at five hundred francs an hour. A woman's point of view, an outsider, might prove helpful.

"I have no suspects and feeble hunches. I'm at an impasse on these cases," Michel declared to Dr. Stein. "The only common thread was robbery." Michel picked up a pile of faxes and computer reports. "We have somewhere around a million couples between here and Nice who are youthful and go to the beach. The women have had their summer hair bleach and bikini-wax."

"Let's concentrate on Louise. I saw the forensic report. It's appalling. From what we know about Louise, I think she was certainly coerced into this *ménage à trois.*"

"Louise wasn't a lesbian."

"The couple have done this before," Stein said, relighting his cigar. Michel felt a new clarity emerging. "It's a component of their sexual dynamics."

"And is a curling iron part of this ritual?"

"I'm not sure."

"They must have brought one along. It wouldn't be an afterthought. In fact, Denise was sure Louise never used one."

Michel was persuaded that the robbery of Louise's jewelry and ready cash was secondary. The expertise of this murder and its sexual elements were interrelated.

"Who brings the curling iron, Leon? The man or the woman?"

"One would think the woman. Maybe she was once burned by her mother. Or by someone she trusted. Possibly at school by a teacher."

Jennifer had not expected to be fascinated by the discussion and burst in. "I'd vote for one of the schoolgirls. The jealous bully. Do you think she might have a scar on her face or her body?"

Michel nodded with approval. "That's a possibility. Well, we can also assume that the curling iron symbolically represents a penis, red hot, burning its way into the female orifice in a godlike engagement."

The suggestion pleased Stein, who still regarded Freud as a king despite his reputed affairs and fondness for cocaine.

"I'm uncomfortable with the thought of a woman physically torturing another one," Michel said, observing Jennifer's reaction.

"Enough of them in the asylum," Stein said.

"I'm thirty and I've spent twenty-five years in schools and my mother's a teacher," Jennifer said. "Girls who behave that way are invariably caught in adolescence. Someone notices their conduct and reports it." The two men nodded. "A man did this. He organized it."

"He's the sadist, the woman's the disciple," Michel added. He closed his eyes. "I see a young woman with a hardened, older man. She'll do anything to please him. He's the stronger of the two. It's like the relationship of a pimp and a whore."

"The man's perversion would have begun in childhood. Certainly before he was ten," Stein said.

"Older women played sexual games with him. And he became a slave? Would that fit this kind of profile, Leon?"

"If it was a mother or sister or a babysitter, he might have killed her. Either that or he worships her. There are always these polarized tensions in this form of pathology. I don't know that your assumption is correct about him being hard. His affect would not necessarily be frightening."

Michel proposed another scenario. "He's a sorcerer, then. He uses his talent for seduction and he finds an impressionable girl."

Stein rummaged for a fresh cigar. "That still doesn't suggest a motive for murdering Louise. I can't conceive of Louise walking in on a burglary and your couple stopping everything to torture her to death." Leon flipped over a few pages of the police inventory. "Here's a Bang and Olufsen stereo system worth thousands. Easy to sell in a market. They didn't take it."

"The motive is obscure and when I find this lovely couple, it'll still be obscure to rational people." Michel was pained by the irony. "So for reasons unknown, they force Louise to have sex with them."

"Against her will," Jennifer cried out.

"That's what excites the man. It's a role reversal. Louise becomes the prisoner he once was," Stein said, warming to Jennifer.

"Let's consider the nature of his sexuality. Is he a homosexual or not? Does he like it both ways?"

"No, Michel," Stein said forcefully. "He's projecting his homosexual fantasy on the women. He doesn't trust himself and he has to obliterate those feelings. They're degrading for him. I'd bet he's had relationships with men. You see, in a normal one-on-one alliance the introduction of another party is anathema. A partnership or joint venture is formed by attraction, trust and love.

"Bringing in another person is an incalculable threat in a heterosexual union. It is a fact that gay men frequently employ more than one partner and that their sexuality is often violent. Now I'm not talking about the roots of homosexuality or implying that it's wrong. In a free society, there's room for everyone."

Michel heard the chords of music at last. The crime had a melody he could hear. The full orchestra was engaged. He had been right to bring Leon Stein and Jennifer in at this stage. She was unfettered by conventional notions of bizarre crime and her background as a teacher was proving useful.

"The male killer was forced into homosexual relationships. And I know where. He's been in prison. And he was raped there. Or even perhaps as a child at school. But raped he was," Michel said with growing confidence. "For a man to take revenge with this degree of savagery, the experience must have been horrible for him and it was one that was repeated. Nevertheless, he loves to kill and has murdered many times."

Stein wearily set down the crime scene photographs.

"I'm glad I cleared you. I can see you're fit for duty."

"Meeting Jennifer did me more good than all our sessions."

Stein smiled at her. "We'll see."

"I have a horror of all this, but I can't let Michel out of my sight. Our time is so precious to me."

"You're a brave woman to listen to all this talk," Stein said. "Now I have one final thought before I have a patient to see. Lasque and Fabret coined the term *folie à deux* in 1877. They promoted the idea of the infectiousness of insanity. They proved that delusional ideas and abnormal behavior could be transferred from one person to another in an intimate relationship.

"Now assume the man has a powerful personality that overwhelms a young woman. We see it in marriages all the time. The woman's a mouse, the husband's a loud bully. Ironically, the woman very often comes to the man's defense if he's challenged or accused of treating her badly. Now in this case your dominant male killer imposes his psychosis on the woman, the weaker partner. He seduces her and the woman submits to his machinations."

"Charles Manson colonized a *family* who killed for him," Jennifer said, chilled by her own suggestion. "Something like that couldn't happen in Provence, could it?"

CHAPTER 35

"And there she is, our *tateleh*," Adam Gold said, embracing Maddie. Wet kisses squelched on her cheeks. "Look at her, Karen. She's so beautiful."

"And she's become an angel," Karen Gold said, squeezing Maddie. "My God, what a lady you are, Maddie. We're so proud of the way you've turned things around."

"Jennifer has praised you to the heavens."

"She's introduced me to a new world of art and the symbolist poets. I've started reading Rimbaud in French. How do you like that, folks?"

"I'm impressed," Adam said remotely.

Maddie squirmed but forced herself to smile. "All I needed was to get rid of you two guys."

"And one other guy!" her father noted ominously.

They sat on the large penthouse terrace, which provided a panoramic view of the Croisette. The hotel had placed a telescope outside so that Karen could indulge in one of her favorite hobbies, spying on the luxury yachts to see who was on board. She and Adam had dozens of invitations for parties.

A waiter wheeled out a cart; on platters were a side of smoked salmon, a sliced pumpernickel and a large bowl of caviar; two bottles of Cristal rested in ice buckets.

"Come on, it's cocktail hour," Adam said, pouring glasses up to the brim. "Eat, drink, be merry."

"I want to buy you some clothes, Maddie," her mother said. "That Armani suit you're wearing looks like *dreck*."

"It's fine, Mother."

"Take it off and put on a robe. We'll have the maid iron it."

"Jesus, it's linen, it's supposed to wrinkle."

"After dark, never during sunlight," Adam observed.

"You'll wear one of my Bob Mackies."

Maddie dug her heels in. "I will agree to an ironing but not Bob Mackie."

"A Valentino or Chanel, then," Karen insisted. "Make Mom happy, come on, pick one, darling."

They babbled on. They would be introducing her to Roger Vergé, the celebrated owner-chef of Moulin de Mougins, and might also run into some friends. Maddie sulked and wondered how she had endured the two of them for her entire life. She wished that Boy had attended to them in California.

"Mother, we're not going to an Oscar night party."

"Okay, okay, let her be, Karen."

"Oui, mon chéri," Karen warbled.

The sound of her mother's phony voice was like a bee sting. "You've still got your check-in French, I see."

"Yes, baby, and check-out as well." She looked at Adam. "Your father and I want to settle some old business with you, then get on the merry-go-round for a good time."

Maddie heard the peal of thunder behind "old business." Adam glared at her for a moment before reaching into his attaché case. He handed her a folder with CONFIDENTIAL typed in bold red.

"This is the only copy of a dossier I was given."

"Paid for," Karen interjected.

"Right, paid for. Now listen up, young lady."

Maddie looked blankly at them. "What's this crap about?"

Adam Gold extended his chubby hands and created the image of a TV screen in the air. It was like a network pitch meeting. He gave Maddie a strained smile.

"Let's do the opening sequence as a flashback, okay?" he said. "It's after Christmas when your mother and I went down to Palm Springs for three days. You didn't want to go because you hate the desert and our five-million-dollar house. Didn't matter that I was being honored with the Good Samaritan Man of the Year Award. Remember, Maddie?"

"I can't keep up with these awards you and your friends give each other." Maddie was losing it and pulled herself together. "But I am proud of you, Dad."

"That's nice to know." His tone turned brusque. "Kevin Sullivan advises all the heavy hitters in the industry about security. He's also a private detective and has a home protection business. He recommended I put in a Las Vegas–type 'eye in the sky' security system. He's also my consultant on cop shows."

"What else is new, Dad?"

"Just hear your father out," Karen said waspishly, panning the telescope.

"Adam Gold does not want to make his home a prison with bodyguards. So he agrees to use this casino technology. Every room is computer-monitored. If there's a problem, help is five minutes away. There are also silent alarms. Maddie, I don't want to live in a fortress. People can come and go. I hate those muscle-bound bozos who strut around with walkie-talkies and guns. All they do is intimidate everybody."

"We've never had them, why start now?" she asked. "I just don't get this, Dad. Where is this going?"

"Exposition, angel. A pilot show can't work without it. So pay attention. "We have millions in paintings and antiques . . . plus Mom's jewelry. There's also the small consideration of our personal safety and the safety of anyone who comes to the house. You know I like to have my show-runners over to brainstorm away from the office phones."

He paused as though entering commercial time.

"I want you to understand that there was no attempt to spy on you. And it wasn't invasion of privacy. It's a system that's monitored twenty-four hours a day. And I forgot to mention it to you when we left for Palm Springs."

Maddie fought to control the sickness worming through her body. She thought she might faint. No, they couldn't have done this to her and Boy. It was inconceivable. She slowly regained her faculties and recalled the events clearly. She had begged off on the Palm Springs weekend. Karen had come to her aid: the desert did not agree with Maddie. She had been given three days' liberty for good behavior.

Her father pushed ahead, oblivious of the wound of this disclosure.

"Kevin was passing the monitoring station when you and this guy got it on. What caught Kevin's attention wasn't that an adult woman—*my daughter!*—was having sex. It was an image. This naked guy in your bed has two snakes, *copperheads,* tattooed on his buttocks! And another one on his penis."

Maddie felt the sweat running down her back and swayed on her feet.

"Kevin was terribly worried. After you went back to Pembrooke, he came to me with great reluctance. Maddie, what you do in your personal life is your business. What you do under my roof becomes family business. Now neither your mother nor I saw the tapes. We didn't want to."

"Never. *Feh*. We don't have the stomach for it!" Karen said.

"There are tapes of me?" Maddie asked, still dazed.

"They've been destroyed," Adam Gold informed her.

Maddie was grim and boiling over, struggling to contain her rage. But she stuck to the plan Boy had devised. Under no circumstances was she to walk out on them. She didn't buy her father's tale about forgetting to inform her that she'd be on video in her bedroom and in the toilet! They had put her under surveillance, rooted through her clothes and drawers, trying to nail her for drugs over the holiday. She did not confront these monsters who called themselves parents.

Her mother turned away from the yacht crowd. "Do you have any comments?"

"No . . . I guess, in a way this pie-eye system was for my benefit." She appeared contrite and shoveled out a payload of Boy's down-home blarney. "It was the first time. And I can't tell you how much I regret the incident. No drugs were involved. I made a terrible mistake."

"Amazing, Adam, she understands, finally. Kevin thinks this snake-man was a psycho. Maybe he does stag films . . . As your mother, I find it too distasteful to consider."

While Adam made himself a caviar and smoked salmon sandwich, Karen stretched out on a chaise longue and with a groan continued her chronicle of maternal tribulation.

"Maddie, when you wanted to bring down some of your friends for your birthday in May, and had a yen for Chinois, I called Wolfgang Puck and arranged it. You had a lovely party. But it was spoiled when you introduced your father and me to this creep who was sitting at the bar. He scared us to death. Kevin had given us a head shot of him. A still. His *eyes* . . . he looked like he belonged in an asylum and not out on the street."

"He's had his problems. He must've been stalking me."

"Really? Well, after that Dad asked Kevin to keep an eye on you at Pembrooke. He did his best. And you and this animal—whatever his name is—pushed Kevin's car over the cliff."

Jaws clenched, and the hors d'oeuvres tray a victim of chaos theory, Adam Gold resumed.

"Kevin was very angry about your making a schmuck out of him. He's a tenacious man—ten years in homicide on the LAPD—and he had to get to the bottom of this and made it his personal crusade. So apart from putting in an insurance claim, he had various parts of the car checked for fingerprints.

"His came up naturally and the police had a record of this Darrell Boynton character. What he didn't expect was *your* fingerprints. So stop lying."

"Okay, it was a sex thing. But it's over."

Adam gulped his champagne. "I had to buy Kevin a new Chrysler, loaded with all his sophisticated gear so he'd forget about this humiliation. I also gave him ten big ones *not* to file a police report on you and the snakeman."

Her parents had been quietly hysterical during her time in Aix-en-Provence. Still, Maddie had not expected this brawl. She had been tutored by Boy. "Let them roll over you and don't give them any lip." She followed his advice to the letter, loathing the two of them more each moment. Oh, how she craved to be there when the valiant deed took place. She had loved entering Boy's world and killing Louise. It was all she could do to restrain herself from picking up the sharp knife that lay on the room service trolley. Her parents were control freaks. They'd never let her be free. If they had given her enough money, she never would have had to prostitute herself at Louise's.

"When you put the flier about summer school in Aix on my dressing table, I immediately told your father. And we went up to Pembrooke to see if Jennifer would go with you. We had to lose this character or you'd be sunk."

"It worked," Maddie said amiably, looking at her watch. "It changed my life. I can't tell you how grateful I am, Mom."

"Oh, my baby," she cooed. "Jen says you've been a diligent student, and that you've found a new romance with a French musician."

"I have. André's very creative."

"Now *him* we'd like to meet, wouldn't we, Adam?"

"I'd love you to," Maddie said, while her father scraped out the last of the caviar. "I'll arrange it as soon as I possibly can."

As if by magic, a pair of masseuses, carrying fold-up tables, appeared.

"You want a rubdown, Maddie?" her father asked, looking drained.

"No thanks, Dad."

"See you both shortly. I've got a few calls to make to the Coast. Have a nap, Karen. And get ready to rumble," he added.

Karen leaned down and kissed Maddie. "Please your father and try on some of my clothes. Shop, whatever. We'll be a couple of hours." She handed Maddie the dossier on Boy. "If I were you, I'd read about this guy. Maddie, you have the world at your fingertips, don't blow it with some maniac loser like him."

For once Maddie followed her mother's instructions and scanned the report. What could it tell her that she hadn't sensed or experienced? Maddie tore the pages into small pieces and savagely threw them off the balcony. Boy's previous history floated down on the Croisette like the confetti she had seen her father pitch at a Cannes film festival.

"Snakes and fire / Will halt desire," she crooned.

Adam was off the phone and came up behind Maddie on the terrace. "You say something, babe?"

"No, Dad. I was humming something André wrote." Maddie snuggled against her father. "Thanks for looking out for me, Daddy. I really screwed up royally. I'm sorry about Kevin's car."

"Okay, sugar. You know—no matter what—you'll always be my baby girl."

At eight, when the Golds left the suite, swanning in the mirrors beside the elevator, Maddie stopped abruptly.

"Oh, can I have the key? I've got to use the bathroom."

Adam handed it to her. "You okay, *chuchie?* I didn't mean to give you the third degree."

"Yes, fine. I won't be long."

"We'll be at the bar," Karen said.

"See you downstairs. You two look fabulous."

Karen held Maddie at arm's length. "And you, was I right or was I right about the Valentino?"

"What a figure she's got. We made a beauty, Karen," he said proudly. "When you're through with school, sweetheart, I'm going to put you in one of my shows."

"How come?" Maddie asked.

"You're a natural actress."

Maddie walked slowly back to the suite. Don't run, Boy had cautioned. Take your time. Look for surveillance cameras and hotel snoops. Maddie opened her purse and dropped her compact and lipstick. She knelt down and lifted the carpet in front of the suite door. Looking behind her and down both ends of the hallway, she slid the key underneath the carpet and pushed back the edge.

Like geometry, the act of murder had its own inviolable laws for Boy. Don't repeat an MO unless there is a reason. Never use drugs or drink. Stay away from bars. Avoid shops, someone may notice. Don't wear bright clothes, shorts or T-shirts. Have on running shoes. Be sure to have at least two routes of escape. Get going early.

Blending in with the crowd of early evening shoppers along Rue d'Antibes, Boy had become invisible. He had meticulously worked his way through Le Suquet's narrow, twisting streets until he had a fix on the watch tower. The place was mobbed with sightseers. He continued his excursion until he reached Mistral Square. It was also crowded, with strollers, couples having picnics, kids playing soccer.

At five-thirty he strolled by Nôtre-Dame-d'Espérance. The sun was a fireball and he walked close to the Gothic church to avoid the blinding light. He was getting antsy. There was a tree-lined terrace and high bushes behind the chapel. He hoped Françoise would be on time.

In a few minutes, he spotted her climbing up the hill. Her new dress was on a hanger and slung over her shoulder.

"Ah, Boy, you're here already. Is Karim inside?"

"I left him at the tailor. He was being fitted." Boy moved closer to her. "He cleans up real good. Just like you." Françoise looked elegant and beautiful. "You're a heartbreaker. I love your new hair color." The shade was very close to Maddie's the night they had murdered Louise.

"All thanks to you. I thought I'd change into my dress when Karim and Maddie arrive."

He affectionately cupped her chin in his palm. "Oh, we won't get you wrinkled, I promise."

She giggled with childlike mischief and he realized that the brassy blond hair had made her look older and hard.

"I'm very fond of you, Boy."

A couple left the church and Boy swiftly turned away. When they walked off, he put his arm around Françoise's waist. She was getting the message. She kissed him on the cheek, then lightly on the mouth.

"You smell so good, sugar." She rolled her eyes. "Maddie's going to pick up Karim. They're going to be at least an hour late."

She looked at Boy with desire. "That's not so terrible."

"Not for me. At brunch, well, kitten, you made me wonder."

"About what?"

"You know what . . . I couldn't get you out of my head all day. I'm really in the mood."

"Oh, are you?" She now had a mysterious coyness that attracted him. "So am I. Aren't we lucky?" Boy slipped on a pair of surgical gloves. "What are those for?"

"You ever play games, like doctors and nurses in France?"

She was ripe. "Ooooh, you want to examine me?"

"I sure do, Nurse Françoise," he whispered, kissing her ear.

"What an exciting idea, Dr. Boynton."

He took a pair of Louise's diamond earrings out of a plastic bag and handed them to her.

"For me?"

"They'll set off your new hair style."

"They're exquisite! They must be worth a fortune."

"Put 'em on."

"What a giving man you are. Come, I know a private place. I'm going to do something for you that Maddie could never dream of."

Françoise led him to a thicket of bushes behind the terrace. In an instant she had unzipped his fly.

"Oh, how I've wanted you." She stroked him. "*Mon Dieu.* It's Hercules. And the tattoo. Magnificent. You'd make a fortune doing porn films."

"I'll have to think about that one," Boy said, restraining the furies that took flight in his mind. "I'll bet you'd like naked pictures of me."

"Yes, who wouldn't?" Her voice was a low hiss. "I'd keep one in my wallet."

"And what would you do with it?"

"What do you think . . . ?"

Boy pulled two thick, garish beach towels from his backpack. He laid one on the ground. Françoise deftly stepped out of her new black silk panties. She dropped to her knees on the towel.

"Come to me, my angel. You're the sexiest man I've ever met."

"That's what they say . . ."

With his back to her, Boy packed the .45 automatic in the other towel. Françoise had her top off and was offering her breasts to him. She stretched out on the towel. Boy leaned down as if to kiss her.

"Françoise, when you promise to split money with someone who's done your trick, it's not a good idea to break your word."

The haunted expression in his eyes and the icy pitch of his voice made her shiver. Her fear became palpable and excited Boy.

"*Je ne comprends pas.* I gave the money to Karim. I told you I had to."

"Doesn't matter any more," Boy said with a smile.

He fired a single shot into her left temple. The report was muffled.

Fingers frozen on her breasts, Françoise lay there with a tortured smile on her face. Boy couldn't resist her white belly. He slipped out his knife.

CHAPTER 36

"I heard voices," **Benedict,** a mite tipsy, growled at the bar of Chez Danton. He was a defrocked priest who had been adopted by Louise to serve as her concierge. He picked up change with clients and the girls by claiming that he had the powers of a psychic and for ten francs ran the Tarot for them or cast a horoscope for newborns. The last time Michel had encountered him he had said, "I knew you were coming . . . You're happy and even more in love with Yvette. In fact, I have a feeling that a marriage hovers." So much for Louise's star-gazer. His recurrent cataracts made him ineffectual as an eyewitness, but through the gray fog he could sniff out a cop as quickly as a cassoulet. He leaned over the bar and collared René. "I may be going blind, but my hearing is excellent. Someone has to listen to me. Michel, come off the boule court."

"How'd you know I was out there?"

"Your stroke makes a particular clack when it strikes the *cochonnet*."

"So if I was on the firing range, you could tell when my bullet hit the target?"

"Anything's possible."

Michel joined him on the next stool. "René, how many drinks has Benedict had?"

"Four. Fortunately, he can't drive."

"Pour him another," Michel said.

Benedict's long mottled fingers reached through the frayed cuff of an ancient blue serge jacket. A black ribbon was tied around his arm like a blood-pressure sleeve; as if this weren't enough, he had on a hand-painted tie of something that might have been splattered ratatouille, with a bulbous knot the size of a Gypsy onion.

"There was a report that you and Celeste were interviewed by Claude when he arrived at the scene."

"No, it was that idiot Courbet." He raised his glass. "*Merci,*

Michel. I must apologize for my prediction about you and Yvette. The planets were in retrograde."

"I forgive you for the starless nights with her."

Benedict caught a welt of phlegm on a bar napkin and was in the mood to ramble on with his drink. He sniffed the humid air, inhaling deeply.

"Boeuf Mironton."

Michel looked at a waiter's tray. Beef in onion sauce it was. "Correct. Would you like Delantier to bring you back a portion tonight?"

"Yes. My nose is good."

René leaned over and pondered the large blotchy instrument fanned by hairs. "It's in the Escoffier range."

"Now listen to me . . . Before Madame arrived, I distinctly heard two other voices, a young man and a young woman. I told Courbet about it. He accused me of always hearing voices and dismissed me as a loon." Michel urged him to continue. "I said goodnight to Madame; she told me to sleep well. Then there were three voices. Hers and the couple's."

"Tell me about the other voices." Michel leaned closer. The soothsayer's breath had the fierceness of napalm. "Another pastis for him, René."

Only when his drink was replenished would Benedict continue. "They spoke English."

"Was it a British accent or American?" Michel asked, containing his excitement.

"More American than British. I couldn't swear to it."

"What else did you hear?"

"The woman used a word that sounded like *bois.*"

"Wood?"

"I may be mispronouncing it, but that's like it."

Michel pondered over this enigma, but it confirmed his surmise. The couple weren't French or European. They might have been university students, tourists. Thousands of them. But he had built cases from even more tenuous leads and elusive witnesses.

After Benedict had been shuttled out, Michel ran into Jennifer outside the restaurant. He felt a new reserve, a wariness that had intruded like a snake at a picnic.

"I came looking for you earlier, Michel."

"Sorry, I was tied up in Marseille with Annie. We were trying to piece together the murders of the young Americans at the dam. They were listening to music on the radio. The station was having a tribute to Streisand. They did an hour of her songs at the time of those murders. My guess is that the couple never heard the killer approach."

"I've been doing some thinking, Michel . . ." He recognized this immediately as a bad sign and waited uneasily. "Let's take a walk."

He considered this another sinister harbinger of Jennifer's disengagement. The silence blossomed poisonously down the Cours Mirabeau all the way to the Nine Cannons fountain where they stopped and observed elderly rheumatics filling their jugs with the water.

"This is becoming too much for me, Michel. I'm blown out. It scares me. I appreciate your confidence in me. But . . . I don't know if I've got the nerves for it."

"No one does," he admitted. "It's a challenge."

"I don't know how to deal with it. I never should have gone with you to Dr. Stein's. Afterwards, I kept having these frightful visions of Louise being murdered."

"You helped me. Jennifer, when these cases are over, we'll discuss my career."

"Would you quit?"

Stein had warned him that he was not ready for emotional weight. "Jennifer, my ego is fragile. I wouldn't admit that to anyone but you. I have to see this through."

She put her arms around him and tilted his face toward hers for fear of losing his attention.

"These cases can take years, can't they?"

He was afraid this might turn out to be true. "It's a possibility."

"That's exactly what's alarming me."

CHAPTER 37

Dressed in a new Armani white dinner jacket, and carrying a bouquet of roses, Karim observed the crowd at the Moulin de Mougins. He was bewitched by the ivy-covered ancient olive mill which had been converted into a world-famous restaurant. It had a superb garden, which he peeked at from the entrance. Waiters were gently heating dishes in copper pans. The scent of truffles intoxicated him and his senses exploded. Here was where he and Françoise belonged. One day they'd have the money to eat with friends at Michelin-starred restaurants. At the moment, he no longer felt alienated from the upper-class French who treated people like him with disdain. He could fit in with this wealthy set.

Karim looked at his watch again. It was exactly nine-thirty. Where was Darrell—and, more important, where was Françoise? If she was still with a date, he'd slap her silly. He told the supercilious maître d' he was going to join the Gold party. He was ushered out to the garden, fragrant with lavender and night-blooming jasmine. Under a towering purple bougainvillea, he spied Maddie and her parents. Alongside them was the distinguished chef, in his whites and toque, leaning down to discuss the menu.

Karim tremulously snuck up on Maddie to surprise her. The diminutive girl had grace and poise in a high-fashion beaded white dress. He pulled her up from her chair, lifted her in his arms and kissed her passionately on the lips.

Something went terribly wrong with this greeting. Maddie clawed at him. Karim tried to back away, but she continued to strike him. Her screams brought the place to an amazed silence. People from other tables rose to come to her assistance. Crying and terrified, she shoved him away.

He found his voice, a weak cheep. "Maddie, it's me, Karim."

Adam Gold confronted Karim. "Who the hell are you?"

The assembly of diners at other tables uncomfortably listened in.

"He's been stalking me for weeks," Maddie shouted.

"Stalking you? Man, you get the hell away from my daughter. Or I'll kill you!"

Maddie spoke in French to Roger Vergé, who was alarmed by this scene at his restaurant. In a trembling, fearful voice, Maddie announced that Karim was an Algerian revolutionary who had threatened to bomb her apartment.

That was enough for everyone. A phalanx of waiters arrived. Karim was frog-marched out and thrown on the pavement of the parking lot with the warning that if he didn't leave at once, they would call the police.

In shock, Karim funneled himself into the backseat of a taxi. He had no idea what had caused this scene. He sat for a moment, staring into space, dazed by the insanity of Maddie's behavior. Finally, he told the driver to take him back to the Pension Martell.

In the ladies' room, Karen and Maddie were surrounded by clucking attendants. Karen Gold listened in horror to Maddie recounting the nightmare of her stay in Aix.

". . . He hangs around the university, selling dope. And he's been after me since I got here. Following me everywhere."

"Did you tell Jennifer?"

"I didn't want to frighten her."

"What about André? Couldn't he have done something?"

"Mother, he tried. This guy carries a gun. He's nobody to mess with."

Karen was crestfallen. "Oh, my poor baby. And everything was going so well."

Maddie shrugged it off. "I guess I just attract trouble."

They returned to the table in the disquieted atmosphere.

Adam hugged Maddie. "We'll call the cops."

"Please, don't. I'll speak to Jennifer's boyfriend. He's a big-shot detective in the French police. They're going to take this Karim out. He must've tracked me from the apartment. Look, I think the best thing would be for me to go back to Aix after dinner. I'll see Michel and Jen and tell them what happened."

Adam Gold was beside himself. "I don't get it."

"The reason we came to France was to spend a little time with you," Karen said.

"I'll meet up with you at the Hôtel du Cap. Look, I'm really upset.

And I can't miss my lecture tomorrow. It's on Rimbaud's poetry. *A Season in Hell*."

The Golds were bemused by the scholar's dedication.

"And what's that about?" Karen asked sardonically.

Maddie decided on this occasion, the last time she would ever see her parents, that they ought to learn something about what she and Boy had shared. She previously through study, and Boy by deed, had lived by the great symbolist poet's credo.

"Artur Rimbaud said, 'Morality is the weakness of the mind. We must create ourselves through a logical derangement of the senses.'"

Adam Gold was bewildered and laughed it off. "ABC will love this. It's perfect counter-programming against *Mad About You*." He forced himself to cheer up the party. "Let's lighten up."

"Oh, Dad, this isn't a sit-com. You'll never know who I am, until it's too late."

Maddie's eyes filled with tears of wrath and humiliation when she kissed them goodbye.

"Do you want to run over to the Carlton casino and gamble for an hour?" Adam asked Karen when they returned to their suite. "Might take our minds off Maddie."

"You go. I don't feel lucky." Karen started to unzip her mermaid Bob Mackie evening dress. She'd worn it because they were supposed to go dancing at the Palm Beach Casino after dinner. "I can't help it. I'm worried sick about her." The stillborn actress tried to reenact the scene at dinner. "How does something so bizarre happen? A crazy man comes into the restaurant and assaults Maddie. I am truly spooked."

No matter what plans the Golds made for Maddie, they could never do the right thing for their daughter. Whether it was picking a school, a party, taking her to the doctor, something always went wrong.

"How does she find these people?" Adam asked, untying his black bow tie. "Wherever there's dogshit, Maddie steps in it and brings it home. She has an affinity for it." He tossed his dinner jacket on the chair. "It's almost like she's got some kind of curse. And we're the ones always taking the rap. I've had it with her."

"What do we do?"

"We'll give her an allowance, let her move out and do whatever she wants."

"How can we do such a thing? She's a troubled girl."

The Golds sat across from each other in the most expensive suite in Cannes and were plainly miserable. Karen unclasped her ruby choker and slipped off her diamond rings. She tossed them on the table.

"Maybe we shouldn't have told her about that goddamn weirdo. Kevin did the report and we could have let it drop."

"Karen, darling, one thing has nothing to do with another. That Arab stalker is yet another freak Maddie's picked up. I'm not getting mystical now. But there are some people in life who have a kind of magnet that draws the blackest side of humanity to them. I believe Maddie is one of them."

Karen turned her face away and sobbed. She didn't want to hear this. She loved the girl and was convinced that, under Jennifer's tutelage, Maddie had made progress and changed for the better.

"Jennifer is a straight shooter," she said. "I have faith in her, and believe her when she says Maddie has turned over a new leaf. Tonight was some kind of accident."

"Please stop crying, Karen."

He was engulfed by her sadness. Since her childhood Adam Gold had tried to make his daughter happy. He played back all the good times he had arranged for her. Studio visits for her school friends; meeting movie stars; visiting a show in rehearsal; seeing it shot and finally watching the edited version in the living room with their parents. There had been a stream of private instructors, exotic vacations in Africa—the best money could buy. No matter what he had done for her, something ugly occurred. On a duck hunt, Maddie had wounded a guide by firing her gun in the wrong direction. When he recounted the event to Karen, she said, "Maybe she was aiming at you . . ."

In high school, there had been suspensions, then reinstatements after Adam coughed up serious money. Maddie had been accused of pushing a girl out of her car on a freeway. At fourteen she was pregnant and could not identify the father. Then the drugs and disappearances began. The lies were well crafted. He and Karen often weren't able to discern the truth. Maddie's history was an ongoing litany of destructiveness, misdeeds that bespoke a barbaric nature.

"I wish I could understand what makes her tick," Adam said.

"I do." A disembodied, mellow voice, with a southern lilt, drifted through the air.

The Golds surged out of their chairs and backed up to the terrace. They were stricken with a passiveness that was incomprehensible to Boy. Karen's eyes were wild with dread when he came out of the shadows. His gun was raised and a peaked hotel cap tilted low over his eyes, cloaking his face. He had on a pair of white overalls with *Montcalm* written on the pocket.

"The problem with Maddie is she hates you," Boy said by way of explanation. "You two have been hittin' on her, railin' at her, since she was a little kid. She can never please you." He gave off an air of calm professional assurance, a psychiatric specialist. "My opinion is that you never wanted her. She's one of them misbegotten kids like me."

Karen dizzily observed the scene as if the man calmly talking, and the gun pointed at her, came from a scene of dailies in one of Adam's TV shows.

"Mr. Gold, please call the hotel operator and tell her she's not to put in any calls till ten tomorrow morning."

"Don't do it, Adam!"

With a lightning-swift reaction, Boy slammed Karen with the back of his gloved hand and smashed her nose. She bounced against the terrace door, keeled over and hit the floor. Adam Gold was dumbfounded and froze in panic. He gazed dimly at Karen bleeding and groveling on her knees.

"Are you the guy from the restaurant?" Adam asked finally. "No, you're—"

"Pick up the phone or I'll blow your head off."

Adam Gold wavered, confused. "You're going to kill us, aren't you?"

"All I want is jewelry and money. And I'll clear out of here. I need some time to get away."

"Okay, that's good news." Adam quickly assessed the situation. "It'll be all right, Karen. See, he's wearing surgical gloves. That's what the professional burglars do."

Karen moaned and groped on the floor. She seized hold of a table and staggered to her feet. Blood spurted on the carpet. She knew she had blacked out from the blow. She was crying, and Boy helped her to a chair.

"Sit down, Karen, and put your head back. Just don't tell your husband what to do when I give him an order. I'll get some ice for you in a minute."

Adam was unhinged and did not recognize his own voice when he spoke to the operator. He remembered something he had been told by Kevin Sullivan: if he found himself in a spot with a burglar, avoid making eye contact. Don't argue. But Karen was not privy to this information. Karen whimpered miserably and stared at Boy. Adam wanted to warn her to look away, but he didn't dare.

"That was good, Adam. Now let's round up the cash and Karen's jewelry."

In a dream state, Adam went to the desk. Under Boy's vigilant eye, he unlocked his attaché case. Stacks of hundred-dollar bills with bank bands were piled high. In a pouch were more of Karen's rings and necklaces. Her rubies were still on the table and Boy scooped them up.

"Take it all," Adam pleaded, "and go."

"For sure. But I think we better all head for the bathroom and go potty," Boy said affably. "We also need some towels and ice for Karen's nose."

"Thank you. Can I help my wife?"

Boy nodded. Karen shakily walked, leaning on Adam. She stopped suddenly and trembled. "I'm so scared, Adam."

"It's okay, doll. He only wants to rob us."

"Are you going to lock us in? she asked hopefully.

"That's a good idea."

When they were inside the spacious marbled room with its vanity tables, his and hers commodes and a large Jacuzzi with a view window over the Croisette, Boy instructed Adam to turn on the water.

"Why?"

"Just do it. And I'd like you and Karen to undress and get in the tub."

"I don't want to undress, Adam." She was now shaking uncontrollably and swayed from side to side. "I'm afraid of him."

"You should be," Boy said.

What hope there was vanished when Karen, still in shock, said, "I *know* you! You cut your hair. It's short now—"

Adam gasped and Karen realized too late what she had said.

"Well, Miz Gold, no, you *don't* know me. You never gave me a chance. You and your husband high-hatted me. Treated me like dirt when Maddie introduced us the night of her birthday party at Chinois. I was so thrilled to meet you. I watched your TV programs when I was a kid." Boy's anger reached a new level. His face was contorted and they flinched. "And you humiliated me, in front of the woman I love."

Karen began to scream.

"Oh, God help us! It's *him*, the snakeman!"

"And how'd you know that?"

"Maddie told us," Adam replied spontaneously.

"Unh-uh. That's a lie. Now if you don't want somethin' terrible to happen, you'll both undress and get in the tub."

Adam Gold's voice cracked. "I always take showers."

"You'll do this to please me. And I won't hurt you."

They both stripped, chilled by the air conditioning and the terrifying serenity of Boy's demeanor, which had changed from rage to something worse. A fawning manner insinuated itself that did not deceive them. They were both in the tub, naked, twitching nervously.

"You have our money and everything, now go, please," Karen pleaded as she tried to cover her breasts with her arms.

Boy looked at them squirming like fish in a tank. He hated to make things simple and undramatic. He really wanted to do a number on them. But this had to be a riddle for the police. Mystery Man's voice spoke to him from a great distance: "No Fancy-Danning." Boy picked up a pillow that he had taken from the bed earlier.

"What's the pillow for?" Adam asked, wiping the sweat out of his eyes.

"I want you comfortable."

"Don't, don't do this. I can pay you anything, Mr. Boynton."

Boy toyed with Adam Gold until the wrath within him was built step by step. Murderous impulses were nothing new to him and the need to harness them required a heroic effort. His mind wandered again: what was it about these two that reminded him of Herm and Velma Gortz in their trailer?

"You gonna write me a check now? What've you done for me, sir? Well, I'll tell you. You wrote that bitch Jennifer a letter, bad-mouthin' me. Sayin' I was some kind of menace. Maddie found the letter and showed it to me. She destroyed it.

"Up at Ojai, when me and Maddie were out on a date, you sicked a goofball detective on us. We was just havin' a drink and shootin' the breeze in the cocktail lounge with the barmaid. Not hurtin' a soul. Kissin'. Lovin'. What's sinful about that? You must've thought I was some hayseed. Even when I was a child, I could've made that Irish detective in two minutes. Watchin' us from the bar at the motel in Ojai and talkin' on a cellular phone to one of his people. I assure you folks, he's lucky to be alive."

Boy's gelid eyes fixed on the Golds, cowering and holding each other.

"Now what kind of behavior's that for parents? You didn't know a thing about me, except I was mad for your daughter. And when someone's under my protection, they don't need *anybody*. Darrell Vernon Boynton looks after his people. Man, I'm a warrior. I could've taken that detective anytime I wanted. After the people I've done, that bag of slush would've been easy."

. . . People I've done . . .

The sinister words hideously tolled over and over again through Adam's mind. Karen huddled with him as the water streamed into the tub. Boy stood over them, ferociously waving the large gun.

"Please, Mr. Boynton." Karen clutched Adam's hand. "Maddie's been involved with some bad people, dangerous people, in the past."

Boy bellowed with laughter. "You might've thought they were dangerous. But darlin', Maddie was waitin' on me."

Karen gasped and Adam started to whimper. The tears dribbled down his cheeks. He fought to control himself. There had to be a way out, a deal to be cut.

"Don't be breakin' my heart, Adam."

For a moment, Adam thought he detected a signal, some hope. "You can have anything. Anything."

"When you cut off Maddie's money on this trip, you stripped her naked. You've got to give people some slack. Man, you took away her dignity. We was so broke, she went to a whorehouse and turned tricks one afternoon. And Maddie wound up *not* gettin' paid!" Boy screamed over the water filling the tub. "To me there's no worse sin. That poor gal I love did it for me. And she busted out. Maddie screwed two guys so as I'd have money to eat."

"Oh God, no, no," Karen bawled hysterically.

Boy's gloved hand savagely pressed against her windpipe.

"It's the righteous gospel, Karen. And then I had to give that young girl a taste for blood. It's a habit without a cure. If you're wonderin' how I got into your room, Maddie left me the key." He began to laugh. "I'm doin' you as a service to my lady."

"No, this can't be happening, Adam!"

Boy was tempted to strike Karen Gold but held back.

"If I was back home, I'd cut you both up in pieces and let you watch me feedin' your parts to my snakes. That's what I'd do."

Boy turned the tub jets on high and savagely glowered at them, curling up in the water. He knew they were too petrified to fight for their lives. There would be no signature to the crime, no clue or hint that this was anything but a grim robbery turned sour. Boy planted the gun in the pillow.

"Maddie said you used to be cast as a body, Karen. Dead, you were a star. Tonight I'm personally handin' you your Emmy . . ."

CHAPTER 38

Michel had discussed with his staff the conclusions he had reached with Leon Stein. In turn he had been inundated with a barrage of reports of strange sightings, violent arguments, suspicious foreign couples in Aix, Marseille—and it seemed throughout southern France. Communications on the mainframe computer from local police filtered in from the beach cities of the Côte d'Azur.

Airport security was put on alert by Richard Caron, but then it was always on alert because of radicals and bomb threats. In this instance, who would they be looking for? Michel wondered if the couple had already left the country. Had they murdered Louise, then caught a plane? Somehow he doubted it. No, they were in France, possibly still in Aix. But no other murders had been reported that bore a resemblance to Louise's or the Americans'. Unless his couple lost their self-possession, got drunk, high on drugs, they would not be conspicuous.

No one in Marseille's *milieu* had come forward with any tips. Louise had enjoyed a good relationship with the Corsicans who also ran brothels. But theirs were working class and not in competition with her high-class trade. The singular aspect emerging from Louise's background had been the absence of enemies. Michel mused over the strangeness of life, its period of carefree romps—the light skipping, like a stone hopping along a lake—and its morbid finales.

At three in the morning, it still nagged him and he was unable to sleep. He crept out of the farmhouse bedroom. He did not wish to wake Jennifer. With Maddie away, at least for the night, he had persuaded Jennifer to bring some clothes to the farm in St-Rémy.

He switched on a dim desk light in his old playroom which was filled with sports memorabilia. He picked up a soccer ball signed by Pelé. There was a framed photograph of the 1981 New York Yankees. They had lost the World Series to the Los Angeles Dodgers. He proudly recalled how a gracious Mickey Mantle, this time only an honored spectator at the series, had signed the brim of his baseball cap on the parking lot.

His collection of Napoleonic soldiers was in place and he idly began to move a brigade away from Moscow. He thumbed through his university books and pulled one down. Lévi-Strauss's *The Savage Mind*. What were the structural and cultural patterns that connected the killers with three different people? Was there a tribal rite involved?

Through the open window the early dew scent of wind-blown herbs entered the room. He spread out the police reports, which had been screened by Corinne before he left the office. He leafed through them, reflecting on his surmises. He tasted the clues.

Benedict had heard voices speaking English. Michel had no doubts about the acuteness of his hearing. Who would be around at that hour? Working people. Perhaps some hotel night clerks. There had been no hotel check-ins after midnight. It would have been too early for the porters or the farmhands to arrive at the markets.

Aix didn't attract the British hooligans. Students and music lovers came to the city for the festival. It was a place of romance, a university center. The English troublemakers preferred the beach. They would go to Calais, stock up on wine and beer; they might drive to the coast of Normandy, or to a cheap weekend in Ostend, where the girls were easy. The south of France was financially beyond their means. Only wealthy Brits and Americans could afford the high life of Cannes and Monte Carlo. People like Maddie and her parents. They would pay ten dollars for a bottle of Evian and not think twice.

The murder had required tremendous energy and ingenuity. One of the killers had been watching Louise's movements and knew where she was going. Someone who didn't have a job and could move freely, silently through the old quarter without arousing suspicion. A young man. Could it be an exchange student?

Michel rifled through more local police reports. Annie had mentioned a complaint made by property owners. He had it before him.

The first week in July a young American had appeared at the model apartments at Pont de l'Arc. They thought his name was Calhoun. He had claimed to be an American investor and duped the manager and the real estate agents. They had spoken with his banker and been assured he was the real thing. He had stayed in a furnished model apartment through July 16 and vanished. No one by the name of Eldon Royce Calhoun had come through immigration.

If this was a lark, it was high risk, Michel thought. The young man was described as well built, not tall, in his twenties, with long blond hair and a charming personality, very attractive.

"It's me, I didn't want to startle you." Jennifer rubbed her eyes.

"Couldn't you sleep?"

"No. I feel lost without you next to me."

She sat on his lap and he wrapped his arms around her waist. She was wearing red candy-striped pajamas. There was a refreshing propriety about her that he found bewitching. Perhaps she could help. Should he ask if she had noticed a young man of this description near the university?

"Michel, I've thought it through. I haven't been fair. You can't quit because of me. It would be like asking me to resign in the middle of a semester because I met someone I prefer to my students. Dumping girls I've worked with who can get into a fine school like Stanford, if I continued to push them. I'd ask you to be understanding and wait."

He was greatly relieved, for the stress was gnawing at him. "Then murder's on the menu."

"For the time being, it'll have to be."

She looked at him quizzically. "I've also been thinking about the three murders against my will. They're almost like late Cézanne paintings."

"How do you mean?"

"I don't know if it makes sense. But it's the way they're colored to create the balance and form with a palette knife. There's no underlying outline. They're almost two-dimensional without any sense of spatial perspective. It's as though, here's the picture, don't look beyond what's present. This is what I want the viewer to see."

Jennifer nestled her head against his broad chest. He was intrigued by her suggestion and wondered if a metaphor could solve a murder.

"Michel, I appreciate that this might be painful, but I want to know everything about you. If we're going to try to make something of this, you have to confide in me. I'm terrified when your mother says you belong back in a mental hospital. Why?'

"It's really between my psychiatrist and me."

He was guarded, then reluctantly gave in. They went out to the loggia and sat side by side on a rocker. A field of lavender stirred in the wind and the scent, combined with the rich beds of herbs, created a sense of paradise. Nothing could harm them except the past.

"About two and half years ago, we had an ugly case in Marseille. Two homeless women and a man, *clochards*, were murdered. Heads smashed in with bricks and shovels."

The local police were stymied but not especially troubled by these incidents. However, Michel's boss, Richard Caron, a man with a social conscience, was outraged and brought Michel in to investigate. The municipal people were delighted to turn over their scrappy files and attend to more pressing high-profile crimes.

"In ten days, I found the culprits. Two boys and a girl who were at the *lycée*. They were about fourteen. I was sick about it when I had to go to the school and arrest them. Émile and Annie Vallon came with me. She was in tears. But it had to be done. You think a case is cleared, everyone's convicted. A year later, you find it's alive.

"The court remanded them and sent them for psychiatric treatment to a special hospital. The parents were all respectable. This shattered their lives.

"I came home for Christmas, relieved that it was behind me. At that point I met Yvette. She was covering the case and she made a play for me. I was vulnerable. She moved into my flat.

"Even though I continued to brood about the case, it was over. And I had new assignments. The point is the case was *not* over. Now we come to the folly of an assumption. I'd been troubled by something. A missing piece. I followed up with social services, even though it was no longer my business. I read the psychiatric reports and they didn't ring true. I reinterviewed the parents and I was hardly a welcome guest."

Michel stared into the darkness. Jennifer held his hand, encouraging him to resume.

"One sunny afternoon, I dropped by the hospital and brought some fruit and sausages from the farm. I visited the girl for the first time. She was a slight, pretty, dark-haired little thing. I took a walk with her in the park. And she told me the truth.

"There was a *fourth* member of the murder party, the ringleader and planner.

"His name was Giorgio Vecchi, the fourteen-year-old son of Ciro Vecchi, head of the Union Corse. Kissing cousins of the Mafia. The Vecchi family moved from Marseille back to Ajaccio, where Ciro was the law. These island societies in Corsica and Sicily have old traditions in which enforcement of people's rights are carried out by these secret societies.

"As it happened, I had my Polaroid camera in the car. I asked the girl if she would let me take her picture. She wrote a little message to Giorgio on the back."

Michel had traveled alone, telling no one in the Legion that he would be investigating. On a whim, he had gotten on the ferry and had bought a ticket to Ajaccio. He located young Giorgio on a school football field. He had watched the boy and when practice was over, he introduced himself to Giorgio and took him for an ice cream.

Then in a spirit of a kindly visiting relative, he laid the snapshot of the girl on the table.

"Giorgio picked it up. On the back the girl had written: *I will love you always.* Giorgio began crying, pounding his hands against the wrought iron table. He was ready to come back with me. He was despondent and tormented for having let his friends take the blame. He'd deserted them. This is against everything his father taught him as well as the Union's ethics, such as they are. Still, in our modern world, loyalty of this kind is admirable. The group had agreed never to inform on each other. Giorgio and the girl were in love. Puppy love, we call it. But because of its innocence, it can be more powerful and binding than the adult version.

"I felt horrible about yet another arrest. Sending a fourth child to prison! My guts were churning. I hated myself. My conscience betrayed me!

"I thought of a line from Camus's *La Chute*: 'We can't assert the innocence of anyone, whereas we can state with certainty the guilt of all.'

"So what if I let Giorgio go? Then I realized what my action would mean. In five, ten years at most, he'd be like his father, the head of a criminal organization.

"Giorgio had already murdered three people for no reason. What's going to happen when he has a good reason? A judge, a cop, somebody who gets in his way over their business. He'll murder them in an instant. Or maybe he'll go to university, become a doctor, save lives, redeem himself.

"What was I thinking? My character has been so deeply flawed by probing through people's lives. At times I feel like Hamlet, incapable of action, because I understand the grammar of motives."

Michel had walked home with Giorgio after ice cream and tears. He met his father. Ciro Vecchi was a diplomat and a wise gentleman. Not a flashy gangster. Calm, reserved, intelligent. He understood everything. Giorgio was suffering and perhaps this was the best solution. Michel had been invited to dinner with the two of them at a local restaurant and he accepted.

"I see corruption in my hometown and I'm sickened by my willingness to let things slide. This one takes a bribe; that one looks the other way. And I'm looking the other way, too. What does it matter? It's so petty and venial. And yet, there's that moment, when I know

I'm God. I can transform someone's life, send him to prison, alter the entire circumstances of his family, ruin a generation, destroy love.

"I need Caesar to tell me what to do—not the Sextius Legion in Marseille. In the last six months, I've had time to think. Yes, it's exciting to solve a murder, but then what? Wait for the next one and the one after that."

He paused, and Jennifer took him in her arms, soothing his fears.

"Michel, I understand."

"Yes, you've been there, suffered."

"Go on."

"The dinner with the Vecchis is cordial, everything implied, nothing settled. I'm wavering. The irony was that I'd decided to let the boy go. What's the purpose of locking up another kid?

"Espresso is served. Giorgio sits glumly, leaning on his elbow waiting for his destiny to be decided. Ciro peels the skin off a peach. He's also confounded. He knows he can't bribe me. He's a father who has been crushed.

"Suddenly a man with a newspaper passes by the table and pauses. He's wrapped the paper around a sawed-off shotgun. I see the muzzle, but I can't move. He fires at me."

Michel's hand flew to his chest. He reeled back, feeling the phantom bullets again. He trembled in Jennifer's arms.

"In that instant, *I* was murdered. I entered a realm of demons, knew the sensation of death, how it feels when your life's been stolen and your soul is torn between two spectral worlds. You have no choice but to yield to the strongest field of spiritual gravity.

"Later when I was in hospital, miraculously recovering, one of the nuns scavenging in the library sale brought me Fouché's memoirs. He was Napoleon's minister of police. After Napoleon executed the duc d'Enghien, Fouché wrote: 'It is more than a crime, it is a blunder.'

"In short that's what I thought of my expedition to Corsica."

Three months in the hospital and a few weeks for what is known in the Legion as "reacclimation" and Michel was ready to return to duty.

"Then one evening I'm in a restaurant in Marseille. A man with a newspaper passes my table. I had a flashback. I leap up, take out my gun and I'm about to shoot him. I thought it was Ciro Vecchi's man, come back to life.

"Of course there's pandemonium. I'm dragged out by my own men. Dr. Leon Stein is called. I'm raving and he has me put in a straitjacket. My boss, the commissioner, Richard Caron, fights to keep me on. But the decision must be made by the Inspectorat in Paris and the Minister of the Interior.

"After much pleading and a review of my record, the Great Powers give me the Légion d'honneur and offer me six months forced leave for psychiatric treatment with Stein. Sometimes he acts like a friend, sometimes he doesn't. But he has the power to decide whether I'm fit to return."

After a long silence, Jennifer knew their idyll had ended.

"What is it that draws you to murder?"

"I think of it as a magnetic field. No, that's just on the surface. My flippancy. Murder resembles a disease which can be cured only by surrendering to the violent fever of its invasion. Without it, I feel oddly unwell. A part of me is missing. I crave it. Or rather the solution." He struggled, then said, "There are times when I think I'm as bad as they are."

"No, you're not. Without people like you, we'd have only darkness and anarchy. We'd revert to savagery."

He clung to her, secure in her firm arms, at last complete, in a union.

"Jennifer, I love you."

"Do you? Can it be this fast?"

"Yes, when it's right." He smiled at her. "You've saved me a trip to the psychiatrist."

The nightmare of his impotence vanished in the sunlight of her faith. He no longer thought of himself as a straw man.

CHAPTER 39

Maddie was revved up, and tried jogging around her room, iron-ing clothes, cleaning the old fridge. It was too late to vacuum. She found some rancid furniture polish and went around the room apply-ing it, buffing tabletops.

It was five in the morning. Time had frozen for her. She stared at the telephone on the bedside table, imploring it to ring. She had saved a last joint of hash for a celebration and she was tempted to light it.

So far it had all worked. There were witnesses at the Moulin de Mougins who had seen her say goodbye to her parents. Another limo had been hired by the restaurant to take the Golds back to the hotel. Maddie made certain she had left first. The Montcalm's night chauf-feur had sped her back to Aix from Mougins. He had accompanied her to the apartment at exactly two-fifteen in the morning. She had offered to make him coffee, but he had said he would stop on the way back.

She had undressed, packed her books and notes for the eleven o'clock lecture. Jennifer had left Michel's phone number in St-Rémy where she could be reached. They would meet at the university. Mad-die could now say that she had spent the night with André at the apartment. Boy's plan was dazzling.

She flipped through the bus schedule. A bus departed from Cannes to Aix at one A.M. It would have arrived at four. Had something happened to Boy? The prospect was intolerable and she bit her lip in a frenzy. Now she was getting confused.

The sun shimmered through the leafy plane trees on the Cours Mir-abeau and the flower sellers sprayed water on small precious arbors in their stalls. The pavement was fiery and the soles of Maddie's sandals simmered in the heat. She squinted through her sunglasses at *Le Clai-ron*. She had her briefcase in one hand and the newspaper in the other.

At King René's fountain, she slumped down in despondency and scanned the news with other students. The murder of Louise Vercours was buried in a brief article on page four. There was no mention of her parents or any sign of Boy.

Dragging herself up, she crumpled the bus schedule and threw it in a trash can. The police might ask why she had one. She turned away from the Cours and gritted her teeth. She had to meet Jennifer at the Rimbaud lecture. A rude wolf whistle pursued her, and she held her head high, ignoring it.

"You're one real tough chick. Do I have to kill someone to get your attention?"

The music of Boy's voice reawakened Maddie to the magic of life; the rhythmic southern cadence charmed her as though she were a snake rising to a flute.

"No hand holdin'. Let's just take a friendly walk."

"You're all right," she said, choking on air.

"Don't hyperventilate, my lady."

"Your gorgeous hair—"

"I'm back to my sweet Soledad look."

"Oh, angel, I've been sick all night, worrying." The imperative question regained its resonance, Boy was back. "Are they *gone*?"

"Yep. But not quite forgotten. Now don't ask any more questions. Will you ever stop that, Maddie?"

"Yes, sir." Still, she whined. "You cut your beautiful hair. Jesus, you'll have to show an ID when you want a drink. You look sixteen now."

"I live right. I think you're one of them horny ladies who likes the idea of messin' with a little boy in the sack. Teachin' him the tricks."

"Do I ever. Everything about you turns me on." She studied his velvety unlined, untroubled face. "Aren't you exhausted?"

"I napped on the bus back from Cannes," he said casually. They paused at the crossroads to Deux Garçons, already filling with smoke and newspapers. "Sugar, don't ever lie to me. The *late* Françoise told me you never asked Louise for money for the tricks you turned."

"Late" registered on Maddie. Now no one could link her to Louise and she wanted to take Boy in her arms. She held back, fearing that he might have been followed.

"Françoise didn't ask Louise for a dime. She would have been fired. I tell you, darlin', people who bullshit me have a problem catchin' their next breath."

Maddie turned toward him, cowed, eyes pathetic, close to tears. He entwined his little finger with hers.

"Yes, yes, I lied about Louise. I didn't want to disappoint you. I was so worried about you. Sleeping rough in parks. Moving in with that disgusting old hairdresser. We had to get some money. I have no regrets."

Boy steered her to the phone kiosk. "You know what to do now. Call the Municipal Police. Got the number?"

"I know the drill."

"Slight change. Ask for a cop, name of Paul Courbet. If he's out, leave your message on the machine. In French naturally."

"Karim Hassad se vante de l'assassinat de Louise Vercours," Maddie repeated by rote.

"Make the call, then go to your lecture and hang on to Jen all day long."

"Okay. Where will you be later?"

"I'll drop by Denise's. See if she needs an odd job. Best if I stay put. I've got a shitload of cash which I'll hide in Denise's shed. We have to be careful about spending."

"Can I sneak by?"

"Maybe."

"I've got an idea, let's check into a hotel."

"No, we stick with the game plan." He grew firm and surly. "Maddie, you've got to learn some discipline." His cavernous cat eyes flamed at her. "If you start gettin' careless—"

"I won't," she said gravely. "I promise. We're in this together. When do you think the police will contact me?"

"Dunno with these folks. Tonight or next week. These guys are lazy and dumb. You could age a barrel of Jack Daniel's by the time they get through eatin', drinkin' and messin' around."

Boy had her laughing. Maddie rejoiced in his exuberance and humor. Nothing fazed him. The scent of him drove her into a sexual fury. She moved ahead of him at the curb and reached behind to feel his crotch.

"They gonna arrest you for impairin' the morals of a minor."

"I'd spend my life in prison for a taste of you now."

"We'll get to it. Say, Maddie, we sure lucked into one thing. Mom had an ounce of primo flake coke."

Maddie's temper flared. "That hypocrite bitch." Her mind quickly shifted to the conqueror's spoils. "You're utterly fantastic, you brought it for us. I want a toot so bad."

"You're such a dumb ass, Maddie. I left half of it, so even Commander Danton could find it. At the rate he's goin', we'd both have gold medals at the Olympics by the time he rolls off Jennifer."

He crossed the wide street, side by side with her. "When you're questioned—and you will be!—you got to get it forced out of you that Mom had a secret coke problem. Don't anticipate, but be ready."

"Yuck, that phony viper blowing coke and shipping *me* off to drug rehab for months at a stretch! I can't wait to see their bodies."

"I think you're a mite too cheerful even for these frogbacks. You better be in more shock than you are now, darlin'. "

Maddie, the diva of death, was filled with herself. "I will give a great performance. I just want to enjoy myself for a while. Never to see them again," she whispered.

She and Boy arrived at the *calisson* stand from different directions and bought the honeyed almond cakes. Boy looked her over. Puffy red eyes, but the black dope bags graven underneath had been displaced by a luminous tan.

"What'd you do when you got back last night?" he asked.

"I thought of you, us . . . me first, doing Louise."

His protégé had developed his finely cultivated tastes and he had forged her for terror.

"Ole Louise was as fine as they get. I can tell you that for a dead certainty."

Maddie looked at Boy's short hair, his youthful unlined face, innocent of folly, romantic, tender toward her. She was filled with June bride ideas and images.

"Let's do something unique for our wedding."

"You bet. I'll see to that. Darlin', I'm goin' to take you back to Guthrie, Oklahoma. Show you off. You'll see where it all started. How I got to be me." The prospects triggered off memories of pleasure and horror for Boy. "We'll picnic out at the Logan Fairgrounds with Barbra Streisand singing 'The Music of the Night.' "

"Perfect. I love her voice. It all sounds wonderful, woodsy and fresh."

"Sure is. Wait till I take you on down to Snake Creek. It'll be a real learnin' experience and not the crap you pick up in school. Then I'll introduce you to someone very special. He'll be our best man." In a whisper that might have come from the ruler of a secret society, Boy added, "He was my teacher."

Boy's hissing fiery breath sprayed on her neck and Maddie could not let go of his magic.

"He must be remarkable. A god, like you."

"He is. Major Eldon Royce Calhoun is our Mystery Man."

CHAPTER 40

In the suffocating heat of the damp sheets, Yvette's skin was coated with sweat. She was kissing Courbet's neck, snuggled in his muscular arms, when the call came from headquarters. He had left word that he would be at Denise's for an hour. He and Yvette had contrived one of their short times. Courbet skipped out of his home a bit earlier than usual, and Denise rushed to open the salon because her manager had been in a car accident.

The quirky danger of the affair brought with it a current of passion neither of them had experienced. From Paul Courbet's point of view, the bountiful sex was less important than the delight he took in deception. It had been even more tingling and wicked when Michel had played the crippled leg of the triangle. But for now his wife would have to do. As a vice cop, Paul Courbet embraced the role of highwayman.

From the rear of the house, Boy watched them and overheard their conversation through the open window.

"Are you quite done with me?" Yvette asked sullenly, after Courbet hung up the phone.

He tossed her thin summer top to her. "Yes, get dressed."

"Can we stay a little longer? Did I do something to upset you?"

Paul Courbet knotted his tie in the mirror and smarmed back the sides of his hair. He suppressed a yawn, narrowed his eyes in the spokes of sun choking the bedroom.

"No, you're always perfect. We ought to make an evening of it when my wife visits her family with the brats."

"What was the call about?"

"A chance for immortality . . . if it turns out to be true."

"Tell me, talk to me."

"I'm thinking . . . Should I let Claude know?"

"About what?"

"Arresting Louise's killer!"

"You're not serious?"

Paul Courbet cast a buoyant smile at her. He was the town buffoon, the casualty of endless jokes and sarcastic remarks by the arrogant Marseille hands. Now he savored the dual pleasures of cuckolding Michel and poaching a murder case from his patronizing antagonist.

"I'll go with you. That way no one will cut you out of the story. And I'll make sure you get the credit."

Boy peered around the front of the house and saw them charge into a rattling old car and speed away in plumes of black smoke.

With a video camera on her lap, and speedily loading a cassette, she asked, "Where are we going?"

"To Aubagne." Courbet finally felt in charge and not her monkey. "How much do you pay Claude for your TV interviews?"

"I think Sardou gives him five hundred francs a show."

"What would it be worth if I were to arrest the killer?"

"Plenty. I'll act as your agent. Twenty thousand for a big Paris TV show. I'd also get Reuters and the British tabloids to cough up some money."

"A series of articles?"

"*France-Soir* can be persuaded. With lots of photos of your handsome mug."

"I like that, Yvette." All at once the virile colossus crumpled up and grew somber. "If it turns out that Karim Hassad is not the man, then you might do a story on La Sex Boutique. Tie Gerard in with Louise. It should be worth a few front pages."

"Ah, you're my editor now."

"Splashy, sexy porn. The housewives lap it up."

"I've done better gutter rubbish than that," she countered. "How do you know this Karim?"

"In case you hadn't heard, I'm a detective. Marseille Vice wanted me," he said huffily. "I've turned them down several times." He pressed a hand between her thighs. "Life's too sweet here."

"And who'll be the lucky girl when I'm in Paris?"

"You're irreplaceable, Yvette."

"We'll see if I can get you posted to Paris. I have friends." For a moment there was a tender silence between them and she dropped her guard. "Paul, I wanted to have your child."

"Children! Get it out of your head. You can't have a life with them. It's the nineties, families are out. Old hat. Rubbish. Kids bleed you when you're young, and toss you into institutions when you stop working."

They had spoken before of the possibility of his leaving his wife.

She liked a man a step slower, one who could summon up towering erections without any strenuous efforts on her part. Michel had been deficient in both areas. He required endless foreplay, exhausting her intellectually, and when he was ready she had become grizzly.

By noon they reached the outskirts of Aubagne, fuming in dust and heavy viscous sunshine. They passed the Marcel Pagnol Christmas workshop, then shot past the Foreign Legion grounds.

She slued the car sharply into a gritty parking lot filled with over-heated trucks leaking oil. They walked on the pocked gravel lot to La Sex Boutique. Yvette pointed at the display in the shop window.

"What's that supposed to be?"

"It's boot fetishist week. Gerard scours hospitals, lunatic asylums, estate sales, searching for old boots, gloves, corsets, wooden wheelchairs, crutches, any kind of lace underwear. He's got an enormous clientele for that crap."

"In this heat?" she said with an amazed laugh.

"Perversion isn't seasonal for truckers or men in barracks."

"Then I won't have to wait for Christmas to wear my boots for you again?"

He also laughed and held her hand. "No, you can wear them with leather gloves and nothing else. Oh, Yvette, I'm going to miss you like hell."

"I've only seen Gerard around town a few times. How did he happen to work for Louise?"

"Like all of us, he stole some money," Courbet said. "But he picked the wrong person. Your boss."

"Vincent Sardou?"

"Yes, he was a notary there. Louise kept Gerard out of prison."

"That's a miracle."

"Wait outside. I'll be back in a moment after I see Gerard."

Yvette stopped at the nearby truckers' café for a bottle of Evian. Courbet trotted back, bewildered. The shop was closed. He spoke to the barkeep who also registered surprise and pointed to the kinky assortment of men furiously waiting.

"Karim has a house in back," the barkeep told Courbet.

"It might be dangerous. Let me check things before you come around," Courbet whispered to her.

Yvette ignored him and trailed with her camera ready. They spied a grimy Deux Chevaux in front of a miserable tin-roofed hovel. From inside, music whined from a tinny radio. Courbet warily inched around the side and peeked at the rear. There was no back door. He found a window blocked with dirty Styrofoam.

He cautiously knocked. Karim came to the door, opened it a crack and peeped out. Instantly, he tried to slam it in Courbet's face. But he was not fast enough. Courbet stormed inside, ramming Karim backwards. He immediately saw the .45 on the bed amid a mine of glinting jewelry.

Courbet reached for his automatic. He ordered the frightened Karim to get to his knees. On a rickety table lay a mirror, a mound of white powder, a razor, and an American hundred-dollar bill rolled up.

"Coke for your wake-up cocktail?"

"It's not mine. I found it here," Karim said haplessly.

"Clasp your hands behind your head!"

Yvette was rapidly panning the camera.

"Smashing, Paul! Tousle your hair and put some dirt on your face."

Maddie sat beside Jennifer in the sweltering lecture hall of the university. It was Jennifer who had first introduced her to Rimbaud and the symbolist poets. Maddie had signed up for her course Arts and Ideas last fall at Pembrooke. She had no inkling that the *fin de siècle* radical innovations in the arts in France would capture her imagination. Maddie found herself enthralled by the course. Jennifer was a stimulating teacher who brought a sweeping enthusiasm to the arts.

While running slides of a Manet painting of boats, she read to the class Rimbaud's seminal poem "Le Bateau ivre." How could a boat be drunk? Manet's listing picture of a sailboat revealed just that. The literary and visual were connected.

Maddie developed a kinship with the outgoing teacher, which slowly blossomed into friendship. It was an awkward coupling. Jennifer had something of the prude in her. Early on, Maddie discovered that Jennifer was shocked by her sexual experiments and her use of drugs. It was at best an uneasy alliance until Jennifer had met Michel.

Maddie had the remarkable capability of blocking out the realities of life when she was absorbed in a subject. The fact that her parents were now dead and that Boy had cleared the path to the future stood still as she listened to the professor's mesmerizing account of the extraordinary life of Rimbaud.

He had been a child prodigy, brutally raised by an insensitive mother. He started writing when he was ten and composed many of his remarkable poems by the age of seventeen. Living rough, he tramped through France and Belgium. He committed a petty offense and was imprisoned in Paris with hardened criminals.

Months later he met Paul Verlaine, an older established poet, who encouraged him. Unfortunately, Verlaine was so besotted by the beautiful Rimbaud that in a fit of violent jealousy he shot the young man.

Rimbaud recovered, gave up his poetry and worked as a laborer and dockhand. Having abandoned his great talent, Rimbaud wandered through Africa and became a merchant. At thirty-seven, he developed an infection in his leg, returned to Marseille for medical treatment and died of gangrene, never to know the fame that would be his posthumously.

When the lecture concluded, Maddie accompanied Jennifer to Chez Danton. She followed Boy's script and stuck with her. Michel had ordered a picnic lunch for them. The two women set off on a walk along Cézanne's immortal trail up Mont Sainte-Victoire. They were dazzled by the shifting hues of the limestone cliffs. For once Jennifer was suffused with a spirit of sisterhood.

When they stopped by a stream, Jennifer served thin slices of Bayonne ham, Nicole's farm sausage, Philippe's roasted peppers, and chèvre. She lathered their baguettes with dollops of green olive oil, and opened a bottle of Tavel.

"My folks were disappointed that you didn't come. But I'm relieved. Our evening was a disaster."

"You didn't quarrel with them again?"

"No, no. We had a wonderful time until this maniac came after me."

"Who?"

"He's an Algerian. His name is Karim. He's been on my back since I got here. Like a shadow, day and night. He keeps threatening me."

"Maddie, you should've told me."

"I didn't want to worry you. Jen, he's frightening. He must've trailed me to Cannes. He attacked me in the restaurant last night and ruined the dinner with my folks."

Jennifer was flabbergasted. "I'll call them."

"No, don't. Let this blow over. We'll spend the day with them at the Hôtel du Cap, next week."

"What did this Karim do?"

"We were at the table with the owner. Karim must've snuck in. He grabbed my hair, pulled me out of my chair and, stuck his tongue in my mouth. I started screaming. I thought he was going to shoot us."

The charming, vulnerable side of the girl emerged, and Jennifer knew that she needed to be protected.

"I can't believe this. In the Moulin de Mougins?"

"Yes. Karim's insane and on drugs. My father was about to break his neck when the waiters booted him out. He threatened my dad. I was in shock. He's bad news, Jen."

Jennifer was appalled by her own insensitivity. Maddie had been suffering in silence.

"He can't get away with that. In Aix of all places to have a creep like that after you. Wait till Michel hears about this."

"Let's forget it for now and dream of Cézanne and Rimbaud."

But Jennifer could not dismiss the episode. She was haunted by the vision of Maddie being attacked.

"You need someone who's really exceptional and understands you. Maybe it is this André."

"Yes, I feel part of him."

"I'm happy you met someone decent. The truth is, we've had a bad time."

"André's the love of my life."

"I want to meet him."

"You'll adore him, Jen."

CHAPTER 41

Michel brooded over his pastis. Jennifer nervously observed his mood and gave him some room. Chez Danton would not be open for another half hour. The staff was in the bar, grouped around the TV, raptly watching Yvette interview Paul Courbet. She paraded her smug prize outside La Sex Boutique. In her summer camouflage gear, khaki trousers and jungle jacket with bulging pockets for grenades and bullets, Yvette played her role skillfully. Her smudged makeup was another nice touch, Michel thought. She might have just returned from the Congo.

". . . Now Sergeant Courbet, I happened to listen in to a police call, which is what brought me to Aubagne. How did you find out that the suspect was Karim Hassad?"

"Karim Hassad?" Jennifer burst out. "He could be the man who's been stalking Maddie."

"You know him?"

She clutched Michel's hand. "At dinner last night in Cannes with her parents, a man by the name of Karim attacked her. She only told me about it this afternoon."

Michel's eyes went back to the TV screen. Courbet's tie was askew and his jacket torn from battle.

". . . Through an intensive investigation alongside my chief, Super-intendent Claude Boisser, I developed various leads. This man may be tied to the terrorist bombings throughout France."

Yvette took over. "I was fortunate to be here during the capture of Karim Hassad. I'd like the audience to know that I witnessed your extraordinary bravery. Walking in on an armed man who may have committed a double murder required extraordinary courage. I refer of course to Louise Vercours and her business associate, Gerard David, who was also found shot to death in his sex shop."

Nicole snuffled into her handkerchief and Philippe held her hand. "At last it's over, Nicole. They've captured the beast."

She looked crossly at Michel. "Can we make preparations for Louise's funeral if you and your experts in Marseille are finished with her? I want to hold a special mass for her at St-Sauveur."

On screen, Yvette waved her hand dramatically at the entrance of Karim's shack. Barking orders to the uniformed gendarmes, Claude Boisser stood restlessly in the background, waiting his turn.

". . . I can personally assure our viewers that Detective Sergeant Paul Courbet is lucky to be alive after the violent struggle with the suspect, who resisted arrest."

Yvette spoon-fed Courbet another question. "Is there more?"

"Yes, there was bad blood between Karim and the victims. There's also the possibility that he was involved in the murder of the two American tourists."

"Incredible! Please go on, Sergeant Courbet."

"We're looking for Karim's girlfriend, Françoise Artois. We need the public's cooperation. If you've seen her, please contact us in Aix-en-Provence."

An excellent series of photographs of Françoise was superimposed on the screen with the caption WANTED BY THE POLICE. Michel wondered who had taken the pictures. It was an expert job and not usual for prostitutes to have elaborate composites.

"Do you have any idea where Mademoiselle Artois might be?" Yvette asked.

"My own guess is she's plying her trade around Cannes. We've sent a police bulletin to every resort on the Côte d'Azur."

"I previously reported in the newspaper that Marseille's Special Circumstances Section was brought in to run this investigation."

Paul Courbet had his opening and plunged the knife.

"Oh, them. They were *supposed* to be on the job. They did some forensic testing at the crime scene for us. And their medical examiner performed the postmortem on Madame Vercours. We were forced to defer to them. They're considered the specialists. They have the manpower and an enormous budget to deal with these cases."

"Did they develop any leads?"

"They had some vague theories that didn't amount to much."

A detective burst into shot.

"There's an urgent call for you, Sergeant Courbet!"

Yvette and the bar audience were spellbound. She trailed after Courbet to the communications van and dribbled some filler about how he was a devoted husband and the father of two children. She insinuated that Michel and his team were bunglers. During her analysis, Delantier sidled up to the bar. He appealed to Philippe.

"Shall I reinstate the Place de Paul Courbet sign over the boule court? It can only help business. He's a patron and our local champion."

Philippe glared at Michel. "Excellent idea."

Jennifer bristled at the pompous waiter's snippiness. But she was delighted that the case had ended. In three weeks she'd be back teaching at Pembrooke. Her contract ran for another year and she wondered how she and Michel could endure the separation. Nicole Danton's attitude had improved toward her and she had begun to treat her with pleasant misgivings. After Jennifer had returned the picnic set, Nicole had given her a cream concoction that she had made for dry skin. Philippe had taken her through the prep for a braised breast of veal stuffed with spinach which would be the *plat du jour*. She was beginning to feel like one of the family.

"Murders sometimes get solved by some bizarre tip," Michel said with a mixture of irritation and relief. "I listened to the recording the operator made of the tipster's call to Courbet. Probably some girl who'd worked for Louise," he told Jennifer.

Framed in a close-up, Courbet made another startling announcement.

"I've just been informed by the police in Cannes that in the early hours of the morning, the body of Françoise Artois was found in the grove of Our Lady of Good Hope. I'm afraid, Yvette, I have to end this interview so that we can interrogate the suspect about his murderous rampage."

Michel was troubled by the turn of events. None of this made sense to him. Why would Karim murder his patrons? Gerard was making him a partner in the porn shop and Françoise would inherit Louise's business. Had they conspired to cut Karim out? Was that the motive? And how did Louise fit in to this enigma? What had she done to set off this chain of murders?

"Do you have to go in?" Jennifer asked.

Nominally Michel had the authority to take over, but a tacit code of ethics existed. The arresting detective was given the first opportunity to build a case and then brought the *procès-verbal* statement to the examining magistrate. Sometimes a suspect gave a better account of his actions after a wait, ripening like cheese. Michel had already sent Annie down to the station to observe the interrogation.

"I'd like to. But it would be bad form to horn in. I'll let Courbet play detective."

A smirking Delantier, with a spring in his step, flaunted the sign when he passed the bar.

"That man's impossible. He gets more spiteful each day," she said.

"Yes, I'm thinking of shooting him with Courbet's gun and framing my father for it. Will you be my alibi?"

She laughed. "I'll do anything. I've got you all to myself without a murder."

"You'll get jaded and bored."

"I don't think so . . . Would you be a sweetheart and take me to the Mahler concert tonight?"

She held Michel's hand and he had a sour smile on his face. He nodded. Mahler would suit his doleful mood.

Boy and Maddie sat in Denise's living room, which was a tribute to her acquisitive spirit; the walls were smothered by huge china chests and loaded with flea market bric-à-brac. The sentries of murder intently listened to the story unfold on the TV news. There was still no word about her parents and Maddie looked at Boy.

"Who's Gerard David?"

"It was his porn shop. He caught me going into Karim's place. I never leave witnesses," Boy said.

For the first time since they'd met, she was horrified by his reaction. She sensed that her fear of him was at the core of the attraction.

"That's what I meant by the discipline of this work."

"Why haven't the police called me?"

"Those lard-asses don't know how to find you," he explained. "They'll probably check with the embassy first. Then call the States to see if they can locate you."

Maddie was reassured. Boy knew how to handle everything.

"That TV girl Yvette is staying here."

"That's convenient," Maddie said coldly.

"Calm down. The cop she interviewed is her boyfriend. He was stuffin' her pretty good this mornin'."

"When does Denise get home?"

"Not till later." Boy had spent the day unpacking shipments of cosmetics and bringing some order to Denise's stockroom. "Some salesman from Paris is buying her dinner. And she's a mooch."

As Yvette was winding up the TV coverage, she suddenly paused. She could not believe the message coming from her earphone.

"Ladies and gentlemen, *please stand by!* We have another breaking story. A very prominent American couple have been found murdered at the Hôtel Montcalm in Cannes. The police are withholding the names until they contact the American authorities." Yvette's voice rose to the heady range of a soprano's. "What a season for murder!"

Maddie leaned her head on Boy's shoulder and gave him a loving smile. He kissed her so hard that he seemed to be consuming her. He carried her into the small bedroom Denise had given him.

"The princess can leave the tower now. She owns the castle."

"And so does my prince."

Maddie looked at him in an attitude of religious rapture. Boy had traveled across the world to free her from a lifetime of enslavement by her parents. Now she would have Darrell Vernon Boynton all to herself forever. Was there a luckier girl in the world?

"You *are* God."

On that late sunny afternoon, Boy evoked the image of Rimbaud in Maddie's mind. A mystical transference had been revealed to her. Boy had become the personification of her idol. In her unconscious quest, she had sought a hero and uncloaked one. She picked up her lecture notes and read some lines to him in French and he smiled as though he understood the meaning.

"Sounds like poetry."

"It's Rimbaud," she whispered.

" 'I will be at your feet . . . Let me penetrate all of your memories . . . Let me be *that woman* who can kiss your hand and foot . . . Then, I will strangle you.' "

Boy's body rocked hard with laughter. "If anybody does, let it be you, Maddie."

CHAPTER 42

Mahler's lyrical Fifth Symphony always made Jennifer cry. It touched powerful emotions within her and brought to the surface her deepest yearnings as a woman. Under an arch of flashing summer stars, the sweeping, emotional music filled the ancient courtyard of the Archbishop's Palace. In the sensual moonglow, she sat clasping Michel's hand and thinking of their future. His was a generous nature and she visualized herself with his children. He would find the time to play with them and they would have an appreciation of everything that was fine.

Michel was distracted throughout the concert and Jennifer realized that he was indulging her. Of course he had grown up surrounded by the enthralling history of Aix and another concert was nothing special. But she was hurt when he leaned over, kissed her on the cheek, then got up in the middle of the bewitching scherzo and said, "I'll meet you later at the restaurant. I have to see the monster who killed Louise."

"It's no longer your case."

"I'll have to complete the interrogation in Marseille tomorrow."

The mood was broken by his fixation on murder. She should have known by now that he was compelled by inner voices beyond his control. Perhaps he was unbalanced. As he dashed down the aisle, she felt her life plans had been dealt a fatal setback.

At the end of Place Jeanne d'Arc the Gendarmerie appeared as a gray cluster of squalid stone which masqueraded as an antiquity for desperate tourists anxious to take photos of any rum bag of bricks. The stench of spoiled food and steamy sweat hung in the air like a toxic cloud.

Annie Vallon's beige summer suit was ringing wet. In the light, her fine angular features were pasty. A stale sandwich lay on the table. She was lighting a Gauloise when Michel approached and she quickly moved it out of sight. She had quit smoking that winter when she'd been laid up with bronchitis.

"What's going on?"

"The evidence is very strong, Michel. They found a rusted old hatchet in the breeze block. It's been sent to our lab for blood analysis."

"Really. Karim might have murdered the American couple as well. Has he confessed?"

"No, he's a tough little *cafard*. Here's the recording of the informer's voice on tape."

"Play it."

He listened to the girl's voice several times, while looking through the evidence verification inventory and the interrogation report. They had collected jewelry identified as Louise's. It was on the insurance schedule that Sardou had sent over. A .45 Smith & Wesson that had recently been fired was sent to Marseille for a ballistics report; a batch of five-thousand-franc chips from the casino at the Hôtel de Paris in Monte Carlo; a box of surgical gloves; eleven grams of cocaine, not yet tested for purity; and ten thousand dollars in cash.

Michel looked up. "American Express traveler's checks signed by Adam Gold? What's that about?"

"There were two more murders reported in Cannes after you and Jennifer left for the concert. An American couple were found shot to death in the bathtub of their suite at the Montcalm." Annie turned the page of her notebook. "I spoke to the investigators in Cannes. It was a husband and wife. Adam and Karen Gold. He's some famous Hollywood producer. We haven't released the names to the media, pending notification to the daughter."

Michel was rattled by this startling information.

"This is incredible. Has there been a positive identification?"

"Yes," Annie said solemnly. "The Golds are well known by the staff at the Montcalm and the daughter's name is written in their passports as next of kin. The manager naturally turned over the passports to the Cannes police."

"Maddie Gold is the daughter."

Courbet had drifted over, glowing with satisfaction. Now he was bewildered.

"How would you know that?"

"She's a summer student at the university. Don't you remember? My friend Jennifer Bowen is her tutor." With a large glass of scotch in hand, Claude Boisser merrily approached the group. "You and Paul did very well. It was a fine piece of work," Michel admitted. "All of this from an anonymous tip?"

"Karim was heard bragging about the killings at Les Deux Garçons," Courbet informed him.

Michel found himself perplexed. "A mass murderer tells the world he's killed all these people in a café in Aix? Paul, if you don't mind, I'd like the original recording of the informant's voice. The one I heard was unclear."

"That was the operator's original recording. We don't have the money for the kind of hi-tech equipment you have in Marseille," Courbet noted.

Michel ignored the taunt but promised himself that when the case was over, he'd settle matters with Courbet.

"Give it to Annie. She'll take it to our sound lab."

"The arraignment's in hand. I've spoken with the examining magistrate and he's all fired up."

"Is Karim also a suspect in the Gold homicides?" Michel asked.

Claude was intrigued by the possibility. "Why would you think that? Is there some connection with the Golds and Karim?"

"Yes, there is."

"Your ballistics staff are testing the weapon. It was an army forty-five," Courbet said.

Michel tried to piece the circumstances together.

"Karim was in Cannes. He followed the Golds and their daughter Maddie to a restaurant. He's been after the girl since she came over to study. According to Jennifer, there was a violent argument at the Moulin de Mougins. And Karim attacked Maddie."

If Karim was also guilty of the murders of a high-profile Hollywood couple, Claude and Courbet could count on worldwide publicity. Careers, especially in the provinces, had been made on less.

"Where are you holding Karim?"

"In the isolation cell. On suicide watch."

Michel was led past the duty guards into the dank bowels of the station. He slid the peephole and saw the straggly young Algerian, frightened and tearful, lying on a cot. He had on leg irons and a straitjacket.

"We'll bring him into Marseille in the morning and let you mop it up with the magistrate," Claude said disdainfully.

Michel was mystified. "What exactly did Karim say about the murders?"

"He denied killing Louise and Gerard," Annie said after a silence.

Michel glanced at the report. "*And* his girlfriend, Françoise?"

"He fainted when Paul asked him about her," Annie said in a tone that Claude and Courbet found unsettling. "And then he became hysterical."

"That's why we had to put him in restraints," Claude said. "We couldn't continue the interrogation."

"You didn't mention the murder of the Golds?"

"Not yet," Courbet advised him. "He was high on coke when I made the arrest and extremely violent . . . as you may have seen when I was interviewed on TV."

Their theory was that Françoise had been an accomplice in the murder of Louise; Karim and she had a falling out. Gerard had been privy to the murder and more than likely set it up in order to take over Louise's business. Karim wanted to control his employer. But how did he have the thousand dollars in U.S. currency and the Golds' traveler's checks if he hadn't murdered them as well?

"Do you want to talk to him, Michel? Or are you satisfied with the way I've done my job?" Courbet asked bitingly.

"You perform wonderfully on the boule court and on TV. But in bed you're a superstar, Paul."

"I'm also a detective, Michel. You aren't the only one in Provence. Maybe you ought to go back on sick leave."

"Gentlemen, please," Claude urged, getting between them. "Let's not bring personal rivalries into a murder investigation."

"There are no hard feelings on my part, Paul." Michel turned to Claude. "You and Annie have a decent relationship. I'd like her to act as the section's liaison."

"Fine with us," Claude said.

"After Karim is booked in Marseille, clean him up, and bring him to my office at ten tomorrow morning. Gentlemen, congratulations on your hat trick. We could have used you for the World Cup."

When he and Annie walked to her car, Michel's mind was still clouded with doubts, which his detective did not dispel.

"Annie, it's hard to believe. Did this pathetic Algerian boy murder seven people? Do you think there's some kind of terrorist connection as well? And if there were, what do the Golds, the American couple and Louise have to do with it?"

"I don't know," she admitted. "Laurent and his staff are doing the autopsies now. We'll have to see if there are any similarities to Louise."

"The Golds were shot in the hotel bathtub. None of this makes any sense to me. Have Émile and Pierre put Maddie Gold under surveillance. There's a chance she's in danger. Karim may have accomplices."

"You'll tell the girl about her parents?"

At this moment, Michel loathed his work.

"Yes, in the morning. We'll bring her to Marseille with Jennifer."

Returning to Chez Danton, Michel found a dispirited Jennifer sitting at the bar with an espresso. He was daunted by the gloomy task that confronted him.

"I apologize for leaving you."

"I won't ever get used to it."

"There was an emergency that wasn't on TV."

"I feel like I'm losing you, Michel. Is there *any* hope for us? Will we ever have a quiet moment together when you aren't thinking of a body count?"

She might just as well have slapped him and he retreated. His sense of duty had impaled them both. There was an urgency in his manner that filled her with dread.

"Right now, the situation is impossible and I'm trapped."

She nodded reluctantly and on her face, he saw indecision and self-doubt.

"Look at it from my point of view. I'm just a normal member of the public. Not a crime reporter like Yvette. All these murders . . . they shock me. I've tried so hard to help and understand. But I can't seem to make you realize what this is doing to me."

"I'll come by your apartment in the morning."

"Are you too busy for me now?" She could not breach his silence and was left in the lurch. "Maddie's got classes at nine."

"I'll be there before."

"Can we have a drive through the countryside and maybe a picnic at the farm?"

"Not tomorrow."

He leaned over to kiss her, but she pulled away, sensing that doomsday lay just ahead of them.

CHAPTER 43

Michel arrived early at Maddie's apartment. Annie came upstairs with him. They carried the pall of death with them. He had been up most of the night reading the shoddy interrogation report on Karim before it had been broken off. Karim had been harangued by Courbet but admitted nothing. The forensic profiles would not be completed until later that morning.

"I'm going to ask Corinne to work with me during the interrogation of Karim if you don't mind."

Annie was alarmed. "Did I do something wrong, Michel?"

"No, she's more maternal than you are. Tell her to meet us at the morgue."

Jennifer was already dressed and Maddie was blow-drying her hair in the bathroom. Jennifer's eyes roved suspiciously over Annie's somber face. "What's going on, Michel?" she asked.

"This is Inspector Annie Vallon, who works with me, Jennifer."

"We'd like you to come to Marseille with us, Mademoiselle Bowen."

Her eyes darted over Michel's somber features. "I don't understand. Why?"

Before Annie could continue, Maddie bounced into the room, breezily smiling. Michel noticed something different about her. Yes, her hair was colored, reddish.

"Let me guess, Michel, this time you brought breakfast for us."

"I wish."

The girl was so high-spirited and vulnerable that he backed off. Jennifer's eyes were riveted on him.

"Do we have time before class to go for some crêpes, Jen?"

Michel shook his head. "No we'll do that in Marseille. I have something to tell you. . . ."

Maddie smiled with uncertainty, and Michel waited until a look of mystification came over her. As he began, the girl's tormented cries of anguish pierced the morning air.

When the bodies of Adam and Karen Gold were returned to their morgue drawers, Jennifer appeared as deeply affected as Maddie. Michel watched Maddie carefully. She was distraught, her body quivered, and Michel caught her when she collapsed.

In the corridor, he signaled Corinne and took the pregnant young detective aside. "Get hold of Leon Stein. See if he's in his office or doing grand rounds. But get him down here." Corinne hesitated and Michel wondered if she was up to the case. "Are you still having morning sickness?"

"No, I'm fine, really. I was up early, checking the dossier on Louise and looking at the photographs of Françoise."

He wondered about his judgment now. Had it been a bad idea to have a pregnant detective on such a gory case?

He put his arm around her. "I promise, it won't hurt your record if you want to be replaced."

"No, please, let me work on this with you. I can manage it."

"Karim's a mass murderer and you'll have to be his comfort zone." She nodded. "Go down to the lab. I need to know as soon as possible if Françoise's pubic hair matches what was found in Louise's murder. I want vaginal fluid swabs, the works." The assignment was sickening for any woman, but Corinne was holding together. "Then take Jennifer and Maddie out to the Bon-Bon."

"For crêpes?"

"Yes, we could all use something sweet." As Corinne was about to leave, he said, "And bring a few back—with apricot and strawberry jam."

The clutter of murder. Reports, tests, ideas, chaos, all of it jumbled on Michel's desk, begging for logic. At least the prefect in Aix had the sense to call in Marseille's forensic specialists. They had taken samples of nail dirt, hair, blood, urine, and saliva from Karim.

Michel compared the photos of Françoise and Louise. There were no curling iron burns on Françoise; she had been shot in the left temple with a single .45 bullet. It had passed through a beach towel which was now in the evidence section. She had also been slashed open from the navel down. Adam and Karen Gold had been shot in the head, but through a pillow. In both cases, the killer had muffled the gunshot.

On the other hand, Gerard David had been shot twice in the back. A third bullet had been fired into his left temple. Michel visualized the executioner standing over Gerard, wounded, lying on his face. The *coup de grâce* had been meticulous. The killer then had dragged Gerard's body through the rear door of the shop and dumped him into the stockroom. Nothing had been found to indicate that the perpetrator had used anything to silence the shots from the .45. Photographs taken of the bloody sand, from the point of Gerard's fall, indicated a distance to the stockroom of fifteen meters. The rough estimate of the shots in the back was about ten meters.

"Gerard was a moving target," Michel said aloud, looking down at the Bay l'Estaque. "Was Karim trained in a Mideast guerrilla camp?"

He made a series of notes.

> Check . . . Karim's car. Clothing. All personal effects. Reflexes. Weight. He had to drag or lift Gerard. No blood of any kind found on Karim's body when Laurent examined him following his arrest. He looked dirty and grimy after his battle with Courbet. Did he have enough time to bathe? Where? No bath or shower in his house. The public bath in Aubagne is ten minutes away. Pierre to make inquiries.

Michel stopped writing abruptly and picked up the postmortem report on Gerard. His weight was ninety kilos. He compared it with Karim's: sixty-five kilos. Was the slight boy he'd glimpsed the previous night strong enough to maneuver Gerard to the back of the shop?

There was a knock on his door and Corinne entered. "The ladies don't want anything to eat, Michel." She laid the warm bag holding the crêpes on his desk. "Your friend Jennifer Bowen would like to see you. Can she come in?"

"Yes."

"The press office is packed downstairs. Yvette is making a terrible racket. But she has competition. The Brits have arrived and so has *Paris-Match* and *Der Stern*. Richard asked them to come back this afternoon before we issue a statement. Did you know that Mr. Gold was one of the most famous television producers in the world?"

"I'd heard. Where's Karim?"

"En route from Aix."

"As soon as he gets here, settle him into an interview room. And bring all the files with you."

Corinne was alert and vigorous. "I'm very excited about this, Michel. I can't wait to start nursing him."

Michel studied her round sensual face and the thin ocher blouse she wore under her suit jacket. "Would you mind if I asked you not to wear your jacket? And open a couple of buttons. Show a little of your bra. I want to see his reaction."

"Annie would strip."

Michel laughed and took Corinne's hand. "That's why I didn't ask her. "Now do me a favor. Let's keep Karim hopping. From time to time, I'd like you to play Lady Macbeth and I'll sink into my Hamlet funk. I'm used to it."

She gave him a droll look. "You're getting back to yourself. By the way, Jennifer is gorgeous."

This pleasing description no longer applied, for Jennifer's eyes were ablaze with pain and anger. She was disheveled and hardly seemed the same woman he had picked up two hours ago. He was tender and vigilant while reassuring her.

"This is a nightmare."

"I know how you feel, darling. But if you break down, it'll be a lot worse for Maddie. We have to think of her."

"She wants to go back to California as soon as possible and bury her parents. Me too." He detected a dark current of antagonism toward him. "You knew they were dead last night."

"I suspected as much."

"Why didn't you tell me?"

"I needed confirmation and time to have the bodies moved from Cannes. Jennifer, don't taunt me. I'm on Maddie's side."

She bowed her head and wiped her tears. "The Golds were generous to me and damn good people." He reached over and held her hand. "Well, you and I had some fun. It was a short, euphoric summer with a viper's sting."

"Not for me."

"I'm going to make plane reservations."

He wanted to hold her, but the approach-avoidance legacy was too compelling to abandon.

"Give it a few days."

"What the hell is this about? You got laid. Isn't that what you wanted? What else is there?"

"That's a rotten thing to say. And let's get the facts straight. You seduced me, remember?"

"Screw you, Michel."

He had not been prepared for Jennifer's hostility and stoically accepted it. He had been the one to break the news to them and she felt betrayed. It was irrational, but it had occurred before in other cases with family members and friends of a victim's. Always the police's fault.

"I'll take care of everything, if you only let me. There's going to be a colossal press problem. But I can protect you from it."

"How?"

"Annie will drive you both to our farm in St-Rémy. She'll stay with you until I get home. They won't bother you there."

"You do have the killer?"

"Everything's under control. Now you've got to stop hurting us."

"I'm sorry." She faltered, lowered her eyes. "How can all these horrible things keep happening?"

"I intend to find out *exactly* how. You'll be the first to know . . . if you want to. Now I'm not asking a lot, but to believe in me and my love."

"I was so happy." Her voice and spirit seemed broken. "Until this madman came along."

"I know. Would you like me to have Dr. Stein prescribe tranquilizers for you both?"

"No, I'm afraid of them. And Maddie's mother gave her some."

"When?"

"Last night, I guess, after Karim assaulted her in the restaurant."

He took her arm and walked her down the hallway. As they turned the corner, four uniformed guards escorted a chained Karim to the interview room.

"Is that him?"

"Yes."

"My God, he's only a boy."

"And not a strong one, from the looks of him." Michel held her tightly outside the waiting room. "Don't let this poison the good things between us."

"I'll try. Forgive me."

Annie was standing vigil over Maddie. Head buried in her hands, Maddie was stretched out on a bench, crying bitterly. The young girl brought out Michel's paternal instincts. He yearned to console her.

"Maddie, you have my deepest sympathy."

"Do you have the guillotine here?" she asked.

"Not any longer."

"I wish he'd killed them in California," she wailed. "They have lethal injection there."

CHAPTER 44

"**Take off his leg** irons and handcuffs," Michel ordered Karim's guards. "And somebody go down to the canteen and get us a pot of fresh coffee. Two cups, and a container of milk for Inspector Toulaine."

Karim Hassad listed and stared into space. Michel and Corinne brought him into a sunny room which overlooked the fish market at the Quai des Belges. He rubbed his bruised wrists and looked quizzically at them.

"Are you going to torture me?"

"No, Karim. Put that out of your mind. I'm Commander Michel Danton of the Special Circumstances Section—"

"I've heard about you."

"Really? Tell me."

"Cops in Aix hate your guts and are frightened of you."

"I'm sorry to hear that. My mother loves me, and that makes me happy. This is Inspector Corinne Toulaine." He paused and stared at Karim. "We want to find out the truth. There are seven homicides and you're the suspect in all of them."

Karim gasped and shook his head with disbelief. "What? Seven! Ridiculous. I never killed anyone."

Michel opened the bag with the crêpes. He cut them with a plastic knife and fork and placed them on cardboard plates.

"We've got apricot and strawberry. Shall we share them?"

Karim blinked at him uncertainly. "They must be poisoned."

Michel smiled. "I'll be the guinea pig and have the first taste."

Karim waited and watched Michel chew and swallow. Then, like a cat, he pawed the crêpe and licked the jam off his fingers.

"There's a sink over there. You can wash your hands when you're finished." Coffee arrived and Michel poured cups for them. "Help yourself to sugar and milk."

"Why are you treating me so well?"

"Am I? Well, it's just the way I operate. I've been away from my job for some time, maybe I'm rusty. I don't know. You've had enough people threatening you, haven't you? Would you prefer that?"

"Courbet almost beat me to death. The doctor said my jaw's dislocated."

"Sergeant Courbet had no option. You were resisting arrest."

"I was not!" Karim furiously replied. "He hit me first, knocked me down and had a gun on me when I was on the ground. I didn't raise a hand to him. I'd never fight him! He's much too big for me."

"Yes, he's a rough customer."

Corinne went through Karim's national record. He'd been born in Paris in 1972 of Algerian immigrants; attended the Luxembourg *lycée* and had a variety of menial jobs as indicated by his tax records.

"How long have you been in Aix-en-Provence?"

"Françoise and I came from Paris last September. We'd met four years before that. She knew a girl in Paris who told her there was easy money here."

"Easy . . . in what way?" Michel asked.

"If you wanted to be a working girl, there was a wealthy clientele. Businessmen who slither in from Marseille. Local gentry. Tourists."

"Your information was accurate. But how'd you come to meet Louise Vercours?"

"Françoise was arrested twice in Aix by the vice squad. That pig Courbet busted her. One of the girls in jail said she was pretty enough to work for Madame Vercours."

Michel noticed how polite he was about Louise. With an emotional wrench, but maintaining his equanimity, Michel slid over a photograph of Louise: alive, vital, smiling. His father had taken it on Easter Sunday when Louise had come to the farm.

"Can you identify this woman for me?"

"Naturally. It's Madame Louise Vercours." Karim began sobbing, then drifted. "How could anyone murder my Françoise? She never harmed anyone. She was so loving."

Michel nodded to Corinne.

"Why did you let her work as a whore, then?" Corinne brought a puzzled delicacy to the question.

"It was Françoise's decision. I had no control over it. She wanted us to save enough money to buy a place and get married."

"How did it make you feel?" Corinne inquired.

"Horrible. But I had to get used to it."

And now Michel silkily refined Corinne's cordial manner in the hope of clarifying the motive for murder.

"Speaking as a man, I would have resented Louise. Selling my fiancée's body to enrich herself."

"And as a woman, I can understand your hatred, Karim. And I also sympathize with you."

Karim sloped back in his chair and clutched the arms.

"Your kind have no grasp of how people like us have to survive. I didn't resent Louise. She put food in our mouths. Françoise and I adored her."

Michel affected indifference, but was intrigued.

"Sometimes Françoise took home two thousand francs in a single day. Madame Vercours bought Françoise dresses and perfume. She ran a business, the way Gerard does in the boutique." He sipped his coffee and it dribbled on his chin. "It's about sex and commerce. But they're not criminal. Men rove. They want a change. Some have secret vices which they hide from their wives. Louise and Gerard catered to people with erotic tastes."

Corinne suddenly slashed at him. "What about the morality?"

"Morality, Inspector? I'm an Algerian. How can you French dare to use the word, when you treat us like scum? We've always been your slaves. The blacks in America have it better than we do. They've got laws to protect them. Algerians are at the mercy of cops like you and Courbet."

Michel sympathized with him. He had to get him off the subject of prejudice. Why had Françoise been discharged and sent to Cannes? "Weren't you and Françoise angry with Louise for sending her into exile?"

"Yes, we were. But Louise gave Françoise some money."

"Why did Louise want her to leave Aix? Did they have an argument?" Corinne asked.

"I don't know the answer. Gerard ordered her to get out."

Karim would obviously have a grudge against Gerard. "You mean to tell me that Françoise never mentioned what the problem was?"

"No. And if she had, what could I do about it?"

Michel gently prodded him. "What were your suspicions?"

Karim sighed, anguished, lost, feral, but essentially harmless, Michel thought. A boy in over his head.

"I think she had someone take her place at the *bordel* when she had her period. Louise had an ironclad rule about the girls never bringing in a stranger."

Corinne reviewed the evidence found in Karim's house: Louise's jewelry, casino chips, tens of thousands of francs, and high-grade cocaine. The hatchet and .45 were still with the forensic techs. For the time being she also left out any mention of the Golds' property and traveler's checks.

"It was all planted by someone. It's a plot to implicate me in the murders."

"A plot? They always fascinate me. I'd like to hear about this one," Michel casually asked.

"I got back from Cannes at about ten yesterday morning and found all this stuff on my bed: The jewelry, my forty-five, cash, traveler's checks. Casino chips. And the coke. I was exhausted. Gerard wasn't around, so I thought, why not get high."

"What time did you meet Françoise in Cannes?" Corrine demanded.

"I never saw her. She went shopping during the day. I was supposed to meet her at the Moulin de Mougins with Maddie and her parents. But she stood me up for a date."

The implicit point of the statement was that Karim had made no attempt to escape or change his identity. It would have been simple to go to Nice airport and catch a flight out of the country. He had plenty of money. Michel was confounded by Karim's actions. What had he been waiting for? If he'd murdered Françoise and the Golds, along with the American couple and Gerard, why come back to Aix where he'd be the primary suspect? Could he be this stupid? He'd murdered seven people without leaving a scintilla of evidence—no clues, signature, fingerprints.

"My forty-five was also back," he observed casually. "Someone broke into my place a few weeks ago and stole it. I couldn't make any sense of it. But with all that money and"—he lowered his eyes—"the cocaine, I didn't bother to work it all out. The gun was back, so what?"

"You got the forty-five illegally?"

Karim stared at Michel and nodded.

"Yes . . . A few months ago Gerard gave me some horrible child-porn tapes. They were revolting. Even Gerard hated that side of the business. American trash. This was the worst. We watched a few minutes of a grainy old film. There was a small blond-haired boy being tortured by four adults. We were both sickened. Gerard wouldn't sell them. He gave them to me to get rid of. There's always a market for monsters."

Michel gave him a kindly nod. "Go on, please."

"I'd heard about a high-ranking Foreign legionnaire who'd been cashiered. He peddles anything. He'd been asking about tapes or films of child torture. One day, he dropped by and I said I had something.

We bartered. I wanted a gun. He'd stolen equipment from the Legion: a forty-five, some sticks of dynamite. I traded with him. Owning an automatic was a dream of mine. It made me feel like a true revolutionary."

Michel was excited now. "Why did you need latex gloves?"

Karim gave a guttural laugh. "Do you French ever look at your garbage collectors? They're mostly Algerian. I'm in that trade also. It's one of my jobs at the shop. Our refined French customers leave Kleenex and rags or handkerchiefs on the floor in the video booths. After they slink out, I put on latex gloves to clean up. There's an AIDS epidemic in case you hadn't heard."

Corinne gave a heavy, wilting sigh. Michel thought about relieving her.

"Let me be clear about this. Your prize forty-five is stolen and magically reappears in time for Sergeant Courbet to arrest you? Is that what you're telling me?"

Karim slumped down in his chair and banged his head on the table. Michel observed that Karim did not intend to injure himself.

"We don't have a neurosurgeon on call, Karim. If you want the inspector to handcuff you, she will."

Michel looked again at Corinne. Her hair was sopping wet and the pupils in her eyes were dilated. He would have to dismiss her from the interrogation and conduct it alone. She'd be upset, but it would be best. Karim was not responding well to her.

"Damn, murder always makes me hungry. I'm in one of my eating moods. I think I'd like hummus with a good fresh pita. Lamb kebobs. Tahini. I'll start with dolmas. Ah, I've got a bottle of Pétrus to go with it." He smiled at Karim. "If you're hungry, you can join me."

"Oh, please stop this, Commander. Don't underestimate my intelligence. I'm an expert in being an alien. I've read Albert Camus. He understood Algerians. I know you intend to torture me psychologically."

Michel found the young man's comment extraordinary. They both shared an admiration for the same writer.

"Camus would have enjoyed a fine Pétrus. Oh, what's wrong with me? You don't know anything about wine. You're a Muslim of course and don't drink alcohol."

Karim stared at Michel, baffled. "I'm a Muslim but not a fundamentalist terrorist or a fanatic. Pétrus costs a fortune. I'll drink it in the next world when Allah takes me to paradise."

"Allah's not invited. In the meantime, you'll have to put up with me and our glowing inspector."

In the hallway, Corinne grabbed Michel and staggered into a corner. "Michel, I'm going to be sick."

"I'll get some water—"

"Oh, no, please don't . . . Excuse me, I have to go to the ladies—"

When she left, Michel smiled at Karim who fearfully averted his eyes. He was off balance as Michel had planned. His suspect had no idea what to expect from this mad detective.

CHAPTER 45

Having built up a degree of rapport, Michel preferred to have Karim on his own. He had shaped the interrogation in order to spare Corinne more grisly details. In the canteen, with guards at other tables observing them with bewildered curiosity, Michel had a Middle Eastern lunch brought in.

Karim wolfed down his food, but was forced to drink Evian. The bottle of Pétrus on the table was a talisman that represented the fine things the young Algerian had been denied.

"If you had a case of this, what would you do?" Michel asked.

"Flog it to a wine merchant for cash."

"These photographs Sergeant Courbet found of Françoise in your cupboard are really excellent. I take photos myself, but I'm not in this class."

"I took them," Karim said, about to break into tears. "I can't believe my angel's dead."

Michel thumbed through the album and stopped at one which showed the lissome girl in a scant bikini. Karim had been a photographer's apprentice in Paris. During this period, he had met Françoise, who had run away from Callac, a small inland town in Brittany. She was sixteen, high-spirited, with visions of becoming a model. They lived together in the back of the photographer's studio. A month later, Françoise was doing nude life studies for art students.

"We struggled for years but couldn't make any real money. Paris broke us. Françoise got into the demimonde. She worked in dance clubs on the Champs-Elysées. When we were broke, she'd pick up men." Michel nodded without reproof, but Karim threw a childish tantrum. "She supported us. I couldn't argue."

In Aix, he had met Gerard David through Françoise and he took a clerk's job in the sex emporium.

"You quarreled with Gerard."

"Only after he sent Françoise to Cannes."

"It's high season there as well," Michel countered.

"But here, she has her regular following and sometimes a few wealthy drop-ins. We had a life of sorts. Cannes was foreign territory. You have to be connected with someone in *le milieu* or it's hopeless."

Along the way, Karim admitted to dealing drugs in small quantities. Most of his customers were students at the University of Aix.

"I have nothing to hide. The truth is I'm a coward and incapable of murder. I can talk you to death and make a woman happy. If Françoise were here she'd tell you. Murdering someone is beyond me."

Michel slid over some other photographs and observed Karim shrink with horror.

"Haven't you ever seen a man decapitated?"

"In the name of Allah, no, never."

Afterwards, as they strolled through the corridor, curious officials and secretaries stared from their cubicles at Michel nonchalantly chatting with this exotic mass murderer.

"Let's go to my office. There's a much better view of the harbor and the afternoon sun won't be so bad. Would you care to look at some paintings?"

"No more bodies, please, Commander Danton."

"You've won me over."

"Paintings? You're a master of deception."

"No. Just getting acquainted. I'd like you to identify a few things if you can."

Karim paced nervously as Michel went through Louise's file. Her artwork had been photographed and he spread out on his desk a number of pictures.

"Come over to my desk and don't be shy, Karim. What do you think of these?"

He glanced at the assembly of photos. "I've been charged with murder and you ask me if I like Renoir. I'm going out of my mind."

"So you recognize Renoir."

"Who wouldn't? I used to take Françoise to the Musée d'Orsay and the Louvre whenever I could."

Michel showed him the *Odalisque* which had hung over Louise's bed. "Who's this one by?"

"Stop, it's Matisse naturally. I've only seen the reproductions."

"Didn't Louise show it to you in her bedroom?"

"I was never in her bedroom."

"Or swam in her pool?"

"Did she have one?"

Michel continued the art show. Karim easily recognized the painters in her collection: a small Bonnard; Picasso; Cézanne; and a Gauguin.

"Excellent. You have a fine eye."

"I'm no idiot. I studied art as well as photography."

"If you had the chance, would you steal them?"

Karim was again flustered. "What do you take me for, an expert thief? If these aren't forgeries, they'd be worth hundred of millions. How could I get them out of her house and who would I sell them to?"

"It would be a delicate operation," Michel admitted. He continued to ask Karim to examine photos of various rooms and furniture in Louise's house. "Are you sure you've never been there?"

"Naturally, do you think I'd forget?"

On the night Louise was murdered, Karim maintained he had been making the rounds of dance clubs, searching for customers in the market for hashish.

"I'd bought a brick of Nepalese Temple from a merchant seaman in Marseille. It's the caviar of hash." He sighed and pressed his slender fingers against his temples. "It's laced with lines of opium. Françoise said it was the best smoke there is."

He provided Michel with a list of clubs he'd stopped in, along with people he'd seen and those who had bought drugs.

"I got home at dawn after a party at the Ground Zero disco in Salon. Françoise must've arrived at—I don't know—maybe around two."

Neither Courbet nor Claude had asked him about his whereabouts.

"Why did you go to Cannes?"

"To see Françoise. I missed her and she was miserable there. The other girls on the Croisette were giving her a hard time. The casinos ran her out. She was staying at the Pension Martell in the old port and the owner was trying to sleep with her."

Then Michel sprang his surprise.

"I was under the impression you were following Maddie Gold to Cannes?"

"Maddie? No. Not at all. Maddie started the trouble. I was humiliated. Americans like idiotic, practical jokes. But what she did to me wasn't funny."

Karim explained that Maddie and her lover had invited him and Françoise to the Moulin de Mougins to meet her parents.

"Maddie's *boyfriend*?"

"Yes, he's an American. Sometimes he calls himself André. To Maddie he's always Boy. I'm not sure about his last name."

"What does he look like?"

"Like a film star . . . He reminds me of James Dean in the old film *Giant*. But built differently. Boy's short . . . very powerfully built, bulging biceps. Blond curly hair down to his shoulders. Sometimes he doesn't shave for a few days. He's a hippie." Karim was fatigued. "He's difficult to figure out. But very nice. When he has money, he treats everyone. He's not a beggar."

"Is he violent?"

"No. What makes you think that?"

"Jealous?"

"Not really."

"When did you meet him?"

"Maybe about a month ago. He had a new model apartment on Pont de l'Arc. River view from the rear. We had drinks on the terrace. Maddie was standing outside the building. I think I understand Americans. But I don't. They tease each other. It was some kind of game. Maddie was pretending to pick me up. But she wasn't serious. Then Françoise came running toward us. We went with Maddie to the model apartment. Boy or André, whatever, came out of the closet with a hammer raised. When he saw us, we all fell down laughing. It was so silly."

"Why do you suppose Maddie and her friend tried to get you into their apartment?"

Karim shrugged. "They were drinking and so were we. The truth is that they were lonely and wanted to meet a couple their own age who knew their way around. We'd have a meal or drink together from time to time. Lovely people. Drinks at Deux Garçons. Chat about this and that. Maddie was interested in Algerian politics and sympathetic to my cause. Sometimes she and Françoise saw each other alone to shop. They're young girls. I'd save a little hash for Maddie and Boy. We would all smoke together in my house and listen to rock music. Until this crazy thing happened at the Moulin de Mougins."

Michel had found his opening and leisurely took it.

"Have you been stalking Maddie?"

"Stalking her? That's ridiculous. Why would I? We were friends. Absurd. And for a fact, she's totally crazy. In Cannes, Boy gave me the money to rent formal clothes for the dinner party with Maddie and her parents at the Moulin. He's from a wealthy oil family in

Oklahoma, I believe. And his check arrived. He spent money lavishly when he had it.

"He said he'd seen Françoise and she was shopping for a cocktail dress. Oh, and she'd made a date with some rich old man. I admit I was incensed when Françoise didn't show up."

"Was this Boy there?"

"No. I think Maddie was playing a bad joke on all of us. Boy may have arrived later. I don't know what happened."

Michel stood with him at the window and put an arm around him. "Tell me all of it, Karim."

"I'm so frightened. I don't see you taking notes." He peered at the walls. "Oh, you're recording this."

"No."

"I like you, Commander."

"Thank you. What happened at the restaurant? I don't have a picture yet."

"I asked the maître d' for the Golds' table, as I'd been told to by Boy. I kissed Maddie to surprise her. Suddenly, she began to scream and scratch and slap me. I was in a fight that I can't explain. Maddie was wild. Then I thought I was going to be beaten to death by a mob."

All of this had been confirmed by the Cannes investigators. Maddie's lover had not joined the party. The Gold reservation had been made for three.

"Let's be honest: you blamed Françoise for this and you were angry at her."

"I was infuriated, pissed at the world. I'd been made a fool of. I still don't know why."

"Did Françoise expect to see you before you went to the Moulin?"

"Yes. But she was out. Look, before I left Aubagne, Gerard called me into the shop. Finally, I was making some headway after years of struggling. Gerard offered me a full partnership in the boutique. He was going to train Françoise to become the town's madam. We'd have everything we dreamed of. She wouldn't have dates. She'd be the one to recruit girls and get a percentage." Karim threw his hands out to an invisible audience. "Gerard was our patron."

"Louise's murder paved the way, didn't it?"

Karim pulled away from the window and collapsed at Michel's feet in tears.

"It was the best thing that could've happened to us."

"You were going to tell Françoise that she was the new madam."

"Yes, I was so excited for us. On the way, my car broke down in St-Raphaël and I telephoned Françoise. But I didn't mention Gerard's offer. I wanted to do that in person and see the look on her face. And now she's dead."

The young Algerian writhed on the carpet. Michel helped Karim to his sofa and propped up a pillow behind his head.

"Did Maddie Gold ever take Françoise's place at Louise's brothel?"

"Absolutely not. We would have lost everything if she'd done that."

"Nevertheless, Louise and Gerard thought Françoise might have used someone to do a turn when she had her monthly."

"They were wrong. The girls spread rumors. They make false accusations because they're jealous and want to steal someone else's customers."

"Are you denying that you saw Françoise in Cannes?"

"Yes, sir. If I had, we'd be sitting on the beach with a cold bottle of wine over a picnic lunch." He began to sob. "And making love afterwards."

Michel studied this ragged bag of bones, shivering in his air-conditioned office and looking longingly at the sea, the bright green Pharaoh's Park across from Fort St-Jean, the elusive freedom beckoning. Unexpectedly, Michel felt a twinge of sympathy for the doomed young man. He was struck by Karim's grief, which contained the element of loss and not the dread allied to guilt.

Michel grappled with his instincts and the evidence against Karim. Had he murdered seven people? Four of them within a day? His fiancée, his employer, the Golds, strangers until the quarrel in Mougins?

"I excused Inspector Toulaine because I wanted to bring up something delicate—man to man." Karim was transfixed. "I want to ask about your sex life with Françoise."

Karim regarded him with disdain. "Are you sick or perverse?"

"No, really rather bourgeois. In fact the woman I lived with for two years threw me over for another man. I'm not very agile, or graceful as you are. And since I was shot, I have difficulty with aerobic positions."

Karim smiled with a certain arrogance, but Michel did not take it amiss.

"So long as you both have a good time," said the young porn merchant. "The sin is frustration."

"That's true. I make up for my gracelessness with enthusiasm."

"That'll do for some women."

"Well, I have to take a course. Something puzzles me about your life, Karim. You spend all day looking at porn, selling fancy gadgets, changing the tapes in the arcade. What happened when Françoise got home at the end of a day? How did you feel about sex with her?"

He was now unfazed. "It was her job. A routine. She'd take a shower. Depending on her shift, we might go dancing at a club. Have dinner, see friends."

"Did the two of you ever have a *ménage à trois?*"

Karim looked at him with disgust. "What a mind you have."

"What do you mean?"

"Will these questions help to capture Françoise's killer?"

"I hope so." Michel thought it odd that Karim was no longer pro-testing his innocence. "I'm curious about your inner world. According to the other girls, Françoise worked six hours when she was on. That could be six dates."

"Or four or eight. It depended."

"Some men come to Louise's for a show."

"There are girls who enjoy other women. It's the gay world. Noth-ing wrong with it. My Françoise wasn't one of them." He reached for a glass of water and picked up a piece of ice and held it against his split lip. "As for threesomes, we never took part in them."

Karim shook his head furiously. "Commander Danton, when you used to get home to the woman who left you, would you bring photos of dead bodies or discuss gruesome murders with her? And say, '*Chérie,* we have a delectable autopsy to go with the Matisse painting and the Pétrus wine?' "

No, not him. Yvette would merrily root through the day's horrors, Michel recalled. He allowed Karim to lead him.

"Obviously not," Karim said. "Or if you did, she'd have a damn good reason for finding another man."

"Actually, I'm attracted to murder. But not at dinner."

"Well, our business was sex. But when Françoise's work hours were over, we talked and made love and slept and woke up together and I would bring her coffee from the filthy café next to the boutique be-cause she slept late. We might drive to Bandol and sit on the beach. In the evening we'd go to the Auberge du Port. We would drink a few Black Labels before dinner to show we had money and then eat *la grillade.*"

"Braised beef slices with anchovies is one of my father's specialties."

"Your father cooks?"

"Yes, he and my mother own Chez Danton."

"Wonderful food. Louise took us there after Françoise's first week. To celebrate her triumph."

Karim's dark eyes blazed with the past glories of a pimp. For a moment, he reminded Michel of Colette's husband Willy, who had forced her to write her books, then stole her money. Karim might have been celebrating the rave reviews for an actress in the gala opening of a play or a diva's recital. But ultimately Françoise was nothing more than the new face on the street. Karim's lofty conscience was not in evidence.

"We went back to Chez Danton one other time without Madame Vercours." Karim began to sag. "An old waiter with a limp treated us abominably. He chased us out when we asked for the hors d'oeuvres to be passed. He was so rude."

"That would be Delantier. The most boorish waiter in Provence."

Karim began to doze. The ice he held on his lip formed a puddle on the glass table. The killer had been meticulous and experienced. He hadn't acted impulsively. Everything was done with precision. If Karim had also murdered Karen Gold, why hadn't she been tortured and gutted? There had to be a reason. Was he trying to confuse the investigators? But that didn't hold up, since the killer had used the same .45 on Françoise and Gerard. Michel raised Karim's head and he threw out his elbows violently and hit the chair.

"I'm sorry, Commander Danton. I thought—"

"Who do you suspect is behind this conspiracy to trap you?"

"I have no idea. I'm so confused and terrified. I can't think. Catch the man." Karim looked up for divine intervention. "Only Allah will ever know the truth."

Michel was troubled by the structure of this symphony. The music was a series of discordant notes. He could detect no melody line or rational purpose in the movements of these crimes which would link the events. He toyed with the metaphor of Cézanne's technique that Jennifer had suggested. The balance was off, the geometry missing. Nothing flowed in a progression.

In the forensic laboratory, he stopped at Andrea's bench. She was leaning over her electromicroscope, projecting the slides on a computer monitor.

"Look at these comparisons," she said gruffly. "There is no way that Françoise Artois was the woman with Louise. In fact, she did not use b-wax. Her pubic hair was cut with scissors. The hair endings are ragged, broken."

"And her hair color?"

"Recent. Her hair was dyed at a salon."

"What about Karim's hair?"

"None of it has been recovered from Louise's crime scene or off any of the victims."

Yet another problem presented itself: Louise had been murdered by a man and a woman—in theory Karim and Françoise. Had a couple murdered the Golds and Gerard? Nothing supported this hypothesis.

In ballistics the news was also bleak. The paraffin test to determine whether Karim had fired a gun had come back negative. Antoine, the burly expert, was in a foul temper. His holiday had been canceled because of these cases.

"And the weapon?"

"This forty-five Smith and Wesson was used on Françoise Artois, Gerard David, and Adam and Karen Gold."

"Where does this leave us?"

"We have a murder weapon and your suspect is locked up, Michel. Isn't that enough?"

Pierre Graslin intercepted Michel as he left the firing range.

"What's going on in the sound lab with the recording of the tip for Courbet?"

"They're still working on the background. There was a lot of noise."

"Make sure they preserve the integrity of the original. There was something there . . . I don't know what."

Had the woman who tipped off Courbet been one of the parties in Louise's murder? And how had she been involved in the other killings? In some ways the arrest of Karim as a suspect obscured the other cases.

He thought aloud. "Karim is the shield . . ."

In the large paneled auditorium, the news conference seemed more like an engagement party of unhappy relatives disapproving of the match. Sweating, half-drunk beefy Englishmen from Fleet Street hurled into the front row alongside their fashion-conscious Parisian counterparts, who were busily cutting deals with the raucous German and suave Italian journalists. The Americans were in their usual running shoes and jogging shorts. But the queen of the proceedings was Yvette, prancing around, whispering, making notes, offering false information to her brethren.

Richard Caron placidly regarded the gluttonous faces.

"Ladies and gentlemen, because of the greater resources of the Police Judiciaire, the municipal authorities in Aix have requested that we take over the investigation of these homicides. On behalf of Commander Michel Danton, who is heading our team, we would like to commend the police in Aix-en-Provence.

"Sergeant Paul Courbet put his life in jeopardy when making the arrest of Karim Hassad. His chief, Superintendent Claude Boisser, was instrumental in organizing the clues leading to this capture. It was an astonishing piece of detection," Caron noted with a wry smile. "Now Commander Danton will take questions."

Michel was uncomfortable before audiences, especially when he had nothing to say. He signaled Caron to leave the podium. They walked through to a covered walkway beside the platform.

"We have the wrong man."

Caron was aghast and for a moment thought that Michel might be suffering a relapse. He'd heard that Dr. Leon Stein had been called.

"You can't tell them that!"

"Oh, I have no intention of telling them anything at this stage. Stein is interviewing Karim now. He'll butter their bread with a steamy psychiatric profile tomorrow."

This was not good enough for Caron.

"Where the hell are we with this case, Michel?"

"At the beginning."

5

HOUSE OF THE HANGED MAN

CHAPTER 46

Dr. Leon Stein had spent several hours with Karim while Richard fended rowdy questions from the press with ambiguous answers. He sat with Michel in the back of Chez Danton with a pastis and a dead cigar.

"Karim's a half-baked revolutionary," Stein said. "Filled with contradictory ideas. I don't believe he's a sociopath or insane in any legal sense. Pitiful. In love with a whore and mourning her."

"That's clear. Leon, he's not faking his grief for Françoise. There's an unusual linkage in these murders. Not quite a signature but close: Louise was killed in a sexual frenzy that featured sadistic torture. Yet it was a disciplined rage. It was very much a composition. The maestro had the time and the voyeuristic arousal to take his time, do it step by step.

"Françoise had to be lured to the church. She was not raped. It looked as though she was preparing for a night out. New dress in a plastic cover with her high heels at the bottom of the bag. It's been confirmed that she left the hairdresser on Rue d'Antibes at five-thirty. Women hate to have their hair messed or touched after spending hours there. They'll accommodate different forms of sex so long as they don't have to put their head on a pillow.

"But Françoise didn't mind. So whoever was with her wasn't a fast trick. And Françoise had more than seven thousand francs in cash and Louise's diamond earrings. I'm convinced whoever killed her was a man she knew . . . a man who attracted her. He was someone who may have given her the money to splurge. She takes off her clothes and spreads her legs for sex and doesn't give a damn about her hair."

Stein nodded in agreement. "Maybe her body was dragged there?"

"No, that's been checked by my people. Now let's try to visualize this: Françoise takes off her panties, lies down on the towel to excite the man. He comes closer, kneels beside her. He has the gun in another towel. When she puts up her face to kiss him, he fires. He knows she's dead. He looks around to make sure no one is in the church grove. He then takes out his knife and slices her open because the blood from the gunshot wound doesn't satisfy him. He has to see viscera. The longitudinal cleavage wound he makes is virtually the same size and angle made on Louise. However, he doesn't have the time to gut Françoise."

The Golds were executed. They were not tortured except psychologically. Why put them in a tub? Ah, yes, his man liked water. Jets thumping away, water running, pillow muffling the gunshot. The police in Cannes reported no signs of forced entry. Hotel keys were easy to get hold of. That's how he came in.

"A forty-five automatic was used on four of the victims. But not Louise."

"The killers were afraid of the shot rousing people at night," Stein suggested.

"Yes, that's reasonable."

"But why not use the gun on the American couple picnicking at the dam?"

"Our lover hadn't stolen it yet."

Michel recounted his interview with Benedict. "He heard English voices at about nine. He can't be sure if they were Brits or Americans. A man and woman. It may be nothing, it may help. I don't know yet. But it tantalizes me. Before Karim became a suspect, I was convinced that the killers weren't French. And even though Karim is of Algerian descent, he's as French as we are."

Stein was unhappy with the direction of the hypothesis. "Michel, you're falling into a trap. It's like the knight fork in chess attacking two pieces at the same time. Clearly a man and woman murdered Louise. As far as the six other killings, there's nothing to substantiate a woman's presence. I think there are three different killers and different motives."

"Go on, Leon."

"If Karim is the sole party and he had a woman accomplice only with Louise and forced them to have sex—certainly Louise was forced—why did he change his technique? We also know for certain that Françoise was not involved in Louise's murder."

Stein fished out a cigar, cut the end and lit it.

"Leon, it looks as though all the murders were planned, except for Gerard's. He may have seen the killer. Gerard was unlucky. Wrong place, wrong time. The question now is: do we believe Karim committed multiple murders and who was the woman he brought with him to Louise's house?"

Stein shuffled through his briefcase and laid his notes on the table.

"From a psychiatric viewpoint, Karim is inept. Mentally he keeps jumping from one subject to another. A magpie. You need resolve and the blood lust to kill all these people. Karim is surprisingly intelligent, with some degree of insight. Nevertheless, as I suggested, his is a disorganized intelligence. Now forgetting logic as we know it, why be sitting on your bed with all this evidence and snorting cocaine with Gerard dead in the shop? You see, Michel, during the examination I conducted, Karim gave no signs of addiction. I believe he uses drugs only when they're available.

"He was stood up by Françoise and thrown out of a restaurant because of some misunderstanding. He returns from Cannes exhausted; up all night; looking in bars and clubs for Françoise; and there's a mother lode of cocaine on his table. He gets high. He's like some starving guest who arrives early and finds a luscious buffet table and makes a pig of himself. Karim isn't reflective, but he's an industrious young man.

"I gave him a variety of tests. Rorschach, Word Association and the TAT. On all of them, he falls within normal parameters. The other conclusion I came to is that Karim Hassad is *not* a liar."

Leon Stein had come around to the impressions Michel had privately formed.

"The cocaine we analyzed came from the same batch we found in Mrs. Gold's purse."

Stein considered this. "Someone put it there. Someone who knew about Karim's habits and behavior."

"It's all so well planned technically that it has the rhythm of a man with military training. Someone who might have been a commando or in special forces."

"There might be a link."

"We also have a good place to begin. The Foreign Legion headquarters is in Aubagne, walking distance from the sex shop Karim worked in."

"Who's the examining magistrate?"

"Charles Fournier."

Stein threw up his hands. "He's going to have a fit. When I completed my tests with Karim, he demanded a polygraph examination. We can of course comply with this request. There's a curious attitude of defiance about him which is not the bravado of a master criminal."

"I agree. Instead of continuing to protest his innocence, he wants us to do whatever we can to solve the crime. Guilty people seldom behave this way."

Stein gulped down the last of his pastis and relit his cigar.

"I've got to dash now. How are you doing with Jennifer?"

"Murder is killing us."

CHAPTER 47

The air cooled on the drive to St-Rémy as the sultry red gloaming dissipated into an ethereal dark blue. Michel could smell and feel the watered verdant pastures he hunted in as a boy. At the end of the road, Jennifer Bowen, his enchantress, would be waiting. Despite the malevolent condition of murder, he was overcome by serenity and the heady flavor of happiness as he got out of the car.

Annie, who had been assigned to guard the women, approached him.

"Were there any problems?" he asked.

"No. The girl's been crying off and on, and Jennifer has been with her."

"Thanks for playing nursemaid, Annie."

"How did Corinne handle the interrogation?"

The women were competitive and he had to protect them from each other.

"She did very well. Karim trusted her. I'll see you in the morning."

"I still think you should have let me do it."

Jennifer was setting the table on the old brick loggia. Silently brooding, Maddie was stretched out on a chaise longue. Michel detected a cold self-absorption that isolated her from time and place.

He sat down at her feet. "How are you feeling, Maddie?"

"Numb, I guess. Like I don't believe what's happened." She reached out for Michel's hand. "You're so generous to take me in this way."

"Consider me your friend."

"I'm glad Jennifer met a man like you. She deserves you."

He was completely disarmed by her attitude. "Jennifer mentioned that you've also met a nice young man. Where's he now?"

"I don't know. Somewhere in Aix."

"Was he away when all this happened?"

He noticed that his innocent question made Maddie wary.

"No, he was with me. We spent the night together in the apartment when I got back from Cannes. You and Jen were out here. I felt it would be okay with Jen."

Maddie was extremely perceptive about providing the two of them with an alibi. She knew full well that Karim had mentioned their relationship. Michel hid his discomfort under a friendly smile. He decided to bide his time.

"After the way Jennifer and I've been acting, you're a puritan. At times, I don't feel like an adult."

"We're all kids when we fall in love."

"You're right, Maddie." He held her hand. "I'm looking forward to meeting your young man. Pity he's not with you at a time like this." He lullabied her with the story she had given to Jennifer. "He's a musician, isn't he?" Again he noticed that Maddie was holding back. "Has Jennifer heard him play?"

"No, not yet. He's very shy."

Michel beamed. "He can't be a Frenchman."

"You're right."

"Do you have classes together at the university?"

"We sort of ran into each other there at a café."

Michel sensed he was on the fox's trail. He came to a decision: he would not mention Karim to Maddie. Let her anxiety build and see where it took him.

He strolled out to the woodshed. The dry olive branches he gathered crackled in his hands. The family hadn't had a barbecue since Easter when Philippe had spit-roasted a suckling pig, and Nicole had prepared a green-apple sauce with honey and Calvados. The memory of the flavors still had a tang. He lit the barbecue and laid out plump entrecôtes. Jennifer motioned him to the side of the farmhouse. He put his arms around her and kissed her.

"I've missed you, Jennifer."

"Me too. I apologize for what happened. I lost it. This is all so bizarre."

"I want to tell you how deeply confident I feel about us and our future together. This isn't a little summer romance for me."

"I think I know that. I'm acting irresponsibly. I don't seem to be able to control my emotions. I'm so greedy for you. I want to be with you all the time."

The touch of her fragrant, silky skin and the sad cast of her features affected him.

"This is an appalling thing to have happened to Maddie."

"She's going to be a problem. She insists on going back to the apartment in Aix."

"Isn't she comfortable here?"

"She wants to pack, Michel. In fact, she's booked airline reservations for tomorrow."

He was intrigued by Maddie's haste. "Has she talked much about her parents?"

"No, everything's very tight inside her."

"What about this musician André. Or is his name Boy?"

She was bewildered. "I'm not sure. She's promiscuous and highly sexed." Jennifer thought for a moment. "There could be more than one man."

He nodded judiciously. "You haven't met either of them?"

"No."

"What about the young man the Golds mentioned in the letter they gave you? Have you seen him?"

"He's not here."

"Would you recognize him?"

"I'm not sure. I only caught a glimpse of him once in a restaurant in Santa Monica. Maddie had a birthday party and a number of girls and I were invited down from Pembrooke." She became unsettled again. "What is this about, Michel? Do you think that creep came here?"

"I'll find out."

"I'd like to know."

Michel reconsidered his position. "Jennifer, I need to confide in you—and you can't mention this to Maddie. She can't leave the country under any circumstances. She's a material witness and I'll have to take an official statement from her."

"This sounds ominous."

"No, just procedure."

"She's so stressed out."

"I'll put it off for a day or two until she's more relaxed. But she's going to have to identify Karim in person. We'll do it in a lineup."

"What?" Jennifer found herself thrust on Maddie's side. "How the hell can you subject her to something like that? She's on the verge of a nervous breakdown." He recognized that Jennifer had a powerful moral obligation to protect Maddie from everyone, including him. "Hasn't she suffered enough? Why put her through another ordeal?"

"Karim's story challenges everything Maddie's told us."

Jennifer drew back as though he'd struck her. "You can't believe him."

"I didn't say I did."

After he had put the steaks on the grill and Jennifer was tossing the salad, Maddie snapped out of her lethargy.

"Would you call a taxi for me, Michel? Or should I do it myself?"

"Where would you like to go?"

"Back to the apartment. I don't like being cut off in the middle of nowhere. The sounds of the country at night make me jumpy."

"I'll drive you in after dinner. How would that be?"

"I said now."

He explained that she would be dogged by the press who were encamped outside her apartment.

"I'll check into a hotel. Tell Jennifer to let me have the American Express checks my father gave her. It's my money."

Her overbearing manner sharply contrasted with her earlier behavior.

"Of course it is."

"I want to rent a car."

"I'll arrange it for you tomorrow. I can get you a preferential rate."

"I don't need a preferential rate."

"I'm worried about you, Maddie. Please stay tonight."

She burst into tears and rushed off the loggia and into the living room. Jennifer started after her and Michel intercepted her.

"Leave her alone for now. Maddie has to act out her guilt."

"Guilt? What do you mean by that?"

"When we lose loved ones, there's a period of remorse for what we've done to them in the past. In some ways, we feel responsible. . . ."

Jennifer turned white. "I guess I understand that better than anyone."

Michel's hands slipped off Jennifer's shoulder. From the bedroom and half asleep, he heard the growl of a cold engine. The luminous clock dial showed it was four in the morning. Silently, he crept out of bed and went outside. His car shot into reverse and throttled down the black driveway. It skirted on a gravel bank, spun, then raced down the road. He had left the keys in the car for Maddie. She and her lover were about to go public. He phoned the duty officers in Aix from the kitchen. They were to track his car from a distance and note where it went.

"Alert everyone, especially Claude's crew that Maddie Gold is driving my Citroën Maserati with my permission. No matter how fast she drives, don't stop her! When she gets to her destination, call Dispatch and I'll check in with them."

Boy was startled by the tapping on his bedroom window. He opened it and climbed out naked onto the sill. The air had a biting chill and the garden was still dark and silent.

"Why the hell're you here?" He reached inside, yanked his jeans and sweatshirt off the cot, and tumbled into his clothes.

"I can't bear being without you."

He dug his fingers into her arm. Maddie longed to have his angry flesh on hers, evidence of his passion. She couldn't survive without it. He shoved her into the garden shed. He had cleaned it out for Denise. It was as immaculate as the gut shanty when Mystery Man inspected it after church on Sunday. Part of the training program to build good habits and never leave evidence. His eyes, grave and deadly, cut through Maddie.

"I don't do time any more, Maddie. We better not be in trouble. You can be unpredictable with everyone, not me."

"Boy, Boy, I couldn't help it. I was stuck in Marseille at Police Headquarters. Afterwards this woman cop took me and Jen out to a farm Michel's family owns. It's in the middle of nowhere."

"What happened?"

"Why'd you cut Françoise open?"

"To throw the cops in a tailspin."

"You screwed her without me?"

"No, little lady. We do these things together." He smiled sedately. "I didn't want to walk in with a big ole hard-on, visitin' your mother. I like to make a good impression when I meet people."

Maddie pressed her body against his. "Oh, God, you're awesome."

He grabbed her hair viciously. "You better have a good reason to be here."

"I do." She loved the pain. "I overheard Michel and Jennifer. Karim told them you use two names."

"We knew he would say that. Look, I watched a news conference in English on the Sky Channel. Karim's their man. Big Michel was on TV being interviewed by that motormouth down the hall."

"He's suspicious. I can feel it."

"You're gettin' paranoid, sugar."

Maddie was gulping air and sobbing. "I can't make it without you."

Boy cradled her head, master of the hunt. Kick a dog and have him bark at other people. He opened the shed door a crack and listened. The church bells rang five times. Calm her down and get rid of her fast.

"I was so cut off, I took Michel's car."

"Brilliant. When I was in the model apartment, I sent you out to hustle. You delivered a pimp and a hooker. And now you steal a cop's car." For a moment he wondered if he should strangle her. He rejected the impulse because he was overcome by actual love for her. "Don't tell me you parked out front of Denise's?"

"No, at Chez Danton. I ran through the alleys from there. No one followed me. Boy, stop worrying, Michel will love the move. I have to act crazy and be unstable for him. It's against my nature to be passive. If I am, Jen'll think it's odd. I'm playing myself," she added with a laugh.

According to Maddie, she had not been impulsive but had thought out her escape. They could not let Michel come to them; they must seize the initiative. Boy was impressed by this assertiveness.

"I want you to come back to the apartment with me. I told Michel you were with me all night. We've got to show him we're out front and not hiding."

"What happens when Jennifer finds me there?"

"I'll say I called you in California and you flew in."

He slammed her head against the wall. "My name's on the fuckin' flight manifest with yours."

"We were going to say I lied about you coming."

He gazed at her. Could he trust her to hold up and play murder games with Michel?

"The story will still work," he said after a moment. "The letter your father wrote to Jen about me is gone. With all this crap going on, and Jen gettin' her rocks off, she won't remember shit."

Maddie silently thanked her lucky constellation of stars that Boy had foreseen this. Did she dare to mention the dossier Kevin Sullivan had compiled? No, she had destroyed the only copy.

"Were you okay with the ID in the morgue?"

"Karen and Adam Gold looked beautiful, chilled. I'm going to go mute and faint at the funeral back in Forest Lawn. How I've hated them. I touched them on the slab. They were silvery and their skin was cold and translucent. My father was always an air-conditioning freak. You could hang meat in there."

Boy gave her his winning smirk. "He'll never have to pay another utility bill."

Maddie savored the moment. She reached into Boy's open fly. "You smell so good."

"Denise's shower ran out and I had to toss some of her herbal slime in the tub and have me a bath."

"Give it to me, Boy. In every part . . . the full snake."

"You'll give birth to a copperhead at this rate."

CHAPTER 48

Michel's detectives were in a foul mood after being roused. They had followed Michel's speeding car to Chez Danton, where it was abandoned. Pierre pursued Maddie on foot through the back passages of Aix's old quarter. Émile maintained contact with his partner over his staticky cellular phone. He trailed him on the small, twisted streets.

"She's stopped at Denise's house," Pierre said, gasping for breath.

"What?"

"Maddie's going through the side gate. Where are you?"

"The corner of Place des Tanneurs. Annie's outside."

"Send her to the back alley of Denise's house."

In a moment, Pierre wearily clip-clopped to the car.

A battered, grimy old Indian motorcycle pulled alongside them. Michel yanked off his helmet. Aware that his car had been stolen, the detectives didn't know what to expect. They were taken off guard by his calmness.

"Where's the girl?"

"She went through the alley of Denise's house. Annie's got her under surveillance."

Why would Maddie go *there*? What possible connection could she have to Denise? Had Yvette persuaded her to give her a private interview?

"Has anyone left the house yet?"

"Annie doesn't think so."

"I'll wait with Émile. Get my car, Pierre. Here's a spare set of keys," Michel said brusquely.

"The girl certainly knows her way around the old quarter," Émile informed him.

"Does she?"

*   *   *

Michel returned to the farm and hauled a belligerent Jennifer back to Aix. She was nettled by something and he accompanied her up to her attic in Maddie's resplendent apartment. Jennifer spent fifteen minutes going through her papers and notebooks. She was fastidious to a fault; he admired the clarity and order she brought to her Cézanne research.

"It's gone."

"What?"

"The letter Adam Gold wrote me. It was about this guy Maddie got involved with. I showed it to you the day we met."

"I didn't actually read all of it."

"The Golds didn't like him."

"Since when do rich fathers approve of their daughters' boyfriends?" Michel was distracted, trying to find the key that drew the murders together. Jennifer was interfering with his train of thought. "Could you have misplaced the letter?" he asked politely and without interest.

While Jennifer scoured through her papers, Michel took the opportunity to search the bathroom. There was no curling iron.

"I don't lose things. I kept all Adam Gold's correspondence separated from my regular letters." She took out an alphabetized accordion folder. "It was under *X*."

"Why there?"

"Because I don't know any Xaviers and I could locate it right away. Look, here are names, addresses, phone and fax numbers for every contingency concerning Maddie. Adam's lawyer, his business manager. A local doctor who speaks English in case we had an emergency."

"Do you remember the name of the man Gold mentioned in his letter?"

Jennifer paced around the narrow room where only weeks ago they had met. She shook her head in frustration. "I'm stuck. Adam Gold didn't mention a name."

"I have to leave now."

"Will I see you later?"

"Dinner certainly. You have my cellular number if you need me." These farewells were becoming increasingly sour for them. "Where will you be?"

"At the research library."

"When you see Maddie, reassure her. Tell her . . . I'm not upset about her taking my car."

*   *   *

Michel had learned little of Maddie's young man from his detectives, who later that morning tracked the couple back to Maddie's apartment. Subsequently, Michel had a phone conference with Richard Caron. The examining magistrate had completed his interrogation of Karim and was prepared to charge him with seven acts of homicide.

"Fournier wants to meet with you, Michel, before acting officially."

"Richard, we have a master killer. I need time to think this through."

There was a long silence at the other end. "Michel, what are the implications of this? If Karim's not our man, who do you suspect?"

"I'm not sure. There are shadows and some correlations in these homicides and I must probe them."

"Are you still trying to connect them all?"

"Or separate them."

"Given the evidence, Fournier will find this objectionable."

"Tell him I'm reviewing everything and doing a follow-up investigation in Cannes."

"Are you?"

"No, but it'll keep him happy."

"Exactly where are you going to be?"

"I've run into interesting company in Aix."

"What does that mean? Are you still searching for a couple?"

"I'll let you know . . ."

During the balmy sun-filled August days, the citizens of Aix were accustomed to sluggish articles praising the music festival, Nicole's recipes for light summer salads, and naturally news of agricultural fairs. *Le Clairon*, however, trumpeted more seductive fare to the locals:

DEPRAVED PORN KING'S MASS MURDER SPREE!

For once Yvette had not exaggerated, Michel thought as he glanced at her article. She may have gotten the killer wrong, that was all. Karim might be surprised to find himself described as a porn potentate, but he could take no remedial action from his prison cell.

Denise was at the cash drawer of her salon making change. A disagreeable expression clouded her face when she caught sight of Michel's bulky figure massed in the doorway. She turned away to stock a shelf with hairspray. He knew she'd be praying that he would vanish.

He gave her a disarming smile, reached up to the top shelf and placed some canisters for her.

"I have someone to do that, Michel. You must have more important things to do with your time than gaping at women under dryers."

"I really enjoy your company, Denise. Your frankness is refreshing."

"Stop this. Haven't you had enough sex talk? There are women who do that for a living. Call one."

"Good idea, it might improve my bedroom conversation."

"All right, what now?"

"You seem to be attracting a number of Americans to your salon."

"We speak English here and advertise during the summer."

"There's a young man working here, and I hear he's also staying with you."

"I always take in students. It's not a crime to help people."

"No, it's not." How could he put this delicately? But then he decided to confront the insufferable woman. "Is he one of the young men you and Louise shared?"

Denise's layers of pancake seemed to expand and melt like tar on the pavement under a blazing sun.

"You're disgusting." Her voice was caustic. "You contaminate everyone around you. No wonder Yvette dumped you for a normal man."

He smarted from the rebuke and grappled to keep his temper. "Please answer my question."

"I tell you something in confidence and you use it to torment me. No, he never met Louise and I wasn't about to introduce them. He's simply down on his luck and there's nothing between us. Dammit. It's innocent. Do you think I'd have sex on my mind when my dearest friend—and your mother's—has been slaughtered? You really need psychiatric help, Michel."

Coming toward him was a short-haired blond young man. Michel realized that he had seen him before. But where and when? He had an extraordinary physical presence, like a Roman Bacchus, with classical features and pellucid innocent deep green eyes that would have pleased Cézanne. Michel thought if a man could be beautiful, Maddie's boyfriend would qualify for that distinction.

"Need me, Denise?"

"Yes, André, please bring out two more cartons of the Fluance Shampoo. I have to go out now." She brushed past Michel, leaving the two men.

Michel looked at him amiably. "Are you Maddie's friend?"

"Yes, sir. Guess you must be Michel." He extended his hand and Michel shook it. "I told her she had no business taking your car."

"It wasn't a problem. Did she come to see you this morning?"

Boy moved his weight from one foot to the other, then gracefully gave in. "Yeah. She's been in a bad way since this horrible thing happened to her folks."

"Is it André?"

"Naw, that was just a gag. I thought if I was goin' to be here, might as well give myself a French name."

Michel exploded with unexpected laughter. "I wish I'd done that myself when I lived in New York and California." He fell easily into the American vernacular. "The guys called me Frenchie. Drove me nuts. I should've told them I was a duke or something like that. They would have loved it."

"Real name's Darrell Vernon Boynton. They call me Boy at home."

"Well, Boy, how are you enjoying your stay here?"

"Very much, sir—until these murders."

"Michel, please."

Boy gave off an air of gentle sincerity, tempered by a refreshing diffidence that Michel found charming.

"How long have you been working here?"

"Few weeks. My money ran out and Denise has a heart o' gold. She's been puttin' me up and I do some jobs here."

"I respect people who aren't afraid of work. Most Americans come here dripping with dollars and think they can buy everything."

They continued to chat outside the salon, both of them congenial and open. What impressed Michel about Maddie's young man was how likable and respectful he was.

"I understand you're a musician."

"Oh, Maddie, she exaggerates. I play a little country and western and Dixieland. I just fool around."

"You're being modest. You've got strong tapered fingers."

"I play some piano and guitar."

"It's a pity you're here in season. When the tourists are gone, Aix is an entirely different place."

"Tell you the truth, Michel, I can't wait to get back to the States and have me an American meal. Food here's too rich for someone with my down-home tastes."

"We all miss our native cooking. I felt that way in America. The only thing I became addicted to was chili dogs and barbecue."

Magic words! Boy let out a whoop.

"I'd kill for a chili dog."

"Would you?" Michel wrapped an arm around Boy's shoulders. "Ah, I remember in L.A. going to Pink's on La Brea at two o'clock in the morning for a chili dog with onions. When I was in the San Fernando Valley, I'd drive miles out of my way to Uncle Hogly Wogly's for Texas spareribs."

"You're somethin' else. A kindred spirit, Michel."

"I've got an idea. Tonight, I can't promise you ribs or a chili dog, but would a good thick steak and fries do?"

Boy's mouth was watering. "That's fantastic."

"My family owns a restaurant. You know what, I'll have my father cut you a special steak. He charcoal-broils it."

Boy's lips puckered. "Sounds great."

Michel moved close to Boy. "Jennifer and I are worried about Maddie. We have to support her. If you see her, tell her she's invited. If it's at all possible, we have to get her mind off this tragedy."

"Will do."

"Is seven o'clock convenient?"

"We'll be there. And thanks." Gratitude suffused Boy's open face. He radiated a guileless purity. "Maddie said you were a terrific guy and she sure was right."

For the first time since this monstrous chain of murders had begun, Michel had a sense that there was an inscrutable order evolving amid these disparate events. He was not exactly making progress, but he was wending his way down an unmapped back road. In the distance he thought he could hear an evanescent note of music.

CHAPTER 49

That afternoon, Boy cleaned up back at Maddie's apartment. He and Maddie showered together. Riding high, they wrapped bath sheets around each other and made love on the terrace, viewed below by Michel's detectives outside. The new life of wealth and comfort agreed with Boy. Later they caressed their freedom at Les Deux Garçons. Aix was fragrant with flowers, gorgeous with its sun-bronzed cast of faces parading by the café tables. They could at last enjoy being young lovers and loll under the canopy of plane trees in the late afternoon sunshine without fear.

Boy strutted in his tight jeans and Tony Lama high-heeled western boots; a bright red-striped Mexican shirt with a black string tie set off his Saturday night outfit. Banging back a Jack Daniel's and conjuring up their future in Los Angeles, he realized he'd never been happier. Maddie scrutinized him with pride of ownership. In a few days she would be truly liberated.

"Got to give you credit, my lady. You're playin' our hand like a champ. We're sittin' pat with four aces. Let Michel draw and try to make a straight flush."

Maddie leaned her head on Boy's shoulder. "Funny thing is I like him."

"Do you?" Boy belted down his drink and waved at the waiter for two more. "That's his number, being liked. Don't you get it?" he said warily. "Tomorrow he's goin' to stuff Karim's story down your throat."

"I can handle it."

"Scream your head off when you see the slimeball. Grand Ole Opry time."

"Where will you be?"

Boy raised his hands, trying to shape the situation. "Maybe Michel will ask me to run in to Marseille with you."

"I can swing it alone, Boy." Maddie moved her soft mouth against his and slipped her tongue along his lips. "Where do you want to go for a honeymoon?"

"Love to see Hawaii." His eyes widened. "I've read about volcanoes . . . and seen burning beds of lava on TV," he said. "Then it'll be your turn. I'll take you down home. Searing red dirt, thunder, snakes, dark gray twister combs comin' at you. Skies speckled with lightning."

"It'll be thrilling."

"Do you think of your folks?"

"Sometimes images flash by."

"What do you see?"

"That fat ugly man and the dead phony actress were born for one reason. To bring me to you."

The thought of murder aroused Boy. Maddie put her hand along his thigh. In plain sight, his jeans bulged. He was hard again.

"I presented her with her Emmy, my lady."

Boy eagerly accepted Michel's offer to tour the glories of Chez Danton's kitchen. In the deep freezer, Michel switched on a light and guided his guest inside. Gleaming sides of beef, girdled with fat, were coated with white frost. Boy inspected them with interest and did not complain of the cold. Earlier they had discussed the possibilities of barbecuing spareribs at the farm.

"These ole hindquarters have good marbling," Boy observed.

"It's Charolais, our best beef. We have the slaughterhouse hang it for six weeks before it comes here."

"Most folks don't realize that when it turns a little green it's a sign of the good bacteria which tenderize the beef."

"I'm really delighted to show someone around who's knowledgeable about these things."

"Oh, I've kicked around slop kitchens and canteens . . . nothin' like this, mind you. Jobs in supermarkets, shootin' the breeze with butchers."

"On the other hand, I was forced to work in this kitchen for years. It's hard, repetitious work. Drove me crazy."

"That why you became a cop?"

"I suppose. I thought anything's got to be better. It would be an adventure. It's not really. The trouble with me is, routines get on my nerves."

"World wouldn't work without 'em."

"You're right."

Michel led Boy back into the kitchen. On a large maple chopping block, a side of perfect ruby beef lay thawing to room temperature. Bone saws, cleavers, and choppers hung from a rack above. The Sabatier chef's knives were laid out on the block. Boy's eyes drifted with shaded enchantment from one stainless steel blade to another and lingered on the razor-sharp ten-inch slicing knife.

"Which cut would you like?"

"Could I have me a porterhouse?"

"My favorite, too." He handed the knife to Boy. "Like to carve your own?"

"Oh no, no, Michel." Boy was momentarily disconcerted by the invitation and became vigilant. "Knowin' me, I'd probably make one holy mess of it. I'm so damn clumsy."

"No problem. We'll let my father do it. He's the expert. How thick would you like yours?"

"Say about two inches, please. Don't let him trim too much fat."

"Too lean and it's tough. A good steak needs an edge."

Philippe was at the grill flipping the sparse early orders, now and then peering curiously over his shoulder at them. Boy smiled at him and sniffed around the range.

"What's this?"

"Our secret house steak sauce. It's beef marrow in a red wine reduction with shallots, garlic mustard and herbs," Philippe said exuberantly to Michel's visitor. He enjoyed having spectators. He followed Boy's eyes. "You're looking for something?"

"Do you keep any Heinz ketchup?"

"Absolutely not!" he said, curtly turning his back.

"Sorry, your sauce sounds great."

"My father's very sensitive about cooking. We'll have it served on the side for you to try," Michel said amiably.

Michel was temporarily back in the family good graces. He had been paying his bills. Nicole was at the bar with Maddie. They were drinking the little-known, highly coveted, Ayala champagne which had just arrived.

Now that the case had been solved by Courbet, and Louise's killer was safely in jail, Nicole was also in a better mood. Her incision was healing and there hadn't been any further complications. She had a long guest list for the funeral and was reviewing the names. The degenerate, married country whoremasters who had slobbered over Louise's girls at the restaurant while their wives ate old cheese and drank sour wine would not welcome her intrusion. No, she'd better not spook that herd.

Michel observed that his mother provided a fountain of sympathy for the orphaned Maddie, whom she'd taken to her heart. She held Maddie's hand and was suggesting a mass for her parents.

"We're Jewish. But it can't hurt," Maddie replied. Her gloom dissipated when she spied Boy's glittering smile over Michel's shoulder. She hugged Michel. "Nicole, I'm so grateful to your son for taking me in and putting up with me."

Nicole cuffed Michel's large chin. "He's not all bad," she said with a smile. "Sometimes a bit tightfisted. He thinks we're running a soup kitchen for the police here."

"That's enough. My account's in good standing."

"Either that or it would have been a court appearance. Delantier suggested we sue you and your fancy group in Marseille. Our bills get lost in your computers. Delantier will serve you dinner properly this evening. Your father gave him your account for collection."

"I'm shocked that he'd stoop so low."

"My dear son, you've charged your tips for two years and he hadn't collected them."

Michel brought Boy into the group like a big brother. "I'm sorry to subject you to our family business. I'm an only child—"

"And the black sheep," Nicole said not unkindly. "Maybe Jennifer will straighten you out."

"Not as far as we're concerned, Madame Danton," Boy chirped. *"Monsieur Michel est très gallant."* He winked at Maddie. "How's that? I'm pickin' up hairdresser's French."

Maddie tapped her glass and René was quick to pour more of the Ayala for her.

Michel leaned forward. "Fresh drinks for us too, René! Mr. Boynton's drink is all water. Open a new bottle of Jack Daniel's."

René grouchily put the dirty glasses on a full tray atop the hatch. The phone rang and he answered it. "For you, Michel."

"I'll take it in the office. Here, give me the tray and stop whining. We're paying customers now."

Michel speedily brought the tray into the kitchen. He handed it to Annie who was waiting and chomping a lamb chop.

"René's prints are in our central computer file, so match them first. I told him to be sure to touch only the stem of the glass. Have the lab scan the prints, put them on the main-frame computer and send them to the FBI. Mark it Priority Urgent. And wipe that grease off your hands."

"Yes, sir." She opened her notebook. "His name is Darrell Vernon Boynton?"

"Yes, that's what he said. I want Pierre to check with immigration on his arrival date. I'm sure it was through Nice. And have Émile get the flight manifests for both Maddie Gold and Boynton."

Annie slipped on latex gloves. She emptied the dregs of liquor and placed the glass in a brown paper bag.

Michel looked at his watch. "The FBI claim they can do a four-hour turnaround. Let them prove it to me this time."

Jennifer arrived through the kitchen and was waiting in Nicole's office for him.

"Are they here?" she asked.

"Yes. You look stunning."

He moved close to her. She wore a short skirt and a green V-necked silk top. He leaned over to kiss her, but she backed away.

"What's wrong now, Jennifer?"

"I can't go through with this dinner. While I was upstairs changing, I heard Maddie laughing her head off. When I leaned out the window of my room, I saw her and this André going at it. They were naked on the terrace. Now I don't give a damn about people screwing. But this was revolting."

"Sex helps when you've been through a traumatic experience." He wondered if he might be talking about himself.

A disgusted skepticism tightened Jennifer's lovely face. "I'm no moralist sitting in judgment. But dammit, there's a time to mourn."

"Jennifer, she's not you."

"That's not the issue. Michel, there's something about this guy that's bad. He frightens me."

Jennifer moved away and took a deep breath. She couldn't bring herself to mention what she had seen. Snake tattoos on the young man's buttocks. The gruesome sight had repulsed her.

"He's a naive country boy."

"You're kidding yourself."

"Was he the one at Maddie's birthday dinner in Los Angeles?"

"I don't recognize him."

"Have you ever seen him before?"

"Stop pressuring me, I don't know." She shuddered in his arms and held him tightly. "I'm so tense in this situation."

"They've probably been dodging you for the last month. You never would have let Maddie have him sleep at the flat."

"Damn right. I'm *not* a madam."

"Stop it, Jennifer." He kissed her soothingly. "Look at it this way: Your duties are over. You've been paid. Maddie's going to do what she wants. Forget about her going to classes and working on conversation. Have a real holiday at the farm. You could come into Aix to do research at the library." Another solution occurred to him. "If that doesn't suit you, move into my flat. I've had it cleaned up. The point is, I want you out of that miserable attic and close to me."

Jennifer was in turmoil. She struggled with an innate sense of duty, and the fantasy he offered. He had never found modesty in women forbidding. After Yvette, Jennifer's conduct bolstered him. She had purged Yvette and helped him gather the shattered strands of his ego.

"You're wonderful, Michel. It's a lovely suggestion. But selfish. I'm a pain in the ass. But I have to help Maddie through this tragedy."

He took her arm and guided her through the busy kitchen.

"If that's the case, act out your convictions and join us for dinner."

CHAPTER 50

Over their massive char-broiled steaks, Delantier was the epitome of the classic French waiter. He sliced, he charmed, brought plates from the warmer, but he still maintained a dash of smugness in his smile. Maddie merely picked at her food, but Boy packed his away.

"I haven't ever had this kind of service anywhere," Boy told Maddie. "And the steaks were out of this world."

Jennifer remained distant and troubled. The women became more relaxed when Delantier gracefully prepared crêpes with a sauce of marc. He gave them a running commentary as though calling a race at Longchamps.

"I'd like to take him home with me," Maddie said.

"I wish you would," Michel grumbled out of earshot. Michel recalled the other morning at her flat. "You wanted crêpes, Maddie. Here they are, made by a master."

Jennifer was astounded by Delantier's transformation from a snarling ogre to an ingratiating enchanter. "Did your parents threaten to fire him or what?"

"It's a long story. . . ."

With everyone happily eating their dessert, Michel added a dash of bitters. Somewhat abashed, he looked over at Boy and Maddie.

"I hate to bring this up—especially after such a delightful evening. But I have to discuss something unpleasant. Maddie, I've bent the rules for you because of my relationship with Jennifer." Boy and Maddie seemed puzzled. "Unfortunately, I have some official business with you both tomorrow. I'll make it as painless as I can."

"Like what?" Maddie asked.

"Well, you know that Karim is the principal suspect in your parents' case and five other homicides. He's made some ridiculous statements that have to be cleared up in my report."

Boy had been waiting for this and pretended to be oblivious. He tucked into seconds of the crêpes.

"Do I have to see Karim?" Maddie asked.

Boy reassured her. "He's in jail, it'll be okay. Trust Michel."

Jennifer took her hand. "Of course it will."

Maddie was still alarmed. "Will he be convicted?"

"Without question. And the sooner I can discuss this with you, the better. I'm afraid it's necessary for the preparation of the case. Legal requirements have to be satisfied, just like the United States. We're probably worse than they are."

"Worse?" she asked. "In what way?"

"I didn't mean to suggest brutal. We're so much more bureaucratic here. We have armies of civil servants—*fonctionnaires*—who have to justify their existence, filling out endless forms and reports. It's a terrible nuisance, going through a tedious chain of command."

"I thought you were in charge of the police," Maddie said in some confusion.

"Only of the Special Circumstances Section in the southern departments. We're all slaves of the state." Michel grimaced. "We have lawyers and courts to deal with and it makes busywork for everyone. The clerks, the stenographers . . . And then we have to wait until mid-September for the fall sitting of the Assize Court in Marseille. It's like your superior court. It hears the criminal cases."

Maddie winced and laid her head on Boy's shoulder. To Michel the affection between them seemed genuine.

"Her parents were so good to her," Boy said glumly.

"Then you can understand that we want our evidence to be solid and without ambiguity. When this goes to court, Karim's lawyer won't stand a chance."

"Airtight," Boy said. "You got to do it, sugar."

Maddie began to snuffle. "When can I take my parents home and give them a proper burial?"

"As soon as possible. I guarantee that. You see, I've had to inform the American embassy in Paris about the situation. There's a protocol. Red tape and technical things have to be satisfied when two countries are involved in a tragedy like this. I'd prefer to do this informally before an official *procès-verbal.*"

"A what?" she asked.

"It's our version of a formal police statement. It has to be taken down. If I know what's involved now, I can fill out details you might not recall later. Nobody has a perfect memory, so if you contradict yourself, don't be concerned."

Neither Maddie nor Boy was forthcoming.

Michel mildly prodded them. "While we have our coffee, why don't you both tell me how you met Karim and Françoise?"

And so their convoluted tale began.

"I shouldn't say this—since you're a cop," Boy said, a model of probity and meekness.

"Think of me more as an adviser and friend."

Boy lowered his eyes. "I ran into Karim around the university and he was dealing drugs. Well, he gave me a little hash."

Maddie took command. "We had some drinks with him and Françoise at Deux Garçons. Boy wanted to find out about the club scene here and see if he could get work with a rock group."

"You do this in California?" Michel asked.

"I work here and there in dance clubs. Been tryin' to connect in L.A."

Michel turned to Jennifer. "Not easy being a musician."

"I wouldn't know," she said coldly.

"Were you aware that Françoise was a prostitute?"

"Not at the beginning," Maddie said. "If Boy and Jennifer had known, they wouldn't have wanted me to hang out with her. See, I liked her. She had a friendly, open personality. She showed me around."

Jennifer sulked, infuriated. She had introduced Maddie to new cultural pursuits, and tried to shore up the girl. She realized how miserably she had failed in the mission she'd undertaken for the Golds. Clearly, her companionship had been rejected for that of a whore.

"Ole Françoise was fun," Boy agreed. With an air of censure, he continued. "I didn't know about the hooker stuff until later. Or else I would've nipped it in the bud. But Maddie's more broadminded than me."

Michel turned to Jennifer. "Did you all fly over together?"

Jennifer was livid. She had been sandbagged. "I damn well didn't know a thing about that."

Boy tried to calm her down. "Jen, blame me. It was kind of a surprise for Maddie. I didn't know if I could get the money together for a ticket or what the work situation was like here. If I'd known, I wouldn't have come."

Maddie and Jennifer had flown first class, Boy, coach, imprisoned with the masses.

Michel was genial, regarding it as a prank. "Maddie, you had no idea that Boy was on the flight?"

"Not till we got here." Boy gave her a sheepish smile. "I almost fainted when Boy phoned me up for a date. Jen said something like '*Dinner with André.*' That's how we all got started calling him André."

"No, honey, I think it was Denise who gave me the nickname."

"Whatever . . ."

Jennifer glared at them. "I was under the impression he was French!"

Michel came quickly to her rescue. "This is no big deal, darling. Students having a lark."

"Right on, Michel. Larkin'. And the reason I didn't want to meet Jennifer was that Maddie was afraid she might think Maddie'd be messin' around with me instead of doin' her course work."

Michel was intrigued by how skillfully Boy had shifted any blame for his deception away from the Golds and onto Jennifer.

Jennifer's eyes were large with indignation. "I wish the hell there weren't these lies for my benefit."

"Come now, they weren't really lies," Michel said, defending the young couple and becoming their champion.

He dared not explain to Jennifer why she had been isolated, made the outcast in the group. Delantier broke the tension. He wheeled over the trolley with cognacs. Michel selected a dense thirty-year-old Borderies from Louzac and poured glasses for Boy and himself.

"Let's stretch our legs on the boule court before we call it a night? I'm not very good but I'll show you how to play."

"If the ladies'll excuse us," Boy said.

Drinks in hand, Michel led him to the court in back.

"I'll give you a lesson another time. I wanted a private word with you."

"Shoot."

"We're in a sticky personal situation and this might suit us both. It's silly for you and Maddie to sneak around. You shouldn't have to stay with Denise. Maddie needs you with her."

"It's been frustrating, that's for sure."

"I can imagine. It's obvious that you and Maddie are in love. Having Jennifer around is awkward."

Boy snapped at the offer. He would move in with Maddie. Jennifer, despite her concerns, would reluctantly stay with Michel.

"Sure make life easier for everyone," Boy agreed.

"Wonderful. You have to understand that Jennifer feels a deep sense of responsibility for Maddie and that's why she's overprotective."

"Bless her. We're all on the same team. Michel, I can't thank you enough for dinner and bein' such a pal."

In the perfect murders of the past, everything Boy and Mystery Man had done had been worked out with precision. Now in France, unforeseen events had conspired to abet Boy. Jennifer, his enemy, had become the instrument of his triumph. Michel had neutralized her danger. Until it proved otherwise, he would allow Jennifer to live.

"I'll have a car pick you both up . . . at about ten. Would that be convenient?"

"Suit us fine."

"In the meantime, here are the addresses and phone numbers at my flat in Aix and the farm. Call me any time there's a problem."

Boy snuggled the card in his wallet. "Maybe this weekend, we'll try to cook up some ribs and a batch of chili."

"That's a wonderful idea. We can really get to know each other."

"Yeah . . . Oh, where do I shop for the food?"

"Don't worry about that. I'll arrange it. My mother has the recipes of the world. I'll get her to research it for us. She'll be glad to help out."

CHAPTER 51

The moment they were alone inside the apartment, Maddie let out a squealing rodeo whoop. She was astonished when Boy clapped his hand over her mouth and spoke in a whisper.

"Don't say a word."

The veins bulged tensely in his forehead and he flicked off a drop of sweat. His eyes had the color of a drowned swimmer. They changed gradually and the pupils enlarged into the vacant stare of an owl hunting in the night. His madness had such a fierce purity as to be beautiful and mesmerizing to Maddie. He peered around suspiciously and led her into the bathroom. He turned on the bath faucets and spoke over the gurgling water.

"We don't know the laws here. Maybe Michel can bug us legally and also tap the phone. We can't discuss a thing about what happened."

"It's working, though."

"Long as we don't mess up."

Boy was jumpy and distracted by Michel's behavior. He was simply too nice and considerate. Boy didn't for a moment consider Michel stupid.

"Look, he's so hot for Jennifer, he can't think straight. He wants us on our way so he can have her full time." Maddie's small child hands enclosed Boy's shiny damp face as though it was a rare cameo. She licked his lips. "Know the feeling, Boy . . . when you can't get enough of someone?"

Jennifer opened the balcony door in Michel's apartment. It was stuffy and she sensed the presence of another woman's intrusive laughter, the sounds of love. Somehow at Michel's farm, with the wind whipping the branches of the tall cypress trees, the night cries and howls of animals and birdsong, Yvette had been absent. Now the ghost of her gaunt face and sharp voice pervaded the enclosed space. Michel came up behind Jennifer and wound his strong fingers around her waist.

"Why'd you push this?"

"You had no option. They're lovers—as we are. Why make things more difficult for Maddie?"

"Maybe you're right. Will you take it easy on her tomorrow?"

"Should I?"

"What do you mean by that?"

"I've cut corners for her and Boy as it is. The three of us have a good deal to discuss. I didn't want to drag her down to the office and subject her to a barrage of questions tonight—questions the examining magistrate and I need answers to."

Jennifer could not identify exactly why she was deluged with misgivings. She had not liked Boy and found his obsequiousness repellent. The southern gallantry and clumsy politesse had been done to death. How could Maddie stand the sound of his heavy drawl, his sham meekness? Of course, he supplied the oversexed girl with heavy voltage. Could Michel have a blind spot about young American men?

"How can you bear this rube? The way he sucks up to everyone. He's a phony."

"Really?"

"This isn't a question of his lack of education. It's an act, this bashful, bumbling, good ole country boy stuff. It's bullshit, Michel."

He had been thrust on delicate ground and dared not alarm Jennifer any further. He hated to lie but was trapped. "I thought I was just being gracious for Maddie's sake."

"She's probably glad her parents are dead."

"Is that a fact?"

"She'd been on dope, and done everything you hear about spoiled rich girls with doting parents. But the Golds got the message finally and stopped rolling over. That's why they sent her to Pembrooke. The school has a very structured environment for girls who have discipline problems. If you don't control yourself and do your work, you're out. In that sense, the college is a refreshing change for what passes for education in America. The dean is tough-minded. No free rides there.

"As soon as this Boynton shows up, he gets some hash for her from a murderous pimp. They get high and I'm sitting in the apartment sweating it, reviewing her notes on the symbolist poets. Like a fool.

"Maybe I deserved it. But I took this job as Maddie's escort or monitor, or whatever I'm supposed to be, in a spirit of dedication.

Yes, I wanted another trip to France. I couldn't afford to come over on my salary and now I'm walking through blood. I can't stand it!" Suddenly she began to cry. He was thrown off balance and upset. "Are we really going to be together? I'm starting to sense an ambivalence in you."

"It's my work that's creating the pressure." He kissed her, tasting the salty drops on her cheeks. "I never thought I would have a woman who'd fulfill me the way you do. You've become the center of my life."

"We don't know each other and yet we do. I love you, Michel, so solemnly that at times it whips at me with such force that I feel myself cowering. And I want to raise my hands to protect myself from it."

He visualized her as the lady in the tower in some medieval rite, a woman for whom men would go to the lists, for the privilege of her hand. At a time of rancor between the sexes, he cherished the fine texture of Jennifer's character.

"I love you beyond anything I could have imagined. When I'm away from you, I can hardly concentrate and I feel guilty about squandering our time on this sordid business. When it gets resolved, I'll show you the country. We'll get away from all this and take a driving trip. I have friends who own small hotels and restaurants all around. We'll go to the beach at Bandol, eat oysters in Brittany, foie gras in Périgueux."

What a sad, mean little existence it had been before him, she thought. The promise of a future and his natural gaiety when they were alone transported her out of the bleak scenes of death.

"Between meals, will we have a chance to make love?"

"Are you busy now?"

"No, are you on call?"

He swept her into the bedroom and they pawed at each other. She lifted her sweater and he was enveloped by the curve of her deep breasts, which he had helplessly stared at all through the evening, waiting for this moment. The touch of her flesh reminded him of childhood and a voluptuous pudding he had secretly stolen from the kitchen.

"You've been a mirage all my life, Jennifer."

CHAPTER 52

Michel reached his office in Marseille at six-thirty the following morning. He struggled to free himself from the dreamy night with Jennifer. He'd have to shop for a new mattress. He didn't remember buying the old horsehair installation. As it aged, it had developed the properties of a concrete slab. He couldn't keep a woman on it for any length of time. Yvette had also complained of it.

He opened his briefcase and removed a package of Arles sausage and fresh nutty-olive cheese. The baguette was still warm and he placed it on his desk.

"No peaches for me?" Annie asked the office's food supplier. His staff seldom made lunch arrangements until they had seen what he brought in.

"Don't be greedy. I didn't have time."

Annie opened a cupboard and took out some chipped plates and tarnished silverware Chez Danton had donated along with deep-bellied breakfast coffee cups.

Annie summarized the salient points in the prolix FBI official report, which was now a year old.

"How's Karim holding up?"

"He's in a trance."

"Has Leon Stein come in?"

"No, he's due at ten when the happy couple arrive."

"What's your feeling, Annie?"

"I adore Mr. Boynton's history. I can't wait to sign my name on his dance card."

DARRELL VERNON BOYNTON
b. January 10, 1972, West Guthrie, Oklahoma
Orphan, Single, Caucasian male.

IN OKLAHOMA

When he was 16, Boynton had been brought to trial for the snake murder of a man called Rico Gonzalez. Gonzalez had been a union organizer of itinerant laborers on the farm where the two had worked.

The defendant asserted that everyone in the area knew that he trapped and bred vipers: rattlesnakes, water moccasins and copperheads, which he often sold to collectors. He admitted that there had been disagreements between himself and Gonzalez.

On the evening of Gonzalez's death, he had apparently locked himself in the changing room where Boynton's snakes were kept. Six rattlers had attacked Gonzalez. Toxicological examinations revealed that the snakes had ingested peyote prior to the attack. Boynton explained that he had been carrying out experiments on the snakes and was attempting in fact to modify their behavior.

The D.A.'s final report had read:

Case circumstantial. Dismissed for lack of evidence. Death ultimately ruled accidental.

At 19, Boynton had been convicted of abducting two 11-year-old girls. It was not a clear case. The defendant said that all he had done was to give the hitchhiking girls a ride. When his car broke down, he attempted to repair it. He only tied up the girls to prevent them from wandering away in the woods. At the trial, the girls made timid witnesses and one of them recanted her original statement.

Charge reduced to unlawful detention of minors. Boynton served two years at Oklahoma State Prison in McAlester.

IN CALIFORNIA

When Boynton was 22, he was charged and convicted of the rape of a mother and daughter in Salinas. The accused maintained he had been a rodeo worker and had met the woman's 14-year-old daughter and the two had a relationship which had received the mother's blessing.

Boynton had been invited to move into their trailer park home. He had resided with them for 3 months. With the end of the rodeo season, he was hired at a cattle mart. According to Boynton, the girl's mother was jealous and had forced herself on him. When he rejected her, she contacted the police and accused him of raping them both.

After 6 months at Soledad Prison Boynton's behavior was judged to be a danger to other prison inmates. His court-appointed lawyer successfully petitioned the court for further psychological evaluations. Court psychiatrists determined that he was "borderline sociopathic" and recommended that he be sent to Atascadero Mental Hospital for treatment.

After state budgets were cut, Darrell Vernon Boynton was released from Atascadero.

EXCERPTS FROM D. V. BOYNTON'S CASEWORKER'S REPORT

Darrell is extremely friendly and personable and has a good attitude. He has not been late or missed an appointment with me. He is working as a sound technician and sometime musician in disco clubs. Although the work is sporadic, it pays well and "Boy" has been averaging $400 p.w.

At a social gathering at my apartment complex, he brought sound equipment and also performed very well. Afterward he offered free guitar lessons to anyone who wished to sign up. Given his background and interpersonal history, I consider his behavior exemplary.

J. R. BYERS

Michel put down his sandwich and considered the progress of the murders. What possible reason could Boy have had for murdering Louise? Had they met? Where and under what circumstances? Was he a young man that she and Denise would have for an evening then dismiss? Was that it, despite Denise's vituperative denial?

Louise had been robbed of cash, jewelry and casino chips. Most of it had turned up with both Karim and Françoise. Why hadn't Boy checked into a hotel or bought himself a new wardrobe if he had ready cash? The murder of someone by an outsider with no apparent motive was the most difficult kind of case to solve.

Boy had known Karim and Françoise. Nothing yet to indicate bad blood among them. Maddie considered Françoise a friend. And how did the Golds fit into the pattern? Boy had praised them as parents, but he might easily have been lying.

According to Jennifer, the letter they had written cautioned her to beware of a man Maddie was involved with. Could this have been Boy? Michel struggled to recall the details of the letter. But he retained only a vague outline.

Gerard had seen the killer and had to die.

Still, why kill five people?

Louise had been eviscerated. Françoise had been cut from the navel to the pubis with the same type of slash. There was similarity and not congruence.

The Golds had only been shot. Karen Gold had not been cut open.

Why? Had this been to spare Maddie?

Finally, apart from robbery, what was the motive behind the murder of the American couple at the Bimont Dam? Robbery, sex? Was there a link?

Michel glanced up at Annie, who was anxiously waiting for his re-action. He handed the report back to her. "Are you sure you want to sign Boy's dance card?"

"Maybe I'll take guitar lessons."

"Send out a bulletin to Immigration. I don't want Maddie or Boynton leaving the country. If they try, arrest them."

CHAPTER 53

A bit past seven, Jennifer arrived at the apartment carrying a large container of espresso and a buttery baguette. She still had Michel's scent clinging to her. Jennifer Bowen cast the murders out of her mind for a moment. She took a gleeful pleasure in the splendors of having fallen in love in Provence. Only a month ago, nothing of the kind seemed possible. Walking up the steps, she was humming a favorite Beatles song from her childhood.

" 'He loves you, yeah yeah.' "

She would pack her clothes and books and bring them to Michel's flat, then head for the library. She and Michel would meet later. She now realized that, for her own good, Michel had tricked her. He had wanted to extricate her from what had turned out to be a sordid situation.

Jennifer unlocked the door, trooped happily through the foyer and was immobilized. She knew that the horror of the depraved indelible image right before her eyes would always haunt her.

Maddie and Boy were naked and sound asleep. As Jennifer tiptoed past them, she made out something attached to Maddie. A gold ring had been pierced through Maddie's clitoris. Boy's index finger was inserted in the ring.

Even asleep he had a grotesque erection. Jennifer now saw a third copperhead snake tattoo. This one was on the shaft of his penis. It seemed to surge before it would strike. The snake's open mouth and the large fangs had been fused on the head.

Jennifer put her hand over her mouth to prevent herself from screaming. She removed her shoes and silently crept up the staircase. She moved slowly, overcome by the shock of their deviancy. She sat on her bed, staring at her bare feet on the grainy wooden floor.

She had heard stories of this kind of piercing among girls in L.A. gangs. But Maddie came from a different background. Beholding her, so slight and slender, a child with a tanned glow, descending to purgatory, overwhelmed Jennifer. What insanity had driven her to do such a thing to the most precious part of her body? Maddie had degraded a woman's sacred place. If an act could be unholy, such a savage violation seemed like the act of murder to Jennifer. She could find no grounds for such barbarism, only perversion of a magnitude that attacked the realm of reason.

In a daze, she packed her clothes, and loaded her books into wine crates. She squeezed her research folders between the books and stopped suddenly. A raucous sound from below startled her and she crept to the foot of the stairs. Leaning against the wall, she was out of view. Maddie was being tickled and giggling. Maddie picked up a pillow and had a tug of war for it with Boy. Maddie abruptly halted.

"Oh, shit, with everything that happened, I forgot to tell you something." Maddie's voice dropped, but Jennifer could still hear. "My father had an 'eye in the sky' put in every room at the house."

Boy dropped the pillow. "The gizmos they use in Vegas to catch cheating?"

"Yes, sir. And it runs video tape to a security service."

"We're on tape?" he groaned, fuming.

"Uh-huh. It was our first time after Christmas in my room."

"Did he say he watched it?"

"No, he swore he didn't."

"Are there copies?"

"No, he destroyed it. I tore up the report the private detective did on you."

Boy sneered and turned his head up to the ceiling as if Adam Gold was above him. Jennifer darted back into her room.

"Well, you piece of lard, you can watch me and your daughter makin' love for the next fifty years."

Maddie soothed him. "He's done, forget it. Come on, Boy, let's get cleaned up."

"Showtime for Michel. No makeup. Remember, you're in mourning."

Maddie laughed hoarsely. Boy's fusion of charm and malevolence intoxicated her. "I wonder why I keep forgetting."

Bile burst into Jennifer's throat and she pitched her hand to her mouth. When she heard the shower going, she decided to make a dash for it. She would return later to clear out for good. She peeped out. Boy was still sitting on the bed. It would be impossible to pass him. She'd have to wait until they left.

She picked up her Skira volume on Cézanne, a treasure bought secondhand in Ojai's outdoor bookstore for fifty dollars. She flipped through the pages, lingering morbidly on the reproduction of *House of the Hanged Man*. With its bare twisted branches jutting out in front of the window of a house, blocking out the light, suggesting the gallows, it provided a deadly correlative of her circumstances. Her house of love had been transfigured into a place of death. She had studied the sinister composition in Paris and spent the better part of a day making notes for her doctoral dissertation. The mood of foreboding gloom cast a spell over her, enveloping her in its pall until she lost track of time.

By nine-thirty, her agitation had settled into a wary stupor. Boy and Maddie left for their appointment with Michel.

Jennifer rapidly resumed packing. In fifteen minutes she had made three trips down to the apartment. She bolted up the stairs for a final inspection of the attic room. She stood stock-still on the landing. She could see a mottled shape on the roof above the grimy blackened skylight. It was a man's athletic shoe. Was it Boy? Had he come back because of some jungle instinct he possessed?

Jennifer edged to the window and observed Maddie standing alone at the curb beside a waiting car. Two of Michel's detectives were fighting back surging colonies of photographers and reporters.

The squeaking footfalls above Jennifer gave way to the creak of the metal roof door and a heavy clang when it was slammed. Jennifer wrapped herself in the window curtain but maintained a view of the street. In a shivering sweat, with bluebottles swarming over her face and arms, she waited for the car to pull away. What was holding it up?

Suddenly, Boy exploded out of the entrance and into the blistering sunlight. He pranced up to Maddie. As the anxious detectives cleared a path to the car door, Boy took Maddie aside and whispered to her.

Maddie turned and cast her eyes up at Jennifer's window.

CHAPTER 54

"What a view of the harbor," Boy exclaimed. He romped around Michel's office like a hyperactive child in a doctor's waiting room. "Wish I had me a camera. This harbor must've once been full of pirates fightin' for treasure. Long John Silver waving his cutlass." He adjusted the eyepiece on Michel's eighteenth-century brass telescope. "Maddie, it works!"

"Not well enough to have spotted Lord Nelson," Michel said grumpily. Earlier they had positively identified Karim in a lineup in mere seconds.

"Huh?"

"He was the Brit who sank the French fleet," Maddie informed him.

"Never got around to anything but Civil War history."

A gilded immaturity imprisoned Boy in a timeless frieze of youth. He might have been de-aging before Michel's eyes. He had never witnessed such a transformation in an adult. Rather than finding this behavior engaging, it created the opposite effect on Michel. He found it chilling in its natural calculation.

Boy's guile and innocence were unified, concealing the dark man. He who was ready to skip rope when chili was mentioned, cultivated snakes, experimented with them, and had been on trial for murder at sixteen. He who had kidnapped two young girls and done what to them? Exposed himself, petted them? Whatever it might be, it would have been unspeakable. Later, Boy had gone to prison for raping a mother and daughter who had taken him into their home.

What could Boy's behavior have been like, if the other prisoners in Soledad felt threatened by him? Ever inventive, he had found a narrow crack in the system and slipped through as silently as a viper in pursuit of prey. Soft time at a mental institution where he would be more at home duping nurses with his mush and playing the eternal child with clod psychologists. Michel knew how American authorities lapped up stormy sagas of abuse delivered by young men with angelic faces. That, of course, was the fundamental problem with questioning someone like Darrell Vernon Boynton. The façade was unthreatening, coded.

They had been at it for the better part of an hour, Maddie and Boy, rambling through their quixotic association with Karim and Françoise. They dodged around, each corroborating what the other said.

"Are you telling me that Karim was attracted to you, Maddie?"

"Yes, he hit on me, propositioned me. Karim's so twisted. I was scared out of my wits. He talked about Louise's place and said he could make a deal with her if I worked as a whore. When he didn't back off, I finally told Boy. He was furious. I mean the four of us started out as kind of friends. Then it became scary."

Boy left his private world of pirates and tall ships at the window and dropped on the sofa. "When I faced Karim down about it, that maniac stuck a gun against my heart." Boy hit his chest and trembled. "Michel, I was terrified of this guy."

Michel evinced the concern of a big brother listening to the younger one recount the activities of a dangerous bully.

"Horrible. What was Françoise's reaction?"

"She was frightened of Karim. We all were," Maddie said with assurance. "He had this vicious side to him. He used to beat her up. One minute Karim's charming, the next, he's planning to make bombs and blow up the music festival."

"Didn't either of you think of reporting these threats to the police? You know we've had bombings all over France."

Boy's tongue roved through his cheek in the manner of someone slow-witted who required patience from an adult. But once the opening presented itself, he took the initiative.

"That's the point. We've read about how dangerous these Algerian revolutionaries are. They're ready to kill hundreds of innocent people for their cause. The other thing, Michel"—Boy grimaced—"truth be told, I had some problems with the law when I was younger." Michel feigned surprise. Boy studied Michel's incredulity and determined it was genuine. "Got into a few jams. It was kid stuff. And, well, sir, I did some time."

Michel nodded. "I appreciate your honesty, Boy."

"We're pals. I'd done my time and I wasn't lookin' for trouble. So we stopped seein' Karim. But Aix's a small town and we couldn't help but run into him. He'd force himself on us. We'd have coffee, a drink. I was afraid of bein' rude and settin' him off."

The day before the murders of Françoise and the Golds in Cannes, they claimed Karim had pursued them and dragged them to an Algerian restaurant where Boy was forced to pay for the meal.

Maddie took her cue. "I mentioned I was going to Cannes to visit my parents. I did that hoping he'd get off my back and leave me alone. I said my father had a hair-trigger temper. Instead, Karim followed me there." Her voice took on a macabre hush. "And you know what he *did* there."

Maddie broke off and mewled on Boy's shoulder. "Easy, easy, my lady."

She responded to his blandishments. He took up the murky story with the craft of a parent bolstering a distraught child's glaring lie.

"Don't let's forget how Karim ran down the Cours after that horrible lunch, Maddie. He couldn't wait to get the newspaper because he thought him and Françoise were suspected of murderin' the madam."

Maddie wiped her eyes. "Right."

Michel gave her some time and his attitude was placid, more of muddled advocate. "Didn't Karim go to Cannes to see Françoise?"

"Not that I know of," Maddie quickly answered. "She was hiding from him."

Boy leaned forward. "She was tryin' to escape from him."

In view of what Gerard had reported to him, this assumption would not bear weight. On the basis of a rumor at the brothel, Françoise had been banished to Cannes by Louise. Karim would be the last one to be battering her and ruining her summer season. Michel listened patiently to more and more discrepancies in their chronicle. He ruminated about his next question. He was afraid to alarm them.

"Boy, why didn't you go to Cannes with Maddie? Or did you?"

"Nope, I stayed here."

"Wouldn't you have enjoyed seeing the Golds?"

"Sure. I loved those folks. But it was strictly a family get-together for Maddie."

"But as Maddie's good and dear friend, didn't you expect to visit with them?"

"I wanted to break the news that Boy and I were going to get married," she said.

"Oh, I see."

"They were the kind of people who put their daughter in a glass cage," he said.

"Nobody was good enough," Michel suggested.

"Right. But they adored Boy. My father was thinking of testing him for one of his TV series. Boy has a future, a career. And my father, God bless, was the key to Boy's future success. Still, well, I really didn't want to use my position with them to further his career."

"I've acted, Michel. And people who've seen me think I'm a natural."

Maddie touched his face. "Star potential, my man."

Karim had assured Michel that Boy was in Cannes and had seen Françoise earlier, then invited him to dinner with the Golds. He had given Karim money to buy evening clothes. Michel watched the young couple now grappling through the curtain of silence.

"Look, everything depended on my parents' itinerary and my classes at the university. Once we got that organized, Boy was going to join us."

"At the Hôtel du Cap," he added, completing her sentences for her.

Michel could imagine how the Golds would react to their princess courting a violent ex-con. As an enormously wealthy man in the communications business, it would have been a simple matter for Adam Gold to collect information on Boy.

"I think I understand now, Boy. You waited for Maddie to return to Aix. At her apartment?"

"No, I was over at Denise's place."

"How did you know Maddie would be home earlier than expected? The same night, in fact."

Maddie's mouth quivered. "I had a lecture to go to with Jennifer. Sorry it killed *your* evening. When you're in love . . . Oh, come on, Michel, you should know—you sense these things."

Boy smiled at her and she leaned her head on his shoulder.

"Fact was, I couldn't sleep. I hit a couple of little bars. Had a beer here and there." And a haircut along the way, Michel thought. "Then moseyed over to Maddie's."

"You knew Jennifer was staying at my farm?"

"Maddie thought she might be." Boy turned to Maddie. "Didn't Jen leave a note, sugar?"

"I'm pretty sure she did. Jen leaves lots of notes."

In the unassailable unity of accomplices, lovers who would back each other to the death, Michel's dilemma was crystallized. If he moved impulsively, he would be planted in a swamp of international lawyers and American politicians. The diplomatic corps would file protests at the Elysée Palace. Maddie and Boy would wave goodbye to him from the first-class lounge on their way to America and immunity.

The O. J. Simpson case demonstrated how the synthesis of celebrity wealth and brilliant counsel had combined to create havoc for the authorities.

"I think we're finished. Thank you both for your cooperation. I realize what an ordeal this has been for you, Maddie. You're lucky to have someone as loving as Boy to look after you."

"I know." She looked at Boy tenderly. "Can we go now?"

Boy played an ace. "Back home?"

"I'm afraid not just yet. There's a short interview with our Mr. Fournier after I've given him my report. He's like a D.A. I know it's an inconvenience. But I'd like you to feel—when you're back in America with a clear conscience—that this tragedy is behind you. Please be patient and let us plod along and resolve this for you."

Boy made the best of the delay. There was an air of arrogance in his manner.

"Still up for our chili barbecue, or are you quittin' on us?"

"My mother's working on the recipe. Suppose we smoke the ribs together? With you in charge, we'll do it right. France could use a barbecue franchise. Business ventures can start with flukes . . . like all of us meeting." He rose from his desk. "I'll have a driver take you back to Aix. There's a back way, so the press won't be after you."

He detected their uncertainty about his offer and wondered what plan Boy had devised.

"No thanks, Michel. I think we'd like to explore Marseille today. You've been super."

Maddie grabbed hold of him and kissed him on the cheek. There was no way to avoid the contact without making them skittish.

Maddie and Boy were escorted down to the basement and left through a side exit to avoid the press. When they turned the corner, they found themselves thrust in the middle of briny fishwives and stallkeepers bellowing on the Quai de Belges. Boy tightly held Maddie's hand as they drifted through veiled side streets, eyed by hawk-eyed hustlers and hookers offering drugs and live sex shows. The glorious Marseille summer sunshine spread out before them like a finely woven tapestry, spotlighting the bustling life of the city.

"What were you going to tell me before we left Aix?"

"Jen was upstairs when we were in bed this mornin'. She was spyin' on us. That's why I didn't go to the car with you. I checked out the roof."

Maddie stopped in midstride, worry pinching her mouth. "Did we say something wrong?"

"She knows."

"How? I don't understand." Her voice was shrill. "We didn't do anything incriminating."

"We had the *wrong* attitude for death."

CHAPTER 55

"Of course I've heard the news about you and Yvette . . ."

The speaker was Charles Fournier, the examining magistrate assigned to the case. He and Michel were friends, but in judicial proceedings they jousted. Fournier conducted himself with the hauteur arrogance of a feudal baron and Michel was the serf. The magistrate functioned as something of a judge as well as a district attorney. He assessed evidence and passed it on to a prosecutor to argue in court. The eccentric judicial role was unique to France. Charles Fournier knew the law to the letter and his habitual pettifogging about details and instructions did not endear him to the Legion members.

"Our local boule champion Courbet did me in."

"I wish he'd taken a crack at my wife while he was screwing everyone else in Aix."

Fournier was in his late fifties, tall but stooped, and had a cowl of blondish hair drifting over his eyebrow which he indolently brushed back like a fashion model. The eyes behind the rimless glasses were deep brown and focused amicably on Michel. Tailored in an English summer herringbone, he was enormously rich and had a keen appreciation of any malicious gossip circulating.

"They say you've been cured by an American *femme fatale*. I've heard from experts that she has the finest set of natural tits between here and Paris."

"Charles, do be sure to tell her that when I bring her to your bouillabaisse festival. She loves compliments like that."

"Well, then I'll strike Yvette off the list."

Invitations to dinner by Fournier and his wife, Melba, were eagerly sought after. They served fish, five courses of it. The best fish in the world. Melba's father owned the largest fleet of trawlers in Marseille and Fournier's widowed mother was the owner of the prodigious langoustine wholesale business on the Quai de Belges. Behind his back, Fournier was known as Neptune. Rather than a trident, he carried a mother-of-pearl Mont Blanc fountain pen, which he tapped over Michel's report.

"I've never had a homicide suspect who declined a lawyer and demanded a polygraph examination," Fournier observed bleakly.

"Let's give Karim the test."

"No. Out of the question. It's the rage in America. There are people who can lie their way through it. Look at this Aldrich Ames who was a KGB mole in the CIA. No, absolutely not."

"I still have some people to interview."

"Michel, I intend to get my appointment as a judge at the Assize Court next year." The cowl of hair was patted in place. I'm going to charge this Algerian mongrel Karim with seven homicides."

"I don't want you to make a fool of yourself, Charles. Be patient."

A frown of displeasure creased Neptune's brow. He adjusted his speckled Charvet tie.

"What are you cooking up?"

"I'm not at the range yet. It's just prep. A young man and woman, both Americans. If I'm not very careful, they could call in lawyers and be on the next plane to Los Angeles."

"Do you have evidence?"

"No, only some whispering doubts."

"What shall I do about Karim?"

"There's plenty to keep him here. Illegal firearms possession, receiving stolen property. Let's not forget drugs and possible terrorist activities under investigation."

"I'm like you, Michel. I love a murder for the entrée."

"Not yet, please."

"Take your father's advice, Michel. Don't overcook this, we like our steaks and women rare."

Michel hurried down to the sound lab where he found his speech expert Georges Gamel doing stretching exercises on the floor. He nimbly jumped to his feet.

"We were going to Cassis to play tennis for the day when one of your minions telephoned me, Michel."

"I won't keep you long, Georges."

Gamel was a sometime police consultant and professor of speech therapy at the University of Marseille. Many of the academics in town enjoyed the prospect of helping to solve crimes, as well as the supplement to their meager incomes. Gamel was ramrod tall with a gray mustache, and he arranged the hair on his head so that, like strands of spaghetti, it covered the plate. When he took off his straw hat, it was with the caution of someone who'd had neurosurgery.

Michel signaled the sound technician to play the tape. The background static and fuzz had been removed from a copy of the master tape.

"Karim Hassad se vante de l'assassinat de Louise Vercours."

Karim Hassad had bragged about murdering Louise. Michel detected the bells of St-Sauveur tolling nine o'clock. There were other muted sounds; a harp, playing the same Debussy suite he had heard near the market weeks earlier. A girl had been practicing. He had looked up and seen her silhouette in the window through a veil of curtains. If he returned to the same spot at the perimeter of the market, he could, through triangulation, locate the telephone. It was certainly outside.

"Excellent French," Professor Gamel observed, "but not native born. Definitely not of Latin descent. I'd say American."

"How do you know that?" Michel asked anxiously.

"The consonants in *Louise Vercours* aren't French. The girl leaving the message softened the *s*, which should be a hard *z*. Also the *i* in *assassinat* isn't long enough. No one who speaks a Romance language indigenously would do that."

"I thought it might be a foreigner," Michel said. "The line sounds as if it was memorized. And the voice is strained, nervous. Would you agree, Georges?"

"Yes, it's forced. Like an actor who knows his part well but whose attention is not on the significance and meaning of the dialogue. The principal concern of the speaker is on accuracy."

"Thank you."

Gamel replaced his beach hat with extraordinary care, lighted a cigarillo and hesitated with indecision. He removed an official envelope from his pocket.

"Would you do me a favor now, Michel?"

"Glad to."

He handed Michel the envelope, which contained a traffic summons. "See if you can get these brutes out of what remains of my hair."

The web of circumstances now had an irresistible logic, propelling Michel forward at high speed. He was thrilled to be composing a case, uncovering obscure themes, clues that hardly amounted to anything and might be overlooked.

This meditation intruded on the memorial service in progress at St-Sauveur. Michel had been baptized there at the font where the priest now stood handing candles to the mourners of the extraordinary Louise Vercours. His mother knelt at the altar, followed by his father and finally he himself. All of them praying for the lady's immortal soul. The hundreds of people packed in the majestic cathedral attested to her good will and benevolence.

Vincent Sardou lost his austerity and was restraining a tear. In his sad, wrinkled eyes and black suit, he himself might have been the grieving husband. He caught up with Michel.

"I know you're still in the middle of the case. But when you have some free time, please drop by the office."

"Do you know something about the murders?"

"No, it's a personal matter. It can wait. Since your forensic people have finished with Louise's house, I've had new locks and a gate put up. It's all been cleaned up. I'll let you have a key when you come into the office."

"Thank you, Vincent."

Nicole walked alongside Michel in the market square. The vendors bowed to Nicole Danton. It had been ages since they had seen her inspecting produce and cheeses. She was an imposing, respected figure and sample tastes were offered. Nyons olives, sugary, baby red radishes the size of a fingernail, violet lettuces. When she nodded, stallkeepers hunted for clean sacks and said they'd deliver her orders. Nicole Danton no longer carried anything but her Chanel bag.

Michel took his mother's arm and sat her down at the Café Printemps across from Louise's house. He ordered espressos for them.

"It's been so long since we've been on our own at the market," Nicole said. "I'm so relieved that all of this is behind us and you've found the killer."

"It was inevitable that he'd make a mistake."

"I've missed our little chats, darling."

"I have as well. Would you do me a favor, Mother? It's very important." She nodded. "Go through your cooking files and get me a recipe for chili. And I'd like you to fix a sauce for spareribs."

Maternal fear swept over Nicole Danton. Could Michel be ill again? She was weighed down by the futility of helping him.

"Are you planning to poison someone?" An insight intruded. "Oh no, it's that Jennifer. She put you up to this. Americans will eat anything."

CHAPTER 56

Michel found Jennifer sitting outside the library, her head down in a book. The sun glimmered on her blond hair. She had it up and tied with a red ribbon. She wore no makeup and had on cut-off jeans and a baggy Pembrooke T-shirt. There was an ethereal innocence about her which unlocked a cluster of emotions within him.

He was passionately in love with her and didn't care about forfeiting his parents' endorsement. But how could he structure his life around her? Could he leave his position with the police and give up the excitement, the challenges? Start a business? But what kind? How would he spend his days? Selling junk in a shop? Handing out menus at Chez Danton? Working at the farm? His immersion in murder was too concentrated and ingrained to abandon. He was haunted by the realization that his obsession would consume Jennifer's love.

A smile crossed her face when he leaned down and kissed her. "Sorry I was running late."

"I called your office. They said you'd gone to a funeral."

"Louise's memorial service."

"That must have been a drain."

"Even more than I thought. I'll always miss her."

She held on to his arm and they strolled in the direction of the Cours Mirabeau. He couldn't remember when they had last walked together. They stopped at King René's fountain, luxuriating in the serene street, cooled by towering plane trees which formed umbrellas over the old buildings. The odd shapes of shade and light created a mysterious chiaroscuro effect. What had become of the loveliness of summer days, doing nothing with the woman he loved?

"Michel, look, I found a first edition of Vollard's autobiography. Imagine, being the first one to have recognized Cézanne's genius and known him."

"It was a good time to be alive."

"Finding the book saved my awful day."

"What happened?"

"I'm all packed." Her soft eyes were grim. "When you've got some time, will you help me get my stuff out of the apartment? I don't want to go back alone."

"We can do it now." He found her apprehension troubling. "What's on your mind, darling?"

"I can't wait to get away from them. Maddie and Boy frighten me. They're mad, Michel. And so perverted that even the most far-out people would be sickened."

When Jennifer described how she had found them asleep, Michel's suspicions received another spur. A woman who had her privates pierced by a ring and a man with a tattoo on his penis had propelled them beyond the boundary of fads and normality. People who treated their bodies that way were capable of anything.

"Aren't you shocked?" When he vacillated, Jennifer was filled with condemnation. "I guess when you've seen people hacked to death, you have to harden yourself to what average people feel and think."

"You're wrong. This is as repelling to me as it is to you. But I've had to develop discipline. I can't act surprised when I'm conducting an investigation. If I show my feelings, I could damage a case. And the guilty parties take a walk."

She accepted his explanation, but was neither happy nor prepared to say she understood. For his part, he knew that he would have to deceive her again so that she'd accept the invitation to the barbecue. If she were absent, Maddie and Boy would be on guard and he might lose them. He wished he could confide in Jennifer, but he fell back on diversionary tactics. He studied her solemn face and began to laugh.

"Jennifer, how would you like to see Louise's collection of paintings? Picasso, Renoir, Bonnard, Monet and Degas? And we mustn't forget your icon. Louise has one of the Cézanne still lifes of apples."

"Oh my God, when?"

"In a couple of days when I've finished the case."

Maddie settled for a blue Mercedes 560SL convertible at Hertz in Marseille. She'd wanted a red Porsche, but Boy had prevailed. It was too flashy, not the kind of car someone in mourning would be renting.

"It gives off the wrong vibes. We have to be . . . conservative." He fastened on the word. Conservative. It had the sound of wealth and position. People with big bucks played it down. "We take it slow for a while. Only a few more days and we're home."

"You think Michel suspects anything?"

"No way. You knocked me out with him." He smiled blithely. "Man, the way you cruised. Didn't get rattled for a sec. There's no evidence and he's got Karim sittin' in the can. Michel wouldn't be knockin' his brains out to entertain us if he thought anything was fishy. But never forget he's a cop and has a big job. So it's a reflex to be watchin' us out of the corner of his eye."

Boy finally had a set of wheels under him and he was jubilant. He hit the accelerator and took it up to a 120, blurring past everything on the road.

"There's one problem that won't go away. From the get-go it's been Jennifer. Miserable bitch. Miss goody-two-shoes with a holier-than-thou attitude." Boy reflected. "If she'd only asked your father to be more openhanded none of this would've happened." The inconvenience of his circumstances and not the murders themselves still rankled him. "I had to take control. No one can pull me along. I am capable of valiant deeds. Now you are. You're in the world I rule."

With the skill of a Michelangelo, Boy constructed an edifice of hatred around Jennifer which he implanted in Maddie. Jennifer had heard something in the apartment. She might tell Michel. Suspicions would grow. Michel would do anything to pacify Jennifer, appear heroic to her. Mystery Man had taught Boy that the seed of an idea was everything. Create a partial outline and the other person completed the form.

"If we get tripped up—"

Maddie was gripped by panic and her face contorted. "What do you mean, tripped up?"

"All those people are dead because of Jen. You saw the way she acted toward me at dinner. She couldn't stand me. She's like your folks. She'll always be lookin' for some way to bag us. She comes in this mornin'. Hides upstairs. Spies on us. Why? You walk in on two sleepin' naked people, you make a noise, give 'em a chance to cover up. Jen was there when we were makin' love."

Maddie's eyes grew large and warlike as she listened attentively.

"Suppose for some reason, Karim beats this case. The first one they'll come after is you, Maddie. And Jen will be pullin' them by the hand. She'll say, 'Maddie has this boyfriend and he's a bad dude who served time. Now he's married to her and livin' in a Bel Air palace.' It's motive. And only Jen can supply it."

Maddie was engrossed by Boy's scenario.

"Let's say Karim gets himself a great lawyer. He might. Never know. He's an Arab, and there are people with oil money who'd contribute to a defense fund. He does a year or two for the gun and the dope, but no murder. Your father's lawyers decide to put up a reward. That private detective who taped us at the house, hooks up with Jennifer. Remember, Jen is a bust-out, a nickel and dimer, or she wouldn't have taken this job of chaperonin' you for a free trip and a few bucks at the back end.

"Jen and that detective are breathin' down our necks. He's ex-Homicide. He has friends on the force. They start sniffin' around. Murder-Money-Beautiful Heiress. They bring in some fat, beer-belly cop and get him to read up on the chickenshit investigation in France by these amateurs. He pulls records and takes a shot.

"He interviews Jen. Prods her memory. She starts imaginin' things that never happened. She dresses it up. Maybe she can walk away with half a million bucks, peddlin' a book or movie. I mean what's Jen got in Pembrooke? Worryin' all the time about the ax fallin'. She's in a no-lose situation. They give her another freebie back to France to jog her memory. That penny-pinchin' bitch, she'd sell her mother for that."

By the time they had reached the village of St-Rémy-de-Provence, the conception was beginning to form in Maddie's mind, slowly at first. As Boy continued, the logic of it became apparent.

He glanced around with disdain at the main street. "Another shitty old town. Why don't they fix these places up?"

"You're wrong this time. Nostradamus was born here. And the Marquis de Sade's ancestors lived here."

"De Sade. I know who he is." He remembered that Mystery Man spoke of de Sade and had a collection of his works. Boy's appetite was whetted. "Let's see the place."

Maddie scanned the map and gave him directions.

The Hôtel de Sade was a forbidding gray townhouse. Inside, Boy examined the votive altars where he imagined men and women had been chained and tortured. His eyes were filled with pleasure and wonder. He imagined he could hear the sound of screams. On the stone floors he visualized ancient blood spatters. Standing in front of a statue of Hercules, he felt empowered, omnipotent.

He glanced around, sizing up the few curious visitors. He maneuvered Maddie into a corner of the chamber, away from the guard. He had a sense of its history. This was a holy shrine. If they could lure Jennifer into this house of punishment, it would be a fitting conclusion. Wild images of Jennifer naked, manacled, pleading, aroused him.

"You'd lash her with a bullwhip. Then we'd do what I call a special handling on her and keep her alive for days and days . . ."

Slowly, he incited Maddie, building the erotic momentum. He conjured up a scene she could visualize. Don't let Jennifer pass out. Keep her awake. Let her feel the pain as he had.

Mouth agape, Maddie listened with the devotion of a high priestess. Nestled in a corner, out of view, Boy slipped his hand under Maddie's skirt. His fingers roved between her throbbing thighs until he clenched the slave ring. Maddie's eyes protruded, glazing over. He continued to probe inside her. Maddie groaned, her body flexed, then shook in repeated orgasms.

He abruptly stopped. She was wobbling and he supported her.

"You're going to have say goodbye to Jennifer for us. Will you do it?"

"Yes, yes," Maddie whispered, joined to him in the ecstasy of the moment.

"How do we get to Michel's farm?"

Boy parked behind a gnarled grove of sheltering olive trees turning black in the melting dusk. They put on the Nikes they had bought at a stall in Marseille. Low stone walls undulated around the property. But there were no barbed wire fences to negotiate.

"Any dogs?" he asked.

"An old German shepherd going blind that sleeps on the porch. A poodle and some cats."

The house was deserted, but in the barnyard he spotted a man feeding chickens.

"His mother's sausage factory is down there with a greenhouse where they grow herbs."

They trod through a copse. The thrash of the wind and the scurrying of animals and birds reminded Boy of his expeditions in the woods with Mystery Man, the two of them carrying warm musky bodies they would bury.

Maddie was uneasy. "Any snakes here?"

Boy had read of the local varieties. "Maybe a snub-nosed adder. But you will come to no harm. I am the savior of snakes."

Boy heard a musical sound that lured him on through the property. Running water. Leading Maddie by the hand, he followed the tinkle, until it grew stronger. They reached a lake enclosed by old clusters of umbrella pines and dells filled with thick rushes of undergrowth. Boy leaned down and tested the water. It was cold and clear. He cupped his hand and tasted the water.

"Perfect for a swim on a hot afternoon while Michel and me are cookin' up a storm at the house."

"Do I tell Jen to take a swimsuit along?"

"No, it's on impulse. You and Jen are on a nature walk in the woods. She'll buy it. You're both hot and sweaty. You strip off your clothes and barrel in naked."

"Jen's uptight about that."

"Sell her. Coax her. She can't be such a prude. Maybe it'll be easy. Don't put up obstacles, Maddie! It's two girls at a swimmin' hole. A lark. Nobody can see you."

In a flash, Boy envisioned the scene in its totality. When the two women were naked in the water, a phantom rapist would attack them.

Boy picked up a stone. "You smash Jennifer's head. Hit her hard on the left temple. It'll paralyze her. Once she's under water, hold her there until there are no bubbles. Grab her by the hair, *not* the throat. If the cops examine your fingernails, they won't find her skin.

"Once she's dead, you bang the hell out of yourself. Hit *your* head with a rock. You've got to be badly bruised. And be sure to cut your legs up with some of these sharp branches. I want you staggerin' back to the house naked and bleeding."

Maddie was daunted by these demands. "Oh God, I'll have to give a description of the man who attacked us."

"You say he's a big man in denim overalls. He had on a ski mask. He came up from behind and hit you first. You're in shock. It's all a blur to you. Happened so fast. Babble, scream. Michel will be flippin' out. He won't be thinkin' of anything but gettin' to Jennifer and trackin' the killer."

Maddie was tormented by the act of murdering anyone . . . alone.

"But Boy, I'll be the only witness," Maddie countered. "They'll keep me in France even longer!"

"No way. You give Michel a statement and we're gone. Back to the States to bury your parents. You're incoherent, a bug case. We get your ole man's lawyers to start screamin' at the embassy. They fly you back for psychiatric treatment. Believe me, Maddie, this is my turf. I'm a specialist."

She shuddered in Boy's arms and he reassured her. He took off her clothes and wormed his tongue along her belly, then he throttled inside her.

"Ohhh, ohhh," she cried.

He took it easy. In the woods, he'd always been gentle with the young girls. Couldn't scare them while they were being initiated.

"Michel spends his time lookin' for the freak who killed Jen. We'll be free!"

"I can't wait till we're back home on our own. Just us, Boy."

"If you do it, we'll have the world by the balls."

She huddled against him, kissing him until she thought she'd choke.

"I'll kill Jennifer."

CHAPTER 57

In Brillat-Savarin's *The Physiology of Taste*, the bible and philosophy of voluptuous eating and cuisine, the esteemed author made an observation which Nicole Danton quoted to Michel in the restaurant kitchen.

" 'No man is a gourmand simply because he wishes to be one. There are certain people to whom Nature has denied this organic delicacy. Such people are as blind to taste as true blind men are to light.' " She paused mournfully. "Obviously, you are such a individual. A barbarian, Michel."

While Nicole was angrily preparing barbecue sauce, Escoffier had been quoted. Michel had not only taken up with an American woman, moved her into the family farm, but also was serving American food in their home!

"This is the death knell of French civilization."

"To me it's a new beginning," he said with amusement.

Flushed with weariness and resignation, Nicole picked up her mortar and with evident repulsion emptied the contents into a plastic bag. The mixture contained ground chili peppers, flour, cumin, oregano, dried garlic, onion, paprika and sea salt. Looking over her shoulder, she placed the pestle and mortar in a sink of boiling water.

"It's a good thing your father isn't back from the market. Here's your chili powder." She handed the bag to him as though it contained some gruesome virus that had to be taken to a laboratory. "Obviously as parents we took a wrong turning, Michel. You've had marvelous opportunities—more of them than anyone I know. You had a future as an academic. Not exciting enough for you. You might have become a chef. Taken over Chez Danton eventually. . . .

"Instead you chose to be a detective, and not a very good one at that. Everywhere one looks—in the newspapers and on TV—there are interviews with Paul Courbet, whom you've treated despicably. But he's the valiant officer who captured Louise's killer and brought him in! And he didn't get shot four times in the process."

Strangled by his indignation, Michel held in his anger. He merely nodded to his mother and glumly shuffled out the back door.

An investigation of Gerard David's records and diaries conducted by Richard Caron revealed that Gerard had been paying Paul Courbet a regular stipend for intimidating the girls at Louise's. Charges would be brought against Courbet. One particular notation stood out:

Françoise must leave for Cannes.
Call Courbet and have him threaten her.
Payment 1000 francs.

Before setting out to St-Rémy, Michel had briefed his detectives and set up positions for them on the perimeter of the farm. Jennifer had moved in the previous day and was unaware of the guests who would be arriving shortly.

With the philosophical meditations of Brillat-Savarin and Nicole's censure ringing in Michel's ears, French cuisine reached its nadir in the mad preparation of chili on a steamy Saturday afternoon. Jennifer soaked the kidney beans and ground the beef. Michel simmered onions and small bite-sized pieces of steak. He wore his precious Mickey Mantle Yankee baseball cap.

"You're full of surprises, Michel," she said with delight. "Of all the people in the world, I couldn't imagine you cooking chili or being a Yankee fan."

"I hope you approve."

"I love it. Are we having a salad with the chili?"

"Cole slaw and spareribs!"

"This is orgasmic! Mind-blowing." He regarded her gloomily. "Did I say something wrong?"

"No, my mother makes me crabby."

"Well, wait till you meet mine. She'll take you to her heart as I have."

With the devilish ragout brewing in the stockpot, they walked out into the garden where the heady scent of lavender and herbs obliterated the psychological horrors of the kitchen. The air was heavy with unspoken intentions. They had met only weeks ago, but the swift passage of days had enveloped them in a different level of intense time that massed and created lifetimes in seconds. This theory had been

Henri Bergson's view of the duration of time, he remembered from his philosophy course at the Sorbonne.

They stretched out on the grassy hillside. Jennifer rested her head on his stomach and he looked down at her tanned face and ran his fingers over her skin. She would be flying back to Los Angeles in a week.

"Do you have to go?"

"My ticket is nonrefundable. And I have a contract at Pembrooke for next year, which I sweated to get. I've still got masses of notes to collate for my courses. But I'm really excited about seeing Louise's collection of paintings. It would give me the inside track for a monograph."

He leaned down and kissed her rapturously. "Would it be folly to ask you not to leave or premature to ask if you'd marry me?"

"No, my darling." Her face clouded with conflict. "We'd have to make sacrifices. I'd make any for you. But I know now that I couldn't be happy if you remained on the police. I can't adjust to that. When we're in bed, and I touch the scars on your body, it hurts me. I can never forget what happened to you."

He was not a man who compromised with equanimity. But he realized he must yield in some manner.

"Suppose I gave up being chief investigator and my position was administrative? I'd be going to an office checking reports and doing legal work with the magistrates. It would be like a D.A.'s investigator."

"You'd be miserable. Be honest with me, there'd always be bodies you'd examine. And monsters to question. If you want to build a life with me, you can't have death on your hands."

Their conversation was cut off by a Mercedes blazing dust on the dirt road, its stereo detonating with rap. With an acrobatic move, Jennifer jumped to her feet. She saw the passengers in the car, then shot an incensed look at Michel. He pushed himself up from the grass.

"What a sucker punch! I actually thought you were doing this for me."

"I wasn't sure if they were coming."

"Oh, cut it out! I know when I've been had." She headed back to the house and he ran after her, grasped her arm. "Don't touch me!"

"Please, it's important. I have to talk to Boy alone. Take Maddie for a walk."

"Why, why would you ruin one of our last afternoons together when you knew damn well how I felt?"

"You won't have to see them again. I promise."

Michel waved at the visitors. Boy was lugging a crate of beer and Maddie was scooping up an armload of tapes.

"Tell me what's going on."

"I can't talk now. I'll never ask for your help again. I need you, Jennifer."

This rare admission, a departure from his self-assurance, was sinister. Jennifer grew chilled, sensing danger. Maddie danced toward her, and she managed to conceal her feelings. Maddie and Boy were exuberant, high or drunk. They smiled pleasantly and Maddie thrust a long box with *Chanel* imprinted on it.

Boy smiled at her. "Come on, Jen, open it."

Michel watched Jennifer carefully and asked, "What's all this about? It's not your birthday, is it?"

"No," she said, staring in confusion.

"I wanted you to have a going-away present. And this is for you, Michel." Maddie handed him a box with a Sulka label. "I adore you, but I hate your ties. I bought you three new ones." It was a role reversal that took them both by surprise. "We've got to dress Michel and Boy, Jen. They've got terrific ladies. Now they need a little fashion in their lives."

"Not me," Boy said coyly. "I'm an ole dust-bowl hillbilly who came on over to France to eat chili."

Maddie had slid into the role of a wealthy, gracious mistress of the manor with hundreds of millions of dollars at her command. It was not so much the cost of the gifts as the brazen condescension she displayed which dazzled Michel. Jennifer reluctantly opened her box and found a violet silk blouse along with a matching scarf.

"I got you a medium, Jen." Maddie smirked and fixed her eyes on Jennifer's breasts, which bulged through her damp T-shirt. "If it's tight, they'll exchange it."

Jennifer was conscious of the lascivious intent behind everything Maddie said. She wanted to throw it on the barbecue along with Michel. His box held three silk ties, the cost of which boggled her mind.

"You really didn't have to do this, Maddie," Jennifer said.

"Ah, Jen, we're not going to see each other for some time."

"Aren't we?"

"I'm not going back to Pembrooke."

Boy wrapped his arm around her waist. "We're expectin' to travel a little—in the States this time. My territory. Startin' Monday."

Michel floundered in this rush. It hardly gave him enough time to interview them again or to bring them before Charles Fournier who, at his urging, would procrastinate.

"I'm sorry you're quitting school," Jennifer said. "Thanks for the gift. I'm little confused, though. Aren't we leaving together on September fifth?"

"No, Boy and I are flying to Paris on Monday and then taking the Concorde to New York. He's never flown on it. Then I'll charter a plane to take us to L.A. and arrange my parents' funeral."

Michel entered the discussion guardedly. "Didn't you understand that you'd both have to see the examining magistrate? He has reports to complete."

Boy took command of the situation with that callous naiveté that disgusted Jennifer.

"Oh Jesus, Mr. Fournier must have got his signals crossed. Didn't he call you yet? See, Maddie has to go home to settle all her family's business. No one else can do it. Her lawyer called the apartment. When did you speak to Bob Mayer, Maddie?"

"About six this morning. He said he'd set up our meeting with Monsieur Fournier on Monday at eight. It won't take long, Michel. Then we'll be on the noon flight out of Marseille." Maddie touched Jennifer as though she were her lady-in-waiting. "Don't worry about your ticket, Jen. You can fly home anytime you're ready."

"The airline will give you a whole new deal." Boy's tone dripped more molasses than Nicole had put in the barbecue sauce. "See, there are exceptions about tragic situations like this. They're called bereavement flights."

His gloating sickened Jennifer. Without a sign from Michel or indeed the desire to please him, she informed him that she was going to show Maddie around the farm. She'd do anything to escape from Boy.

"Good idea. Let's go, Boy. You're our expert and I want you to check the chili with me and do the ribs."

"Michel, I tell you, it's just like down home. Women out of the kitchen when the men are fixin' dinner."

"You'll do the cole slaw?"

"Lead me to it. Hey, where'd you get the baseball cap?"

"I worked at Yankee Stadium one summer."

"Really? I'm a Yankee fan, too. You an' me have so much in common."

Jennifer and Maddie were already walking past the sausage factory, climbing the hill through the orchard of almond trees.

"All we're missin' is the red dirt from Oklahoma, Boy."

For a second Boy was disconcerted, then he flashed an easy smile. "Hell, this is better. Took some doin', but I've found us a case of iced Bud." He flipped a bottle of beer to Michel. "Let's line up a squad of dead soldiers."

During his foray in Chez Danton's kitchen, Boy had behaved timidly, as though he didn't know the first thing about cooking. He had, however, demonstrated considerable knowledge when inspecting the sides of beef in the deep freezer. Now in the farm kitchen, amid the glistening network of brass pots, casseroles and utensils, he disclosed the hidden craft of a short-order cook.

"We need some more garlic powder, and something to thicken it. At home we use mesa flour to give it the tang of Mexico."

"Do you want to make a roux?" Boy gave him a blank look. "That's a paste of flour and butter to thicken the sauce."

"Sure. By the time I get through, there won't be any lumps."

"I suppose you and Maddie will hire a first-class chef."

Boy stirred the pot. "Some dishes a man likes to cook himself." He added some beer, tasted it with a wooden spoon. "Do you have some hot sauce?"

"What kind?"

"No jalapeños or anchos around the markets." He thought aloud. "Habañeros might be too hot for the ladies. What do you use in France?"

Michel offered him a bottle of cayenne, which Boy sprinkled delicately along with some coarse sea salt. Michel was astonished by the enthusiasm and affability of the young country cook. Could he possibly be wrong about him? Finally, he was forced to taste the concoction and pronounced it excellent.

"Are the ribs in the fridge?"

"No, they're down in the sausage factory."

With extra Buds under their arms, as though celebrating a college football victory, they lazily ambled down the hill.

"I hope you'll come to America and visit us."

"I don't know when I'll get the time."

Boy was surprised by Michel's reluctance. "Is there a problem? I thought you and Jen were serious. She needs someone cultured like you. Somebody who'd understand her."

"You don't really like Jennifer, do you?"

"I wouldn't say that. I don't think I'm educated enough to suit her. Maybe she expected Maddie to fall for some intellectual so they could rove museums and travel the world."

But the reluctant tourist had enjoyed the Hôtel de Sade. Pierre and Annie had watched him inside with Maddie before they set out to explore his farm.

"I got the answer." Boy smiled luminously. "You'll stay with Maddie and me. And believe me, I'll never let you put your hand in your pocket. Goes without sayin' that Jen's included."

Michel marveled at Boy's performance. Overnight, this vagabond, diagnosed as sociopathic, had transformed himself into a grand seigneur, extending invitations, all expenses paid, while Karim languished in prison accused of the bestial homicides. How thoughtful of Karim to have murdered Adam and Karen Gold so that Boy could live like a king.

Boy examined Nicole's emporium with the approval of an experienced hand. Knives and machines gleamed. The white marble counters were spotless. The large elm cross-grained chopping block had drawers. Knives, saws and choppers were displayed in a wooden boutique built into the block frame. Boy ran his hand across the wooden grain.

"It's state of the art, Michel."

"My mother's a perfectionist." He took a pull from the bottle of beer and surveyed Boy. "Amazing how things can change. Last month you were camping out in a model apartment in Pont de l'Arc. Then before you were caught, you found a cozy spot with Denise. Now you'll have a mansion in Bel Air."

Boy did not flinch and smiled wryly. "You knew?"

"The real estate agent complained. A police report was filed mentioning a mysterious Mr. Calhoun."

"The places were empty and I didn't hurt anyone."

"Of course not. Where did you live between there and Denise's?"

"I got me a sleeping bag and found a good spot out of town. I'd hitch a ride or catch a bus and troop out to the base of Mont Sainte-Victoire. I like the outdoors. Red clay at the base reminded me of home. I'd make a fire and strum my guitar."

"Weren't you afraid of animals or snakes?"

"Snakes, hell no. I haven't seen a single one since I got here. Anyway I grew up camping. Only time I ever ran was from a grizzly bear. Some bastard shot him and he was on a tear. Can't say I blame him." He scanned the empty building. "Goin' to get us the ribs? Time I get through, you'll die for 'em."

CHAPTER 58

Trudging through the farm's fruit and olive groves, Jennifer carried an old burlap sack and was passing time with Maddie gathering wild herbs and almonds. Deep inside, her anger built, until she could no longer contain it.

"Take those gifts and burn them. I don't want a damn thing from you."

Maddie stared at her with surprise. "What's this about? Can't I spoil you a little?"

"Please stop this con. I'll go back to L.A. when I'm supposed to. Now as soon as this freakin' day is over, I want you out of my life. Don't ever get in touch with me. Is that clear?"

"What is it with you?" Maddie asked, fuming inside.

Jennifer picked a bunch of ripe figs from a branch and put them in her sack.

"I was wrong about you. I thought you had some sense of decency. But you let a hideous animal latch on to you and destroy everything that might've been good in you. It's a travesty of what a relationship is really like."

"Don't talk about him that way!"

"Snake tattoos all over his body. Yes, I saw. And I wasn't snooping or trying to catch you. You're a liar and freak just like him. He's twisted and he corrupted you. But you were all too willing. No wonder your parents were afraid of him. They loathed him. Anyone in his right mind would.

"You hated your parents so much that you were gloating and celebrating when you found out Karim murdered them. It wouldn't surprise me if you put him up to it. Or maybe that maniac did. Now you can have all the orgies you want."

Rage fomented and twisted within Maddie like a wild, unnavigable river, fed by snowmelt and coursing tortuously in every direction, devastating everything in its path. She wished that Boy had given her his knife.

"I thought I cared about you, Jennifer." Maddie face was flushed. "I was kidding myself. You're no different from my parents. All you ever did was disapprove and reprimand me. Let's *control* Maddie, keep her groveling on her knees. You're a self-righteous bitch. You make me sick. You don't have a clue about what sex is. How it takes over and claims everything . . . even your soul. You'll never know what Boy and I are to each other."

Maddie's manner had become threatening and Jennifer realized that she could not defuse the situation. Maddie's eyes bulged and she pressed her face close to Jennifer's.

"We're wild animals. Because we've been locked up by hypocrites, like you. You want to destroy our natural instincts. You're the loser, Jennifer, not me. You can play pitty-pat with Michel. But you're nothing. You're incapable of defending yourself or acting on your true feelings. You're the one who's blind to life. Boy taught me the meaning of valiant deeds. To act, not to cave in, to stand up and not be trampled by people like you."

With revulsion, Jennifer backed away. "There's nothing inside you, Maddie. You're hollow. Boy found a vein already opened so he could fill you with his poisons. You can't see what you've done to yourself. The two of you have created a jungle without rules or respect. Without love, even for your own bodies."

Madness admitted itself and confronted Jennifer. A hideous mask obscured Maddie's face, transforming her features into something depraved and unnatural. She lashed out at Jennifer and viciously struck her across the face.

"I'll tear you apart," Maddie bellowed.

Jennifer began to run, barreling forward, sweat dripping so heavily that she could barely see ahead of her. She smashed into low-hanging branches and furiously ripped undergrowth out of her way.

When she reached the lake, she fell breathlessly to her knees and sucked up the cold water.

In the reflection of the water, she saw Maddie behind her. Jennifer heard a horrendous, demented sound. Maddie's footsteps thundered, rampaging toward her. Maddie held a large rock, raised over her head.

The crashing blow stunned Jennifer and she dropped face forward into the water. Maddie raised the rock again and Jennifer rolled away and staggered to her feet.

"Don't, Maddie! I can hurt you."

"I'm going to kill you!"

She vaulted over the rocks in the water and again thrashed at Jennifer. Jennifer chopped at her arm, dislodging the rock and the two stumbled down in the water. Maddie's hands locked around Jennifer's throat and she wildly bit her. Then she forced her under water. Suddenly Jennifer's knee came up and caught the girl in the pit of the stomach. Coughing and choking, Jennifer lurched through the water.

But Maddie lunged at her again. Jennifer stayed close to her, thrust her foot behind Maddie's, and flipped her over on her side. When Maddie fell, her head smashed into a jutting rock.

Jennifer caught her breath and lifted Maddie up in her arms. The rock had dug a deep gouge in her temple. Blood spurted from the wound, spraying on Jennifer. Jennifer cradled Maddie's head against her chest. But she was turning blue as Jennifer desperately pressed her lips against Maddie's mouth and blew air down her throat.

"Maddie . . . Maddie . . . !"

CHAPTER 59

In the sausage factory, Michel's temper flared. He was at his wits' end.

"These idiots at the slaughterhouse have ruined everything," he stormed. "They got the damn order wrong. I asked for spareribs and they sent a whole pig."

"Don't get upset, let's see what we can do."

Shoulder to shoulder, Michel and Boy hoisted the hog carcass and finally angled it so that it was impaled on the hooks of a steel gambrel. They hung it with its head down. Boy spread-eagled the pig and inspected it with professional authority.

"It's a sow. It'll have tender meat." He gave Michel a consoling smile. "We haven't fixed ourselves a world championship chili just to pass up baby backribs."

Boy went over to a rail where rubber aprons were hung and put on one. He attached a butcher's bandoleer to his waist. The rubber swished and squeaked. He collected two large stainless steel metal pans, which he placed below the pig. He studied the animal with professorial concentration, then ran his palm across a white band which encircled the middle of its otherwise black body.

"Never saw a porker like this one."

"They're raised in an area called Bresse, which is also famous for its chickens. It's under government control and nothing artificial is introduced into their diet."

"If we had ourselves a Jarvis circular saw, I could split this sucker in a minute."

Michel watched Boy checking through the butcher's tools. "The other night in the restaurant kitchen, I offered to let you cut your own steak. I didn't know you were familiar with butchery."

Boy seemed puzzled. "I don't do beef, porkers I can handle. Back home, we specialize. It's assembly-line packing."

"Really?"

Boy checked below the cabinet and located several electrical outlets. "Where there's an outlet, there has to be a saw to plug in," he explained. "Oh well, never mind. I can handle this honey with what's here."

Boy selected the knives and inserted them in the sheaths. With a curve-tipped knife and a deft stroke, he split the sow down the middle. Blood gushed into the metal pan. Michel watched him separate the stomach and intestines.

"If you had a saline solution and a hose, I could run it through and clean the casing."

"This is a part of the operation I don't know anything about."

As Boy scooped out the innards, he expatiated on worms, bacteria, the illegal sale of lungs by unscrupulous packers.

"Inspector sees anything funny when you're slaughtering, he pours black powder on the whole lot and you got to dump it. But the Mexicans will eat anything: cheeks, lips, jowls and make a stew out of the lungs. They whack everything with hot sauce and salsa so it doesn't really much matter."

Boy laid half of the pig on the chopping block. Bone gristle filled the air as Boy sawed with dexterity, neatly cutting the bacon and trimming it. Had he been this self-possessed when he was decapitating the young American man, strangling his girlfriend, and later gutting Louise while illustrating the lesson for Maddie?

"She's as pretty as Petunia Pig."

"Who?"

"She's a cartoon character—Porky Pig's girlfriend. God, they used to make me laugh when I was a kid." Hands slick with dripping blood, he inclined his head to the bottle of beer. "Beer, please."

Michel held the bottle up to his lips. Pointing with his knife, Boy pared the flesh expertly and lectured about the various parts—from jowl butt through picnic shoulder and finally into the spareribs.

"Beautiful and pink," he said, proudly holding up the trophy for Michel.

"You're a virtuoso in this job as well."

Boy scrubbed his hands in the sink with the deliberation of a surgeon.

"Well, yeah, I do like to cook. Except for a steak at your folks' place, I hadn't had a decent meal since I got here."

"I think you misunderstood me, Darrell."

"How so?

"In the years I've been working as a homicide investigator, I've developed some theories. Everything we do in life is to feed and satisfy our appetites, no matter how special, how exotic and diabolical they are. Food and sex are necessary, but in a sense they're substitutes for the real primal craving."

Boy appeared detached and sipped his beer. "And what might that be?"

"Man has never lost his taste for blood. At one time we were cannibals, killed other people, ate their flesh, drank their blood. Religious rituals celebrated it. Witchcraft and demonology were outgrowths of this stage. There's something magical about controlling life. But we can only reach this godlike state by depriving others of it. Laws have always existed to prevent us from exercising our instinctive desires. The majority find other ways to tame their rage and can disguise this lust. But some men can't find substitutes, can they?"

Boy was reminded of the teachings of Mystery Man. Wear the mask, veil the purpose.

"All this is real interesting," Boy replied. He was growing restless and looked at the wall clock behind Michel. Maddie should have been back by now.

"But the passion for blood is never far away, never entirely absent. It boils up within us, under the skin. We have jobs, ambitions, religions and tribal rites which help control the drive.

"But for some people the desire to cause pain after they've suffered pain is relentless. We don't actually understand it. But what occurs is that someone else's pain—the pain *you* yourself might have felt at some stage—becomes pleasure. It's the ultimate euphoria. Most of us are terrified of these feelings. We repress them. When we dare to act our fantasy, it takes on the trappings of a religious experience, doesn't it?"

Boy read Michel's face and was convinced that he knew everything, but had no hard proof.

"You're a fascinating guy, Michel. Never met a cop like you. Maybe we ought to check on the chili."

Michel perceived the tension growing in Boy.

"I turned off the burner when we came down here. Let's finish this. This all began—at least my part did—when Jennifer complained to the vice squad about Maddie working at Louise's brothel. On the surface, it was ridiculous that Louise would allow anything like that. But of course she didn't know that Maddie had been delivered by Françoise. She suspected Françoise and got Gerard to send her to Cannes. Another thing: we're close to finding the men who were with Maddie."

Boy shook his head ruefully. "You think I'd let my girl—the love of my life!—screw anyone?"

"You didn't know. But when Maddie told you, and you were broke, you decided to get back at Louise. She was the devil and you had to prove yourself to Maddie. You went after Louise with a vicious premeditated detachment. In precisely the same way that you butchered the sow. I had the electric saws taken out and the sow delivered whole. I wanted to watch you in action."

Boy's face was impassive.

"And I can prove that you killed the couple at the dam and all the others."

In Boy's impassive eyes and his facial expression, devoid of change, Michel glimpsed the horror of a voracious human black hole sucking people in—alive yet dead, antimatter, killing light, time, everything.

"Françoise could link Maddie to the brothel, but she couldn't admit that she'd brought her there. You see, Karim had no motive for any of the murders. Before Karim left for Cannes, Gerard offered him a partnership in the sex shop. Gerard was also planning to make Françoise the new madam in Aix. That was a bad miscalculation on your part, Boy. Karim wouldn't murder his meal ticket.

"Now if Karim and Françoise had planned to rob Louise and they were forced to kill her, they would have taken her art collection. Karim has a fine eye for masterpieces. And Karim and Françoise weren't interested in forcing Louise into a sex orgy. They're heterosexual." Michel fought to restrain his fury. "You, you filth, you and Maddie murdered Louise!"

Boy calmly studied Michel and stood his ground fearlessly.

"Out of the blue, Maddie's parents came to visit her. And you thought everything fell into place, didn't you? Karim was the perfect foil for you. He was going to see his girlfriend in Cannes. You and Maddie invited him to dinner with her parents. And before they went out, Maddie left the key to their suite where you could find it. I assume you decided not to carve up Karen Gold to spare Maddie.

"And speaking of Maddie, when she phoned the police with a tip for Sergeant Courbet, a recording was made. Our experts have identified the voice as American. We can match it with a voice print. And there're other tests we've been doing: on vaginal fluid and pubic hair. When Maddie gets back from her walk with Jennifer, I'm sure she'll be cooperative. We'll make a series of forensic comparisons."

Boy made a move toward the door but Michel blocked his way.

"This is all garbage. There's no proof. I'd like to go now."

"Without your lady?" Michel said, mocking him.

A woman's plaintive screams distracted them. Slashed and bleeding, Jennifer was stumbling down the hill toward Michel. Her T-shirt had been ripped off and mud caked her chest and face. Michel nervously called to her, but remained blocking Boy. Jennifer wobbled the last few steps and dropped beside Michel, wailing. He turned away from Boy.

"Maddie, Maddie—"

Michel shouted, "What happened?"

Choking on the words, she said, "She tried to kill me."

From a shelf above, Michel seized a clean towel and wiped the blood off Jennifer's face. Teeth marks had gouged her neck.

"Where is she now?"

"Oh Christ, God, Michel," Jennifer cried, "she's in the lake— dead."

Boy whirred past the counters like a satanic wraith. He leapt up, swinging from a wire above the gambrel and reached a low support under the skylight. When Michel looked up, the sun illuminated the shimmering knife blades.

A cleaver whipped past Jennifer's head and gouged the wall, shattering the tile. Boy climbed to a rafter at the end closest to the door. He dropped down like an acrobat. The carving knives whirled and spun in his hands with such speed and dexterity they seemed almost to be flashing dervishes in a ballet. He rushed toward Michel, who seemed mesmerized by the performance. The knives were weaving and flicking at Michel, then Jennifer.

She screamed when the knives came toward her face. Michel bounced against her and shoved her outside. He slid behind the door as Boy stabbed wildly at him, impaling a knife in the wooden frame. Boy yanked the door and lunged at Michel. Swiveling out of the way of the long blade, Michel's hand was on the automatic he'd hidden on the shelf above him. Boy raised the knife again. As he was about to thrust it into Michel's chest, Michel fired his gun twice.

Boy screeched in pain, reeled backwards and slammed into the chopping block where he supported himself. He tried to right himself and staggered to the other end of the counter. Michel rushed after him and smashed his fist into the bridge of his nose, shattering the bone.

Boy corkscrewed to his knees, his bleeding hand still clutching a knife. He laid it across his chest to staunch the wound, bucking on the floor like a wild horse. Michel stepped on his wrist until Boy released the knife.

"Jennifer! Jennifer." Michel shouted. "Run up to the house and call emergency. Tell them to send an ambulance."

Michel kicked the knife away and stooped to examine Boy's

wounds. One bullet had gone through his left shoulder, the other was low in the abdomen where a geyser of blood gushed over Michel.

"Get me a beer, Michel."

"An ambulance will be here very soon. Tell me the truth now. You murdered them all, didn't you?"

Boy had a hollow smile on his lips. His eyes closed and he found himself adrift in the dream phase of the warrior's sacred grounds where valiant deeds and totems celebrating them awaited him. He had visions of himself and Maddie entwined by snakes. He heard the cries of young girls and Mystery Man's laughter. In the darkness, he imagined he saw thorns bursting from the fist of Goliath.

CHAPTER 60

A week had passed since the fatal summer afternoon barbecue at Michel's farm. The tourists had at last packed up. The country squires came out of hiding from their estates, but the suffering natives were not entirely free to reclaim their town. Michel watched them, filled with silent anguish, strolling by the boarded-up Hôtel Estaque. They would wistfully glance up at their favorite balconies as they remembered, with Proustian sorrow, moments of sexual conquest and Madeleines of a different texture. Reawakening to bleak reality, they would scurry to catch up with their wives, who were buying designer ensembles in boutiques. Many of them could now afford a Chanel, for Aix was without a madam.

Despite the evacuation of tourists and summer students, Aix's history remained unchanged. It was forever defending itself against the barbarians. Hotels were bursting with foreign invaders. Pernicious hordes of attorneys, complaining of the heat, had flown in from the United States, offering to represent Boy and protect his civil rights.

Boy's gentle, fawning manners and soft friendly voice bewitched them. Along with these transient scavengers, there were hardened TV news teams, villainous tabloid journalists, and gruesome film producers of every nationality. All of them were driven by a single purpose: to thrust checks into Boy's hand for his story.

At first, Michel had been convinced that Maddie had attempted to murder Jennifer in the heat of their argument. But this theory was contradicted by Boy when Michel interviewed him at the hospital. With a businessman's stoic attitude, Boy informed him that this was a planned event in the curriculum of execution *Maddie* had masterminded. Alive, Jennifer would always be a threat to her. This would be Maddie's final opportunity "to close her out." Boy himself admitted to complicity but with mitigating circumstances.

"Look, I was a slave, bought and paid for by Maddie Gold," he protested. "I was crazy in love and she used me. I wanted to get out of here the minute I arrived. But I couldn't change my ticket. I was trapped. I had no money. I was at Maddie's mercy. She was perverted. She did those guys at Louise's, then demanded that I help kill Louise because she didn't get paid."

Michel switched off the tape recorder. He had enough of what Boy called shuckin' and jivin'. Boy had brilliantly covered his tracks.

"Listen, Michel. I worked sweepin' up for Denise and stayed at her house. If I'm such a menace, how come I didn't kill Yvette and Denise? I'm the fall guy who was suckered in by a twisted woman, an insane criminal!"

A strange nightmarish, insightful relationship had developed between them. It was clear that Boy felt nothing. He inhabited a nihilistic universe. At another stage of his ravings, he had explained to Michel that for him murder was the ultimate creative act.

"I'm the spirit of the century. You can kill me, but I won't die. You have music, art, books, but you get everything secondhand."

He was implacable, atrocious, blatant in his manipulation. Michel had had enough of this monster and turned over the interrogation to Charles Fournier. Boy continued to deny knowledge of all the murders except for Louise's, which had been planned as retribution by Maddie. There was no one left alive to refute his testimony.

As the days passed, from his guarded hospital room, Boy continued to recuperate and held court for the constant stream of well-wishing visitors, government officials and lawyers. All signs of mourning for his once beloved Maddie vaporized under the spotlight, and his good humor returned. Michel found Boy's calmness as frightening as his violence.

Boy refused all press requests for interviews and designated Yvette as his representative. She claimed, with some logic, that as former housemates, they had developed a special rapport.

Still the locals could drive and walk through Aix, sometimes find a table at Les Deux Garçons and quietly savor Yvette's graphic series of interviews with the monster.

Michel had left Jennifer asleep in his flat and had tried to escape the blaring publicity by stopping off at Chez Danton. This was his first day off since the morning of Louise's murder. But he stumbled into a hornets' nest. Over their coffee at the bar, Delantier was feverishly reading aloud the latest headline of the saga to René:

The Gods are Mad: King Tut and his Snake Tattoos!

The Egyptian connection and snake worship are allied in Darrell Boynton. He lies wounded in a hospital bed, his bow-string broken and quiver empty, a young Apollo with glorious emerald eyes that would meld with the sky above Mont Sainte-Victoire. A model for our great Cézanne's *Bathers*. But he has tasted blood many times . . ."

This new legendary approach was introduced after Yvette had breathlessly interviewed herself and Denise on her TV show. Both women shuddered as they recollected grotesque moments when they shared Boy's company under Denise's roof. Michel had declined to be interviewed by the Queen of Murder, the title bestowed on Yvette by the *Enquirer*.

"Give Yvette a Fail both in mythology and art," Michel said irritably.

"To think I served Boy dinner and fixed crêpes for him," Delantier said. "Now what about this: Maddie's forensic tests—What the devil is DNA?"

"Never mind! Will we ever get rid of Yvette? When is she going to Paris?"

"Haven't you heard?"

René informed him that Yvette was attempting to round up a syndicate of investors and planning to buy *Le Clairon* from Vincent Sardou.

"Please God, no!"

"Discussions are already under way." Delantier regarded Michel with a despotic sneer. "Michel, I think that since you've come out of this without bullet holes or completely disgracing yourself *or* the reputation of Chez Danton—that as intimate friends—we're entitled to some grisly nuggets to retail to our regulars."

René was already reaching for the bottle of pastis, and Michel swiftly bolted from Chez Danton. He had a variety of errands: stops at the chemist for Jennifer's Xanax prescription; the cleaners, to drop off and collect their clothes; Lascombe's, to pay for a new bedroom suite which would be delivered later that afternoon.

Richard Caron had implored him to get a haircut and a new suit because of the impending visit of the slick opportunists from the director general's office in Paris. A delegation would be flying to Marseille on Friday. The prospect of Denise snipping him and the tailor sticking pins in his crotch during a fitting was too daunting even for him.

Michel found his freedom restricted. He could no longer wander aimlessly through the market square beside St-Sauveur and chat with the stallkeepers. He had transcended the easy familiarity of native son. The news media had given him a public persona. The bows and compliments, the finger-pointing of people he'd known all of his life, distressed and embarrassed him. For once he was not at home in town. Although his star had never been brighter, he walked with visible forlornness.

Jennifer Bowen had changed her mind and would not marry him. She was now a daily patient of Dr. Leon Stein's. He had advised her not to rush into anything! The sweet summer of their love had ended with a violent eruption that would mark the rest of her days. Although she stayed at Michel's flat in town, she was moody, withdrawn, and guilt-ridden toward him. An aura of alienation drifted over them like a toxic cloud and intimacy drifted away with the heat wave.

She had clusters of nightmares, reliving the brutal fight with Maddie. She'd wake up in a sweat, screaming. He would calm her down and wait until she dozed off. He watched her until his insomnia greeted the morning light. He was a detective and knew that the woman he loved had secrets. They came to light when she was called in by Charles Fournier and Richard Caron for an interview.

Jennifer recounted the events at the Special Circumstances office of the Police Judiciaire in Marseille. She had a disoriented expression and avoided Michel's eyes during her statement.

"Maddie and I had a quarrel which turned violent. I said some things which maybe I shouldn't have. I tried to reason with her. She was my student. I wanted her to see that this Darrell would destroy her."

Jennifer slumped in her chair and the ever gallant Fournier was at her side, staring at her breasts.

"Maddie lost control and hit me in the face. I started running. I was out of breath and I thought it was over. I stopped by the lake on Michel's property. I was leaning over to drink some water and wash my face when Maddie came at me from behind with a rock and hit me. I was dazed and fell into the water. I couldn't get away from her."

A stenographer and a video camera were recording her official account.

Michel sipped cold coffee, listening intently. Tears streamed down Jennifer's cheeks. When Michel rose to comfort her, she waved him away.

"Take your time, Mademoiselle Bowen," Richard said, offering her his handkerchief.

"It's okay. I have to handle this in my own way. You see, my fiancé was murdered in San Francisco several years ago. And I vowed that I'd never be a victim. If I were ever threatened. I'd be able to put up the fight of my life!

"So I enrolled in a karate school. I've been going for two years. Three times a week. And I'm a Second Dan Black Belt. I don't talk about it, but I can kill someone in minutes." She grimaced when she continued. "I've also had training with handguns. I shoot at the range once a week."

The men stared at Michel, who was as shocked as they were. Fournier seemed dismayed by Jennifer's candor.

"Did you attempt to tell Maddie about your special training?"

"Only *after* she struck me. I warned her that I could hurt her."

Richard was impressed by her courage. "Try to remember exactly what you said to Maddie."

"I don't—she was wild. Totally out of control."

"You were still in the water?" Fournier asked.

Jennifer sighed. "Yes. I was trying to get away from her. I backed up. Then she leapt on me. I was still very groggy. We struggled. She got me in a headlock and began to bite me. Then she was strangling me and I was under water."

The left side of Jennifer's neck was still bandaged. A plastic surgeon had been called in to stitch her wound.

"I . . . I thought Maddie would back off even when she was strangling me. She didn't. I was fighting for my life. I got my knee in her groin and kicked her as hard as I could. When I came up from under the water, she had a branch or a stick. And I got close to her to stop her from getting any leverage to hit me again."

The men glanced over at Michel. He found no safe ground for retreat. When Jennifer had first told him about her karate expertise, he had dismissed her claim.

"Then what happened?" Caron asked.

"I elbowed her in the gut, shifted my weight and flipped her over my hip. Maddie went down and hit her head on a sharp stone. It was jutting out of the water. She went under.

"I caught my breath and waded over as fast as I could. There's a drop-off there and the water gets deeper. I pulled Maddie up. Blood was spurting from her temple. And her mouth. I dragged her out of the water and she was dead in my arms."

Dr. Laurent had slipped into the room and presented his report. The postmortem he had performed on Madeleine Gold confirmed Jennifer's statement.

The men rose and bowed gracefully to Jennifer.

"I'll see you punctually at six-thirty," Fournier informed Jennifer. "No fish for the preceding eight hours. No lunch or alcohol. And definitely no strenuous exercise."

Jennifer was aghast. She finally reached out to Michel for support.

"What is this? You can't send me to prison without allowing me to get a lawyer! I know my rights."

"Mademoiselle Bowen, you're not going to prison. You'll be the guest of honor at my bouillabaisse festival tonight."

It was past four when Michel returned home. He found Jennifer ushering out the grumbling, sweaty delivery men. She returned to the bedroom. Through the open door he watched her bouncing on the new bed. He could not keep up with her mood swings.

"It took two of them to lift that horsehair monstrosity out on the balcony and another two downstairs to lower it on the hoist to the street. No wonder you didn't want to take me here on our first date."

"I was concerned about your back and safety," he said with a smile.

He examined the sleek modern lines of the new bedroom set without enthusiasm.

"I picked up your tranquilizers. Maybe *I* ought to take one. What about you? Want one now?"

"No, toss them out."

Jennifer's attitude had changed. The spirit that had so attracted and infuriated him had returned. She unzipped her jeans and beckoned him.

"Can I get you anything?"

"You sure can." She pulled him down on the bed. Her freshly washed damp hair tingled on his face. "I want a toe-curler, Michel."

"Before Neptune's bouillabaisse? He warned you about strenuous exercise. You'll need all your strength. Put this in your bag."

"Mace for dinner?"

He handed her a pocket-size Evian atomizer. She was astonished and looked at the small tubular can. "Why do I need a *brumisateur*?"

"You may have to spray your skin and your tongue. People have been known to become demented from the *rouille*."

He slipped off the plastic from a dark dress.

"What're you doing now? I was planning to wear my white one."

"Saffron stains are fatal. And put on comfortable shoes. There's dancing afterwards, if you can still move."

"I'll go along with you on one condition. I want you to make love to me when we get home on our new bed. All night long!"

Our resonated in his mind. Michel rolled her over and dizzily kissed her.

"I thought Dr. Stein put you on a love-free diet."

"I fired him."

"Well, I'll have to think about it."

"Like hell, you will."

"Don't men have rights anymore? What if I refuse?"

"I'll flip you on your ass and then do you on the floor."

Dressed in a handsome gray pencil-striped double-breasted suit, Michel might have been a comfortable burgher and not a detective. Shedding his gloom, he uncovered a side of himself that he had alienated. Optimism, the hope of a future with this courageous, brilliant woman. He waited like a jittery teenager and contemplated a glorious, sunny life with her. But tonight, they'd dance naked through his apartment.

Jennifer emerged finally, hair upswept, in a navy dress with a lace jacket that was modishly old-fashioned. Beaming with happiness, she wrapped her arms around him, then suddenly withdrew.

"Bouillabaisse and bullets don't mix. Give it here."

Reluctantly, he handed over his loaded Glock automatic, which she placed in the drawer of the telephone table near the door.

"I feel naked."

"I'll be your shield."

CHAPTER 61

It would be necessary to return to the Middle Ages during the time of plague to find a case in which communal ostracism so devastated an individual as profoundly as it did Paul Courbet. In spite of Richard Caron's covert investigation, news of Courbet's role as Gerard David's gladiator leaked out. Among Françoise's clientele, there was a general conviction that Courbet was responsible for her murder. He had threatened her and forced her to go to Cannes.

The prefect of police suspended the sergeant, his wife finally lobbed him out, and he descended into that quicksand reserved for outcasts. Shopkeepers refused to wait on him and he was rebuffed by members of the police. Lawsuits by news organizations, who had paid him thousands for interviews, abounded.

Only Yvette stood by him. But not in the manner he had been accustomed to previously. Courbet served as her lackey, bodyguard and legman. He performed these menial functions while the Queen of Murder was now being courted by an editor from the *Globe*. She was offering photos of Boy's erect penis which she had not yet taken or, in fact, seen. Nurses she had bribed reported that his body art contained a triptych of copperhead snake tattoos.

Staggering by five-thirty, Courbet had the drunken effrontery to poke his head into Chez Danton. He came in through the rear, wandered past the boule court and flinched when he saw the sign with his name spray-painted with the word *punaise*. He was too intoxicated to object to being called a dirty whore. Nicole was in her office on the phone with her back to the door. He crept by and heard a familiar voice.

Although Claude Boisser was on self-imposed protracted leave, he still graced Chez Danton's bar at the hors d'oeuvres hour. Bellies shaking with laughter, the country squires guffawed at his jokes. They had sent their wives back to the estates with Yves St. Laurent packages. One of them waved to René to refill Claude's glass.

"Go on, Claude," René said as he poured.

"Yes, yes," the chorus bellowed.

"Ah well, if you insist . . . This large law firm in Los Angeles has a hundred partners and they are at a meeting which lasts three hours. Outside the door, the young lawyers are waiting anxiously. Who will be fired and who promoted?

"The meeting ends and the managing partner calls in this brilliant young Harvard trial magician and says, 'We've made you a partner . . . but there is a stipulation.'

" 'Yes, sir.'

" 'The partners want to know if you've been screwing the red-headed receptionist?'

" 'No, sir!' the young man replies.

" 'Fine, then you can fire her.' "

The loudest laugh came from Paul Courbet, who had crept up to the bar. He applauded wildly. Everyone solemnly turned and regarded him with lifeless stares.

"René, bring me a drink."

The barman glared at Courbet and strove to subdue his anger. With a clattering of silverware, Delantier emerged from the alcove. He was perhaps eight inches shorter than Courbet, and thrust himself against his chest.

"Only gentlemen may be served here. You have dishonored the noble game of boule, Chez Danton, and the gallantry of Michel Danton."

Delantier removed a white glove from his pocket and slapped Courbet on both cheeks.

Like marathons, bacchanals require rigorous training, conditioning coaches perhaps. Knives and forks, spoons and nutcrackers clashed as violently as cymbals in an orchestra without a conductor, as servants dressed in fishermen's costumes furiously served bouillabaisse from giant soup tureens around the Fourniers' baronial table. The center-piece was a massive ice sculpture of a spiny langoustine that once might have lived during the Jurassic era.

Jennifer was already flushed and giddy. At the outdoor oyster bar, set up beside fountains of weathered green dolphins which seemed to be leaping above the fish topiary in the gardens, she had consumed a dozen each of Belons and Marennes, countless shrimp, medleys of lobster, washed down with four or five glasses of Cristal champagne.

A wine steward, one among several assigned to every quartet, placed a second bottle of Bâtard-Montrachet in her ice bucket. She sat beside Michel, surrounded by an assembly of forty or more. Nets and tridents hung from the coffered ceiling, Flemish masterpieces of fish and fowl and fruit were on the walls, and the Gipsy Kings' frenetic music lashed out from loudspeakers.

Suddenly another bowl was placed before Jennifer, dark as ink.

"What's this?" she asked Michel.

"Part Two. The cuttlefish version, a delicacy."

"Everything is," Nicole informed her. She and Philippe were scrutinizing her conduct at this eating event. Jennifer raised her spoon quizzically from the bowl.

"What am I eating now?"

"Rascasse, scorpionfish," Michel whispered. "Don't raise your voice, there may not be enough to go around for seconds."

"Seconds?"

"Yes. There was a small catch and the Fourniers are furious. You've been served this, because you're the guest of honor."

She surreptitiously dropped an ice cube down her neckline in the hope of shocking her system.

"Michel, before we arrived, your parents dropped us off at the old port. You wanted some privacy. We took a walk around. And there on the jetty, you asked me again to marry you. I couldn't answer then, but I can now." She seductively wrapped her arms around his neck. Eyes luminous with expectation, he grasped her hand. "I will marry you, if you'll allow me to stop eating."

He gave her a chilly look. "That's out of the question. Neptune will never invite us back."

Philippe had got wind of the dispute and waved with his spoon for her to drink up. "Now taste Part Two!"

"How can you all be so ruthless, Michel?"

"My parents and Marseille's society are observing your every move. Chez Danton's fish supply could be compromised if you quit now."

With a groan, Jennifer hoisted up her spoon, tasted the black brew, smiled at the Fourniers and never knew that her head had hit the table until Michel sprayed her with Evian. She had lost consciousness.

"Have you had blackouts like this before?" Dr. Laurent asked, taking her pulse.

She gave the coroner a glazed look and asked, "I'm not dead, am I?"

But again she seemed incoherent, whimpering through mountains of exotic cheeses and tubs of sorbets. Laurent acted decisively and helped her up from the table.

"She needs some air and a good dance," the coroner advised Michel.

He led her out to the terrace where a Latin orchestra had been installed during her blackout.

"This will get your blood pressure going, Jennifer."

CHAPTER 62

When Courbet staggered into the hospital, the police guards outside Boy's hospital room were grumbling about their shifts and balancing dinner trays on their laps. Everyone hated this tedious watchdog assignment.

Yvette felt grimy. Her new Armani suit was a wreck of creases. She rose from her chair at Boy's bedside. She alone had complete access to him and used every device to win him over. Damn the rules. She was paying thousands a day to the hospital staff and police. The urchin from the provinces owned them all. She was on her way to becoming an international celebrity, speaking out on abortion, Algerian affairs, whatever wasp stung the public that day. And now she had makeup, wardrobe, and cameras ready to roll at the snap of a finger.

"Did you get Boy his hamburger and fries from Chez Danton?" she demanded.

Courbet could not bear to admit how he had been treated. He had bought a sausage pizza at a takeout stand. Boy spied the square box and howled when he smelled the garlic.

"I can't eat this shit any more! I'd rather take another bullet from Michel."

"See how you've upset him? How will I ever get the rest of my story?"

Courbet retreated to the doorway, where the guards scowled at him. "There's someone downstairs to see you—"

"What are you talking about, you drunk? To think that I ever slept with you!"

Courbet composed himself. "A special envoy arrived with me from the American embassy. Medals all over him. He's very important. Military attaché, legal or whatever. He has extradition papers for Boy. They want to fly him back to Los Angeles tonight."

Boy became incensed. He did not want to be extradited.

"What is this, Yvette? You gave me guarantees! Said if I told only you the whole story about how Maddie planned this, I'd get immunity."

Yvette held his hand. "Calm down, my precious Boy. This may work in our favor." Yvette changed tapes on her recorder. "Paul, stop your pathetic sulking. What is the officer's name?"

Courbet handed Yvette a card he had nervously crumpled in his hand. She straightened her skirt and slapped some life into her pale cheeks.

"Well, Boy, you certainly have drawn out the forces. Major Eldon Royce Calhoun has come to see you."

The name transformed Boy's pouting face and brought with it the elation of a religious experience. He had a magical mood swing.

"Maybe extradition will work in my favor," Boy said.

His heart pounded wildly and his hope was renewed. Mystery Man, his savior, had arrived. Boy checked his fresh dressing. The wound in his abdomen had stopped draining. He could walk without too much discomfort.

"Wonder if Major Calhoun brought me a Big Mac."

The distinguished visitor, fit and tanned, sparkling with military precision, was outside. His eyes darted to Boy and there was an imperceptible nod. He glanced at the two police officers slathering heels of bread in the last of the gray hospital gravy.

"May I present my credentials along with this signed document from the Interior Ministry?"

The guards blustered and Yvette intervened. "You know Boynton is an American citizen. He has a right to see counsel."

On the scent, Mystery Man edged closer. He took in everything.

"Mademoiselle Molyneux, I have read your brilliant articles and watched you on television. Your fame has spread across the world . . . even to the red dirt of Oklahoma's back roads."

"We're not supposed to let anyone in, Yvette," a burly guard informed him.

The major's courtly bearing impressed Yvette. She was beside herself. Again she was at the right place. Her timing was perfect. This was an exclusive aspect to the story which she could file before the wire services.

"That's enough!" Yvette stormed. She took the guards aside and railed furiously at them. In a moment she was back. "I've been working very hard on this case, Major."

"We all have, ma'am. Surely, Mr. Boynton, a United States citizen, can have a private moment with his government's representative."

"Of course. But a guard is required to be present," she said, snarling at the men nervously fidgeting outside.

Mystery Man noticed Courbet teetering against the wall. "May we have this official with us and close the door for a confidential chat?" he inquired.

"All right. He's on leave, but he'll do."

Courbet thrust out his chest. "I've had to surrender my firearm, Yvette."

"There will be no need for one, sir."

Yvette again approached the guards. "You take a break. Bring your trays back to the kitchen. It's all right, there'll be three of us with the prisoner." The guards continued to balk, igniting Yvette's temper. "If you don't leave us," she snapped, picking up her cellular phone, "I'll call your wives this minute and tell them the way you've been carrying on with the nurses." She pointed at several of them scurrying back to the station. "I know what goes on in the room next door."

The two guards no longer demurred. They bolted up from their chairs and meekly carried their trays down the corridor. Yvette grasped Major Calhoun's hand and guided him into Boy's room. She closed the door.

Boy's eyes focussed on Mystery Man's large attaché case.

"Major Calhoun, I'm sorry about this nonsense," she said.

He was sympathetic. "I know all about red tape."

She looked at the parade ground of decorations on this gallant soldier's jacket. Boy began to get ready. He took some fresh dressings from the side table and packed them into his bathrobe pocket.

"You've been through the wars, sir," she said respectfully.

"I have indeed."

Yvette was dazzled by the array of ribbons. "Vietnam, I see."

"Yes, ma'am. Tortured by the Vietcong for three years."

She turned up the volume on her recorder. This would add human interest to Boy's story. "How did you survive?"

Mystery Man gave her a long penetrating look that troubled her. "I didn't."

Old war stories bored Paul Courbet. He needed a drink. He slipped behind the screen and took a nip from his flask. He was revived, leaping over his humiliation, and thrust himself back to his official mode.

"I'll have to inspect your attaché case, Major."

"Of course."

Everything conspired to prevent Yvette from getting her story.

"Oh, do get this over with, Paul. We're not playing games."

Boy watched Mystery Man calmly settle the case at the edge of his bed and hand Courbet the keys. He stood behind Courbet and his eyes blazed. Boy's body tensed with the excitement of this magic moment.

"Landlocked Okies have historically been drawn by their futile and misguided aspirations to California's beaches and glamorous women. It is a deadly tropism—this thrust to the sea."

"I'm puzzled by your remarks, Major Calhoun," Yvette said.

"I'm bein' dressed down, Yvette, and I deserve it. I should've stayed put," Boy said.

She looked at Boy, bewildered. This comment only added to the enigma.

The major pressed close to Yvette. "We all have a bad, mean streak. But Boy has a gift right up from hell. Without me, he has been unable to control it."

Courbet was oblivious to this exchange and unlocked the attaché case. A musky sweat scent infused the room. When he lifted the top, he gasped and cringed in terror.

"There's something alive!" Shocked by what he had seen inside the attaché case, he turned to the major.

Mystery Man's attack was instantaneous. The scalpel slashed across Courbet's throat. The major agilely moved back to avoid the fountain of jetting blood. He instantly seized hold of Yvette.

Boy got out of bed. "Don't scream, Yvette, or the major'll tear your eyes out." He stepped over Courbet whose body jerked spasmodically.

"Do we kill her too, Boy?"

"No, Major, ole Yvette, she's our seein'-eye dog out of here."

Mystery Man stuck his hand into Yvette's mouth and grasped her tongue. He dragged her to the open attaché case.

In a mesh cage, the slender copperheads angrily fixed their long front teeth into the wire mesh.

"If you start anything, I'll turn the snakes on you. I brought Boy's pets along as a diversion for you folks in case I needed one. Then we'll kill everyone in this hospital. I've got enough semtex to blow up the whole place.

"Boy, I got you some morphine and Percocets." He looked longingly at Boy and then to Yvette. "You see, he's mine . . . my Boy. And I'm takin' him home with me."

Yvette nodded and he released the grip on her tongue.

"Get goin', Boy, there's an outfit and automatic weapons in the case."

Yvette's terror so overwhelmed her, she could hardly breathe. Her eyes fixed on the coiled snakes, then down to the blood congealing on the severed artery in Courbet's throat.

Major Calhoun hiked up his trouser leg and brought out a small automatic. He placed the muzzle between Yvette's eyes.

"Now the Vietcong, they taught me how to treat invaders. I lived with a mamba snake for three years beside my rice bowl. Belongs to the cobra family and has enough venom to kill ten people. Always bites the head or trunk. This copperhead is a match for it. I assure you snake bite is an agonizing way to end . . . paralysis, convulsions, and death follow in minutes."

Every nightmare fear Yvette had known or written about existed and found expression in the dead pool of the major's frozen eyes. The madness of Boy and this man reached out and devoured her.

"This will be a wonderful story, if you live to write it. Speak very softly when I tell you to. And remember, I understand French."

Jets of sweat dribbled down her neck, along her back and thighs. What had been tangible reality faded into a nightscape of dread. Her knees buckled and he supported her back while Boy swiftly dressed. The major flipped out his stopwatch.

"Four minutes have gone by. Where will the guards be?"

She was trembling so violently that she could barely move her tongue. There was no saliva inside her mouth.

"I don't know," she whispered.

"We're both going to see." His eyes roved her face, seeming to read her mind. "If they're back outside, ask them nicely to come in."

Yvette cautiously cracked the door and she and the major peeked out. The guards had not returned. When she spun around, Boy had on a baggy dress and a long black wig. He was at the mirror applying her lipstick and he smiled at her.

"We're clear, Boy."

Walking between them down the corridor, Yvette's body shook. She had virtually lost control of her reflexes. She wrote about such trage-dies. She could not be a part of this—a victim. She listened intently to their hushed discussion. A boat would take Boy and the major from Marseille at four in the morning.

". . . He's an old renegade Foreign legionnaire whose ass I saved in Vietnam. Runs contraband and some dope from Corsica."

They had reached the stairwell. No, this couldn't be happening to *her*!

"It's gettin' to Marseille. That's the problem," Boy said. "We need us some hostages."

Yvette prayed silently that they would let her live. "Please, I beg you—"

Their footsteps clanged on the metal staircase. Yvette felt weightless, in an immutable dream state.

"What about her as a hostage?" the major asked when they reached the basement.

"Nobody likes this slut. They'd let her croak in a minute. Now if we get Michel and Jennifer, we'd have ourselves an American citizen and a French detective. That's a pair to draw to. Everybody'd be easy then." Boy tightened his grip on Yvette's arm, his fingers dug into her flesh. "Is Michel with Jennifer at the farm?"

"No, not tonight."

"Where are they?"

She had a vision of this date a year ago: arriving on Michel's arm, kissing the Fourniers in the garden, flirting, eating bouillabaisse, and dancing with Laurent. She had been hacked off the guest list.

"At a dinner party in Marseille."

In the hospital basement, the custodians and engineers were hunched over a card table playing bridge. Yvette looked in their direction but they were too deeply engrossed to notice the trio. The gun was pressed against the small of her back. She stifled her tears. In a moment, she was pushed out into the street. She closed her eyes and shivered in the misty cool night air.

"Where'll Michel go afterwards?" She was silent. "Will he stay here in Aix?" Boy asked.

"I think so. He has an apartment. I'm peeing!" she cried when they approached her car.

"Don't worry, Yvette. Boy and I have seen that before. Get us to your car."

They walked cautiously to the reserved parking spaces in front. Yvette spied the new red Citroën she had bought when the money began to flow in. She fumbled with the keys. The major opened the driver's side door and shoved her in. He stood with his gun against her forehead, waiting for Boy to get into the backseat. After Boy was inside and had his hands around her throat, the major slipped into the passenger seat.

"Jennifer would never go back to the farm after killin' Maddie there." Boy gave a sharp chortle. "Hey, Yvette, you were Michel's ole lady. Bet you've still got a key to his apartment."

"I'll give you directions. Let me go now."

"No, my lady, you're goin' to be our tour guide and take us there."

She turned the ignition key, heavily pumped the accelerator, hoping that the engine would flood.

The major grasped her thigh. "Don't even think of it," he said.

The pinpricks of light from oncoming cars blinded her. Tears trickled down her gaunt face. In a daze, she pulled out into traffic.

"You'll let me go when we get there?"

Boy's fingers stroked the back of her neck. "This crazy lady wanted to take pictures of me naked. Imagine that?"

"You ought to satisfy her curiosity, Boy."

Yvette almost hit a passing car wheeling around La Rotonde Fountain.

"No, no, it wasn't my idea!"

Her voice sounded distant and bodiless as though she were talking from a different spatial plane. When he'd been shot, Michel had told her that he had been lost in a maze of time which was static and terminal. She began to search for herself but could find nothing.

"You got any ladies' swimsuits in that case, Major?"

"No . . . I got a better idea. Maybe you can talk Yvette into giving us a lingerie show. You're good at persuasion."

"I'll do anything you want. . . . You'll let me go when we get there?" she said again, desperately trying to prove to herself that she was still alive.

"Mystery Man and me, we never forget our friends."

CHAPTER 63

Jennifer's feet were swollen and throbbing from a series of tango bouts with Neptune, the indefatigable coroner, and Michel's boss. Her stomach churning, her brain mush, she drowsily snuggled against Michel in the backseat of Philippe's ancient Facel Vega.

"With the exception of a ten-minute bouillabaisse intoxication, Jennifer acquitted herself much better than I thought possible," Nicole said.

Jennifer decided she'd have to break Nicole of the habit of discussing her as though she were not present. But that would have to be on another day when her brain cells were reconnected.

"It was Jennifer's first time, Nicole. Her coming-out into the world of great cuisine. Evenings of this kind require experience and maturity." Philippe had become her advocate. "We mustn't forget the stress Jennifer's been through."

"I'd call it trauma," Michel piped in.

"At least tonight was a fair preparation for Christmas when the family gathers," his father said, straying above the speed limit.

"I'll be in Ojai teaching French."

"No, you won't," Michel said firmly. "You have to meet the family and come to the Santon fair in Marseille."

"We expect you here," Philippe added. "And it's going to take all your fortitude and character to deal with my cassoulet."

"Your cassoulet?" Nicole's tone turned acerbic.

"Cassoulet!" Stomach still bursting with cuttlefish ink, Jennifer's mind leapt to the surface and bounced back from the bends. "I love it. It's my favorite dish. I know it's the wrong time of the year for it, but Nicole, I've had a craving for cassoulet since I came to France. Whenever I mention it, Michel practically has a convulsion."

Nicole swiveled around from the front seat and determined that the time for intimacy with Michel's lady had arrived.

"You'll need your heart checked—and one of those balloons inserted to dredge the plaque out of your arteries after eating Philippe's version."

And so the evening that had begun so promising turned ugly for Michel. Jennifer might survive a variety of homicides, but the resumption of the cassoulet wars might wreck their future.

It was midnight when they were dropped at his apartment on the Rue Goyrand. Grumpy kisses were exchanged, briefly interrupting the Danton's merciless quarrel.

". . . At this rate neither of you will be invited to meet Jennifer's mother," Michel bellowed.

When the bickering Dantons drove off, Jennifer gazed at groups of lovers illuminated at the monumental Baroque Fountain of the Four Dolphins, which faced Michel's balcony.

"Do you mind if we walk for a few minutes? I've got marine life swimming against the tide in my stomach."

Michel was still fuming. "That's a good idea. I need to clear my head."

Jennifer was flabbergasted by the acrimonious contests waged over recipes by the Dantons.

"Do these brawls about food always go on in your family?"

"It's a question of temperaments. I've been brought up in a tradition in which food isn't simply sustenance. It's the matrix of existence. In Aix what you put into your stomach is a reflection of your soul, your philosophy, and how you feel about yourself. I've seen people come to blows over a tapénade. Friendships have been ended and forged by a ratatouille. When you go to market with me, I'll point out brothers and sisters who haven't spoken for years because someone dared to change a family recipe that might be a century old."

Jennifer's mind was on romance and the tenderness she had avoided since Maddie's death. She had locked up her emotions until this afternoon when the new bedroom suite arrived. Yes, she and Michel had a destiny to fulfill. He, however, still had bouillabaisse on the brain.

"Take tonight: the cuttlefish version was also served to keep from offending some of the guests who regard it as the only true one. On the other hand, the fact that langoustine and mussels appeared might have outraged some of the others. Neptune has to be politic."

She leaned her head on his shoulder. Music was playing at a café.

"You all think with your stomachs."

"It tells us everything about our health and our mental state. In my world—and it's an old one that goes back to the Romans—your blood gets heated when the subject is food. You can say things to people about a dish that can never be forgiven."

"Michel, be patient with me. I'm a simple American and I've never witnessed hysteria over food until tonight."

They circled the block. Michel stopped abruptly a few feet from the entrance to his flat. What was Yvette's new car doing there? The windows were down and her IBM laptop was on the backseat. Could she be in the apartment—bouncing on Jennifer's virgin mattress? Having heaved Courbet out, she'd probably snuck in, intending to make a scene.

Earlier that day at the hospital while interviewing Boy, he had told Yvette that she would never again be invited by the Fourniers. Neptune had tolerated her out of loyalty to him. Yvette's scabrous articles and idolatry of Boy had turned everyone against her. Nonetheless, Michel hadn't expected reprisals from her this quickly.

"Jennifer, would you go over to the Café Mazarin and wait for me there? We'll have a Campari and soda. Order one for me. It'll settle your stomach and you'll sleep better."

"What's wrong? Aren't we going to bed? I've got some surprises for you." He had another glimpse through the secret skin of this woman. She pressed his hand against her breast. "I'm so excited. . . ."

His erection was unbearable. "Unfortunately, there's a gas leak."

"I don't smell anything."

"These old buildings . . . We've had dangerous incidents before." He'd heave Yvette off the terrace if necessary. "I'll join you at the café in a few minutes."

Before entering the building, Michel made certain that Jennifer had turned the corner to the café. The building was preternaturally silent. Two tenants were away until the middle of the month. When he got into the lift, there was the strong scent of Yvette's perfume, Joy. It commingled with her sweat. The floor was wet with urine. He saw something metallic on the floor. He bent down and picked up his grandmother's cameo ring. Yvette had refused to return it. She had said he'd have to cut it off her finger. Why had she left it? Her behavior made no sense to him.

The perils of stillness troubled him. Michel closed the lift gate, reached in and pressed the button for his floor. He'd trap her. On the first landing, he slipped off his shoes and crept up the stairs, listening warily before he eased open the roof door. Yvette would be sitting naked out on the terrace and spring at Jennifer. Her setup was clumsy, absurd.

On tiptoe, he negotiated the angular roof until he was behind the rusty iron frame, girding the skylight of his kitchen. Light crept from under his bedroom door. Had Jennifer left it on? He had no recollection.

Damn Yvette . . . She was probably in the bedroom rifling through Jennifer's things. What a hellish fight this would be.

He was puzzled and distracted. Then he noticed something. Beside the roof rail, tilted at a crazy angle, was a large cardboard carton. Why would the delivery men bringing in a bedroom set leave it there? He moved toward it without making a sound. He lifted the flaps. They were wet and slick. He looked at his hands and saw blood.

Yvette's slender body was doubled in half and stuffed in it. Her throat had been cut so deeply that it quivered on flimsy nerve endings.

Rage and grief paralyzed him. He struggled to hold himself together, but he could not stave off a low, lamenting moan. The anguish of seeing Yvette dead tormented him. Their love affair had been dominated by confusion and anger. The very nature of their failure filled him with grief. He knew now that Boy had escaped and was below in his apartment, waiting for him.

Michel's fingers reflexively reached for his automatic, but he realized that Jennifer had insisted that he leave it. She had put it in the drawer of the telephone table. The lift clanged to his floor. He tiptoed to the shaft and peered down. No one was there. After a moment, the hallway lights went out. Silence tolled.

He moved back to the rail at the side of the roof. His terrace was below. In the faint moonglow, he could make out the silhouettes of the table and chairs, the Chez Danton umbrella, and his old barbecue. A gust of wind thrust the living room curtains back inside the room. Boy was not outside.

Michel took off his jacket, climbed over the rail, and reached for the fire rungs. How many of them were there? Six, ten, more? Why didn't he know? He climbed down. The hard encrusted round metal spokes dug sharp rusted slivers into his palms. The discarded umbrella from Chez Danton had begun to flap in the wind.

He saw four more of these narrow rungs below him. He dropped to the terrace. He was surrounded by clumps of ticking from the horsehair mattress, bric-à-brac, plants that he had forgotten to water. The living room doors were partially open. Through the blowing curtains, he saw his TV and armchair.

Where was Boy?

Michel turned his head. He was unexpectedly distracted by the clatter of heels along the street. Jennifer had her second wind and was returning, rejoicing, singing "La Vie en Rose." She carried bottles and a bucket of ice on a waiter's tray.

Michel picked up a small garden fork which lay under the deck chair. The handle was loose. The wind parted the curtains and he caught a glimpse of a man wearing a military uniform.

At the same moment, the man spotted him and leapt through the curtains and onto the terrace. He had a gun. As he pointed it, Michel stabbed the fork into his wrist. The gun fell and the man cried out. He agilely wove low and struck Michel in the groin with his fist. Michel staggered back, grunting.

Suddenly a scalpel came out of the man's other sleeve and he slashed Michel's arm. Michel dodged away, unaware of the pain. He made a lunge and seized the man's arm, twisting it until he backed him against the wall. Then Michel butted him hard, smashing his nose.

Roused by the struggle, Boy forced his way out. "Shoot him, Major!"

"I can't. You get him!" came the hoarse shout.

Boy kicked at Michel wildly, like a horse gone berserk. Michel hit Boy in the gut and he fell back shattering the glass door.

The major had regrouped. He was waving the scalpel and slashing at Michel.

The front door burst open. Jennifer heard Michel gasp, and saw him struggling with a man outside on the terrace. She dropped the tray and screamed in terror.

Boy staggered over the glass slivers and came toward her, waving something that was undulating in his hand.

It was a snake. He was waving it at her like a lasso and she heard the hiss of the viper. She froze, stunned by panic. The room was wavering, jumping, walls moved. She stood paralyzed by shock.

"Jennifer, run!" Michel shouted, still grappling with the man.

She backed up. The violence of the fight on the terrace had reached a crescendo of barking grunts and howls. Michel shifting from side to side.

Boy slithered toward her with the snake. She backed up into the doorway corner and cringed.

Suddenly a grotesque scream boomed from the terrace. A man's body went over the rail and she and Boy heard it explode on the ground.

Boy turned back to the terrace. Michel was on his knees, groaning and flailing his arms.

Boy was shrieking "Major, Major!" He stumbled back to the terrace with the spitting snake and raised it above his head.

Jennifer fought to regain her focus. She opened the drawer of the telephone table. Her hand roved over papers and books, reaching Michel's gun. She yanked it out of the holster and flicked the safety catch under the trigger.

She fired at Boy, again and again, until silence encroached upon the universe, swallowing it into the dead mass of eternal night.

6

A
MISTRAL
FOR MICHEL

CHAPTER 64

With Boy and Major Eldon Royce Calhoun dead, the investigation into the deadly summer of homicides came to a conclusion. While Michel recuperated from his wounds at the farm, nursed by Jennifer, they learned that she had lost her position at Pembrooke College.

"Michel, listen to what the dean wrote:

> 'Dear Professor Bowen,
>   Regrettably, the trustees are enforcing the terms of our agreement and consider that you have been in breach of contract. Given the circumstances, our attorneys, however, have advised us to pay your salary in full. We enclose a check for $26,754.32 after deductions. No references will be provided should you seek another teaching position.'

"Looks like you're stuck with me. Acts of God don't seem to count with these people," Jennifer said wearily. "The truth is, they know I've been directly involved in two deaths." She had been deeply marked by the murders and the violence of her role. "I'll never be acceptable to the faculty or the parents of these miserable students." She tousled his hair and rubbed her face against his. "Well, I can pay for our honeymoon. What do you think of that?"

He was sprawled on the sofa with his head on her lap and pleased by this turn of events.

"You're full of wonderful ideas. The hell with everyone. I'll resign from the police. We'll live out here and travel for a few months." He stirred. "Let's drive into Aix. I need to see Vincent Sardou on some business."

"You up to it?"

"Yes, and there's a surprise for you."

"Tell me, tell me."

"I had the cassoulet cook-off moved up to tonight. My parents are making the his and hers versions."

"Oh God, I love you!" She leapt up. "How'd you manage that?"

"Three Sulka ties for my father—"

"You couldn't—"

"A Chanel blouse and scarf for my mother."

"You didn't tell them where you got them?"

"It wouldn't matter to them. When they're not fighting, my parents cook for a living. They don't care about the origin of things—like we do."

She held him tightly only for a moment and the delirium of passion surrendered to the profound pleasures of anticipation.

"I'm in the shower—"

Later, as they drove through the farm, the profusion of ivory light illuminated the fields. On the hillside, the threadlike silky branches of smoke trees, which in summer had given them a gray hazy look, now had leaves of bright red, and the land appeared to be covered by small fires. Just as she had been changed, the tones of autumn were already transforming everything.

Jennifer knew that she had never been happier. She thought that the madness she and Michel had endured had brought them closer.

"Please sit down, Michel," Vincent Sardou said. Michel wondered why the elderly barrister seemed so nervous. "Will you have a drink?"

"All right."

"I think you like Johnnie Walker Black Label."

"Yes, fine. Neat, please."

The afternoon shadows of the plane trees on the Cours Mirabeau cast Sardou's face in a medley of crisscrossing lines like a map grid. Michel's eyes rested on a precious eighteenth-century Provençal *salière*; this salt box was carved out of walnut, adorned with acorns, a symbol of health and fertility. Now Louise Vercours's ashes resided inside. Only a few months ago, he had sat laughing with her on the roof terrace eating *calissons*, the almond cakes he had loved from childhood.

He and Sardou tapped glasses. Sardou reached over for a file.

"I drew this up ages ago and reread it this morning. It's all in order and straightforward."

"What exactly is this about?"

"Louise's will. Her collection of paintings—the Matisse *Odalisque* that hung over her bed, a Watteau, two Bonnards, a Picasso from his Blue Period, three Renoirs from the 1850s, a Degas of ballerinas, an early Monet seascape, a Gauguin from the period when he was living with van Gogh, and finally the three Cézannes. I remember when she bought the still life of apples from a client of mine.

"In all, fourteen masterpieces with provenances." Sardou removed his glasses. "They are to go to you."

Michel was astounded by the bequest and could hardly concentrate on what Vincent Sardou was telling him next. The lawyer would stop to explain, then continue to read extracts from the will. Michel's head was swimming.

"I don't understand."

"Let me finish. She's given her vineyards and herds of Charolais and the restaurant buildings, which she owned, to Philippe and Nicole. The rest of the fortune—her homes and property—are to be sold and the proceeds to go to the university. Scholarships for needy girls will be given each year and she's asked you to oversee this."

"Of course."

Michel banged down his drink and reached for the bottle. "I can't imagine myself owning her paintings. Why did she make me the heir to them?"

Sardou seemed to be floundering and finally spoke. "Are you sure you want to know?"

"I certainly do."

"I didn't give you all the facts when you came to see me during your early investigation into her murder. I didn't want to divert you. You'd been under psychiatric treatment after Corsica."

"That was behind me. It was my impression that you were withholding information. But as her barrister, you had a legal right to confidentiality."

Sardou popped a nitro tablet under his tongue.

"I didn't feel that the time was right to discuss other aspects of Louise's life."

"And now you can?"

"Yes."

Louise had come from Toulon after the death of the American test pilot she had been in love with. She had been carrying his child.

"She was living with Philippe and Nicole. And she was suicidal. She took an overdose of sleeping pills shortly before she was due to have her baby. Her contractions began while she was unconscious. Philippe and Nicole couldn't get her to the hospital. They delivered *you* in their bedroom."

The moral and psychological consequences of the truth overwhelmed Michel. He sat stunned by the revelation. He was inconsolable and struggled to suppress his emotional turmoil and confront the reality of who he was.

"I arranged for Nicole and Philippe to adopt you. Louise wanted it that way. Nicole and Philippe couldn't have a child," Sardou said in a broken voice.

Michel rose heavily and stared out of the window, vainly trying to compose himself. Had he subconsciously known or felt this connection with Louise. While investigating her murder he had discovered everything about her personal life and still loved her.

"I suppose that explains why she spoiled me all the time. I was *hers.*"

He recalled a brief, wry conversation he had had with Nicole while visiting her in the hospital. She'd said something to the effect that she and Philippe were married because she was pregnant with him. How could he confront her about this fabrication and the collusion that molded it? It would humiliate her. He couldn't bring himself to darken the maternal love and effort she had brought to him under these circumstances.

"Do my parents know you've told me about this?"

"No. It's up to you to decide what to do about that."

"My real father . . . is there anything more?"

"He was an admiral in the Navy and apparently very well connected socially and politically. In reviewing my notes, I failed to mention that his name was Michael. That's all there is." He handed the detective a sparkling set of brass keys. "I loved your mother as well. Do you want her ashes, or may I keep them?"

Michel wiped a tear from his eye and shook Sardou's hand.

"Keep them. Of course. We have our memories of her. My parents and I will build a memorial to her at the farm. Thank you, Vincent, for your discretion all these years."

A limpid, autumnal tranquility seemed to have settled over Aix, banishing the chaos of the previous season. Shopkeepers, newspapers furled under their arms, were already closing early and scurrying home or out for a drink. The smiling jeweler, anxious for trade, greeted Michel and reminded him that he was having a sale; and Michel realized that he needed a new watch, possibly an engagement ring.

The noble, old mansions had regained the grace of solitude, and a fresh calm breeze barely rustled the trees or swizzled the jets of water dancing from the mossy fountains. Michel bought a bunch of white roses from the flower stall and headed over to Les Deux Garçons.

Jennifer was at a table outside, poring over an art book. To his surprise the espresso saucers were piled high. She was drinking a martini which, along with the scourge of cigars, had made something of a comeback in Provence, and outraged the locals.

Watching her for a moment, Michel felt a surge of power and a release from the ghosts that had obsessed Louise. The discovery of his birth and parents had brought him the missing part of himself. It was now clear to him why he had become a detective, for the inquiry into these murders had unveiled his own history. He had been the son of a warrior and a courtesan. This unforeseen, unimaginable alliance might clarify the composition of his own personality, but he doubted it. He had found some answers but only a temporary reprieve from the confusion which had shaped his character.

He sat down beside Jennifer. She finished her drink and flourished a hundred-franc note.

"The utter luxury of buying a new book and then having a drink and not worrying about the change," she said gaily.

"You're a woman of means now."

"Absolutely, and I'm prepared to keep you."

"That may not be necessary."

"I made the offer. Now when are we going to have our cassoulet?"

"We've still got a couple of hours. I thought I'd pick up the last bottle of Krug champagne."

"That's a lovely idea."

"I've got a special place to take you to and we can drink it there." She held him close to her and was puzzled by the distant look in his eyes. "I'm going to show you Louise's collection."

Jennifer's face filled with elation. "Cézanne's apples."

With a sense of having been liberated from the secrets of the past, he strolled with her to Louise's, his mother's house, which was behind the Cours Mirabeau and close to the Cathedral of St-Sauveur in the old quarter of Aix. The choir was practicing the *Gloria* of the mass which Michel had sung as a boy.

This *maison de jouir*, or house of joy—the name Gauguin inscribed on the portals of his last residence in the Marquesas—over which Louise had once presided, was a stately eighteenth-century house blessed by archbishops under the guise that it was a hostel for runaways.

Michel unlocked the gate. As they walked through the porte-cochère, Jennifer admired the sinuous bronze mermaids expelling water from their mouths in the fountain. Michel led her inside.

As a child he had wanted to take off his clothes and submerge himself in the perfumed bouquets of the house. There were painterly designs on the bowls of fresh, tangy potpourri placed on the hallway tables. They touched gourds, filled with choice lemons, firm peaches, melons and apples, as they passed into the gallery. Louise had balanced the actual presence of nature's bounty with the artistic daubs of people who had been nobodies at one time.

Jennifer gasped at the breathtaking spectacle of Cézanne, Gauguin and Renoir paintings.

"She lived like a queen."

"She *was* a queen for me," he said softly.

Michel opened the champagne and selected two Lalique flutes from Louise's crystal cabinet. He and Jennifer touched glasses. While Jennifer studied the paintings, he filled a Venetian goblet with water and placed the roses inside. He looked up, almost expecting to see Louise smiling with approval. She'd be standing at the top of the marble stairs, wearing a soft celadon green ensemble, her arms open to welcome him. With a bow, he raised his glass to the fugitive apparition.

His mother was still dazzling and mystical to him. She had been masked, illusive, and he felt a captive to his imagination and her impenetrable veils. The atmosphere was impressionistic, no black or white clouded the palette, nothing appeared distinct or fixed in space.

With the brothel shuttered next door, he basked in the ambiance of her beautiful home and the great art with which she had surrounded herself. The two buildings themselves reflected the duality of her life. But the structure and the basic nature of this paradox remained buried.

What had possessed her to become a madam? How did a woman make such a decision? Why, for that matter, were some people drawn to criminal behavior and murder? Was *this* process a decision, or some instinctive reversion to an uncharted former life? These questions would, he knew, endure as unfathomable mysteries and elude him.

"I wish I'd brought my camera! I'd have the only slides of her collection," Jennifer said.

"You won't have to bother with slides. We'll take the pictures home. You can look at them whenever you like."

Jennifer leaned her head on his shoulder. "Will you ever stop putting me on?"

"I'm not sure. Maybe, after we're married."

ACKNOWLEDGMENTS

Apart from the pleasure of composition, one of the extraordinary gratifications of writing a novel is the opportunity to celebrate the contributions that friends have made to my book.

Lori Cohen and her husband, my lifelong friend Dr. Benjamin Cohen, have been there from the beginning. Lori's astute and painstaking reading, her constructive criticism and discerning eye have enriched my work.

My other early readers, Christopher Keane, Laird Koenig, Robert Hamilton, and Jann Robbins, made valuable suggestions.

Rick Hall, who is also kin, was formerly of the Edmond, Oklahoma, police force. He spent time with me driving through the red dirt of Guthrie and its outlying areas and provided important background knowledge.

My friends on the Police Judiciaire prefer to remain anonymous, They have families and careers to protect.

Through the years of feast and famine I have been fortunate to have the friendship of Jim Parks, who has always been there for me.

The same may be said for John Nicksic, Brian G. Hutton, Dr. Lawrence Greenman, and Robert Mayer.

My indomitable agent, Susan Crawford, will only take yes for an answer and was in the trenches with me.

I would like to express my gratitude to my editor and champion, Natalia Aponte, of Forge-Tor.

This list would be incomplete without expressing a father's appreciation for his sons' forbearance over the years: Jonathan, Nicholas, and Alexander have tolerated my absences, wanderings and obsessions with good grace.

By rights I owe all of these people dinner with a bottle of Pétrus in Aix-en-Provence. My thanks will have to suffice for the time being.